STALKED BY THE ALIEN ASSASSIN

ALIENS AMONG US #2

TIFFANY ROBERTS

BLURB

An alien assassin. A tempting human female he can't resist. Will she allow a killer to claim her?

Avery Watson moved to Denver to escape her controlling mother. Sure, it not easy, and she has to budget every penny, but her new friends don't care if she doesn't wear makeup, don't glare at her if she laughs too loud or snorts. For the first time, she's content.

But then she meets Hunter Coleman.

This powerful, mysterious man isn't the sort that small, freckled, awkward women like Avery usually attract. His intense eyes follow her every move. She should be worried, but he makes her feel safe. He makes her feel...wanted.

Yet Hunter is even more dangerous than he seems... And he's not a man at all. He's everything Avery should fear—he's everything she desires. And he'll stop at nothing to make her his lifemate.

There's just one problem—he's not the only one targeting her, and his rivals don't have Avery's best interests in mind.

Dedicated to my true love. Thank you for the patience, support, and laughter.

ONE

THERE WAS no doubt in Fyran's mind—the three males standing outside the convenience store were not human. They were vrokars, members of a species with a culture steeped in ancient tribal traditions despite their advanced technology, a species that considered themselves warriors.

The vrokars were standing just on the other side of the store-front window, bathed in the artificial glow of the gas station's exterior lights. The glass separating them from Fyran muffled their low voices.

One of them had his back toward the window, displaying the insignia on his leather jacket. The vrokar's companions wore matching symbols. It had been those insignias that had initially caught Fyran's attention about half an hour ago. The stylized alien skull with its elongated fangs and intricate markings represented the Kurghan tribe, but Fyran didn't recognize the patterns woven around the symbol or the vertically aligned spears set behind the skull, both of which would've denoted the subtribe.

He was familiar with vrokari culture, but he wasn't a fucking expert on their convoluted heraldry.

"Is this everything, sir?" asked the cashier in front of Fyran, a human male who might've been as young as fifteen or sixteen or as old as his mid-twenties.

Even after all the material he'd been made to study before coming to Earth and living amongst these people for over a year, Fyran had trouble guessing the ages of some humans. Regardless, this cashier had a certain air of innocence about him. He had honest eyes.

The kid wouldn't stand a chance if the vrokars outside decided to make trouble.

Karak'duun, *I'd be lying if I said I didn't want them to...*

"Yeah," Fyran replied, tugging his wallet out of his pocket.

The cashier scanned the two items Fyran had set on the counter—a white and orange box of taquitos that had been proclaimed *spicy and delicious* by their signage and an oversized cup filled with what could only be described as semi-frozen sugar mixed with a hefty dose of red food coloring.

"That'll be six eighty-two," the cashier said. His gaze flicked toward the window, lingering momentarily on the males outside.

All three of the vrokars were around Fyran's height—about six and a half feet—and seemed solidly built. They were clad in leather and heavy boots, their clothing possessing that worn but carefully maintained look that his own clothing had taken on so often during his prolonged deployments on alien worlds.

But it was highly unlikely that these vrokars were deployed here; they were probably exiles or fugitives evading capture. Of course, vrokari pride and tradition left them unable but to display their tribal affiliation for all to see. Humans didn't know any better, but Fyran did.

"Nervous?" Fyran asked as he plucked a ten-dollar bill from his wallet.

The cashier looked back at Fyran. "I mean...a little, I guess? It's just really late, and it's so quiet, and those guys..."

Fyran dropped the bill onto the counter. "They give you a bad feeling."

"Yeah."

"Good. There might be hope for you yet."

The cashier's lips moved as though he meant to reply, but no words came out for a couple seconds. "W-what? What does that mean?"

Dropping his gaze, Fyran returned his wallet to his back pocket and collected his taquitos and slushie. "Nothing. Good night."

He turned away from the counter and strode toward the exit.

"Sir, don't forget your change," the cashier called.

"Keep it," replied Fyran before stepping out into the night.

The air was crisp and cold, and it still bore a hint of the unique, clean scent of the earlier snowfall. Far stronger were the odors of gasoline and motor oil. Fortunately, Fyran found both of those smells oddly comforting.

The vrokars fell silent, and Fyran felt their gazes on him as he walked past. The sound of his boots striking the concrete seemed the only one in all the world for those moments.

Make a fucking move. Say something stupid so I don't have to. Give me what I crave.

But the vrokars hadn't said a word by the time Fyran reached his car. Though he recognized the absurdity of his disappointment, he couldn't shake it. He'd followed these motorcycle-riding vrokars out here from central Denver, hoping to catch them at some nefarious deed, wishing for a reason to engage. Hell, he didn't even need to make a kill to satisfy his desire—a decent brawl would've been enough.

Fighting three hardened vrokari warriors would've been a fulfilling challenge. So what if such a scuffle would undoubtedly cause collateral damage?

Clenching his jaw, he unlocked the car door, tugged it open, and climbed into the vehicle. His tail, currently hidden in his pants, twisted around his leg and squeezed tight.

Why am I being so stupid? So careless?

He'd walked past the vrokars twice, both times drawing within twenty feet of them. The vrokari sense of smell was comparable to that of Fyran's kind, the falorans—and there was a good chance they would've recognized his scent as inhuman had they picked it up. Was he really so desperate for a release for his frustrations? Was he really so eager for action, for violence?

...yes.

He dropped the slushie into the console cupholder. It nearly toppled over; only the very bottom fit in the holder, leaving the top wildly off-balance. Was the forty-four-ounce cup excessively sized or was the cupholder sized too conservatively?

Svesh, why was he wasting time thinking about meaningless shit like that *now?*

Fyran pulled the door closed. Its slam helped force those erroneous thoughts out of his mind, but his lack of focus and caution was still troubling.

Three vrokari warriors were staring at him with hard gazes from less than thirty feet away, and he knew almost nothing about them. Their skills, their demeanors, their reason for being on Earth—all were unknowns. He'd never been prone to distraction, especially when the situation was so uncertain and potentially dangerous. Why now?

Muttering a curse, he set the taquito box on his lap and started the engine. The radio came on, and a deep, smooth human voice came through the speakers, extolling the virtues of some insurance company.

Why now? Because of this planet. This fucking planet had thrown him off, this mission had ruined his focus. Why the hell had they sent Fyran here? Of all the *althicars* they could've assigned, why him?

Keeping his gaze directed down—but watching the vrokars on the upper edge of his peripheral vision—he opened the box and removed one of the taquitos. It was long and thin, glistening with grease, and oozed a cheese-like substance that may or may not have been actual cheese. He lifted it to his mouth and took a tentative bite. There was a slight squish of grease over his tongue as he tore off a piece of the taquito.

The vrokars, apparently satisfied, broke their hard stares and resumed their conversation.

Fyran chewed slowly. The taquito's outer shell was simultane-

them. Looking at it logically, he knew it was because none of those aliens were meant to be here—of course they would be incredibly cautious. But there *had* to be more going on. There had to be something nefarious happening, waiting to be uncovered, especially with that elusive ilventyr he'd tailed a few times.

The vrokars' motorcycles roared to life, causing painful feedback on the listening device that rippled through Fyran's head before his neural transceiver auto-adjusted the volume.

"*Karak'duun*," Fyran growled through a mouthful of greasy food. He deactivated the listening device, plucked the pen from his ear, and dropped it into his pocket. After devouring the final taquito in two quick bites, he tossed the empty box into the small trash can he kept on the floor of the back seat.

He frowned down at his leg, where his jeans were stained by a blotch of grease left behind by the box. A glance at his hand confirmed that his fingers were covered in the same glistening substance.

"Really?"

And I didn't grab any napkins. So much for attention to detail, huh?

Still chewing the remaining taquito, he flicked his gaze to the left, watching the vrokars back their motorcycles out of their parking spots as he wiped his fingers on his already stained pants. That he was tailing the vrokars at all was shameful enough, but that he was being so sloppy, so stupid, was on an entirely different level of foolishness.

Yet Fyran knew he couldn't stop himself. He wouldn't accept the situation Command had forced upon him. He wouldn't let them destroy the life he'd made in the *Exthurizen*. It was all he knew.

Without looking away from the vrokars, he reached down with his right hand to shift the car into reverse. Instead of the shifter, his hand struck the cup. There was a faint pop, followed by a spatter of icy sugar on his hand—and the soft sound of more of it spilling across the passenger seat.

Brows falling low, he slowly turned his head to look. The cup's lid had popped off, and the unbalanced cup had tipped out of the cupholder, dumping its red-dyed contents across the passenger seat, where it was rapidly melting.

"Fucking *really?*" he snarled.

He needed to punch something—or some*one*.

Svesh, what kind of turn had this night taken? What kind of turn had his life taken?

The motorcycles roared louder. Fyran glanced back to see the vrokars speed out onto the main road, turning in front of a big tractor-trailer that was kicking up a torrent of mist from the wet road. They were heading north.

If Fyran delayed even a few more seconds, he risked losing track of them.

He flicked on the headlights, slapped his sticky hand down on the shifter, and threw the car into reverse. Melting cherry slushie flowed across the passenger seat and dripped onto the floor as the car pulled out of the parking spot and turned.

Though he knew better than to get attached to anything on any planet, Fyran couldn't suppress his flare of anger on his car's behalf. He'd needed an automobile for transportation, and for whatever reason, this black Dodge Challenger SRT Hellcat had spoken to him. So what if it was excessively priced compared to other functional vehicles? Command had provided him with essentially unlimited funding.

He'd known little about what the vehicle's specs meant at the time, but he'd certainly come to appreciate them. Modifying this vehicle and driving around Denver and the surrounding areas had been his only means of distracting himself outside those brief windows, like now, during which he'd been investigating other non-humans.

He liked this car. And now it had been fucking desecrated.

This was what happened when he was placed on missions that didn't make proper use of his skills. This was the conse-quence of wasting his talents.

You know that's wrong, Fyran. This is the consequence of you ignoring *your mission.*

He shut that voice up, cramming it down into the deepest, darkest part of his mind where it could rot for all he cared. He pulled out onto the road without stopping at the parking lot's exit, grateful that the wet roads had not yet begun to ice over, which they were likely to do before the night's end.

The tractor-trailer and the motorcycles in front of it had already gained a significant lead, but it was nothing his excessively powerful vehicle couldn't handle—and he always enjoyed opportunities to put the car to use.

Fyran pressed down on the accelerator. The car sped forward, its engine giving off a satisfying roar, and devoured the distance between itself and the semi-truck ahead, which was currently visible as little more than mist-blurred taillights. The landscape to either side of the road was draped in white with tufts of brown grass jutting up through the snow, granted eerie luminescence by the overcast night sky.

It was almost barren enough that Fyran could pretend nothing existed but himself and his quarry—nothing but the hunt.

As he neared the tractor-trailer, he had to use the windshield wipers and washer fluid to clear away the dirty water being kicked up by the larger vehicle. Fyran eased to the left, peering around the truck. The vrokars were about a hundred yards ahead of the semi. Passing the big vehicle would've been no trouble, but after having already been so close to his prey, Fyran thought it best to hang back. The vrokars would certainly take notice if he drew up behind them again. He'd close the gap when it was necessary.

Besides, they were approaching the end point of this road, where it connected to State Highway 128. The stoplight there would likely act as a balance.

Fyran recentered the Hellcat in the right lane, lifting his foot off the gas to back away from the tractor-trailer and reduce the filthy mist spattering his windshield. He wasn't sure how anyone could make it through a Colorado winter on a single tank of washer fluid.

The semi-truck's taillights flared brighter red as the vehicle slowed. A quick check confirmed that the stoplight ahead was red.

The vrokars had nearly reached the intersection, and they were in the left turn lane.

One corner of Fyran's mouth tilted up. The land to the west was remote and sparsely populated. It was the perfect area for an altercation between non-human beings to occur without witnesses.

He brought his vehicle to a stop behind the tractor-trailer. The melting slush on the passenger seat flowed forward, more of it spilling onto the floor. Fyran's tail stiffened, and his grip on the steering wheel tightened, his claws extending to dig their tips into the heels of his palms.

That can be cleaned up later. This opportunity can't wait. I need to know where they're going, what they're up to.

He refused to acknowledge what he already understood—he *didn't* need to know. This wasn't his duty. This was, in fact, in direct violation of it. But it was too late to care now. Fuck his assignment, and fuck Command for giving it to him. If he was going to be on Earth, he was going to make a real difference while he was here, and this was the only way he knew how to do that. He was safeguarding humans from potentially dangerous aliens.

The vrokars' motorcycles rose in a rumbling chorus ahead, and Fyran watched as all three turned onto the highway. The tractor-trailer was slower to move. *Much* slower. It rocked on its chassis as it lurched forward at an impressive speed that could've been topped by a crawling human infant.

Fyran turned his head to glance at the vrokars, who were getting farther and farther away with each passing second. When he looked at the truck again, it seemed to have barely moved.

The Hellcat crept forward behind the semi. Fyran barely resisted the urge to slam his hand on the horn, barely resisted the urge to dart around the truck and get ahead of it, shouting profanities the whole way. Finally, the tractor-trailer completed enough of its turn to make the stoplight visible from Fyran's much lower vantage.

The stoplight was red again.

Fyran stopped his vehicle at the white line and glared at the red light, a crease forming between his eyebrows. He tightened his tail around his leg, its hold so strong that it threatened to cut off circulation to his foot. The steering wheel creaked in his grasp.

This night was working extra fucking hard to make him hate the color red.

He glanced from side to side. Apart from the motorcycles—their taillights little more than pinpricks of red in the distance—and the semi-truck, there were no vehicles within sight. The countryside was dark, quiet, and still.

Fyran's eyes fell upon the stoplight again. Seconds passed, each weighing upon him more heavily than the last. For all his anger and dissatisfaction over the last year, he'd held to the simple rule all *althicars* tried to follow—*do not draw unnecessary attention to oneself*. Often, that meant operating within the local laws as often as possible.

But *karak'duun*, this light didn't seem willing to change. It was mocking him, taunting him, looking down upon him with malicious mirth.

"Fuck it," Fyran growled. He pressed down on the accelerator and turned onto the highway. As soon as the car was straight, he depressed the pedal further.

He'd barely made it a hundred yards before movement in his rearview mirror caught his attention. He looked back to see a vehicle pull onto the road from where it had been parked—beside a fenced in power substation. The vehicle's lights came on in two stages—first the headlights, and then the flashing red and blue lights on its roof.

"What the fuck?" Fyran snapped. How had he missed that vehicle sitting on the side of the road?

How the fuck was he about to be pulled over?

Fyran knew at least fifty curses in half a dozen languages by heart, and not a single one—not even all of them combined—seemed strong enough for this.

What was it that humans were fond of saying? *Fuck my life?*

Clenching his jaw and doing all he could not to crush the steering wheel in his fists, Fyran slowed down and pulling onto the shoulder. The motorcycles were out of sight now, and even the tractor-trailer was almost too far ahead to spot.

What am I supposed to be? An althicar? *The most dangerous assassin in the* Exthurizen's *ranks?*

Fyran dropped his head back against the headrest.

This would've been laughable were it not so immensely frustrating. He knew better. He fucking knew better.

The police car stopped behind Fyran's vehicle.

The Colorado State Patrol drove Dodge Chargers, which were like cousins to Fyran's vehicle—well, if one cousin was a highly trained, world-class athlete and the other sometimes went for morning jogs. The Hellcat could outrun this law enforcement agent, but what then?

He'd have to delve into some hefty hacking to erase all record of his vehicle and license plate number from State Patrol records afterward, and that brought along a whole new set of potential complications—foremost amongst them being that his dwelling wasn't far from here. It seemed likely that a state trooper would recognize a vehicle that had fled justice, and Fyran was not willing to give up his car.

Fyran lowered his window, letting in a rush of cold air that did nothing to ease the building heat in his chest, killed the engine, and settled his hands atop the steering wheel. He curled his lip is disgust; the fingers of his right hand were still sticky.

His heart thumped restlessly, and the tip of his tail twitched against his calf. All the energy that had been building within him during the burgeoning chase, all the anticipation for the potential confrontation—for some fucking action after so long with *nothing* —had nowhere to go now. Every sound seemed sharper, every smell more potent, and the air felt so much crisper and clearer on his skin. His body was ready for combat.

And Fyran was incredibly aware of the knife tucked in his boot and the pistol in a hidden holster under the waist of his pants. His claws extended; fortunately, his holoshroud rendered them invisible.

After what felt like an hour of waiting, the state trooper

opened the door of his silver patrol car and climbed out. He strode forward casually, one hand resting atop the gun on his hip. As he neared Fyran's car, he tugged out a long flashlight, clicked it on, and pointed it at Fyran.

The beam of light hit Fyran directly in the eyes, blinding him momentarily. He closed his eyes to slits and turned his head away, barely stopping himself from growling a curse.

"Evening, sir," the trooper said nonchalantly. "Any idea why I pulled you over?"

"A few."

The trooper snorted a brief laugh. "I'm going to need to see your license and registration."

"I'll need to reach into my pocket," Fyran replied, keeping his gaze averted from the flashlight. "That all right?"

The trooper took a step back. "Just keep it slow."

That's all I've been doing dealing with you people. That's all you can fucking handle.

Fyran reached down and dug his wallet out of his pocket. He plucked his license from within, grateful that the *Exthurizen* had been nothing if not thorough in establishing his human identity, and set it atop the dashboard. "Registration is in the glove compartment."

"Go ahead."

Fyran leaned aside, dropping his right hand onto the passenger seat to support himself. That hand, of course, landed in a cold, sticky puddle.

He pressed his lips into a tight line, released a long, slow breath through his nostrils, and opened the glove compartment with his left hand. After removing the registration, he held both it and his license out to the trooper, whose name tag said *F. G. SULLIVAN*.

Trooper Sullivan accepted the documents. "Guess there's so much red in your car you didn't even notice it on the traffic signal, huh? Hope that washes off all right. Shame to muck up a car like this."

"Sure is." Fyran placed his hands atop the steering wheel

again. Tension thrummed through his limbs, making them tight and achy, but managed to keep his fingers relaxed.

"Hang tight and keep the engine off. Just going to run your information, and we'll get this sorted out." Trooper Sullivan walked back to his vehicle. The sound of his shoes on the pavement was surprisingly loud on the otherwise silent road.

Fyran strained to still his mind, to contain his growing irritation, his growing rage. He glanced into the rearview mirror to see Trooper Sullivan sitting in the driver's seat of his cruiser. The trooper's attention was focused on a computer mounted to the console.

Time passed with little meaning, each second stretching out into what felt like days, months, *years*. Fyran's awareness of his weapons heightened with every moment. The solidness and weight of the human-made pistol called to him, the balance and precision of his faloran-forged knife beckoned softly, and the restlessness at his core answered.

More than once, he lifted his eyes to look west.

The vrokars were out there somewhere, having eluded Fyran due to his own impatience. At least he was aware of them now. At least he'd be on watch for them. They'd been added to his list of aliens to monitor—which also happened to be the list of aliens he couldn't do a fucking thing about.

"*Karak'duun*," he rumbled.

Eventually, Trooper Sullivan emerged from his vehicle and sauntered back to Fyran's window. He held a notepad of some sort in his hand, with Fyran's license and registration lying atop it. "All right, Mr. Coleman, just about through. Your record's clean, but I'm afraid I can't let you off with a warning tonight. With these road conditions and the nature of the vehicle you're operating, I need you to understand the importance of being responsible and obeying all traffic laws. They're in place for your safety and that of the other drivers out here. That's how we keep Colorado a great place to live, right?"

Fyran grunted and curled his fingers tighter around the steering wheel.

Trooper Sullivan frowned and tore a paper off the pad. "Guess you're lucky I pulled you over before I could tack on a fine for speeding, huh? Bet this thing can hit sixty in what, five seconds?"

"Three-point-two after a few modifications," Fyran replied, accepting the citation and his documentation as the trooper passed them over. "So I guess *you're* lucky I chose to stop, huh?"

The trooper's frown deepened, and his brows fell low.

"Joking, Officer. I would never even consider it. Car chases are best left in the movies."

Trooper Sullivan narrowed his eyes and lifted a finger, pointing it at Fyran. "Good. High speed pursuits are extremely dangerous for everyone out on these highways."

As though in response, a gust of wind blew across the open fields. Its howl was the only sound along the now empty stretch of road apart from that of the patrol car's idling engine.

"Nice car, anyway," Trooper Sullivan said with a grin. "Imagine if they issued us these, huh? No one would get away." He stepped back from Fyran's vehicle and lifted his ticket book in a wave. "Have a good night, sir. Drive safe."

"You too," Fyran said, turning on the engine and closing the window. "Right into a fucking ditch."

He was about to toss his license, registration, and fresh citation down on the passenger seat, but he halted his arm before he could release the items. The seat was still wet and sticky. That hadn't changed. He ran his tongue over his teeth and fangs.

What the fuck is this planet doing to me?

Fyran watched in the rearview mirror as Trooper Sullivan entered his vehicle, turned off the flashing lights, and pulled out onto the road, driving west.

Fyran's hand hesitated on the shifter. His instincts said to continue in that direction himself. There was still a chance he could catch up to the vrokars, still a chance he could follow them to wherever they were going, but those chances were miniscule. The vrokars would have easily reached Highway Ninety-three by now, where they would've had to turn either north or south.

If Fyran chose the wrong direction, he could drive for hours without ever spotting them, moving farther and farther from his quarry. Even if he chose correctly, there was a chance he'd never make up for their lead—not without risking another encounter with Trooper Sullivan.

"What a fucking waste of a night," he grumbled as he shifted the Hellcat into drive and turned it around to head back to Westminster.

TWO

THERE WERE no other vehicles in sight as Fyran drove south. There was just the glow of the instrument panel, the rumbling of the engine, and the low, rolling hills and wide fields blanketed in snow. Again, he had a sense that the was universe falling away around him, but this time there was no target to hunt, there was no battle to win. There was no purpose to fulfill.

There was just...nothing.

Emptiness settled in his chest, spreading down into his gut. It was a void, hungry, dark, and cold, ready to swallow him up at any moment. And that would be it. The end. Without his duty, without the hunt...what was he?

Releasing a heavy breath, he squeezed the steering wheel and pressed his foot down on the accelerator. The engine purred as though eager for more, as though yearning to have its full potential unleashed, and Fyran was tempted to oblige it—was tempted to push both the Hellcat and himself to the limits.

At least the danger of driving at one hundred and fifty miles an hour on slick roads would've been thrilling enough to fight back some of that emptiness.

The speedometer crept higher and higher, passing sixty miles per hour, creeping toward sixty-five, seventy...

Fyran gritted his teeth. The tension within him, the turmoil, was almost unbearable. He'd never been so at odds with himself. He'd never been so foolish.

So...restless and reckless.

"*Karak'duun,*" he growled, easing off the gas pedal.

He turned up the radio and flipped through the stations until he landed on suitably loud, distracting music—*rock*. For good measure, he cranked the volume higher. All he needed was to keep his thoughts at bay until he arrived at his dwelling. No more complications, no more bad decisions, no more searches for confrontation. He could be as angry as he wanted so long as he was inside and out of sight.

He just had to make it through the drive home. Just a few more minutes.

The night was peaceful despite everything that had occurred, imbued with a silence and stillness that should've made it serene. There were no hostile forces to evade, no dangerous places to infiltrate, no threats lurking in the shadows. Just a few miles of quiet roadway between Fyran and his dwelling.

That should be laughably easy to overcome for an althicar *with years of experience, shouldn't it?*

By the time he'd reached the road upon which his dwelling was located, his insides were a maelstrom of fire and ice, of anger and emptiness, of frustration and something deeper, something more insidious. Something he refused to acknowledge.

What did the peacefulness of his surroundings matter? Peace wasn't for the likes of Fyran. His place would forever be at the hearts of conflicts, thriving against overwhelming odds, facing mortal danger at every moment, never certain if his next breath would be his last. He belonged behind enemy lines with a knife in hand, stalking the Azmus Protectorate's enemies. *That* was his life.

There was nothing for him out here on the edge of these tall, majestic mountains, nothing for him in these snowy fields, nothing for him in Denver's urban sprawl. It was not for him to stargaze on quiet, clear winter nights or let his mind drift through fanciful dreams while reclining in the summer sun.

It was certainly not for him to take a human female as his lifemate.

Fyran adjusted his hold on the steering wheel, but his right hand was hesitant to move, stuck in place briefly by the sticky residue clinging to it. Snarling, he turned onto his dirt driveway. The sound of dirt, gravel, and snow crunching beneath the tires had become a comforting one, but it didn't soothe him now.

In all the years he'd served in the *Exthurizen*, he'd never felt like this.

His tail coiled tighter around his leg, and the steering wheel creaked in his grip. In his youth, Fyran had developed skills that had later proven useful to the *Exthurizen*. The Azmus Protectorate's covert military organization had offered him a purpose, a chance to make a meaningful difference, to contribute to what they deemed the greater good. Perhaps more importantly, they'd given him an outlet for all the anger he'd carried since his earliest years. They'd honed his skills through years of training and covert operations. They'd turned him into an *althicar* who excelled at one thing above all else.

Killing.

A signal sent through his neural transceiver deactivated the security field protecting the garage. He hit the button on the garage opener, slowing his vehicle until the rollup door was high enough to drive the Hellcat into the garage. Shifting the car into park, he shut off the engine and stared at his reflection on the windshield. His reflection, lit partly by the dashboard's glow and partly by the dim orange light on the garage opener's motor, was ghostly.

Despite the effect of his holoshroud—which made Fyran look human—he could not help but feel like that face was out of place here.

That face, that male, was out of place everywhere.

With another curse, he closed the garage, exited his vehicle, and walked around to the passenger side. He cleaned the fallen slushie with whatever towels—paper and fabric alike—he had on hand, splashing red-dyed water on himself in the process and muttering profanities under his breath throughout. A growl escaped him when he picked up the cup and tossed it in the garbage.

He'd only had one sip before spilling it, and a small, smug voice in his head suggested that was most tragic of tonight's occurrences. His frustration was only heightened by his inability to decide whether that voice was correct.

When he was done, he threw the paper towels in the trash and carried the soiled fabric towels into the adjoined laundry room. He flicked on the light and dumped the towels into the washing machine.

The house was currently quiet—what the humans might've called *deathly quiet*. He'd never been bothered by such silence, but he'd found himself inclined as of late to put on music or the television just to have *something* to focus upon. He always could have adjusted the sound dampeners he'd installed throughout the house so they'd let in sounds from outside, but he didn't think that would help tonight. There'd be nothing to hear but the whisper of wind across the snow countryside.

That seemed lonelier than no sound at all.

He removed his boots, setting them on the floor mat to dry. Then he withdrew the listening device from his pocket and took off his jacket, tossing it atop the dryer. He paused as he was exiting the laundry room.

"*Svesh*, this fucking night," he muttered as he sent the neural signal to reactivate the forcefield at the garage door.

Was he losing his edge, or was he losing the will to care?

Lifting both hands, he dragged his fingers through his long hair, tugging it back out of his face. The amalgamation of emotions in his gut was like a slavering beast stalking him, hungry but still too uncertain of its prey to pounce. Were he to ignore that beast for too long, he'd provoke its aggression, and it would strike—likewise if he stared at it too long.

He muttered curses in half a dozen alien languages—most of

which he'd learned before his tenth year of life—as he walked upstairs, unfastening his belt along the way. The moment it had enough leeway to do so, his tail slipped free to swing in the air behind him. The tuft at its tip bumped the walls to either side again and again, but it refused to slow, responding only to his inner turmoil rather than his conscious commands.

Once he was in his bedroom, which by itself was easily the largest quarters in which he'd ever dwelled, he let his holoshroud fall away, barely noticing the faint tingling it sent across his skin.

Fyran needed a shower, and then he needed to get to bed—not because he was tired, but because sleep was the only thing likely to provide a respite from his anger.

Yet what he needed most of all was to be extracted from this fucking planet and sent on a mission that would actually utilize his skills. He needed to be sent on a mission that wouldn't punish him for success.

Crouching, he peeled back a corner of the rug and opened the hidden compartment in the floorboards with a scan of his genetic code. The compartment contained all the faloran gear he'd been issued for this mission. For most any other operation, it would've been considered a woefully inadequate kit, though he'd gone into hostile zones with far less on numerous occasions. Here on Earth, this equipment was laughably excessive.

Especially since he'd *requisitioned* several items before deployment.

He sneered down at the equipment as he tossed the listening-pen into the compartment. The communication disc, a device small enough to fit comfortably on his palm with room to spare, was lit up. The blue light meant Command was reaching out to him. Why did they bother asking for reports every few weeks? They didn't want the sort of information he'd been giving them.

Fyran stood up and pulled the adjustable restraints out of his front pocket. They looked like strips of fabric—a blend of silk ribbon and the thicker material humans used for things like seatbelts. But these would not yield to any blade; they were even stronger than they were flexible.

There hadn't been any situation during which he could've justified using the restraints since coming to Earth.

He dropped them unceremoniously into the compartment. They fell atop the comm disc, obscuring its blue light. Fyran closed the panel and kicked the rug back into place. "*Svesh*, so clumsy of me."

Turning, he walked into the bathroom, pulling his shirt off over his head as he moved. He tossed the garment aside and paused long enough to turn on the shower before continuing to the counter.

While the water warmed, Fyran removed the holstered pistol that had been hidden against his upper thigh and set it on the counter. There was a faloran plasma pistol in the floor compartment, the sort of weapon that was coveted by intergalactic criminals for its power and reliability, but Fyran never carried it.

He spent most of his time in Denver, where there were far more humans. A gunshot from a human-made pistol would cause panic enough; he couldn't imagine how the humans would react if plasma bolts started flying through the air around them. To the people of Earth, that sort of tech existed only in fiction. The human handgun, while not as efficient or effective, was more practical.

Not that he'd ever have reason to fire a weapon again with the way this mission was going.

After removing his pants and boxer briefs, he braced both hands atop the counter and stared at himself in the mirror. He didn't look directly at his own face; instead, he trailed his gaze over the scars on his arms, chest, and abdomen, each of which carried its own memory. The oldest of those scars were faded by now, but even if they were to vanish completely, he would always see them, he would always remember.

He shifted his attention to the tattoos banded around his arms. The flowing Faloran script, which glowed crimson to match his eyes, marked him as an exile from his people.

That was standard for the *Exthurizen*; every *althicar* was marked as an exile so the Protectorate could deny responsibility should their secret soldiers be captured. Those marks hadn't meant anything to Fyran when he'd first received them. He'd been disconnected from his people for his entire life when he'd joined the *Exthurizen*. What did it matter if he had to bear the mark of an exile, especially when he knew it was in service to the faloran people?

What did it matter if he'd never really felt at home amongst his people, or that the tattoos essentially meant he never would?

He halted those thoughts just before his fingers curled so hard that his claws would've gouged the countertop.

Fyran shoved away from the counter and stepped into the shower. The water was scalding, but he didn't adjust the temperature. He scrubbed his body hard, washed his hair, and combed his fingers through it mercilessly, tugging out every knot and tangle without hesitation. He barely felt any of the pain or discomfort.

Command wanted a report.

Command wanted progress.

It wasn't the place of a soldier to make demands, but when would they consider what *he* wanted? He had nothing to say that they'd want to hear. His history with the *ultricar* didn't matter; this wasn't personal. Just a case of bullshit orders, and a severe misuse of an *Exthurizen* asset.

Fyran opened the shower door and reached for his towel only to realize it wasn't hanging in its usual spot. He'd tossed it in the wash the night before and had neglected to hang a new one.

"How could it go any other fucking way tonight?" With a growl, he closed the glass door, shook as much water as he could from his body—like a damned dog—and exited the shower, hurrying to the linen closet to grab a fresh towel and dry off the rest of the way. He wrapped the towel around his waist when he was done.

By rational standards, tonight hadn't been a disaster. He'd avoided a dangerous potential altercation, had made it through a traffic stop without rousing the trooper's suspicions, and had identified three more non-humans. That was good. His list of aliens in the area was growing.

But his frustrations were growing even faster.

"*Karak'duun*," he snarled as he combed his hair. As much as he wanted to spite Command, as much as he wanted to blow them off—or was the human saying blow them *up*? No, he was sure it was *off*—he knew he couldn't. Without the *Exthurizen*, his life would've gone very differently, and his skills would've been employed for very different reasons. The Azmus Protectorate had given him meaning.

But he could still be furious about this assignment.

When he was done with his hair, he brushed his teeth twice, just to be sure the lingering taste of the taquitos was eliminated, and dumped his dirty clothing in the hamper. Holding the towel in place around his waist, he returned to the bedroom and retrieved the comm disc from the floor compartment.

Fyran double-checked the blinds, curtains, and bedroom door, confirmed via his neural transceiver that the security fields and sound dampeners around the dwelling were still functional, and activated the comm disc—though he disabled its holographic functions.

The disc scanned his identity, just as the floor panel had. A moment later, there was a faint crackling sound that faded when the *ultricar* said in Faloran, "*Althicar* Voltanix."

"What do you want?" Fyran asked, slipping back into Faloran with ease.

Ultricar Khelvar Bathiras grunted. "Your report, *althicar*."

"Three positive classifications today. Vrokars, one possible chieftain, based on the way the other two deferred to him. Kurghan tribe, unknown subtribe. Disguised as bikers. Last sighted traveling west, just outside Westminster."

After a long, heavy sigh, Khelvar said, "I'm growing tired of repeating myself on this, Fyran. You are not to engage *any* non-human lifeforms."

Fyran gritted his teeth, nostrils flaring. "I've been observing, sir. Not engaging."

But not for lack of desire.

"*Karak'duun*, Fyran, you're not even supposed to be doing

that much. Your sole objective on Earth is to find a suitable female human, form a mating bond with her, and reproduce. That is *all*. Anything else, all this chasing renegade aliens across your area of operation, can be considered a dereliction of duty."

Fyran's fingers curled around the comm disc. His hand trembled, and his tail, kept down by the towel around his waist, lashed erratically, slapping the backs of his legs. "Fuck my duty, Khelvar. I don't know why you thought it was a good idea to send me here, but I don't belong on this planet, and I have no place on this mission. You know what I am. You've known it since you found me, and it hasn't changed."

Khelvar was silent for several seconds. In his mind's eye, Fyran could see the *ultricar's* stoic face, could see the tiny glimmer of carefully guarded, indecipherable emotion that sometimes crept into Khelvar's eyes.

"I did know, and I still do," Khelvar said, voice maddeningly calm and steady. "You were a faloran—you *are* a faloran. A faloran with limitless potential. That is what you are, Fyran."

"I'm a killer, Khelvar."

"You're an *althicar*."

"Don't pretend there's some distinction because you gave me a rank. You want someone dead, you send me in. You want a target and his whole inner circle killed? You send me. You have dirty work to do, you send *me*, and I've never complained about it because that's what I'm made for. I'm a killer. That's fucking all."

When Khelvar spoke again, there was an edge to his voice. "You are a master of linguistics who knew more as a street punk at sixteen years old than most of our experts know after decades of training. You are an unrivaled infiltrator. You are a hunter with patience that could outlast the cosmos. You are an improviser, a problem solver. You are an *althicar*, Fyran, and to try to act like you are a nothing more than a killer is either being willfully ignorant or intentionally disrespectful."

Fyran shook his head, squeezing his free hand into a fist that pressed his claws into his palm. More than anything, hearing Khelvar praise his patience stung. He sure didn't have much of that lately. "I have nothing to offer on this mission. Nothing to contribute. You know my place, and you know it's not here."

"If I believed that, you wouldn't be there, *althicar*." Khelvar had seemingly regained his calm, which was somehow worse than him finally starting to slip and show emotion. "This is the most important mission for our people. This is our future as a civilization, as a species. This is all that matters, Fyran."

"You don't even know if it will work. You have us here on a fucking hunch, Khelvar. You sent us here to become breeders when you don't even know if it's possible."

"It will work," the *ultricar* replied firmly. Those words hung in the air for several seconds, seeming to grow heavier with each moment. "We have confirmation. Mating bond and impregnation."

Releasing a huff through his nose, Fyran directed his gaze toward the floor. His jaw was clamped shut, the muscles locked, and his throat felt like it was being constricted. So, it was as he'd feared. They were keeping him here, on this mission, so he would find a mate, so he would have no choice but to leave the field.

To retire from his post. Mated falorans were forbidden from dangerous work; such bonds were too rare to risk.

But what would any sane female see in him? What could he possibly offer to a mate? What could he possibly offer to...to a child? Fyran didn't know anything about relationships like that, didn't know anything about raising offspring. All he remembered about his parents was that they'd taught him to speak Faloran—his only tie to the people he'd descended from—and that they'd disappeared when he was five or six years old. He wasn't even sure what the fuck a father was supposed to do.

Fyran knew how to take care of himself. Adding a mate and a child to that was asking for disaster. He couldn't be a mate, couldn't be a parent. It just...it wasn't in him, wasn't possible.

"Focus on your mission, *althicar*," Khelvar said with an oddly gentle air of authority.

"Success is possible, and if you apply yourself, you will find it.

Stop chasing random aliens and do your job. Our people are depending upon you."

"Our people were nowhere to be found when I needed them," Fyran said in a low voice. He knew it wasn't fair, knew it didn't apply, but it felt good to say those words. "I'll let you know when I find another non-human."

Khelvar started to say something, but his words were cut off by Fyran deactivating the comm disc. The bedroom plunged into suffocating silence.

"Fuck," Fyran snapped, stalking back to the floor compartment and shoving the disc inside before he could crush it in his fist. He tilted his head back, grasped a fistful of his hair, and paced along the bedside with his tail swinging.

Not only had he been ignoring his mission for over a year, but he'd been aggressive with his commanding officer and had essentially told Khelvar, the one who'd found Fyran on Vabos all those years ago, the one who could've shot him on the spot but had chosen to extend mercy to a fellow faloran, to fuck off.

Releasing his hold on his hair, he looked down at his hands. There were little drops of blood welling on one palm where his claws had punctured his skin.

"Resorting to fighting myself now, am I?"

He pulled the towel off his waist and used it to wipe the blood from his hand, keeping it against his palm as he tugged on a pair of underwear.

Apparently, I'm determined to soil every towel I own today.

Tossing the towel into the hamper, he scooped up the dirty laundry and carried it downstairs. He needed something sweet to drink. Why not get a load of laundry started when he went down?

It wasn't like he'd be getting to sleep any time soon.

<h1 style="text-align:center">THREE</h1>

Despite the wintery cold that had gripped the city, downtown Denver was bustling. The streets were packed with vehicles, and the walkways were crowded with pedestrians, many of whom streamed in and out of the stores and restaurants along the Sixteenth Street Mall in a seemingly endless flow of human bodies.

Well, not all human—at least one faloran and an ilventyr were amongst them.

Fyran wove through the mall in pursuit of his quarry, dodging distracted humans with practiced ease. Having grown up in an overpopulated city, he'd spent much of his childhood navigating crowds. He was at home in this environment. He could read gatherings of people the same way he'd seen other *althicars* read tracks in alien wildernesses.

He instinctively understood the ebb and flow of the humans. Each individual or subgroup moved at their own pace, creating flows that were not unlike water currents, sometimes eddying around clusters of people who'd decided to stop and stand as still as rocks surrounded by the moving tide.

Fyran snickered at himself. Apparently, he'd retained more

information from the documentary series he'd watched about Earth's oceans than he'd realized.

But Fyran's true focus wasn't on comparisons to tides and currents; it was on the ilventyr up ahead.

Gregor—as unlikely a name for an ilventyr as Hunter was for a faloran—walked with purpose, scarcely slowing his stride whenever he passed slower pedestrians. Several times, he'd seemed agitated, as though on the verge of plowing through the crowd, but largely seemed to take care in avoiding physical contact as often as possible. Fyran guessed the ilventyr was held in check by something simple—the desire to avoid undue attention.

An announcer on the radio earlier had declared that the holiday shopping season had officially begun, and this overabundance of shoppers was both the perfect cover for Fyran and the perfect distraction for his quarry. Gregor hadn't checked if he was being followed a single time since Fyran had begun tailing him.

This was where Fyran belonged—on the hunt, stalking his prey, using his skills to eliminate those who would cause harm to innocents. Gregor seemed to fit that description, even if Fyran was basing that guess on instinct. The ilventyr tended to talk in the vague way many intergalactic criminals did, never quite referring to anything directly, always using euphemisms or codes, always taking roundabout routes when he traveled. Fyran didn't know what, but he knew Gregor was involved in something illicit.

And he couldn't deny the petty satisfaction of the thought that Command would be furious if they knew what he was doing right now.

A group of females emerged from a clothing store and stepped directly into Fyran's path. They were engaged in conversation, arms laden with bags bearing the logos of the clothing store and a few other nearby shops.

They were in that human default operating mode of obliviousness.

Fyran halted abruptly, nearly colliding with the closest female.

The women turned their wide eyes toward him as they scrambled to stop.

"Oh my God, I'm so sorry!" The closest woman placed her hand on Fyran's forearm and looked up at him through thick, dark lashes. "Don't know how we didn't see you there."

Fyran's muscles tensed, his claws reflexively extended, and his lip curled. Despite the leather of his jacket separating his skin from the woman's, her touch created an unpleasant, prickly heat just under the surface of his flesh. It took a stunning amount of willpower to keep himself from shoving her away.

Why the fuck were so many humans so touchy? It was one thing to bump shoulders by accident, but to deliberately place a hand on someone...

That was justification for a stabbing where he grew up.

"Don't think I'd mind him bumping into me," said one of the other females.

Fyran clenched his jaw and looked over the women's heads and down the street just in time to see Gregor step into a business on the corner. The sign jutting out over the sidewalk said *Jerry's Diner—Breakfast-Lunch-Dinner-ICE CREAM*.

"Maybe we should give you a good look over just to make sure you're all right?" offered a third woman with a giggle.

"Can we, uh...buy you a coffee or something?" asked a fourth female. "You know, to make up for this?"

"I sure am thirsty," said the second.

"I'm sorry about them," the first female said, cheeks pinkening as her lips curled into a shy smile. "But really, I am—"

Barely managing to keep his expression neutral, Fyran took hold of the first woman's wrist, plucked her hand off his arm, and released his hold on her. "Best of luck rehydrating."

He stepped around the group and continued along the street, not sparing them another glance.

There was no fucking way he was going to let Gregor get away now.

The ilventyr had been on Fyran's list for over a month, and keeping tabs on him through that time had been difficult. Fyran had been out searching for Gregor when he'd spotted the vrokars and followed them to Highway 128 a week ago. Hunting this particular quarry had become a regular routine, one that often left Fyran with nothing show for it but wasted time.

As long as it's time not spent on Command's bullshit mission, is it really wasted?

Spotting Gregor today had been mere chance, and Fyran wasn't going to give up the opportunity. Eventually, he'd find real evidence, he'd hear what he needed to hear, and then he would act.

Fyran scanned his surroundings as he neared the diner's entrance. Nothing stood out as abnormal except one individual—a male standing on the corner, his shoulder resting against a light post. He was taller than the average male human, with a shaved head, a bulky coat with a tuft of brown fur around the collar, and dark sunglasses over his eyes. None of that necessarily meant anything, but there was something in his posture, something in the way he was scanning the crowd, that seemed off.

Maybe he was simply waiting for someone.

Or maybe he was a lookout. His build and features certainly fit an ilventyr in disguise, and there was no question that Gregor had associates here on Earth who he was regularly in contact with.

Fyran didn't allow his gaze to linger on the male. As far as anyone was concerned, Fyran was just another human going about his business, seemingly as lost in his little bubble as everyone else was in their own. These people were oblivious to the problems and struggles in the universe—and to the problems and struggles happening right here on Earth.

Oblivious to the aliens amongst them.

As an embedded *althicar*, Fyran was in a unique position to defend humanity from the likes of Gregor, and they never needed to know he was doing it for them. They could remain blissfully ignorant.

So could Command, for all he cared.

He entered the diner.

The place was filled with people, several of whom were

standing near the entrance, and there didn't look to be a single open table or booth. The floor was covered in a black-and-white checker pattern, and all the seating was upholstered in what appeared to be glittery red leather. There was a considerable amount of chrome trim everywhere. Though he wasn't familiar enough with human fashion and history to know for certain, the place had the feel of being decades out of style—but it was maintained so well that it all looked like new.

It only took Fyran a few seconds to spot his quarry. Gregor was at a booth in the far corner, seated across from a burly man in a black knitted cap who Fyran had never seen. They were speaking to one another, but their voices were swallowed up by the buzz of conversation, the sounds of plates and silverware clanking and rattling, and the music playing from a tall, wide, brightly lit machine against the wall.

"All our tables are full up right now," someone said, calling Fyran's attention forward.

The speaker was a male human standing behind the counter ahead, near the cash register. His short brown hair was streaked with gray, and he wore a red and white striped apron over his white shirt and red vest. He was a tall, sturdy man, but there was something decidedly kind in his eyes and his smile. His nametag read *JERRY*.

Jerry gestured to his left. "We got a couple seats open at the counter if you're alone, otherwise it'll be about twenty minutes."

Fyran flicked his eyes toward the side of the diner where Gregor was seated. The long counter, lined with stools that had glittery red seats, ran in that direction. It was possible he could get close enough to listen in on the ilventyr and his unknown associate.

"Counter," Fyran said.

Jerry picked up a menu and held it out to Fyran. "Take whichever spot you'd like. I'll have someone come around and take care of you in a few minutes."

Fyran accepted the menu and walked along the counter to the farthest unoccupied stool. Gregor and his companion were within twenty feet of Fyran now. It was dangerous to get so close to one's quarry before being ready to act, and that danger was only increased by the fact that ilventyrs had exceptional senses of smell. There were a great many scents in this diner between the humans and the food, but all it would take was one whiff for an ilventyr to potentially recognize that Fyran wasn't human.

And yet, some part of him thrilled in the danger, in the risk, in the taste of his old, pre-Earth life.

He placed the menu on the counter and removed his leather jacket, draping it over his lap once he'd sat down. Though he directed his eyes toward the menu, Fyran turned his attention toward his hearing, sorting through all the other sounds to isolate the voices of Gregor and the unknown male sitting with him. It took several seconds, but he homed in on Gregor's deep, gravelly voice.

The ilventyr was speaking Ulgrok, a bastardization of several common intergalactic languages that was used in many major inter-species cities throughout the universe. It was a language Fyran had learned to speak in his youngest days on Vabos, right alongside Faloran, and even now it still came more naturally to him than his ancestral tongue.

Gregor was saying something about it being risky to meet in this place. That they were...too close? He couldn't hear every word over the diner's ambient sounds, and knew he was missing bits of information; that only prompted him to focus harder.

He just needed to overhear something that confirmed his suspicions about Gregor. Anything.

"Big sale," said Gregor's guest in the same language. "Need to see it first before you carry through. Buyer is...very particular."

Fyran's ears perked at that, and his tail twitched within the confines of his pants. He braced a hand on his thigh, pressing it over his jacket, and leaned an elbow on the counter. He dared not turn his head toward his quarry, but it was hard to resist the urge.

"Told you, it's perfect. Nothing to worry about," Gregor said. "Big sale, easy sale."

Gregor's companion grunted and muttered something Fyran couldn't make out.

"You know it is. You see it with your own eyes, don't you?" There was a hint of smugness in Gregor's voice now. It sounded like he was smirking; were it not for the holographic disguise Gregor was wearing, his pointed teeth undoubtedly would've been on display. "Give me a timeframe. Tell me when you—"

"Sorry about the wait," someone said from the other side of the counter, their welcoming voice drowning out Gregor's lower tones. "Can I get you started with something to drink?"

Fyran's tail stiffened along his thigh, and its end wrapped around his calf in a grip that would've put any of Earth's constricting snakes to shame. The surge of frustration—of *rage*—that swelled within him was as strong as anything he'd felt the night he'd followed the vrokars.

Maybe humans didn't deserve his fury, but they were making it easy for him to direct it toward them.

He glanced up from the menu to see one of the servers standing before him, a young human male dressed in the same uniform as Jerry with dark skin and a wide, welcoming smile. Noah, according to his nametag.

Fyran could hear Gregor and the unknown individual talking in those same low voices, but his concentration had been shattered. He'd been so fucking close to getting *something*, to obtaining a bit of information he could work with, only for it to be snatched away.

"Water," Fyran replied tightly.

"Sure thing. Have you had a chance to look over the menu and—"

"No."

"Well, we have a couple specials today, and they're both delic—"

Fyran squeezed his jacket in his fist, making the leather creak, and growled, "Just the fucking water."

Noah raised his hands—one of which was holding a small notepad that, while not at all alike, reminded Fyran infuriatingly of Trooper Sullivan's ticket book—and backed away, his eyes wide. "All right, man. Just water."

Fyran stared at Noah until the human, with an uncertain glance at Fyran over his shoulder, disappeared through a set of swinging doors that led into the kitchen.

Karak'duun, Fyran, so much for not drawing any fucking attention to yourself.

He returned his gaze to the menu, but his brain didn't register any of the words. The incident with the vrokars should have served as a lesson to him. It should have served as a reminder of what he'd already known—patience and caution were paramount. Allowing his frustrations to get the better of him was only compounding the challenges he faced. And yet here he was, making the same mistakes, only a week later.

Releasing a slow, heavy breath, Fyran eased his grip on the jacket, relaxed his tail, and willed his thumping heart to settle. But his body seemed little inclined to obey his commands, and his simmering anger made it difficult to reclaim his focus.

Though Gregor was still talking, Fyran couldn't separate the ilventyr's voice from all the rest. He just needed a few more moments to concentrate, to reestablish his self-control.

A scent struck him then—no, *scent* wasn't quite right, wasn't elegant enough a word. This was a fragrance, calming and mellow, sweet with a hint of spice. Cinnamon, vanilla, and cloves, underlaid by something decidedly feminine and alluring but much harder to identify. He breathed it in deeply.

Something tightened low in his belly, and his cock twitched. Fyran's brow furrowed.

What the fuck?

Closing his eyes, he filled his lungs with that fragrance again, chest swelling and nostrils flaring. The sensation in his groin intensified.

He sensed someone in front of him. A moment later, he heard the distinct sound of a glass being placed on the counter, followed by a similar sound made by something larger. Fyran opened his eyes to see a glass of ice water and a plate with a slice of cherry pie set before him.

"You seemed like you were having a bad day," the woman in front of him said. "Pie makes everything better."

Fyran lifted his gaze, ready to tell her to fuck off even though he knew better, but the words died on his lips. He felt his face go slack, and he couldn't do anything about it.

The female before him was...*beautiful*.

He was captivated by her big, thickly lashed, gray-blue eyes, which peered at him through the lenses of large, round glasses. The eyeliner on her upper eyelids swept outward like little wings, enhancing the beauty of her eyes, and her dark, gently arched eyebrows led down to a nose that was sprinkled with tiny brown freckles that reminded him of her scent—they looked like a dusting of cinnamon. The cinnamon dust was scattered across her cheeks, too, with just a little on her chin. A thin silver ring piercing gleamed on the right side of her nose. Her brown hair was pulled up into a messy bun atop her head, with wisps of it hanging on the sides of her delicate face.

The female's lips, shapely and pink, were curled up in a wide smile—a smile she was gifting directly to him. No one had ever smiled at Fyran that way. It was the sort of expression that could make him forget his name, that could make him forget his purpose. He could blissfully lose himself in it.

She was small and thin-framed, and he'd undoubtedly tower over her if he stood up. Her uniform was similar to Noah's and Jerry's, with a red and white pinstriped apron that molded to her curves, but she had a skirt on instead of pants, and it took all his willpower to keep from rising to get a look at her legs behind the counter.

Her nametag said *AVERY*.

Fyran's heart was pounding even harder now, and it had nothing to do with his anger; he couldn't even recall being angry.

As he stared, she averted her gaze, and her smile turned uncertain. "I mean, if you don't like cherry, I can get you something else." She stooped down so her face was level with his and lowered her voice. "It's totally on me. Just don't tell Jerry."

There were millions of words in dozens of languages stored in his head between his mind and the neural transceiver, but for a few moments, Fyran couldn't recall a single one. Her eyes, so big and round, captivated him.

Her brow creased, and she frowned. "Are...you okay?"

The transition from smile to frown on Avery's lips was like a bright summer sun suddenly dropping behind the horizon to plunge the world into darkness, and it jarred Fyran from his stupor. He sat up straight, flattening a hand atop the counter to brace himself.

"I...yeah. I'm okay," he said. *Oh, Fyran, you fucking liar.* "Cherry's fine."

Her smile returned with a flash of white teeth. "Great. Just wave me down if you'd like anything else."

I want you.

Karak'duun, where the hell had *that* thought come from?

Avery turned and made her way along the counter, pausing to inquire if an elderly customer needed anything. She patted the man's hand affectionally before moving on. Something rumbled in Fyran's chest, and it took him a moment to realize what it was.

Jealousy.

What the fuck?

Fyran finally glimpsed her legs—or, at least, the backs of her calves. Like the rest of her, they were slender but shapely, leading down to dainty feet clad in red canvas sneakers that matched the color of her skirt. She wore a silver chain around her left ankle.

A pulse rippled through his groin, and his tail twitched. That anklet was sexy as hell, and it filled his head with images of him cupping her heel in hand so he could run his thumb across the skin beneath that delicate chain.

Avery stopped next to Noah, who was filling glasses with ice at the soda fountain, and smiled up at him. She said something Fyran didn't catch. Noah chuckled and said something in response, nudging Avery's shoulder with his elbow. She laughed.

The rumble of jealousy Fyran had felt a moment before flared into something he could never have anticipated, twisting into a monster that made his fury look tame. He didn't like seeing her smile at another male, didn't like seeing her touch another male, didn't like seeing her laugh with another male.

He clenched his fists and clamped his jaw shut, battling his surging jealousy, that illogical, unnecessary, unwelcome emotion, battling the growl that threatened to rise from his chest.

Avery turned her head and locked her gaze with Fyran's. Her smile widened for an instant before it turned shy, and she glanced away. And just like that, the possessive rage burning in his chest dissipated.

He forced his attention down to the cherry pie in front of him. He'd liked cherries since his early days on Earth. He also liked cherry flavor, even though it wasn't usually comparable to the real thing.

But now...he *really* fucking liked cherries.

Fyran unwrapped the little bundle of silverware that had been laid out on the counter, took the fork in hand, and cut off a large piece from the tip of the pie. As he lifted the fork to his mouth, he glanced in Avery's direction.

She was talking to another customer at the end of the counter, still smiling, and she somehow looked even more beautiful than she had moments ago. As Fyran slipped the pie into his mouth, a song came to mind, one that he'd heard on the local classic rock station several times—*Cherry Pie*. He'd known the song was filled with sexual innuendos, but much of them had eluded his understanding, and he'd never bothered looking into it further.

He felt as though he'd garnered some new understanding of those hidden meanings now.

He wanted Avery to be his cherry pie. He wanted her taste on his tongue. Somehow, he knew she'd be even sweeter than the filling in this pie.

Dropping his gaze to the food, he took another bite. Such a simple kindness, despite the way he'd behaved. Such a moving gesture.

What the fuck am I doing? I'm here for one *reason, damn it.*

Holding back another growl and a torrent of curses, Fyran turned his head from side to side, forcing himself to move slowly and smoothly to create the illusion that he was simply studying the restaurant. He stilled once Gregor's table entered his peripheral vision.

Both the ilventyr and his guest were gone, leaving only a pair of coffee mugs and some empty sugar packets on their table.

"Fuck," Fyran muttered, turning back to his food. He shoveled another bite of pie into his mouth before standing up, holding his coat in one hand. The sign pointing to the restrooms was on the far side of the restaurant; that would give him a chance to search without being too conspicuous.

He strode across the diner, maintaining a natural pace despite his roiling impatience and anger. He'd allowed himself to be distracted by a female. He'd allowed his prey to escape without collecting any actionable information. For all Fyran knew, Gregor and his companion were plotting to smuggle those little paper packs of sugar to some alien buyer.

Big Sale.

You see it with your own eyes now, don't you?

Either there'd been something on the table between the two aliens that Fyran hadn't seen or there was something here, in this establishment, that they'd been referring to. His instinct told him it was something far more nefarious than smuggling some fucking sugar packets, and that wasn't just his yearning for action manifesting itself in his subconscious.

He discreetly scanned the other patrons and the crowd outside the big windows that ran along the diner's street-facing walls, but there was no sign of Gregor or the male with the knitted hat. They were gone. In the space of a minute or two, they'd slipped out.

Another coincidence?

Part of him was really coming to hate this planet.

Another part of him suggested there might be reasons to love it.

The stalls were empty in the men's room, and there was only one other male inside—a human at one of the urinals. Fyran clenched his jaw, narrowly resisting the urge to punch a hole in the fucking wall, hung his coat on a hook, and stepped up to the open urinal to relieve himself.

It was probably the angriest piss of his life.

Twice in the span of a week he'd fucked up and botched his surveillance. This wasn't the first time Gregor had eluded him, and it wasn't likely to be the last, but this was almost too much to bear so soon after the disaster with the vrokars and Trooper Sullivan.

He washed his hands at the sink, scrubbing hard and working the soap to a lather so full that he had to rinse twice before the soap was all gone. That certainly didn't improve his mood. Worse, this restroom didn't have paper towels—only those noisy dryers that blew semi-warm air for fifteen or twenty seconds at a time and barely dried anything at all.

Fyran just shook his hands off, knowing that he likely would've put his fist through the dryer if he'd tried to use it. He snatched his coat off the hook and exited the restroom.

As he returned to his stool at the counter, he glanced at Gregor's table again to discover that it had been cleared. Fyran could have stepped outside to continue the search, but given the crowds and the amount of time that had passed, the chances of spotting either of his targets were low. All Fyran knew was that Gregor and his anonymous associate had *something* planned.

Something involving this diner somehow.

No, he wasn't going to actively seek more frustration by heading out onto the streets in another blind search. His temper was already dangerously difficult to control. He didn't need to provoke himself further.

Not while he had cherry pie to finish.

Fyran sat down on his stool, laid his coat over his lap, and let out a long sigh. When he took his next bite of pie, he forced aside all his anger, dismissed all his racing thoughts, and focused on the taste and texture of the food. He focused on the gooey sweetness of the cherry filling, on the flakey, buttery perfection of the crust.

How the fuck could a planet that was behind in so many ways have such delicious food?

His eyes wandered, stopping only when they fell upon Avery.

Even if she wasn't deserving of it, he should've been angry with her. He should've been, at the very least, irritated with her. She'd been the distraction that had allowed Fyran's targets to slip away. She was the reason he'd ignored his self-appointed objective. She was a human female, and as he'd made clear to Command, he wanted nothing to do with her kind.

But he couldn't stop his gaze from returning to her time and again as he finished his pie with deliberate slowness.

She really was a tiny thing, flitting along the length of the counter and between tables with a subtle grace, often standing aside to let others through whether they'd seen her or not. It seemed as though she never stopped moving for more than a few moments at a stretch in all the time he watched her. There was a light sheen of sweat on her forehead, only noticeable when the light hit her skin just right, but her smile never wavered.

She was a ray of sunshine in the darkness, brightening every place she went.

Fyran grunted to himself. That wasn't the way he normally thought. It was sentimental, sappy...*human.*

Even when one of her customers put on an angry face and raised his voice slightly—complaining about his egg yolks touching his toast or some bullshit like that and demanding to know how anyone could mess up such a simple order—Avery maintained that smile and spoke to the man in gentle tones.

Fyran's muscles tensed as he watched the exchange, preparing to shove away from the counter so he could race across the diner and intervene.

Delicious as the pie had been, it hadn't dulled Fyran's overwhelming urge to punch something.

Fortunately for the man, he seemed to calm in response to

whatever Avery had said to him. Fyran was at once impressed and disappointed.

Those emotions shifted aside when she turned and walked back toward the kitchen with the man's plate in hand. Though she maintained that friendly expression, Fyran didn't miss the glimmer in her eyes—that tiny flicker of hurt.

His fist tightened around the fork, and he stilled it only when he felt the metal start to bend. Something inside him—instinct, perhaps, operating on a deep, primal level—demanded justice for her hurt. It insisted *he* deliver said justice. That he avenge this slight toward his female.

Hold on a fucking second, Fyran.

My female?

Avery glanced his way in that moment, catching his eye, and her smile widened before she disappeared into the kitchen.

Warmth blossomed in Fyran's chest. Though he'd seen her give a smile to every customer and co-worker she'd interacted with, he couldn't help but see something more there when she smiled at him. Something just for him.

My female.

No! He...he wasn't seeking a female, wasn't seeking a lifemate. He refused to take part in this mission.

A low growl rumbled in his chest as he dipped his head and scooped the remnants of the pie—the outside crust, where it was hardest and thickest—into his mouth. He chewed quickly, in a hurry to be done with it, to escape.

And fuck if it still wasn't delicious despite everything.

His attraction to this female was natural, and it had nothing to do with wanting a lifemate or a family. It was sexual. He was a male, she was a female. An incredibly attractive female, with big entrancing eyes, an intoxicating scent, and an alluring gracefulness.

Sexual urges were nothing new. He'd had them before, and he'd ignored them. This was no different. It wouldn't be a detriment to the work he was attempting to do here on Earth.

Except this felt *very* fucking different. He'd never felt desire this strong, had never felt so instantly, powerfully attracted to anyone.

Fyran dropped his fork and snatched up the glass of water. Condensation had gathered on its exterior, cold against his palm, and the water was even colder as he drank. He drained it all in one go. As he set the glass down, that sweet, spicy, cinnamon fragrance blasted his nose, making his cock twitch. A second later, Avery appeared in front of him.

"I take it you liked the pie?" She grinned as she dropped her gaze to his plate, which was empty save for a few crumbs and a red smear of cherry filling.

His tongue slipped out unbidden, running across his lips to gather the moisture lingering upon them, and he cleared his throat. "Yes. Thank you."

Her eyes dipped to his mouth, and her cheeks flushed a soft pink. She cleared her own throat, reached up, and pushed her glasses farther up the bridge of her freckled nose. "Is there anything else I can get you? More food, a refill, maybe some gift cards?" She picked up his empty plate. "Maaaaybe another piece of cherry pie?"

How about a piece of you?

Fuck.

Fyran's cock was instantly hard, straining against his pants and throbbing painfully. He'd never reacted like this to any female in all his life—not with a sliver of this intensity, not with a fraction of this speed.

Her hand was still on the plate, right in front of him, so close to his own. It would've taken barely any effort to shift his hand closer and touch hers, to feel her skin against his. To make that simple, intimate connection he'd railed against for so long. What would she feel like? Was her skin smooth and silky, warm and welcoming?

He pulled his arms back, dropped his hands into his lap, and squeezed his coat in both fists, pressing it down on his aching cock as though that would alleviate his discomfort.

"No," he said gruffly.

Avery leaned toward him over the counter. "I know it's crazy out there with all the post-Black Friday chaos, but I hope the rest of your day is better."

Fyran found himself staring into those gray-blue eyes again, and his response, spoken deeply, came out unbidden. "It already is."

She ducked her head as her cheeks darkened. "Good." Avery stood up straight. "Happy holidays, stranger."

Though his heart was beating hard enough that he swore she must've heard it, he managed to say, "Hunter. My name is Hunter."

Avery smiled softly. "Have a good day...Hunter."

He watched as she lifted the plate, grabbed his glass, and walked away, his grip on his jacket only strengthening. Helpless to look away, he kept his eyes on her until she'd vanished into the kitchen. Even then, his gaze lingered on the doors just in case she reemerged.

His cock was still throbbing. Oddly, so was his foot. It was only then that he realized his tail was coiled around his leg in a crushing grasp, squeezing impossibly tight.

With another muttered curse, he tore his gaze away from the kitchen door. If he let himself look upon her again, he'd never leave this damned place, and he had important matters to attend to. He had a purpose to fulfill, and it sure as hell wasn't the one the *Exthurizen* had thrust upon him. No one else would stop beings like Gregor. Fyran couldn't allow himself to be distracted from that work.

He stood up, tugged his wallet out of his pocket, pulled out the first bill he could grasp—a twenty—and tossed it on the counter. She'd said it was on her, but he couldn't accept that. He hadn't earned such kindness and consideration from her.

Without even pulling on his coat, he hurried toward the door. Every step of the way, he battled the urge to turn around and seek her out, to catch another glimpse of those enthralling eyes. To look upon his female.

Karak'duun, it's finally happened. Earth has shattered my mind. I'm insane.

As he stepped out into the cold and joined the crowd of holiday shoppers, it seemed impossible to deny it—he'd gone mad. Just being here now was sign of it.

"Not coming back to this place," he growled as he walked back toward the lot where he'd parked his car. Avery had been a pleasant distraction, but she'd been a distraction, nonetheless. That was unacceptable. And if he couldn't trust himself to maintain control, he'd simply have to lessen the risk of losing control in the first place.

His life would go on just fine if he never returned to Jerry's Diner.

However, there was a good chance the place was somehow involved in whatever Gregor was scheming.

And that pie really was delicious...

FOUR

"WE HAVE one BLT with a side of cottage cheese," Avery announced as she set one of the plates she was carrying in front of Mary. She placed the other in front of Mary's husband, Harley. "And one patty melt with extra cheese and pickles and a side of fries."

Harley leaned over his plate, making the booth's red leather cushion creak, and inhaled deeply. "Mmm. Looks and smells good, Avery."

"With as much cheese as you eat, I'm surprised your arteries didn't clog up twenty years ago," Mary said.

Harley grinned, sat back, and patted his stomach with both hands. "Nothing wrong with enjoying life's many pleasures." He wagged his bushy gray eyebrows at his wife. "Though there are *other* pleasures I enjoy even more."

Mary reached across the table and playfully smacked Harley's arm. "Oh, stop it, you rascal! We're in public."

Avery chuckled, and the wholesome warmth she always felt when watching the elderly couple interact spread through her chest. Harley and Mary had been visiting Jerry's forever, since long before Avery had started working here nearly two years ago— since long before she was even born. From what they'd said, Mary and Harley had been regulars since the now-septuagenarians had been teenagers, back when Jerry's parents had run the diner. They were regulars; they came every Sunday for lunch and sometimes stopped in for breakfast on weekdays.

Just recently, the two had celebrated their fiftieth anniversary. They'd come into the diner for the occasion, and Jerry had gone all-out, cooking them a veritable feast and charging nothing for it. Avery had found the whole thing even more special when she'd learned that Mary and Harley's first date had been in this very diner all those years ago.

Avery loved being their waitress. They were always kind, polite, and unhurried, always happy to chat with her, and their relationship was always flirty and sweet. There was no mistaking the love they had for one another. Though they'd aged, their eyes were as young and carefree as their souls.

They had the sort of marriage most people could only dream about—the sort of marriage *Avery* had always dreamed about. Was it still possible to have a relationship like theirs? Was it possible to find that true, undying love, or was it a relic of a past, a fairytale that existed only in books?

Cheeks burning red, Mary turned to look at Avery. "I'm sorry. You didn't need to hear that."

Avery grinned. "It's fine. I love it. My parents never showed affection to one another, so your relationship is inspiring."

"Do you have a lucky man in your life?" Harley asked.

"Not yet. Just haven't met the right one."

Mary reached up and gently patted Avery's shoulder. "You will, sweet girl. And I hope he shows you all the love you deserve."

Avery's heart clenched. Love wasn't something she'd experienced much of in her life. Her father was always indifferent and too busy with work, when her mother wasn't too self-absorbed, she was always finding flaws within Avery to remark upon, and though Avery was on good terms with her older sister, Eliza was focused on her own life, her own goals. The only experience Avery had with love was through romance novels and movies—and being an audience to couples like Harley and Mary.

"Thank you, Mary," Avery said with a smile. "But look at me taking up your time while your food is getting cold! Is there anything else I can get you both?"

"I'm good, dear. Thank you."

"Nope. You go on now," Harley said. "We know you're busy."

"I'll be back to check on you both soon. Enjoy!" Avery walked along the dining area, eyes sweeping her tables, noting the drinks were low in booth two. She stepped behind the counter and snatched up a couple clean cups. As she scooped ice into them, someone nudged her arm.

"*He* is back," Noah said, voice low.

Avery glanced up at him. "Huh? Who?"

"Mr. Tall, Dark, and Angry." He tipped his head to the side.

Leaning forward slightly, Avery peeked around Noah. Her breath caught, and her heart skipped a beat. There was no mistaking the man sitting at the counter. Even if it hadn't only been yesterday that she'd first seen him, she didn't think she could ever have forgotten him. Something about him had lodged itself inside her, and Avery wasn't sure if that was good or bad.

Hunter had his forearms propped against the edge of the countertop and his head bowed slightly, looking down at the menu. His long, wavy brown hair, streaked with gold, hung about his face. Even hunched over, his size was apparent. The man had to be at least six and a half feet tall. He'd tower over her five-foot three-inch frame.

Though she couldn't see his eyes now, she knew they were as black as pitch. Eyes so dark should have seemed unnatural or inhuman, should have looked empty and cold, but there had been such anger in them, such fire and passion. And when they'd met with Avery's...they had filled her with such *heat*. Her body's reaction had been instantaneous; her belly had fluttered, her core had tightened in arousal, and her nipples had hardened into aching peaks. She'd never experienced anything like it, and she felt the phantom sensations of that desire as she looked upon Hunter now.

Was that what it feels like to experience lust at first sight?

Except it felt like more than lust. It was...powerful.

"He gives me bad vibes," Noah said.

Avery blinked and forced herself to look away from Hunter, focusing instead on filling the cups. Because, you know, she had a *job* to do, and that job wasn't to stand around staring at customers longingly or daydream about handsome strangers. Not to mention staring at people was just rude.

And makes me look like a crazy person.

"Why do you say that?" Avery asked, pressing the button on the fountain and watching soda spray into the cup.

"Dude just about bit my head off yesterday."

"He was just having a bad day."

"Avery, everyone has bad days sometimes. Most people don't look like they're gonna murder you for suggesting the daily specials."

"Oh, I see. So you sacrifice me to the hungry lion instead?"

Noah looked down at her and raised his brows in an *Are you kidding me?* expression. "You practically had him eating out of your hands yesterday. I don't think the same thing would have happened if I offered him a slice of pie."

"You won't know until you try."

"Ha. Very funny."

Avery chuckled and placed the other cup beneath the soda fountain to fill it. "Noah, are you waiting for me to offer to my services to him again?"

He pressed his hands flat together in front of him. "Pleeeeese?"

"You know you're being ridiculous, right?"

"You said he was a good tipper. What do you have to lose?"

"What do *you* have to lose?"

"My fingers. I'm serious, Avery. Dude looked ready to bite them off." Noah held up his hands, fingers splayed. "You know I got nice fingers. I want to keep them." He grinned lasciviously. "I have ladies to please."

Avery laughed, rolled her eyes, and gave Noah a shove. "Don't be disgusting."

She looked in Hunter's direction to find him staring at them—

or more specifically, at Noah. A chilling gleam flashed in those dark eyes, there and gone in an instant. But it was enough to tell her that maybe Noah's worries were justified.

"Hey, what are you two gossiping about?" Brandy, one of the other waitresses, asked as she came to stand next to Avery with an armful of empty cups. Her bright red hair was pulled up and curled in a vintage fifties hairstyle with a white bandana tied in a bow atop her head.

"Just trying to get Avery to take a customer for me," Noah said.

"Really? Which one?" Brandy asked.

Noah twisted slightly to shield his hand as he pointed toward Hunter. "Dude in the leather jacket at the end of the counter."

Brandy leaned to the side, and her brown eyes rounded. "Wow. He's hot. I'll do him."

Noah snorted. "I'm sure you would."

Brandy elbowed Noah. "Don't be such a hypocrite. You're more of a ho than I am."

A wide grin spread across his face, and he shrugged. "Guilty."

"I'll take care of him," Avery said, a bit quicker and more enthusiastically than she'd intended. "I've already established a good rapport with him."

"You already do him, then?" Brandy asked with a sly grin.

Avery's cheeks flushed. "What? No! I just gave him a piece of pie."

"You gave him a piece, huh? Did it happen to come with a cherry?"

Noah laughed.

"Oh, my gosh," Avery said, pinching the bridge of her nose, feeling her body heat with embarrassment. "My sex life"—*or lack thereof*—"is none of your business."

"Hey!" Jerry called from the kitchen window. "Get your butts moving! I got orders up here."

"Sorry, Boss Man," Brandy said, taking her armful of dirty cups to the kitchen.

Avery, thankful for Jerry's intervention, pressed the two sodas into Noah hands. "Take these to booth two and check my other tables."

"You're a life saver, Avery," Noah said.

Pushing her glasses up her nose, tucking the loose strands of her hair behind her ear, and smiling, Avery walked along the counter toward Hunter. When she looked up into his eyes, her stride nearly faltered. They were so dark and intense.

He was...beautiful, in an unearthly, dangerous sort of way. His dark, golden-streaked hair framed the face of a fallen angel. He had pronounced cheekbones, a strong jaw, and a chiseled nose. His lips were defined and full, and for a moment, Avery wondered what they might feel like against hers. Would they be hard and brutal, or soft and giving? Thick, dark, slashing eyebrows rested above his black eyes.

"You're back," she said as she stopped in front of him. "Are you going to be a new regular?"

His gaze trailed over her unhurriedly, gleaming with something that should've made her uncomfortable, but Avery couldn't deny the little thrill his gaze had awoken in her.

"Pie was good," he replied in his deep, rumbling voice. "Figured I'd try something else."

He spoke with a hint of an accent. It was nothing that Avery could place, but it was still sexy as hell.

She grinned and swung her fist in front of her. "Well, if you love burgers, you came to the right place!"

Smooth, Avery. Can you be any cornier?

He tilted his head slightly. "That what you recommend?"

"The cheeseburgers with Jerry's special sauce are great, especially with sweet potato fries."

"I'll have that, then."

"Is there anything I can get you to drink while you wait?"

"Something"—his dark eyes flicked over her again, and seemed to light up for an instant—"sweet."

Oh, God...

"We...we have soda, Italian cream sodas, lemonade, milkshakes. I swear we have some of the *best* milkshakes you'll ever have. Jerry's is like, my milkshake brings all the boys to the... Eh, I think I'll stop talking now." Avery let out a nervous laugh.

The corner of his mouth quirked just a tiny bit. That little change somehow softened his expression while making it outright rakish. "What's an Italian cream soda?"

"It's carbonated water, flavored syrup, and cream. It's delicious. I...kind of have a thing for cherry, so that's my favorite, but we have so many other flavors."

Hunter ran a hand through his hair, tucking the strands back from his face. "Cherry would be perfect."

Avery smiled wide. "Great! I'll get your order in and be right back."

As she walked to the kitchen window, she dipped her hand into her apron and pulled out her order pad. She quickly scribbled down his order and attached it to the order wheel. "Order in, Jerry."

"Will be about ten minutes, Avery," Jerry called over the sounds of sizzling meat and fries.

"Got it."

She checked on the other customers at the counter—which were thankfully few—and hurriedly refilled any drinks and fetched condiments before she set about preparing the stranger's Italian soda. Just like yesterday, she felt Hunter's eyes upon her, watching her, studying her the whole time.

She wasn't sure how she felt about it.

Avery had dealt plenty with men's stares and their crude comments. She'd learned to ignore most of it. She'd even survived a few of them touching her inappropriately. None of that had been pleasant, but at least when they'd been direct and open, it had given her something to stand up against.

Hunter hadn't done anything but look, and something about him felt different from all the other men who'd done so. His attentions felt somehow...safe. And it made her feel strange things—pleasantly wicked things. It made her skin tingle, made heat bloom low in her belly, made liquid heat gather between her thighs, and made her heart pound.

I'm going crazy.

Once she'd finished mixing the Italian soda—making sure to add a cherry on top of the whipped cream—she returned to Hunter and set the red and white concoction on the counter. "Here you go!"

"Looks good," he said as he wrapped his fingers around the glass and dragged it closer.

Avery couldn't help but notice that his eyes hadn't left her as he'd spoken. Despite that spark lingering in his dark gaze, she didn't know if he was being flirty or was actually talking about the soda.

It became clearer when Hunter plucked up the cherry and slipped it between his lips, biting it off the stem—without breaking eye contact.

"You'll, um...have to tell me what you think." She glanced down at the glass.

Hunter lifted the glass to his mouth and took a long sip. When he lowered it, there was whipped cream on his upper lip, smeared across his moustache stubble. "You were right."

She couldn't stop a small giggle from escaping her. "Oh! I forgot your straw."

Dipping her hand into the pocket of her apron, she took out a wrapped straw and placed it on the counter while trying so hard to resist the urge to lean forward and lick the whipped cream from his lip.

Totally inappropriate, Avery. Jerry would have words.

But it would be so worth it.

If only she could be that bold.

"You have some, uh, you know." She lifted a hand and pointed to her upper lip, wagging her finger back and forth.

His tongue slipped out and slowly—*sinfully*—swept away the whipped cream, drawing it into his mouth.

Avery's core clenched. There had to be some sort of law against making something like that look so damned alluring.

"Wouldn't want any to go to waste," he said.

"I-I...uh...right?"

Tongue tied, Avery? What is wrong with you?

There is a fine ass man flirting me with me. How else am I supposed to react? I'm no good in these situations!

I'm just going to sigh and daydream, that's what I'm going to do. He's just...

"So hot..."

Wait. What did you just say, Avery?

She gasped, her eyes widening as she realized what had spilled out of her mouth. "I mean your food! Your hot *food* will be ready soon. I didn't mean to say you're hot. Well, I mean you *are*, but...oh jeez." She slipped her hands up beneath her glasses and pressed her palms to her face, hiding behind them. "Just kill me now."

"Why would you say that?" Hunter asked.

Avery slowly lowered her hands, allowing her glasses to fall back into place as she opened her eyes to look at him. His brows were drawn, and there was a troubled expression upon his face.

"You mean...the hot thing?" she asked, cheeks burning in mortification. "I am so, so sorry. It was inappropriate and unprofessional of me. You're the customer and—"

"No. Why would you tell me to kill you?"

He...he didn't think she meant to *literally* kill her, did he? He had to be foreign. That would explain the accent she thought she'd heard earlier, though it was difficult to detect now. Maybe this was one of those lost in translation things?

"It's just an expression," she said. "It means that I'm so embarrassed that death would be preferable to, you know, the humiliation of my own actions. But not *literally*."

"Ah." He nodded and plucked up the straw from the counter, his long fingers moving dexterously as he tore off the wrapper. "So, when you say I'm hot—"

"Welp, would you look at all those tables and empty drink glasses," she said quickly with a giant smile. "Lemme know if you need anything else, okay?"

Hunter smirked as he slipped his straw into his drink. "I will, Avery."

The way his voice caressed her name sent a shiver through her, making her skin prickle with goosebumps. She turned and stepped away, rubbing her arms.

He is definitely flirting with me.

And she...she wasn't sure how to handle it.

She continued taking and delivering orders, refilling drinks, and clearing tables, and before long a large group entered the diner. It wasn't unusual at this time of day on a Sunday.

"You got this one?" Brandy asked as she walked over to Avery with a tray of dirty dishes. "My section's pretty busy."

"Sure. Can you take these?" Avery asked, nodding at the small stack of plates and silverware in her hands.

"Yeah." Brandy took the plates from her. "Noah and I will help keep an eye on your other customers."

"Thanks, Brandy."

"You got it, hon. Good luck."

Well, there goes my chance to talk to Hunter again.

Not like I could consider that talking. More like stuttering, blathering, and bumbling. I can write 'em, but I sure can't say 'em.

Avery sighed. If only she were more like her sister, able to stand tall, talk, and flirt with men confidently. But she'd always hear her mother's voice in the back of her mind, pointing out all her shortcomings.

If you'd just put on some makeup to cover those freckles and do something with your hair, you wouldn't have any problems, Avery.

Wear something flattering, something that shows off your assets. It's too bad you didn't inherit my figure like your sister did.

Why must you wear those horrendous glasses? Everyone is wearing contacts now.

If you looked like you care about yourself, men would be all over you.

Why would Avery want a guy who wanted her just for the way she looked? What good had that done her mother? Allison Watson had a husband who ignored her as much as he ignored his kids—though that seemed to suit her just fine.

Avery refused to settle. She wanted a man who loved her

whether she wore makeup or not, a man who loved her for her freckles and all. She wanted what she'd seen from Harley and Mary. She wanted a deep and loving relationship. She wanted forever.

A forever with *passion*.

She sighed morosely.

Still believing in fairytales and happily-ever-afters, Avery? Maybe you spent too long with your nose stuck in a book.

FIVE

Avery plastered on a smile as she approached the large party gathered at the entrance. "Hi! Welcome to Jerry's. How many in your party?"

"Twelve," the man in front said.

"You got it. Just give me a minute to get your tables set up."

As she moved into the dining area, she glanced at Hunter just in time to see Noah delivering his meal. Fortunately, Hunter didn't bite off Noah's fingers; he didn't even bark, snarl, or growl. He just glanced down at the food for a moment before swinging his gaze around the rest of the diner.

Naturally, that gaze met Avery's, and it nearly made her freeze in place. She could have taken the directness of his stare, its heat and intensity, as a warning, as a sign that this man was dangerous. She really *should* have, but... Corny as it sounded, even in her own head, she felt seen. All the other stuff aside, she felt like he was actually seeing her for her.

Which was ridiculous considering he knew nothing about her.

Focus, Avery. Guys like him are not for you. He might flirt with you, but he's not after a happily-ever-after. He's likely more interested in the bow-chicka-wow-wow.

Mood plummeting, she tore her gaze away from Hunter and

went about pushing some tables together and placing the menus and silverware. She swore she could feel his eyes on her the whole time, but she dared not look at him again. She had work to do.

As soon as she was done, she hurried to the waiting party and led them to their tables. Avery stood back while they all removed their coats and, amidst a lot of loud conversation and a bit of bickering, eventually sorted themselves enough to take their seats. She wasted no time in taking their drink orders.

All twelve ordered water alongside their other drinks. That didn't necessarily mean anything, but it was one of those little things that always made her subconsciously brace herself.

Brandy jumped in to help fill and deliver the drinks, and then the real fun began—half the table was ready to order, half wasn't, and they all seemed keen on contradicting each other. Avery kept her smile in place and gave them a few more minutes to decide.

She checked on a couple other tables, cleared Mary and Harley's table, grateful for their always-generous tip but sad she'd not had a chance to say goodbye before they'd left. As she kept herself busy, she made a willful effort to *not* look toward Hunter. Brandy and Noah had him covered.

When she returned to the large group, they were finally ready to order. The process took a while, and it wasn't quite as smooth as she'd hoped—not that it ever was. A few of the people were still uncertain on what they wanted, a couple were extremely particular with their orders—which was fine, but always made Avery nervous—and one changed his order at the very end. Several of them had already finished their drinks.

Avery smiled through all of it, confirmed their orders, and fetched refills. Jerry and Levi, the other cook, were like whirlwinds in the kitchen, but she knew she had at least a little time to breathe. Those big groups could be so draining, even when everything went right.

Of course, it didn't help that her mother was still there in the back of her mind, saying *I told you so* regarding Avery's current job while looking down her perfect nose.

Noah gave her a hand when the large party's food was ready.

Even with two people, it took two trips to get it all to the table. As always, Avery asked if they needed anything else, and there were the usual requests for more condiments and napkins, along with one snide declaration that she'd messed up an order—from the man who'd changed his at the last moment. Apparently, he'd forgotten having changed his mind, and hadn't corrected her despite her having read back their orders.

It was times like these that wearing a smile hurt, but Avery kept one in place regardless. After calmly explaining that he'd changed his order—which only angered him further—she apologized, assured him she'd make it right, and gathered up his plate and a few empty glasses before heading back to the kitchen.

Only there did her smile falter, and Jerry knew as she relayed the new order that something was wrong. She explained the situation while he quickly put the new meal together.

"You're doing good, Avery," Jerry said, handing her the finished order.

She delivered the food along with fresh refills. Sweat dripped between her breasts and down her back, and her hair was damp at her temples. Between the heater, all the people in the diner, and constantly being on the go, she was sweltering.

After Avery had made several more trips to refill drinks and serve desserts to the few who'd requested them, the large party gathered their belongings and left, allowing Avery a moment's respite.

She moved to their table to collect the signed receipt.

Tears of frustration filled her eyes as she stared down at the paper, and she curled her lips in, biting down to keep them from trembling. She crumpled the paper in her hand as she looked up and blinked the tears away.

Assholes. Those damned, cheap assholes.

The handwritten notes customers sometimes left on the receipts were often heartwarming and uplifting—especially the ones Mary wrote. The note on this receipt was not of that sort.

Try being more attentive and remember—the customer is always right!!! Merry Christmas.

The numbers on the tip line were written quite boldly. Zero point zero zero.

She took in a series of deep breaths to calm herself.

It's done, Avery. They're gone, and there's nothing more you can do.

Tucking the receipt into her apron pocket, she began the task of cleaning up the giant mess on the table and floor. Thankfully, the busiest time of day had passed, and the diner had slowed down, allowing her to hear the jukebox. It was currently playing *Love is Strange.*

Someone set a large plastic bin on the table next to her.

"I'll finish up here, Avery," Noah said. "Go take a break."

Avery smiled and set the partially filled cups in her hands into the bin. "Thanks, Noah."

Wiping her hands on her apron, she made her way to the register, adding the receipts in her pockets to till. As she turned, her eyes caught on the handsome man sitting at the end of the counter. She started, her eyes widening.

Why was Hunter still here?

His plate was clean—it looked like he'd licked every crumb off it—and his glass was empty, with only a bit of leftover cream, tinged red by the cherry flavoring, clinging to the sides.

She wiped her hands on her apron again, this time due to nervousness, as she approached him. Her lips curled into a smile.

"You're still here," she said, bending forward to fold her arms on the countertop.

Even with the counter separating her from Hunter, she felt exposed, vulnerable, and...oddly excited about it.

Hunter raked his gaze over her. "Seems so."

"Is there...anything I can get for you?"

His face remained unreadable. Though she couldn't quite call his expression neutral, she couldn't really call it anything else, either. But his eyes...

Grave. Smoldering. Intense.

Okay, so maybe there were words that fit.

After a moment of silence that should've been uncomfortable, he said, "No."

"All right." Her smile widened. "Has anyone brought your check yet?"

Hunter nodded. "Already paid."

"Great. Well, thank you for coming in again. I hope you enjoyed your meal, and hope you have a good evening."

Avery flattened her hands on the counter, pushed herself upright, and turned to walk away. But she hadn't even lifted her palms off the countertop when something big, strong, and warm fell over her left hand. She froze, breath hitching.

When she was finally able to look down, she found Hunter's hand atop hers, covering it completely. He curled his fingers around her hand. She snapped her eyes back up. His hold on her was firm but not painful. She could feel the calluses on his fingers and palms, could feel the pricks of his nails against the center of her hand. Strange. His nails hadn't looked long, but they almost felt like...claws?

It was thrilling.

"What's wrong?" he asked, his voice a low rumble she swore only she could hear.

"What?" she replied—or at least tried to; the first time she opened her mouth, nothing came out. It was only on her second attempt that she actually produced the word.

"You're troubled," he said.

"Um...yeah." Her tongue slipped out to wet her suddenly dry lips. "People usually look that way when strangers unexpectedly grab their hands."

Hunter's eyebrows sank low over those deep, dark eyes, and his lips fell into a slight but impossibly heavy frown. His fingers flexed around her hand. "You were troubled before this, Avery."

"What do you mean?"

He seemed to search her face for several seconds, maintaining his hold on her hand. Avery didn't try to pull away from him. She couldn't bring herself to do so, even though she knew this wasn't right, this wasn't okay.

Wasn't it?

It was just...his touch felt so good.

"Those people"—Hunter tipped his head toward the other side of the diner—"at the large table. They made your smile seem strained. And there were tears in your eyes when you picked up the bill. What'd they do?"

His voice had taken on a slight edge, and his grasp had tightened further.

Heat flooded her face, and she looked self-consciously to where he held her. "It's nothing. But...thank you, Hunter. For your concern."

What was wrong with her? Why wasn't she feeling unsettled or threatened by his behavior?

His frown deepened, and she knew in that moment that he really was worried for her. However mysterious or dangerous this man was, however odd this whole situation, his concern was genuine.

"Really," she said gently, "I'm okay."

A low sound came straight from his chest, a combination of a grunt and a growl that somehow signaled both a mild acceptance and skepticism of her words. She dared not lift her gaze to look directly into his eyes again. Hunter's were the sort of eyes you were warned about in romance books—the sort of eyes a woman could lose herself in.

Finally, his hand relaxed. His fingers twitched, that prick of his nails on her palm strengthened the tiniest bit, and then he released her. His now empty fingers curled loosely as he lowered his hand to the counter.

"Thank you for the recommendations," he said gruffly.

Of their own accord, Avery's fingers curled, too, and tingles pulsed across her skin.

"I, uh... Any time." She forced a smile onto her lips—not that she had to force it too much—and lifted her gaze to his. "Hope to see you again soon. I have a lot of other things you can taste." Her eyes widened. "Uh, I mean, *we* have other things you can taste... on the menu. Obviously."

Hunter smirked. "Can't wait to taste it all."

The flush on her cheeks intensified, but her eyes remained on him for a little longer before she turned and made her way through the kitchen door.

She walked to the breakroom in the back, where she took a bottle of water out of the fridge, dug her phone out of the bottomless pit that was her green bohemian messenger bag she'd stored in her locker, and sat down at the empty tables. Unscrewing the lid from the bottle, she took a drink and unlocked her phone. She pulled up the e-reader app and attempted to read, but she couldn't focus. Her thoughts kept returning to Hunter.

Clearly too distracted to give the book the attention it deserved, she closed the e-reader app and checked her text messages. The only new message was from her sister. Avery tapped on it.

Mom is going on and on to me about the upcoming photoshoot. Eliza had attached a meme of Bill Lumbergh from *Office Space* saying, *Yeah if someone could just kill me now that'd be great.*

Avery snickered and typed back. *My heart goes out to you, sis.* After searching the gifs, she selected one with Celine Dion singing and pressed send.

"I'm so glad I'm not you right now."

Locking the screen, she sat back and glanced at the clock. Only ten minutes had passed. She sighed. Bored, she took a couple deep drinks from the water bottle, stood, and returned her phone to her bag. She'd rather continue working than sit in here in silence. It'd make the time go by faster so she could get home.

When Avery returned to the dining room, her gaze instinctively returned to the place Hunter had been seated. She frowned. His plate and cup were still on the counter, but he was nowhere to be seen. Had he just left?

She walked to the end of the counter and picked up his plate. Beneath it was a folded napkin that had something written on it in bold, precise capital letters—*AVERY*.

Tilting her head, she opened the napkin and gasped. Tucked within was a one-hundred-dollar bill.

Avery had come from a wealthy family. Though she'd been grateful for all that she'd had, she'd never felt like she'd earned any of it. And all that money...well, it had never resulted in happiness for her or her family. She'd tried to escape from that over these couple years, to find her own way, and she'd worked for every dollar she'd made.

To her parents, a hundred bucks was a single plate of food at a half-decent restaurant. To Avery, it was a week or two of groceries. For Hunter to have left this...

She turned her head and sought out Noah, who was clearing one of the booths along the window nearby. "Hey Noah?"

He looked up at her as he stacked dirty plates in a plastic bin. "Yeah?"

"Did the man who was sitting here tip you when he paid the bill?"

Noah grinned and returned his attention to the table. "Yep. Left forty on a fifteen-dollar check. Best tip of the day."

Avery looked back down, folded the napkin over the money, and traced a finger over the writing. Hunter had given her a large tip the day before, something she hadn't expected but for which she'd been immensely grateful, but this...this was too much. Tears blurred her vision.

Was this because of what that big group had done? Because he'd seen her upset, had seen her cry?

Was it because he was...interested in her?

No. Why would someone like Hunter want anything to do with her? The man was gorgeous! He was big and strong, brooding and mysterious. He looked like a biker, or a rock star, or a Viking transported to modern day America.

And she was...she was just Avery. Small, plain, and awkward. She didn't exude sex appeal like her mother and sister. They were bombshells, and she was a cute little nerd. Nothing about her said that she'd be the wild ride a man like Hunter was undoubtedly after.

But still, he *had* been flirting with her. Blatantly flirting. He hadn't tried to hide his interest even one bit.

Avery didn't know what to make of this tip. She didn't want him to pity her or think that she needed his charity—there were so many people who were so much more deserving of help than her —but she didn't think that was his motivation. Though he'd been unreadable for so much of the time, she had the sense that he'd simply done this out of kindness.

She picked up the napkin and clutched it to her chest, absently stroking her thumb across those neatly printed letters.

Whatever his reasons, Avery knew one thing—she wanted to see Hunter again.

SIX

"Goodnight, Jerry," Avery said, pulling on her cotton gloves as she walked past her boss, who was counting money at the till.

Jerry looked up at smiled. "Night, kid. Enjoy your day off. I'll see you Tuesday."

Avery pushed open the front door and stepped outside. She shivered as the cold winter air bit at her face. Large snowflakes fell lazily from the sky, glowing gold when they drifted into the luminescence of the lampposts. It made her surroundings surreal, majestic, enchanting, and despite having been on her feet all day and having a twenty-minute walk to her apartment ahead of her, she simply stood there and took in the beauty.

With it being late on a Sunday night, there were no shoppers wandering the mall, there were no bustling crowds, and it was easy for Avery to pretend she was the only person in the world as she stood beneath the falling snow. It was quiet. Peaceful.

The hibernating trees along the walkway were decorated with white Christmas lights, and there were wreaths hanging from the light posts. Christmas day had never held any special meaning for her growing up—it was just another excuse for her mother to throw cocktail parties and show off—but she'd always loved the season. She loved the lights, the snow, and festiveness. It was like living in a fantasy world.

For an instant, she had a childlike impulse to stick her tongue out and catch a snowflake. She didn't fight it. She extended her tongue and tipped her head back, catching a huge snowflake on the tip of her tongue. Its delicate, icy touch was invigorating, but it was also fleeting. The snowflake was already melting before she could draw it into her mouth.

Avery took in a slow, deep breath, ignoring the sting of the winter air in her nose. She ran the toe of her boot through the snow in front of her. Though it wasn't coming down heavily, it'd been snowing long enough to leave at least an inch-deep layer of the white stuff upon the sidewalk.

She adjusted the strap of her messenger bag, which had been lying uncomfortably over her bulky coat, raised her hood, and started her trek home. The air flowed around her legs and swept up her skirt, making her glad she'd pulled on her leggings. It would've been one heck of a chilly walk with frigid air blowing directly on her ass.

She'd have to start taking her car if it kept snowing like this. That would mean spending money on gas, an expense she was trying to minimize for as long as possible. But the weather wasn't the only reason for her to start using her car—it was dark outside this late at night, and everything was always more dangerous in the dark. Her practice of varying her route every night wasn't enough.

Avery stuck to the main, well-lit roads until she reached the more residential area, where the streetlights were dimmer and more sparsely placed. Other than the occasional passing car, she was all alone out here tonight. She fiddled with her keys in her coat pocket.

She loved nights like this, though, loved the quiet. Even when things were busier and the sun was shining, she enjoyed walking. It gave her time to think, time to breathe, time to decompress after a hard shift, and it just felt *good*. That had been a big motivation for using her car less. But Avery couldn't deny that walking home after dark put her on edge sometimes. The pepper spray in her bag didn't exactly instill her with a sense of security.

I should invest in a taser. Zap zap.

Or a gun.

The thought gave her pause, and shudder coursed through her. She couldn't imagine shooting anyone; she wasn't sure if she could even pull the trigger if it came down to it.

Snow crunched beneath her boots as she walked, the noise made strange by the eerie quiet all around her that happened whenever it snowed. It was like all sound had been muffled.

The hairs on the back of her neck rose.

Avery halted, turned to look behind her, and furrowed her brow. There was no one there.

So why do I feel like I'm being watched?

Because you started thinking about tasers and guns and all the bad things that could happen. Way to go, Avery. Psych yourself out, why don't you?

Rolling her eyes, she faced forward and continued at a brisker pace until she reached home.

Her street was lined with brick buildings that had been constructed many, many years ago, most of which had lovely adornments in their architecture, little touches that weren't common in modern design. By and large, they'd been well-maintained.

The rundown three-story apartment building where Avery lived seemed so out of place amongst the beautiful structures around it. The building's exterior walls were flat and plain, lacking in imagination. Its once red bricks were faded and crumbling, the awning over the main door was missing a few shingles, and one of the iron-barred windows on the lower floor had a crack in its glass that stretched diagonally from the top left corner to the bottom right.

Here in the dead of night, with snow enhancing the quiet, this seemed like the perfect setting for a horror movie.

My mother would have a stroke if she knew I lived here.

She followed the sidewalk up to the door and pulled it open.

Sometime long ago, well before Avery had lived here, this had been the sort of door that required the entry of a code—or a buzz-in from a resident—to get through. Now, it was open to anyone who wanted to enter.

Avery stomped her feet, clearing the snow off her boots, and stepped inside.

The combined smells of cigarettes and marijuana struck her immediately. They hung in the foyer, hazy and thick, and passing through them was like pushing through a solid brick wall.

She drew back her hood, tugged off her gloves to stuff them in her coat pockets, and walked toward the stairs. She was forced to tilt her head down slightly to look over the rims of her glasses—which had annoyingly fogged up—to make sure she didn't bump into anything. As she climbed the steps, she detected other smells—the mustiness of old wood, the mildewy smell of the old, stained, dark red carpet on the floors and stairs.

By the time she reached the third floor, where her apartment was located, the smoke-stench was thankfully barely noticeable.

There was death metal music blaring in the apartment across from hers. That was nothing out of the ordinary. The man who lived there, Ian, was in his late forties and kept odd hours. He was often active at night and in the early, early mornings, hanging around outside his door or down in the foyer smoking with his friends. Though he seemed nice enough, he liked to stare at Avery—mainly at her chest.

Okay, so maybe he wasn't so nice.

Thankfully, Ian was inside his apartment now, allowing Avery to slip into hers without having to interact with him. He had a habit of drawing out conversations that should never have progressed past the initial exchange of helloes, seemingly oblivious when the person he was talking to sent every signal that they were ready to leave.

She flipped on the lights, closed the door, and locked it. There was a thump on the worn hardwood floor behind her, followed by a series of excited meows.

Avery turned as Beau, her two-year-old ragdoll cat, raced toward her and rubbed against her calf.

"Hey Beau, did you miss me?" She dropped her keys into the small pocket inside her messenger bag, lifted the strap off over her head, and hung the bag on the hook beside the door.

Crouching, she smiled and ran her palm along Beau's back all the way to his dark, fluffy tail. His long fur was soft to the touch, and his body vibrated with his purring.

He arched his back into her hand and paused. For a moment, he stood still, as though waiting for something. Then he turned and forcefully bumped his head against her hand, demanding another pet.

Avery chuckled and complied. "I take that as a yes."

He meowed again, placed his front paws on her leg, and leaned his head toward her, whiskers twitching as he sniffed. She lowered her face and tapped her nose to his. In return, he nuzzled her chin.

This one-bedroom apartment had been so lonely before she'd come across Beau on her way home from work one day. An older woman had been sitting in front of her home with a cardboard box set on the ground and a handwritten sign—*Kittens free to a good home*. Beau had been just a tiny, fluffy, mewing kitten, one in a litter of six, similar in coloration to his siblings. But he'd been the most vocal of them all, climbing over his brothers and sisters when Avery had peered into the box so he could stare up at her with his big blue eyes. Avery had adopted him on the spot. He'd been her constant, loveable companion ever since, and she couldn't imagine coming home and not having him here to greet her.

Avery closed her eyes and rubbed her forehead against his. "I missed you, too." Pulling back, she scratched him behind his ears. "Are you hungry?"

He meowed enthusiastically.

"Let's go fill your dish, then."

Standing back up, Avery took off her coat and hung it next to her bag. After removing her boots and digging her phone out of her bag, she walked through the living room, heading toward the kitchen. Beau raced ahead of her.

The compact kitchen was sectioned off from the living room by a thin wall. It had very little counter space, but came with a fridge, an oven, and a microwave. The flooring was aged yellow vinyl covered with knicks and scrapes that had probably been white at some point in the distant past. The oak cupboards—which were a shade lighter than the hardwood floor in the living room and bedroom—were separated from the counters by a tile backsplash.

The grout between those tiles was stained so deeply that no amount of scrubbing would ever remove it. Avery knew that because she'd given herself sore arms trying to clean it when she'd first moved in.

This place wasn't much to look at, but she was renting it all on her own. And that meant something.

Beau was sitting expectantly beside his food dish. Avery opened the cabinet under the sink, scooped a cupful of cat food out of the bag, and poured it into his dish. He immediately stuck his head in and started chomping away. After making sure his refillable water bowl had plenty of water, she left him to eat, making her way to the bathroom.

It was just as cramped and aged as the kitchen, but it did have one feature she loved—the clawed foot bathtub. Unfortunately, it was late, and Avery was tired. All she wanted to do was cuddle up with Beau on the couch and watch a little bit of TV before bed, so that meant no luxuriating in a hot bath tonight—just a quick shower.

At least she didn't have to worry about fixing dinner; she'd eaten not long ago at the diner.

Yay for free food!

She turned on the water to get it warmed up and removed her glasses, setting them on the counter next to her cellphone. After she let down her hair, she undid the buttons of her uniform and peeled it off, pushing it to the floor. Her bra and underwear came next.

The water was hot by the time she'd finished undressing. She made a few adjustments, turned on the shower, stepped into the tub, and closed the curtain.

She washed her hair and body, relishing the hot water against her chilled skin. One thing she didn't have to worry about was shaving. Her mother had taken both Avery and Eliza to get their body hair removed for their eighteenth birthdays. *All* of their body hair.

Avery closed her eyes and sighed. As much as she wanted to stand under the hot water—and possibly fantasize about Hunter— she wanted to get off her feet more. She was exhausted, and fantasizing would only leave her unfulfilled and wanting. Masturbating was a nice way to relieve some pressure, but that was all. It was scratching an itch. Fleeting and meaningless.

She wanted something...deeper. Wanting something *more*. She craved the feel of calloused hands upon her body, of warm lips against hers, of a man's body atop of her, between her thighs, his cock thrusting into her.

And it was Hunter, with his long, gold-streak hair falling around her, that Avery imagined now; it was Hunter inside her, it was his smoldering black eyes locked with hers.

Her core clenched, and heat coalesced low in her belly.

Her eyes snapped open. "Ugh. Not helping, Avery. Didn't we decide *not* to fantasize?"

She could almost hear her body say it had never agreed to that; it was totally willing to explore this fantasy a little longer. Maybe until she'd climaxed?

Avery snorted.

Turning off the water, she wrung her hair out, opened the curtain, and pulled her towel off the hook. Cold air touched her heated skin, and she shivered. The chill was enough to dampen her arousal.

"Stupid crappy heating and insulation," she muttered, rubbing the towel over her hair and quickly dried her body.

Stepping out of the tub onto the rug, she wrapped the towel around her body, combed her hair, and brushed her teeth. Once she'd applied moisturizer to her face and arms, she plucked up her glasses, perched them back on her nose, and gathered her phone and dirty clothes. She walked into the bedroom, where she dropped the clothes in her laundry basket. At her dresser, she grabbed a clean pair of panties, her coziest pajamas, and some fluffy socks, and pulled it all on.

Beau was already lying atop Avery's favorite blanket on the sofa when she emerged from her bedroom. He looked at her as though asking, *What took you so long?*

"Not everyone can laze about all day, you loaf." She crossed the room to flick off the light switch near the front door.

Without the overhead light on, the lights from the small Christmas tree she'd placed on a stand beside the TV cast a golden glow across the room, making it seem cozy and warm.

Avery smiled and walked to the sofa. She put her cellphone down on the end table and scooped up the fuzzball, cradling him in her arm as she moved the blanket aside and sat with her back against the armrest. She draped the blanket over her lap and set Beau down atop it, letting him get situated as she turned on the TV.

He kneaded his paws on her chest, purring as he pressed his weight against the center of her breastbone, but he thankfully lay down after a few seconds.

"What should we watch?" Avery brushed her hand down Beau's back as she flipped through the selections on Netflix.

She'd seen most of the popular shows and movies, and most everything marked as *new* had been out for months—and some of it hadn't looked interesting even what it was actually new. She steered clear of horror movies—*I'm such a wimp*—which cut the options down quite a bit, and she'd already watched all the romcoms.

Where were the *real* romance movies and shows? The stuff that didn't need to rely on comedy or end with tragedy? Avery didn't care what Hollywood thought—if either the hero or heroine was dead by the end of the movie, it was *not* a romance.

After some more scrolling, Avery selected a British comedy-drama called *Sex Education*. She was laughing within the first few minutes. The show had just reached a scene in which Adam had wandered into Otis's mother's office and was holding two huge dildos when Avery's cellphone rang, startling her.

Avery reached back, careful not to disturb Beau too much, and picked up and her phone. She wrinkled her nose when she saw the name on the screen.

"Talk about buzzkill." She paused the show, glanced at the time displayed on the upper left corner of the phone, and groaned before accepting the call. "Mom, it's eleven twenty. Why are you calling so late? Did someone die?"

"Oh, don't be so morbid, Avery, of course no one died," Allison said. "Can't a mother call her daughter just because?"

"Yeah, at a normal time of the day. I could have been sleeping."

"Well, you're not."

Avery pressed her lips together. *I would've been if I had work tomorrow.*

It's not like I had to pick up the phone...

But she is my mother.

"And it's an hour earlier here, anyway," her mother continued.

Avery closed her eyes and pinched the bridge of her nose above her glasses. "Mom, after ten o'clock is still late."

"Who cares what time it is? You know I usually stay up late."

Avery could picture her mother waving her hand dismissively. It was just like Allison Watson to not care about anyone but herself.

"Anyway, how are you, darling?" Allison asked.

A padded paw tapped Avery's chin. She opened her eyes and find Beau watching her. He stretched out his leg, tapping her chin again. This was his gentle way of saying *give me lovins, human.* He wouldn't remain gentle for long. Headbutting would come next, and if that failed, he wasn't above nipping at her exposed skin.

Avery smiled and resumed petting him. "I'm doing great.

Work's been busy because of the holidays, but I've been pushing forward on my book and—"

"Speaking of the holidays, dear, when are you coming home? You know Christmas is less than a month away, and I'm planning a grand party. I would love to have *both* my daughters here to show off."

Avery clenched her jaw. She shouldn't have been surprised. Allison had never cared about her daughter's interests unless they overlapped with her own. So why did it still hurt to be ignored? Why did Avery still feel this tightness in her chest and the sting of tears in her eyes every time her mother brushed her off?

Because she's my mother.

Stop it, Avery. This is why you moved away. To get away from that abuse.

She took in a slow, deep, fortifying breath. "I'm not."

"You're not what?" Allison asked.

"I'm not visiting for Christmas."

"What do you mean you're not coming home for Christmas? You've already missed every holiday for the last two years! I won't have my daughter ignoring her family any longer."

"I'm not ignoring you. I just don't..." She clenched her jaw, steeling herself. *Here it goes.* "I have bills to pay, and money is tight."

"Ugh. I don't understand why you decided to work such a lowly job. Waitressing? Really, Avery? If money's an issue, I'll pay for your ticket."

"No."

"Nonsense, Avery. I'll book a—"

"Mom, no. I don't want your money."

"I'll come visit you, then. How about next week? You can show me your...*apartment.*"

Why? So you can criticize me and tell me how much of a dump it is?

"I'd rather you not," Avery said.

"Why are you being so *childish?* We've humored this rebellious behavior long enough. I don't understand why you refuse to tell us where you live, or why you won't come home. After every-thing we've done for you? I haven't seen my daughter for two years and all I ask is for her to come home for Christmas, but that's too much? I'll call you in a few days to make the arrangements. Hope-fully, you'll have moved passed this ridiculousness and will be in a more reasonable mood by then."

The line went dead.

Avery lowered the phone and tipped her head back, staring up at the ceiling through a blur of tears.

Let it go, Avery. You did nothing wrong. She's trying to guilt you.

She took in another deep breath and slowly blew it out through her mouth.

"It's all about appearances. You not being there looks bad on her. That's why she wants you there so much. It's not because she...misses you."

It wasn't like Avery's father missed her, either. He hadn't contacted her once since she'd moved a little over two years ago.

She snorted. Nothing had changed when it came to her father. He'd barely noticed her presence even when she'd been living with them.

Avery lifted her head and looked at Beau, who'd settled his chin on her chest. "I made the right choice moving out on my own." She rubbed the side of his face with her thumb, and his purring intensified. "I made the right choice for *me*. I'm happier away from all that."

Happier...but no less lonely.

Her mother had never really allowed her to get too close to anyone when she was younger. It had been some combination of being far too busy for friendship while simultaneously judging everyone as unworthy of her daughters' company. Avery had never been allowed to go to anyone's house for a sleepover, and she definitely hadn't been allowed to bring anyone home. Her parents had little patience for other people's children.

So, Avery had kept mostly to herself, escaping reality by playing games, reading books, and writing stories of her own—

grand adventures and swoon worthy tales of love. Well, at least they'd seemed grand and swoon worthy at the time. It was best if she never revisited those early attempts at writing.

Moving away had allowed Avery the freedom to make connections with others. Her boss, Jerry, was more like a dad to her than her own flesh-and-blood father had ever been, and she had a good relationship with Brandy and Noah, but beyond going out for a drink here and there and gaming with Noah from time to time, she wasn't really close to any of them outside work. She'd never formed that deep, meaningful, BFF relationship that so many people had in their lives. And though she occasionally talked to her sister, they'd never been close, either.

It was just her and Beau.

And his love wasn't always unconditional.

Where does Hunter fit into all that?

It was silly to even think of him right now. They'd only seen each other a couple times, had only had a few brief conversations, and he was a customer. That was his relationship to her. Not a friend, not a...a *romantic* interest, just a customer. A stranger.

But she couldn't stop thinking about him. She couldn't stop thinking about the what ifs...

"You're just setting yourself up for disappointment, Avery. You...were just a diversion. A friendly face on a bad day. What could you offer a guy like him?"

And why would he bother with her when he could have his pick of any woman?

She turned her face back toward the TV, but she'd lost all interest in watching anything.

With a sigh, Avery turned it off.

So much for a quiet, relaxing night.

Cradling Beau against her chest, she gently kicked off the blanket and stood up. "Come on, Beau. Let's get to bed."

SEVEN

Fyran didn't like this place.

The building was three stories tall with a half-basement at ground level, and its cracked, faded bricks bore unidentifiable stains. Iron bars had been installed over the lowest windows. The alley between it and the neighboring building was dark and foreboding, and only one of the wall-mounted lights over the entrance worked, leaving the place bathed in the sickeningly orange glow of the nearby streetlamp.

Though the apartment buildings a couple blocks away were nothing he'd consider beautiful or modern, they made this place look small, ugly, and ancient in comparison. It was far from the worst place he'd ever been, far from the worst place he'd ever seen —he'd have to make a pretty damn long list for it to even rank—but he still didn't like it.

Avery deserved better. Much, much better. He barely knew her, but he was certain of that. If only for her kindness, her compassion, she should've had better than this place. But Fyran had never been naïve enough to think the universe went out of its way to reward good people.

Fyran released a huff through his nostrils that formed a large, fleeting cloud in the cold air and raked his gaze across the building again. By now, he knew it down to every individual brick, the result of staring at the damned place for the last few hours. His tail ached from being confined for so long, and the tips of his ears were freezing.

Habit had kept him out here in the snow, staring at this building. Reconnaissance, as the humans called it, had always been vital to him as an *althicar*, and he'd fallen into it naturally after following Avery. Some small part of him hoped even now that she would emerge at any moment, even though he knew she wouldn't. It was late, she'd worked a long day, and by now she was likely asleep.

His eyes lingered on each of the visible windows one by one, only a couple of which were still lit from within. Which of those was Avery's? Were any?

He assumed the building was divided into apartments like so many of the places in this neighborhood, but he didn't know which apartment was hers. He didn't even know her last name, or where she was from, or how old she was.

Fyran shifted his weight on his feet, and the fresh snow crunched under his boots.

He barely knew what he was doing here now.

I shouldn't be here.

He'd lingered outside the diner after leaving his seat at the counter, and he'd watched through the window as Avery discovered the napkin with her name beneath the plate. His curiosity had been too great; he'd *had* to see her reaction upon finding it, had to know if it would cheer her up after the discouragement and upset she'd suffered.

Even now, hours later, Fyran was uncertain of what her tears had meant. Humans were usually so easy to read, their emotions so simple to pick up on, but he hadn't been able to tell what she was thinking. Were they sad tears or happy tears? Had they stemmed from relief or weariness, disappointment or gratitude?

So long as her upset had been cancelled out, he didn't care.

Fyran tugged his phone out of his pocket and unlocked the

screen. He didn't like Avery's building, didn't like that she was here, and he couldn't bring himself to leave until he knew all was well. He hadn't come this far, hadn't spent half a day waiting in the Colorado cold, for nothing.

He activated the hacking functions of his neural transceiver and interfaced it with his phone, glancing up and down the dark, quiet street as the connection solidified and the transceiver accessed human networks.

In all his time as an *althicar*, Fyran had always been hesitant to use his neural transceiver for such purposes. Though its technology was extremely advanced and had been reinforced with the most powerful security protocols known to the faloran people, it wasn't infallible. There were risks even here on a primitive world like Earth.

But he had to know. He had to know that she was well, had to see her one more time tonight before he went to his own bed.

Using her first name and her address, minus any apartment number, he delved into local governmental records.

As the technology worked, his attention settled on the apartment building again. When he'd returned to Jerry's diner earlier today, he'd told himself it was to keep a look out for Gregor. The *ilventyr*'s business involved the diner in some way, so Fyran couldn't ignore the place, could he? The plan had been simple— were there no sign of Gregor or the male with the knitted cap, Fyran would leave.

But his eyes had been immediately drawn to Avery when he'd first glanced through the diner's window. He'd told himself to turn around, to walk away, that there was no reason for him to go inside.

He'd pushed through the door and taken a seat at the counter in a daze. By then, it had been too late; he couldn't leave.

That restaurant was proving itself a distraction. *She* was a distraction. By ignoring Gregor, Fyran was potentially endangering innocent lives. And yet he'd waited outside as Avery finished her shift, unable to tear himself away even as the sun had set, the temperatures had plummeted, and the snowfall had begun.

He couldn't ignore that Avery had been seared into his mind, that she had invaded his every thought, that she had become a drug to him—and he craved his next fix.

Since the moment he'd first smelled her, first seen her, first spoken to her, she'd been in his head. And the things she made him want, the desires she'd awoken in him, the fire that was now burning deep within him... Fyran didn't know how to deal with any of it, and it had made his long wait far more torturous than the weather ever could have.

But when she'd finally emerged from Jerry's Diner, well after nightfall, he understood one thing at least—the wait had been worth it. Seeing her stop and stand there, shivering, as she absorbed the beautiful scene around her, as she'd stuck out her tongue to catch a snowflake, had made him smile like he never had before. The sight of Avery on Sixteenth Street, surrounded by falling snow and golden light...

It had made him realize that beauty ran far below the surface, that it was only loosely rooted in the physical. The scene had been brief, but so innocent, filled with such wonder, that he'd felt a tiny pull toward everything he'd missed in his life. Toward all those little moments he'd ignored or been unable to appreciate.

Having looked upon her in those seconds...now he understood what humans meant when they said the eyes were the window to the soul.

In that moment, returning directly to his dwelling had ceased to be an option.

He'd trailed her through the silent Denver streets, never taking his eyes off her. The snowfall had muted everything, including the visibility, which left him with the sense that he and Avery were the only two people in the universe.

And some part of Fyran had liked that notion.

At the same time, he'd raged at the knowledge that his female, so small and precious, was walking home alone late at night.

She needs a fucking protector.

"Oh, and who chose me to do that?" he muttered.

He lowered his gaze to his phone. His transceiver had pulled information from the Colorado Department of Revenue, Division of Motor Vehicles—her driver's license.

Avery Watson, twenty-two years old—twenty-three in a few weeks. Five foot three inches tall, one hundred and twenty-one pounds. He paused to study the picture of her, and a corner of his mouth quirked up. She didn't have her eyeglasses on, and her big eyes were rounded in a slightly bewildered expression. Had they caught her off guard with the photograph?

Of course, the most vital piece of information was included in the address line. Apartment eleven.

Fyran severed his neural transceiver's connection with the human networks and tucked the phone away. He swept his gaze up and down the street, scanning every shadow, scrutinizing every window.

All was still but for the falling snow, and all was quiet. There wasn't a single human in sight, though Fyran knew they were all around, tucked in their warm, relatively safe homes. No one was watching him as far as he could tell, and even if anyone was, they weren't likely to see much. The shadows around him were thick, and human eyesight was poor in the dark.

He just wasn't sure of how poor. And it wasn't like he could just pluck random humans off the streets and ask them to help him gauge their vision in various lighting.

Can you see me now? What if I back up a few steps?

Shaking his head, Fyran engaged his holoshroud's cloaking field. The air around him seemed to bend and warp for an instant, brightening and darkening to impossible degrees before reverting to normal. When he glanced down, all he could see of his body was a faint, transparent image, broadcast into his vision by his neural transmitter.

He emerged from the shadows and strode across the street, his invisible boots leaving quite visible prints in the snow, most of which was too fresh and unbroken to avoid. The cloaking field would account for the snowfall in its holographic projection, making it seem as though the snowflakes were passing directly through the space Fyran occupied, but it couldn't affect the snow on the ground that was disturbed by his passage.

Once again, he scanned his surroundings, but he did not slow his momentum. Under almost any other circumstances, the tracks would have been a small but important matter; he'd either have attempted to walk only in existing tracks or cover up the signs of his passage as he moved. But here and now, he almost wanted a human to notice the footprints mysteriously appearing on the street.

That would've been nothing if not entertaining.

When he reached the building's front entrance, he found himself regarding the iron bars over the lowest windows. They seemed pointless not merely because the entrance door had a large glass pane built into it, but because that door was also completely unsecured.

His dislike for the building deepened.

Fyran stomped the snow off his boots before opening the door wide enough to slip inside. His lips fell into a frown. He never expected security here to rival anything employed by the Protectorate's military, but this would barely be acceptable even in the slums back on Vabos.

A myriad of potent smells struck him immediately, making his lips peel back in an involuntary sneer. Some of those odors were almost universal to old, rundown buildings across the universe— mold, must, mildew, a lingering stench of sweat and unwashed bodies. The air was also rife with smoky odors. He knew the tobacco smell from cigarettes, but the more pungent one was unfamiliar to him.

Buried beneath all that was something small, sweet, and fragile—Avery's scent. He focused upon that fragrance as best he could.

He stalked along the dimly lit, dark-carpeted hallway, and could only imagine how all the stains and wear around him would look under more intense light. The doors to the apartments were marked by brass numbers, each of which was so dulled and beaten up that they might as well have been relics of some ancient war. One, two, three, four; that meant Avery's apartment was somewhere upstairs.

Heart thumping and tail curling restlessly, Fyran ascended the staircase, careful to minimize the creaks and groans of the steps under his boots. The other odors only strengthened as he moved, soon overpowering Avery's faint scent and coaxing a low, frustrated growl from his chest. He didn't want anything in the way. All he wanted was her fragrance.

All he wanted was...*her*.

Before he could reflect upon that notion, he reached the second floor, and a baby began crying behind one of the closed apartment doors. Fyran stopped at the top of the stairs to check the nearby apartment numbers—five through eight.

The baby's cries grew louder, achieving a piercing keen that was enough to make Fyran wince. Barely audible beneath those wails was the muffled voice of an adult, their words indecipherable but their tone a blend of soothing, weary, and desperate. Seemingly unrelated despite the timing, two more voices rose from one of the apartments below, engaging in a shouting match that may well have carried through the entire building.

With a few plasma burns in the walls and some shady individuals lurking in the hallways, this place could've stood in for any of the buildings Fyran had lived in as a child.

He continued up the steps and had only made it about halfway when a door opened upstairs. Fyran stilled.

"Come on, man. I bet she'd be down," said a male from above, his words slurred.

"Ian, dude, just forget it," said another male who sounded more coherent and sober. The door closed.

"She always looks so stressed though," said Ian. "A few puffs and she'd be like...relaxed and stuff. I just wanna help her out, you know?"

"So just leave her be."

"But she's such a nice girl."

"Exactly, dude."

There were heavy, shuffling steps on the landing above.

"Wrong way," said the second male. "For real, Ian, let's leave the girl in eleven alone. She doesn't want to take a hit with us. She's probably sleeping."

Fyran clenched his jaw, lips drawing back to bear his fangs. Were these men talking about Avery? *His* Avery? He squeezed his fists, digging his claws into his palms. The instinct that had arisen within him, deep and primal, was almost overwhelming; it was unlike anything he'd ever experienced. And it urged him to destroy these humans for daring even speak of her.

Perhaps it was jealousy, but it was something more than that, too—it was possessiveness, it was a driving need to protect her from *everything*, no matter how big or small, no matter how overt or subtle the threat.

Ian scoffed. "Whatever, man. Dunno why you gotta be such a drag."

After a few more shambling footfalls, the stairs above Fyran creaked, and the males began their descent.

It was only Fyran's *Exthurizen* training that held him back as the humans rounded the landing and came into view on the steps ahead of him. He didn't see them as people in those moments; they were merely objects to be destroyed, unruly beasts begging for slaughter. But some part of him—unsettlingly small but thankfully strong—remembered his mission. For all the time he'd spent actively ignoring that mission, he couldn't bring himself to do anything here that might have actually compromised it.

He couldn't bring himself to do anything that could risk exposing the other *althicars* embedded here on Earth...but only just barely.

Fyran eased down the steps ahead of the humans, any sound produced by his movement swallowed by their heavy footfalls and continued conversation. He shifted into the second-floor hallway as soon as he was able. The unsuspecting males continued past him and onto the next flight of stairs. Both men reeked of the same smoke stench that dominated the building, but it was paired with another smell on them—the sour tang of beer.

Fyran drew in a deep, steadying breath. His fists were clenched tightly enough that he was on the verge of drawing blood with his own claws, and if he gritted his teeth any harder, he'd break his damned jaw. But all he could allow himself to do was watch until the humans were out of sight.

He forced himself to move again, albeit slowly to avoid making too much noise despite the echoing laughter and thumping footsteps from Ian and the other male downstairs. The heat that had been poured into his blood by his protective instinct lingered, but its cause changed as he reached the third floor.

Avery was close, so damned close, and he was about to see her again.

Svesh, *it's not like I didn't see her a few hours ago.*

That thought faded quickly as a wisp of Avery's scent teased his nose, drawing Fyran down the hall and directly to the door marked eleven.

Fyran double checked the hallway to ensure he was alone before leaning forward and pressing his ear to the doorway. For a few moments, all he could hear was the thumping of his own heart and the continued noises from below. Slowly, he willed all those sounds, all those distractions, out of his focus, relegating them to the edges of his awareness.

Silence behind Avery's door.

No, not *full* silence. He could just make out a faint hum, likely produced by a fan or the heating system. He listened for a while just to be certain, but he heard nothing else from behind the door. No sounds of movement, nothing from a television, phone, or computer. That didn't mean she was asleep, but...

Without further thought, he checked the doorknob. Locked. His omnikey was already in hand, the result of muscle memory built up over years of infiltration.

Inserting the malleable end of the omnikey into the keyhole, he activated the device. The tool worked quickly, reshaping itself into the proper configuration for the tumblers and springs within the lock. When he twisted the omnikey, the knob unlocked. He pulled the device free and slipped it into the deadbolt keyhole. It turned without having to readjust itself.

The advantages offered to him by his faloran equipment would render the security of many places on Earth ineffective, but this building, where innocent, beautiful Avery lived, was amongst the least secure places he'd ever been.

He really fucking didn't like this place.

There wasn't a single thing here that could serve as a true obstacle to someone determined enough. Even the apartment doors seemed flimsy, as though they'd buckle against the mere suggestion of force.

Avery was too precious to be left so vulnerable.

Nostrils flaring with a long, heavy exhalation, Fyran withdrew the omnikey and tucked the device away. Taking firm hold of the doorknob, he slowly turned it.

The latch released with a soft click. Fyran scanned the hallway one last time before he eased the door open and peered through the widening gap to find a dark, quiet room beyond.

He slipped through, closed the door with even greater care than he'd used to open it, and locked both the handle and the deadbolt.

His first breath was so laden with Avery's scent that his eyelids fell shut and a thrilling shiver raced up his spine. He dipped his head, leaning his forehead against the door, and breathed. Each inhalation was bliss, a hint of paradise, a sweet torture in its promise of something he did not yet have. Here, her fragrance reigned. Gone were the cloying odors from the hallway, the aromas of food and tightly packed human bodies from the diner, the myriad smells of the snowy Denver streets. Here, it was all Avery.

Well, Avery and a feline. That secondary smell was unmistakable.

Likewise, he could not mistake the absence of any male scents. Just Avery and the cat.

Opening his eyes, Fyran pushed away from the door and turned around. Though the apartment was dark, his eyes adjusted quickly, and he absorbed every detail laid out before him. The modestly sized television, the tiny, fake fir tree on the stand beside it, the bookcase stuffed full of books, the sofa with a rumpled blanket piled on one cushion. The coffee table had a few small decorative knickknacks atop it along with a plugged in, closed laptop computer, its angle suggesting that it had been placed there by someone who'd been reclining on the couch.

The wear and tear evident in the building's hallways was far less pronounced here. The paint on these walls looked relatively fresh, the wooden floorboards, though no longer quite straight or even in some places, looked like they had been polished recently, and the baseboards, though worn, were clean.

Fyran crept forward. There was an open archway to the right that led into a small kitchen. A partially open door straight ahead led into what was likely a bedroom, and the bathroom, the darkest room of all, was to the left.

He stopped at the coffee table and glanced down. There was a book beside the laptop from which a great number of colorful note papers protruded like spikes from the carapace of some reptilian beast. As he reached for the book, he heard a soft sound from the bedroom. Something small had just hit the floor.

Freezing, Fyran shifted his gaze to the partially open door.

A pair of eyes, very close to the floor and glowing with reflected light, stared out through the gap. A moment later, a creature emerged—the feline Fyran had scented upon entering the apartment.

The cat hesitantly stalked forward, its shoulders hunched, its nose twitching, and its tail flicking erratically from side to side. Not afraid, but uncertain; Fyran recognized it on an instinctual level. Those reflective eyes rose as though searching for something that wasn't there.

Or rather something that couldn't be seen.

Fyran watched with quiet fascination as the feline prowled toward him. From what he understood, these creatures had descended from powerful, predatory beasts. He could see hints of that ancestry in the way the feline moved, but this animal was harmless. It was little more than a pampered pet. A shadow of its predecessors, its true nature denied.

And that is what Command means to do to me.

A flare of angry heat rose in Fyran's chest, tensing his muscles as it spread up into his neck and face, and his claws lengthened. The end of his tail curled around his leg against that wave of frustration, against that sense of...of what? Betrayal?

The purpose of this mission on Earth was to take some of the Protectorate's longest serving, most dedicated, and deadliest soldiers and domesticate them. Even if this feline had not gone through that process itself, he could sympathize with its ancestors, with the predator it might've been without such interference.

When he drew in another breath, Avery's cinnamon and vanilla scent washed over him anew, and his anger faded. Part of his mind was desperate to cling to his rage, but it was powerless against the effects of that tantalizing fragrance.

A voice in the back of his mind told him that being here was playing directly into Command's plan; he'd come in pursuit of a female. But he couldn't latch onto that thought because of *her*. How could anyone, human or otherwise, smell so fucking *good*?

The cat was within a foot of Fyran's leg now, having slowed its pace to a glacial crawl as it sniffed the air, its whiskers wiggling.

Fyran shifted his boot, producing a soft scraping sound.

Hackles rising, the cat leapt straight up into the air, landed heavily on all floors, and scrambled away. Though the feline was an otherwise small, stealthy creature, its panicked retreat sounded like a stampeding herd of wildebeests Fyran had once seen on an Earth nature documentary.

Chest tight and blood heated, Fyran swung his attention to the bedroom to watch and listen for Avery. He couldn't decide if it would be good or bad for the cat to have woken her with all the noise it had just made.

But after twenty or thirty seconds, the only sound in the apartment was that of wet, vigorous licking. Fyran turned his eyes to the source—the cat, now sitting on the kitchen floor with one leg raised as it lapped enthusiastically at its own asshole as though nothing had scared the shit out of it half a minute ago.

Or, perhaps, *because* the shit had been scared out of it.

Releasing a huff through his nostrils, Fyran sat down on the couch. He reached forward and flipped through the book with his thumb. The pieces of note paper spread throughout it all bore handwritten notes, the cursive letters scrawled so hastily that Fyran couldn't make out what some of them said. Each was marking a different section of the book, some with hand-drawn arrows pointing to specific passages. None of it meant much of anything to him.

After another glance at the bedroom, he carefully lifted the laptop's lid. The display flickered on, presenting him with a login screen.

Well...done it once already tonight. Why not one more time?

Fyran linked his neural transceiver to the computer through its wireless network. Within a few seconds, it had deciphered the password and initiated the log-in sequence.

The laptop switched to a loading screen for a few seconds before presenting an open document. Brows knitting, Fyran looked over the text. It was a scene—or at least part of one—from a story.

Was his female a writer?

He knew there were poets and writers in the Azmus Protectorate, that there were hundreds, *thousands* of years of history behind those traditions, but his early life had left him decidedly detached from all that. Language to him had always been, first and foremost, a thing spoken, and he'd exceled at that aspect in numerous tongues long before he'd become an *althicar*. He knew how to read and write in a number of languages, as well—having most recently learned to do so in English—but writing for entertainment, crafting stories, engaging readers... All that required a set of skills for which he didn't possess the talent, patience, or need to develop.

And yet he was intrigued now. Even if the words on the screen had nothing to do with Avery directly, her writing could've granted insight into her to which he'd wouldn't have had access otherwise.

His finger hesitated in the air over the laptop's touchpad. Humans embedded so much of themselves on their electronics—far more than just credit card information and search histories. Just half an hour with this computer could tell him so much about her, but...

He couldn't bring himself to read more of the story, and he refused to satisfy his curiosity by scouring her personal files and communications. He needed to know everything about her, right down to the most minute details, but not now. Not like this.

The time would come soon enough. When it did, he'd learn all about Avery from the female herself.

Fyran gently lowered the laptop lid until it latched closed. He placed his hands on the couch cushions, meaning to push himself up, but paused when his left hand pressed down on something soft and fuzzy. The blanket.

Taking hold of the blanket, he lifted it to his face, drawing in a deep breath through his nostrils. The blanket was saturated with Avery's scent. Without thinking, he took it in his other hand and pressed it to his skin, rubbing it against his cheek and neck, drinking in the fragrance and the softness, thrilling in the knowledge that the blanket had been wrapped around Avery much in the way he longed to be wrapped around her.

His cock throbbed and stiffened, run through by a deep ache.

What the hell am I doing?

But he couldn't stop himself, not until his scent was mingled with hers on the blanket. For some reason, that blend of smells was soothing. He couldn't understand why, couldn't even guess why he'd done it to begin with, but it was *right*.

Through sheer force of will, he set the blanket down. He'd violated one of the primary rules of such infiltrative work—leave everything as it had been before his arrival. It'd be impossible to get the blanket into the exact shape it had held before he'd picked it up, but he did his best. His efforts only coaxed more of her scent out of the fabric.

Barely suppressing a groan, Fyran pushed himself off the couch, fixed his gaze on the bookcase, and walked toward it, not allowing himself to look away.

Based on the sounds coming from the kitchen, the cat had not yet finished its tongue bath.

Wouldn't mind giving Avery a bath with my *tongue.*

That thought sparked a tremor in his erection that rippled through his whole body.

Aggaan sin thar, *focus, damn it!*

Tail stiff and muscles tense, he crouched to examine the contents of the bookcase. The row of books standing atop the case were held in place by polished chunks of stone on either side. The left half of them seemed to all have *writing* or *writer* in their titles, and a few had the word *romance*, while the right appeared to be books about several different eras of human history.

The shelves below that were crammed with colorful books of varying thickness that somehow seemed to belong together despite their variety. A couple of the books were facing outward. One cover had a clawed gray wing draped in red fabric with *rhapsodic* written across it. The text crawling down the cover read, *make a deal if you dare.*

Fyran arched a brow and shifted his attention to the other book. *To Love a Monster* depicted a blonde human female on its cover with the shadow of a huge beast looming behind her. At the bottom it said, *The most terrifying is the beast inside him.*

Though either cover could be read as ominous, there was also something alluring about them. Something tempting in the hints of fear. Did his female have a wicked side? He couldn't know for certain without reading more, but the notion brought a smirk to his face.

When he rose and turned away from the bookcase, he swept his gaze around the room again. It was modestly furnished and had minimal décor, but there was personality here regardless. It felt like...a home. Like Avery's home. His own dwelling severely lacked that feel.

Fyran's eyes focused on the entrance to the bedroom. Considering his sudden obsession with Avery, the wisest course of action would be to leave. Something about this female severely hindered his self-control. As ridiculous as it seemed, walking into that bedroom now would be the greatest test of willpower Fyran had ever faced.

He wasn't sure if that fact was amusing or tragic, given the life he'd lead.

Despite all that, he walked toward the bedroom, his every step silent, deliberate, and irrevocable, as though he were being drawn along by an invisible tether.

He extended a hand, grasping the bedroom door loosely in his fingers and easing it open wider. His eyes immediately fell on the bed. Just enough light streamed in through the blinds to cast Avery in a soft, ethereal glow.

His heart quickened as he walked toward the bed, feeling simultaneously as though he were floating and sinking, as though he were permeated by cold and burning up from within. He halted at the bedside.

Avery was lying on her back with her face turned toward him. One of her hands was curled loosely beside her head, and the other rested on her belly. Her dark hair was loose, spread over the white fabric of her pillowcase. Her glasses were on the nearby nightstand. Without them, she looked younger and more innocent than ever, especially with her features relaxed in sleep.

Karak'duun, someone like him didn't deserve to be in the presence of a female like her. So small and delicate, so kind, so different from him. So...beautiful.

He sank into a crouch and reached toward her, running the back of a finger over the soft skin of her cheek with the lightest of touches. His eyes followed the sprinkling of freckles from her cheek and across her nose before he dropped his hand lower to trace just beneath her bottom lip with the pad of his thumb. He barely suppressed a desirous growl.

He forced his hand to move again, stroking her jaw to her long, silky hair, down her graceful neck, to her collarbone. His gaze dipped lower, stopping on her chest.

The blanket was at her waist, leaving her torso exposed, and the fabric of her shirt was molded to her breasts tightly enough that the outlines of her nipples were visible through it.

Fyran hissed through his teeth, stilling his hand. His palm itched with sudden want, and his fingers twitched as pressure built in his groin and his cock strained painfully against his jeans. It would be so easy to settle his hand over her breast and knead her tender flesh. To feel its softness. To peel that shirt off her skin, to touch her and feel her heat, to lower his mouth over one of those hard little buds and taste her as he climbed onto the bed and...

He snatched his hand back with enough force that he threw himself off balance, only stopping himself from falling on his ass by dropping his other hand to the floor to catch his weight.

The pounding of his heart rivaled the booming of an artillery barrage as he stared at her. Avery didn't stir; she continued her slumber in apparent serenity, unaware of the alien three feet away from her who was primed and hungry to rut. Cold sweat beaded on his back, made all the worse in comparison to his inner heat.

Fuck, he'd never wanted anything so badly. He'd never *needed* anything so badly.

It was time to go.

Somehow, he pushed himself to his feet and tore his gaze away from her. He strode toward the door, only for something to catch his eye—a bit of cloth at the top of her hamper beside the doorway.

Unable to resist his curiosity, he plucked the white cloth off the pile of dirty laundry and held it up. It was a pair of Avery's panties. They were simple, dainty, and trimmed with lace. His hands trembled, and he clamped his jaw shut as a new urge swept through him and annihilated what limited control he'd managed to reclaim.

Fyran pressed the panties to his nose and drew in a deep breath.

Avery's scent—her *true* scent, her most intimate, feminine scent—filled his nostrils and sent tremors through his body. His balls ached and his cock pulsed, overcome by a surge of pressure so immense that a drop of seed seeped from its tip.

He bared his fangs, and the muscles of his neck strained as he held in a growl. Faloran males weren't supposed to just leak their fucking seed like that. It wasn't that simple.

Svesh.

Don't look back. Can't look back.

It was time to fucking go. Fyran had to get out of here before he did something stupid. Or something stupider than he'd already done, anyway. He stuffed the panties in his pocket as he strode into the living room, moving directly to the door, but as his hand touched the deadbolt he paused.

There were voices in the hallway—Ian and the other male human.

Stepping out there now would draw attention. Attention to Avery, who was sleeping peacefully, innocent and unaware, in her bed. Avery, who deserved to be safe and secure. Who didn't need *any* fucking attention from Ian.

He could wait the males out, but there was no telling how long they'd be in the hallway—especially as they seemed to be deep in conversation. And every moment he spent in here, enveloped by Avery's scent, knowing that she was so close, was another moment spent fighting a losing battle.

For the first time in memory, Fyran couldn't rely upon himself. He was used to not being able to depend upon others, but this was something new, and it was disheartening. And it still wasn't enough to curb his raging desires.

The feline released a soft, mewling call, drawing Fyran's attention to the living room window where the creature was perched on the windowsill, staring out into the night.

Fyran hurried to the window. The cat straightened, appearing startled, and made another questioning meow. Fyran made a soft hiss. It was enough to get the feline to leap down and scurry away, fortunately without all the noise of its earlier fright.

He checked the window quickly. There was a lock, but it didn't seem to latch properly when he fiddled with it, allowing the window to slide open no matter which way the little lever was turned. As much as he hated the idea of her window being unsecure, at least he could take some solace in knowing it wouldn't be his fault for leaving it unlocked. He opened the window as high as it would go.

Frigid air swept in, carrying a few errant snowflakes. Fyran scrunched his shoulders and pulled himself through the opening. His muscles strained to anchor him in place as he precariously guided more of his body out of the window, uncertain as to what was instilling him with a greater sense of urgency—that Avery could wake up at any moment and discover this, or that she was still so close, that he was only an instant away from being beside her again, from touching her.

He dug his claws into the mortar between some bricks, clamping down as hard as he could, and pulled his legs free of the window to plant his boots against the exterior wall. The end of his tail curled into a tight coil against his calf as he glanced down at the alleyway three stories below.

Reaching back, he slid the window shut with as delicate a balance between haste and care as he could manage. The moment it was closed, he thrust himself away from the building, aiming for the snow piled along the edge of the alley.

He landed heavily, crunching the packed snow beneath his weight, and ended up on his ass with his legs buried past his knees.

"*Svesh*," he growled as he extracted himself from the snow. The cold crept through his clothing and ran its icy fingers along his skin as he brushed snow from his clothing, but it did nothing to ease his yearning or slow his racing heart.

Standing in an alleyway in Five Points in the middle of the night, wet, cold, and hard enough to drill through concrete. What the fuck is happening to me?

Fyran turned to glance up at Avery's window, and the image of her in her bed flashed through his mind. His cock pulsed, prompting him to clamp a hand over it and squeeze. He couldn't tell whether that hurt or felt good.

Though he didn't know what was happening to him, he had a twenty-minute walk to his car and a half-hour drive home to figure it out. But something told him that wasn't nearly long enough to determine why Avery Watson had such a powerful pull on him.

Only one thing was clear—the beast dwelling inside Fyran had chosen Avery as its own, and it wasn't going to be denied.

EIGHT

TREVOR CAPTURED *Emma's lips with his. His kiss was hard, punishing, and merciless, forcing her to open to the thrust of his tongue. He ravaged her mouth with a demanding mastery that left her no choice but to submit.*

And Emma realized she wanted it—she wanted him. She wanted it all.

For too long, Trevor had held back a part of himself from her, a part he'd feared would harm her should he let it loose. He thought he'd lose her. But he'd never lose her. She was his. She had always been his, and she always would be. And tonight, upon his bed, she would show him the truth of that.

She returned his kiss with fervor, and she moaned as his hand fondled and squeezed her breast, further setting her aflame. She burned for more of his touch, more of his kisses, more of him.

With a growl, Hunter tore his mouth from hers and trailed his lips down her throat. She gasped, back arching as his mouth latched onto her nipple. He sucked hard, sending a sharp bolt of pleasure straight to her core. She thrust her hands into his long, golden streaked hair and clutched him closer.

"Hunter," she rasp—

Avery's fingers stilled over the laptop's keys.

"Dang it, Avery, it's Trevor. Not Hunter. And Trevor has black hair. *Short* black hair." She tapped on the touchpad and made the corrections, muttering, "Your fantasies are not supposed to cross over into Emma's. Daydream on your own time."

Well, technically, it was Avery's day off, so this was her own time, but...

"Ugh."

The words had flown from her fingertips, coming easier than they had in days, and it was all because this very scene had happened in her dreams last night.

It *had* been Hunter who'd positioned himself over Avery in that dream, had been Hunter who'd taken her mouth with such passion it bordered on violence, had been Hunter's hand that delved between her thighs. It'd been his fingers that caressed her pussy and brought her to an explosive orgasm—an orgasm that had carried over into reality, waking her up and leaving her wet and throbbing in need.

Avery had lain there staring up at the ceiling, her skin flushed and tingling, her breasts aching, her legs tangled in the blanket. Her need had been too great to ignore. She'd slipped her hand beneath the waistband of her underwear and touched herself. It had taken no more than a few strokes of her clit to make her come.

It'd been a very nice start to her morning.

Only thing better would've been if he were here...and it had been his *fingers.*

Avery groaned and closed her laptop. There'd be no more writing for her this morning. She was...restless. Aroused. Her breasts ached, and there was a heavy warmth low in her belly. Just recalling the dream had triggered a response from her body and reignited her hunger. She wanted more; masturbating had only taken the edge off her true craving.

Hunter.

This had never happened to her before. Sure, she'd grown excited while writing sex scenes in the past, but this...this was something powerful. All she could think about was Hunter. Even more bizarrely, she could have sworn that she could *smell* him, right here in her apartment. She kept catching whiffs of sandal-wood, fir, and leather, but whenever she breathed deep to take those scents in fully, they'd be gone.

Something bumped against her leg. Avery looked down to find Beau standing beside her, his paws sinking into the couch cushion. He peered up at her, meowed, and rubbed his head on her knee before flopping against her thigh.

Avery chuckled, set her laptop on the coffee table, and picked him up. She hugged him to her chest and scratched his head. "Hey, Beau."

Vibrating with enthusiastic purrs, he kneaded her chest with his paws. Avery ignored the pricking of his claws through her sweater as she glanced around her apartment. Bright sunlight was pouring in through the blinds, illuminating the living room. Though it had snowed overnight, it was a beautiful day today.

Apart from her walks to and from work, she'd been cooped up indoors all week. And she'd been working so much lately, covering extra shifts at the diner, squeezing in writing whenever she could find a few minutes... Maybe it was time to go out and do something? Maybe she could take a trip to the mall not to go to Jerry's, but to walk around with a hot drink and window shop. Maybe... maybe she could even buy herself something.

Avery knew it would've been best to put the money Hunter had tipped her away for when she really needed it, but when was the last time she'd bought herself something nice? Something she wanted?

Something she'd earned?

"What do you think, Beau?" she asked, looking down at her cat. "Should I treat myself today? Maybe even take the car and blow a few bucks on parking?"

His eyes were half-lidded and indifferent. Were Beau able to talk, all he'd likely say was *keep the scratchies coming, human.*

She grinned. "I'll see if I can find a special kitty treat, how's that sound?"

Beau shut his eyes.

With her decision made, Avery lifted Beau off her. He resisted for a moment, his claws snagging in her sweater, but she carefully dislodged him before he could pull all the threads apart and set him on the couch. As she pulled the blanket off her lap, she stopped abruptly. That spicy sandalwood and fir fragrance bloomed in the air, stronger than ever. Brow creasing, she dropped her gaze to the blanket, raised it to her nose, and inhaled.

"Oh, my God," she groaned, voice muffled as she buried her face in the soft material.

All this time, that smell had been coming from her blanket? How was that possible? How had she not noticed it before this morning? She closed her eyes, taking in another deep breath. It smelled so damn *good*. She could see herself sitting here all day, cuddled up all snug and warm, sighing dreamily every few minutes.

With great reluctance, Avery swept the blanket off, folded it, and set it aside. "Okay, enough blanket sniffing. People might think you're weird or something."

Her gaze met Beau's. He stared at her. She stared back.

And she felt judged.

"Don't give me that. Least I'm not sucking on it like *someone* I know."

Unfolding her legs, Avery stood and made her way to the bathroom to fix her hair and put on a little makeup. Once she was finished, she pulled on her black snow boots and threw on her coat, zipping it up nearly to her chin.

"I'll be back soon, Beau," she said as she lifted the strap of her messenger bag over her head.

Beau, currently sitting on the floor and vigorously licking his paw, ignored her.

Avery rolled her eyes and opened the door. "Love you, too."

She stepped into the hallway, pulling the door closed behind her. The building was thankfully quiet. Digging her keys out of her bag, she locked her door and made her way downstairs.

The apartment's parking lot was a fenced in area off the back of the building. There were only a few cars within, including Avery's little frost green 2009 Volkswagen Beetle, all of them covered in a fresh layer of snow. She unlocked the car with her key fob as she walked toward it. When she tugged on the handle, the door stuck for a moment before the ice holding it shut broke away. Avery tossed her bag onto the passenger seat and started the engine. Thankfully, the car battery had plenty of juice to get things going.

She'd learned the hard way during her first winter in Colorado that cold weather didn't play nice with a car that tended to sit unused for days at a time. California certainly hadn't prepared her for anything like this. This winter, she'd made sure to start the Beetle and let it run for ten minutes or fifteen minutes every few days, and had driven it to work a couple times when the weather was particularly bad.

"All right," she said, pulling her gloves from her coat pocket. "Let's get started."

Picking up her scraper out of the small door compartment, she set to work on the ice and snow covering the vehicle. By the time she was done, the car's interior was nice and toasty—and her fingers were freezing. She tugged off the damp gloves and laid them out on the passenger seat.

Her phone chirped.

Avery reached into her bag and fished out her phone. There was a new text from her sister. Unlocking her phone, she tapped on the message.

Found out mom called. Sorry. How'd that go?

Avery smirked and typed a reply. *As expected. She wants me to come back for Christmas.*

Are you?

No. I can't. You know I can't.

I know. I understand. Mom is a bit...much.

Their mom was *more* than a bit much. Eliza knew it. She'd been just as trapped in their dysfunctional family dynamic as Avery had been, even after moving out to live her own life, though Eliza happened to have a natural affinity for the profession their mother wanted them to work. Eliza was gorgeous—tall, thin, blonde, and blue eyed, with an expressive face and a seductive smile. A perfect model. But unbeknownst to Allison Watson, her eldest daughter had been attending classes in her spare time, working toward a degree in astrophysics.

If she'd ever put any effort into learning about her daughters' passions, Allison would've understood that Eliza had been fascinated with space since she was a little girl, or that Avery had been wanting to write stories for as long as she could remember. They weren't phases, weren't things the sisters would forget about once they *grew up a little more.*

Eventually, Eliza would have to transition to fulltime schooling to pursue her field of interest. That would undoubtedly draw their mother's ire.

Avery couldn't help but feel relieved about that. She didn't want *anyone* to have to deal with Allison Watson's disapproval, but it'd be nice to have less of it directed toward Avery. Then she wouldn't be the only daughter to disappoint their mother.

Another message from Eliza came through before Avery could respond. *I do miss you though, Avery. I should come visit you in spring once things calm down after the season is over. That is if I don't drop dead from exhaustion the way mom is running me.* The gif that followed the text was of a yellow cartoon dog all shriveled up with the words *I'm dying* on the bottom.

Avery chuckled. *I'd like that. We'll have a slumber party, eat all the chocolate and pizza, and watch old, raunchy comedies.*

It's a date!

Smiling, Avery dropped her phone back into her bag and buckled her seatbelt. Though she hadn't seen Eliza since moving to Denver, they'd kept in touch. They didn't text often, but each knew the other was there for them if they needed it. As kids who hadn't really been allowed to have friends growing up, they'd spent a lot of time with each other—at least when their mother wasn't parading them around parties or forcing them into modeling gigs.

As adults, they'd both escaped home in their own ways, and they were both coming to terms with their childhoods in their own ways. It sucked that the process had put distance between the sisters, both literally and figuratively, but Avery had faith that their relationship would heal and strengthen with time. A visit from Eliza would be perfect to help that process along.

After checking her mirrors, Avery backed out of her spot and exited the parking lot, turning onto the main road.

She sang along to the music on the radio as she drove to the Sixteenth Street Mall. The drive was short, and the snow that had fallen on the roads last night had either been cleared away or melted by now. But the best part? Because it was a Monday morning, she found easy parking.

Slinging her bag over her shoulder, she exited the car and locked it.

First things first.

Before she was doing any shopping, she was grabbing that hot drink because...*chocolate.* Did a girl really need a reason to have chocolate?

No. The answer would always be no.

Avery walked down to Sixteenth and turned onto the patterned walkway that ran along the mall's length. She bypassed the more popular coffee places in favor of her favorite café, The Sweet Spot. The exterior was black and white, those colors broken up with bright, colorful paintings and chalk drawings of flowers, steaming mugs, and cupcakes on the windows and wall. From spring to autumn, there were usually some tables set up outside for diners. It was one of Avery's favorite places to sit and write during the summer while nursing a tall glass of fresh-squeezed lavender lemonade.

Avery opened the door and stepped inside. She was immediately struck by the delicious aroma of brewing coffee and sugary pastries, two of the best smells in the world even if she wasn't much of a fan of the way coffee tasted.

Those scents had dropped in their rankings recently, however, as a certain blend of sandalwood, fir, and leather had rocketed to the top of the list.

The soft pinks, yellows, and greens on the walls and furnishings made the café feel far more open. The owners had gone with an antique chic aesthetic; everything had that lightly distressed look, and most of it, right down to the ornate mirrors and candle-holders, would've been right at home in a Victorian manor. Faux vines and silk flowers in pinks, peaches, and whites added a sense of life to the place. Combined with the floor, which was fashioned to look like it was paved with stone, it made Avery almost feel like she was in a spring garden. The café was warm, charming, and comfortable, a perfect setting in which to unwind and indulge one's sweet tooth.

The woman working the register looked to be in her mid-thirties. She had blonde hair and dark eyes. Another employee was facing the rear wall, decorating cupcakes. But Avery's attention settled on the large glass display case beside the register. It was filled with cupcakes, cakes, muffins, and other decadent pastries. Avery's favorite choice here was the gooey lemon bar.

Though the café wasn't terribly busy, there were at least five people in line ahead of her. She smiled as a mom with two young children, the oldest of whom couldn't have been more than four or five years old, stepped up the register. The children darted toward the display case to point excitedly at the cupcakes as they pressed their hands and faces to the glass in delight. Their mother laughed and told them to calm down, that they'd each get their pick.

The scene was bittersweet for Avery. Her mother had never taken her or Eliza to places like this as kids. Allison Watson would never have set foot in a place like this to begin with, and she would've scolded her daughters for even looking at the café with a hint of longing in their eyes.

Because sugar makes you fat, Allison had always said.

The café door opened briefly, letting in a rush of cold air. That crisp breeze bore just a hint of sandalwood and fir.

Surely, she'd only imagined that smell. Right?

Blanket sniffing withdrawals, Avery?

Whoever had entered stepped into line behind her. Her skin prickled in awareness. She felt the newcomer ease closer, and, without looking, knew they were tall.

The stranger grunted. It was a deep, masculine sound, rough but somehow warm, too. "Morning, Avery."

Something tightened in her belly, making her core clench. Avery knew that voice just as well as she knew that smell.

She turned and looked up to meet Hunter's dark gaze.

He was just as gorgeous as she remembered. He wore a cross zip leather jacket, open at the top to reveal the black shirt beneath, dark blue jeans that hugged his muscular legs, and black boots. His long hair hung loose and wild, as though ruffled by the wind.

Well, don't just stand there and stare! Say something, Avery!

"Oh, my gosh. Hi! I...can't believe you're here."

The smile he offered her—little more than one corner of his mouth slanting up—was positively rakish. "You can touch me if you need to be sure."

She was tempted. Oh, how she was tempted.

Avery smiled and clutched the strap of her bag to keep her hands right where they were. "It's just strange running into you here."

"Why's that?"

"Well, I mean, it's a big world out there. What are the chances?" She ran her eyes over him. She wasn't sure whether his look was more biker or metal musician, but it certainly didn't fit the café's decor. "I guess I wouldn't expect this to be your kind of place. I could picture you better at...a biker bar?"

Really, Avery?

Warmth flooded her cheeks, and she winced. "I'm sorry. I'm stereotyping, and that's really not—"

"It's all right," he said, glancing around the café. "I wouldn't be here if I hadn't seen you come in. But I'm not big on bars, either. I prefer quiet when I can find it."

"I come here a lot, especially when the weather's nice. Normally I'm not big on crowds, but there's just something about the atmosphere of this place that helps me write. The conversations just hit that perfect level of white noise that helps me focus."

His eyes returned to Avery, sweeping up and down her body. "You're a writer, then?"

"Well, an aspiring writer." She stepped up as the line moved forward. "I'm hoping to finish my first book someday soon."

Oh, God, now he's going to ask me what I write, and I'm going to have to explain to him that romance books aren't porn right here in the middle of this café...

Hunter fell into place beside her, keeping his gaze upon her, standing so close that she could *feel* his nearness. But she wanted him closer still. Wanted to take him up on that offer to touch him.

"You will." He said those two little words with more confidence than she'd ever thought possible. "I'd like to buy you a coffee."

Avery's brows raised. "You...want to have coffee with me?"

Hunter's smile faltered. "Did I ask the wrong way?"

She would've expected almost any other guy to sound irritated when asking that question, but Hunter just sounded mildly confused.

"Oh! No. No, you didn't. I just... I mean..." Avery caught her bottom lip between her teeth and glanced around. "You...don't have to feel obligated just because I waitressed for you and gave you a free pie."

"I'm interested, Avery. In you."

Her eyes flared wide and snapped back to his. "You are?"

He moved infinitesimally closer to her, his scent immediately strengthening, and inhaled deeply through his nostrils—as though he were smelling *her*. His voice had more gravel in it when he said, "I am."

A shiver coursed through her, and her cheeks flushed.

"In fact," he continued, "I went to the diner this morning to see you. As you can probably guess, I was unsuccessful."

Avery chuckled. She was definitely going to hear it from her co-workers tomorrow. "Uh, yeah. Today's my day off." She tilted her head. "So this coffee...is like a date-date?"

Hunter tilted his head to mirror hers. "Is a date-date different than a date somehow?"

Her face flushed further. Jeez, could she be anymore

awkward? "Well, no, I just meant, well...like it was a serious date. Not just a hangout with a friend kind of thing, but a...you know."

"Ah." He nodded and extended a hand, placing it on her lower back. It was so big, so strong, so solid. With impossible gentleness, he guided her forward.

The line had moved up by two people, leaving a wide gap between Avery and the next customer. Somehow, when she was around Hunter, everything else just fell away. Hunter kept slightly behind her as she closed the gap—and kept his hand on her back. It was possessive, in a way, as though he were claiming her right here in this café.

He leaned down, his cheek coming close enough to brush her hair, and huskily whispered in her ear, "It's a date-date."

What the heck was that? Had he just used his bedroom voice on her? That had definitely been a fuck-me voice.

She released a shuddering breath. Her pussy clenched, and her nipples hardened into points, aching with the need to be touched.

To be sucked.

Avery swallowed thickly and turned her face toward his, meeting his gaze. Their lips were so close that all it would take was for her to tilt her chin up and they'd touch. "A date-date on one condition."

His eyes, so impossibly black, held hers. "What condition?"

"I pay."

He chuckled. "Unnecessary."

"Well, technically, you're still kind of paying considering that, um....tip you left me yesterday. Which I seriously can't thank you for enough. That's why I want to cover this. It's the least I can do."

He narrowed his eyes, staring into hers as though searching for an answer to an unspoken question within her gaze.

"Please," she said.

His dark, thick brows fell low. "Fine."

Avery grinned. She'd almost expected him to get offended, to deny her this, but he'd relented—albeit reluctantly. And though she couldn't say for sure that her smile was the reason, his expression softened in the face of it.

"What can I get you?" asked the woman behind the counter.

Avery looked forward to discover that she was at the front of the line now. It was her turn.

Hunter straightened. The blonde woman glanced up at him, and her eyes widened. There was no mistaking the interest in them as they ran over him from head to toe.

For an instant, a spark of possessiveness flared in Avery, and she imagined herself growling and gnashing her teeth at the woman, but she tamped it down. Hunter wasn't hers. Sure, this was a date-date—*oh my gosh, I can't believe I'm on a date with him!*—but they weren't exclusive or anything. They weren't *together*. She didn't want to present herself as a rabid beast, hissing, spitting, and clawing at any woman who dared look at him.

Don't be crazy, Avery.

Avery put on a friendly smile and stepped up to the counter. "Hi. Can I get a large hot cocoa with cinnamon and whipped cream and a lemon bar to go?"

The woman blinked and turned her face toward Avery, though it took her eyes much longer to follow suit. "Uh...yeah." She tapped the tablet mounted on the counter in front of her. "Anything else?"

"Whatever he'd like," Avery said, gesturing at Hunter.

"Oh. You're...together?" There was no mistaking the disappointment in the woman's expression as she lifted her head and flicked her eyes between Avery and Hunter. She cleared her throat. "I mean, on the same order?"

"Yes, please."

"I'll take a large hot chocolate, too," Hunter said.

The woman smiled. "Great." She added the total into the register. "If that's everything, that'll be ten dollars and thirty cents."

Avery slipped her hand into her messenger bag and pulled out her wallet. She took out a twenty-dollar bill, handed it to the woman, and returned her wallet to her bag. When she received her change, she dropped it into the tip jar.

"Thank you!" the woman said. "I'll get those hot chocolates started."

"So, what do you do?" Avery asked, looking up at Hunter.

His eyes were roaming the café again as though searching for something. "I was in private security for a while," he said as he returned his gaze to her. "Made enough money that I'm semi-retired now, but I still take on the occasional odd job to keep myself occupied."

"Wow. You seem so...young to be retired. Was it home security, or are we talking like military kind of stuff?"

"Military stuff. Specialized in covert operations. A lot of sitting around and waiting, broken up by nights of sneaking around in the dark."

"Was any of it dangerous?"

"It was all dangerous."

Avery's eyes widened. She glanced from side to side and leaned toward him, lowering her voice. "Did you...*kill* anyone?"

He chuckled, brow furrowing, and shook his head. "Really want to know that on our first date-date?"

She grinned. "Yes? No? Maybe? I mean...you're not going to turn out to be some kind of homicidal maniac or anything, right?"

"No, I'm not. I can assure you that I'm very cold and methodical."

Avery chuckled. "You don't seem very cold."

"Only because I have a warm jacket on." His smile faded after a moment, and his expression grew serious. "You're safe with me, Avery. I would never hurt you. Would never let you get hurt, either."

Before Avery could more deeply consider the meaning of his words or respond, the blonde woman reappeared on the other side of the counter, setting two lidded cups of hot chocolate and a small brown paper bag on the counter.

"Here you go," she said. "Have a wonderful day."

Avery picked up the paper bag and her drink. "Thanks. You, too."

She stepped away from the counter to allow Hunter to grab his drink. The cup looked tiny in his big hand. He placed his free hand on the small of her back, scanning the café again as he guided her toward an open table in the far corner, weaving through the dining area with a grace belied by his size.

When they reached the table, he lowered his hand from her back and pulled out a chair for Avery. She smiled up at him as he seated himself across the table with his back to the corner.

Avery couldn't help but be reminded of that old role-playing game cliché of the mysterious hooded figure sitting in the dark corner of a tavern. Of course, this café was anything but dark, especially with all the pink paint and flowers, and Hunter didn't have a hood up, but he certainly had that air of mystery—and of danger, too.

Well, he didn't deny killing anyone...

And that wasn't necessarily a red flag, was it? Thousands of people had seen combat in the military or had faced life-threatening situations as members of law enforcement. Having taken a life didn't mean they were bad people. And she understood, too, that most people didn't like to talk about such experiences.

She placed her drink and food on the table and grasped the strap of her bag, lifting it over her head. Tucking the bag on the floor between her chair and the wall, Avery unzipped her coat and pulled her arms free. She glanced at Hunter to find his attention focused on her chest. Against her will, her nipples hardened, and a thrill spread through her.

She cleared her throat and wrapping her chilled fingers around her cup, absorbing the heat it emitted.

He lifted his eyes to meet hers, but did so with a deliberate slowness. There wasn't an ounce of shame on his face.

"So, where are you from?" Avery asked.

"Birth certificate says Cheyenne, Wyoming," Hunter replied as he removed the lid from his cup, "but I don't remember it. My father was in the military. We moved around a lot, never stayed in any one place for more than a year or two."

"Did you travel overseas?"

"A few times as a kid, yeah. A lot more as an adult."

"Is that why you have an accent?"

"Accent?" He didn't look up from what he was doing—gathering several packets of sugar and tearing them open. He dumped them into his hot chocolate all at once, at least four or five packets worth.

Her brows furrowed. Was he trying to put himself into a diabetic coma? She'd never seen anyone add extra sugar to hot cocoa before. "Yeah. I can't place it, though. It's usually too subtle to tell."

Hunter shrugged, plucked a coffee stirrer out of the container that held the sugar and cream cups, and dipped it into his drink. "Never thought about it. It's probably from traveling so much, picking up bits and pieces of accents from everywhere. But you..."

Avery's eyes locked on his hand as he stirred his drink. His fingers were long, strong, dexterous. They were *sexy*.

"Your accent's pretty neutral," Hunter continued. "Not easy to place, either. I'd guess...West Coast?"

"California. More specifically, LA."

Those tantalizing fingers continued their steady motion, stirring the hot chocolate. "Don't know much about LA. It's a little warmer than Denver, right?"

She chuckled. "Yeah. Much."

"What brought you here?"

Avery looked down at her cup, watching the steam rise from the hole in the lid as she worried her lip. She'd never been on a date before, so she wasn't sure how much to say about her life, her family problems, and the baggage that came along with her. Self-consciously, she pushed her glasses up her nose.

"I guess I just...really needed to get away," she finally said.

Hunter's hand stilled. He braced his arm on the edge of the table and leaned toward her. Avery met his gaze as he lowered his head so his eyes were level with hers.

"You in some kind of trouble, Avery?" he asked, voice low.

"Trouble?" Her brows creased. "Why would I be in—Oh! No. I didn't leave because I'm in any kind of trouble. I just...kind of have a really controlling mom." She cringed. "I scare you away yet?"

He frowned, tilting his head slightly to the side. "Why would I be scared away?"

"Well, any mention of crazy mothers is a red flag, right? Like, what am I getting myself into? The whole monster-in-law thing? Don't most guys *nope* away when a woman says her mom is controlling?"

Hunter laughed and shook his head. "Your mother has no effect on my interest in you."

God, he looked so *handsome* when he laughed...

Avery's lips curled into a soft smile. "Thank you for that."

Shifting the stirrer aside, Hunter lifted his cup to his mouth and drank. A satisfied hum rumbled in his chest as he lowered the cup. Avery couldn't keep her gaze off his lips; she watched, transfixed, as his tongue slipped out to lick away the hot cocoa left behind on his upper lip.

"How long have you been free, then?" he asked.

She took a sip from her drink. It was still hot, but not enough to stop her from enjoying the small taste of chocolate and cinnamon. "Almost two years. She's been trying to convince me to go back, especially with Christmas coming up, but I just...can't. And I'm happy here. I mean, I work hard, and things are rough at times, but there's just something fulfilling about knowing I've earned what I have right now, you know?"

And Avery certainly didn't miss having it thrown in her face every time her mother gave her something, especially as Allison's *gifts* always came with the expectation of something in return.

"I do," he replied, a hint of rawness in his voice. His gaze fell to his cup, and he stared at it with furrowed brow for several moments, seemingly lost in thought.

She tilted her head, wondering what he was thinking, what might have happened in his past that suddenly made him so somber. But she wouldn't push him. They were on their first date together. She wasn't entitled to the entirety of his past.

"So what brought you here to Colorado?" she asked, taking another drink of her hot chocolate.

"I just wanted somewhere to..." Hunter frowned. "To settle down. Someplace to stop and just...live. Wasn't really looking for anywhere in particular, but there's something about stepping outside in the morning and looking at those mountains just as the rising sun hits them... It's"—he lifted his eyes back to hers—"beautiful."

He's talking about the mountains, Avery. It doesn't matter how he's looking at you right now.

"It is," she said. "I'm still not used to the cold, and there are times I miss the ocean, but I love it here."

Avery dragged the little brown bag holding her lemon bar closer. "You said you were semi-retired," she said, opening the bag and breaking a small piece off the corner of the treat. "What do you do when you're not working?"

She looked up at him as she slipped that piece into her mouth to chew. The tartness of the gooey lemon combined with the sweet, powdered sugar topping and the butter crust nearly made her close her eyes and groan.

Best. Lemon Bar. Ever.

No foodgasms in public, Avery.

She didn't miss that his eyes were focused on her lips as she chewed, or that there was an intense light in his deep, dark gaze.

"I spend a lot of time wandering around," Hunter said distractedly. "Enjoying the scenery. A bit of, uh...people watching. Taken to tinkering with my car, too. Never had the chance to work on one before, so I've kept myself busy learning how." He lifted his gaze. "What about you? Anything besides writing?"

"Not really. I occasionally play video games or go out with my co-workers, but mostly it's just work and writing. In a sense, the writing is work, too, so..."

"But you love writing, don't you?"

"I do. I struggle with it at times, but no matter how hard it can be, I still love it. It's such an escape, like reading, except *I* dictate the setting and what happens, who gets to fall in love, and who must grovel and earn forgiveness—usually the hero. It's like bringing my fantasies to life." Avery stilled, realizing what she'd just said—and how loudly she'd said it in her excitement. "Eh... sorry. I got kind of carried away."

Hunter chuckled, his smile making a return. "Don't apologize for your passion."

Avery smiled. "It's just that I was never able to talk about it with anyone else growing up. My sister would listen, but we didn't get a lot of time to ourselves. My co-workers aren't really into reading and such. All I have is Beau to talk to about books."

Hunter's expression hardened. "Beau?"

His voice was dark and low, carrying an edge to it. It was thrilling. And she could've sworn it was due to jealousy.

She laughed. "My cat."

"Ah." Something akin to relief softened his features again. "I don't know anything about books or writing them, but you can talk to me about them. I'll listen."

Avery tilted her head as she studied him. She didn't know whether he was serious, didn't know where any of this would lead or what would happen after this date, but his offer touched her deeply. How amazing would it be to have someone to talk to openly about her passions and interests, to talk to about her day, someone to provide support without judgment or ulterior motives? To have someone right there when she needed them?

How amazing would it be to have someone there every morning when she woke up and every night when she went to sleep?

"Thank you," she said softly. "I'd like that."

Smiling, she brought another little chunk of the lemon bar to her mouth. Hunter's gaze locked on her fingers, following them, and the light in his eyes intensified as her tongue slipped out to lick the sugar off her lips—it was a hungry gleam, like a predator fixated upon its prey.

She chewed, and still his focus remained upon her lips. A spark of heat flickered low in her belly.

"Do...you want a taste?" Avery broke off another bite-sized piece and held it out to him.

Hunter extended his hand. Avery's mind went wild in anticipation of the light brush of his fingers against hers as he accepted the piece, of that fleeting, tantalizing bit of contact and connection.

But he didn't take the chunk of lemon bar from her.

Instead, his big hand took hold of her wrist, fingers closing around it in a gentle but firm grasp. Her eyes widened as he dipped his head and drew her hand closer to him. As her fingers neared his mouth, he caught her gaze and held it, his dark eyes like a pair of black holes drawing her in, leaving no hope of escape.

Not that she wanted to escape. Not even a little.

Hunter's sculpted lips parted, and his hot breath fanned over her hand just before his mouth touched her fingers. His tongue slid out, hooking the morsel deftly and drawing it into his mouth. Avery's breath hitched and her heart quickened as Hunter closed his lips over her fingertips and sucked.

That tongue, so confident and strong, swept along her fingers, licking away the powdered sugar and lemon curd. A deep, satisfied groan sounded in his chest, powerful enough for her to feel the vibrations rumble into her all the way down to her pussy. She squeezed her thighs together as her core pulsed with a heavy, needy ache.

He slowly drew back, sliding her fingers out of his mouth but not releasing his hold on her wrist. His tongue slipped out to run across his lips. "Delicious."

Avery's breath fled in a soft whoosh. All she could do was sit there and stare at him as desire thrummed in her veins. Never in a million years would she had imagined anything like this happening to her. This was the stuff that only happened in romance novels. This was...this was intoxicating, this was too erotic to be real.

Was it possible for her to have come just from this? She was sure her panties were wet right now.

Avery had no idea how much time passed as they sat there with his thumb sensually stroking her inner wrist, right over her pulse, and his eyes blazing with a look that said he'd take her right there on the table without giving a damn about the other customers in the café. Her heart was racing, and she was burning up from within, and she never wanted it to end.

"Avery..." he growled.

The loud scrape of a chair over the floor nearby startled Avery. She yanked her arm back, turning her head to see a young couple seating themselves at the next table over. It wasn't until a moment later that she felt the sting on the back of her hand. She glanced down. A fresh scratch ran from her wrist to her knuckle, about three inches long, with a couple droplets of blood beading at its top.

Strange. She could've sworn Hunter's nails weren't that long, but maybe she'd caught the corner of one just right?

Hunter snatched a napkin from the dispenser on the table and pressed it over the cut, his hand covering hers completely. "Sorry," he rumbled, mouth falling into a deep frown.

"It's fine. It was my fault for pulling away so quickly." She looked up and smiled at him, though her skin was still ablaze from he'd done only moments before.

Now that she'd been jarred from the spell he'd woven over her, she was aware that the café was busier—and louder—than it had been when she'd first entered. The start of the lunch rush, undoubtedly.

Hunter huffed through his nostrils and looked up at her, but his eyes quickly shifted aside and narrowed. He turned his head slightly as though watching something pass, and his hand flexed atop hers.

"What's wrong?" Avery asked, glancing over her shoulder. The pedestrian traffic outside the window had picked up, and most of the tables inside the café were now full, but she didn't see anything amiss. Just the usual flow of strangers back and forth, in and out.

"Nothing," Hunter said, his hand relaxing. "Thought I saw someone I knew."

She smiled. "That happens when you spend a lot of time around here. You kind of become a regular. I've seen quite a few faces from Jerry's in the area."

He hummed, though that troubled gleam lingered in his eyes for a second or two longer. "There's only one face from Jerry's I want to see again."

Avery's shoulders hunched slightly, and her finger twitched. She could almost feel his lips around it, could almost feel his tongue, warm and wet as it stroked her. "Well, you can...come to Jerry's any time to visit me, or maybe...I can give you my number, and we can meet each other again like we did today. Another, you know, date-date?"

He shifted on his chair and reached back with his free hand, retrieving his phone from his back pocket. "Both options, but I'd pick the number if I had to choose just one."

Avery couldn't stop her smile from stretching wider. "Really?"

He leaned toward her, his dark gaze steady and serious. "Once I set my eye on something, I do not let it get away, *vaerina*."

That intense stare made it quite clear what his eye was currently set on.

She pulled her hand free from beneath his big palm—immediately missing its heat—and retrieved her cellphone from her bag. She tapped in the code to unlock it, created a new contact, and held it out to him.

He placed his phone down as he accepted hers, his long thumbs moving with surprising dexterity as he entered his information. When he'd finished editing the contact, he opened a new text message and sent it. His phone vibrated on the tabletop.

Hunter spun her phone around and handed it back to her before plucking up his own. The text message, which he'd sent to himself, of course, read, *Another date-date?*

A moment later, her phone chimed, and a response appeared from him. *Absolutely*.

Avery laughed and looked up at him. "I can't wait."

"Unfortunately"—Hunter returned his phone to his pocket, flatted his hands on the table, and stood up—"I have a few other things to take care of today. Thanks for the hot chocolate and the...*taste*." His gaze dipped to her lips. "Looking forward to the next one."

Heat suffused her at the memory of his lips around her finger, and suddenly her thoughts were similar to what his must've been —what would his lips taste like?

"Me, too," she said breathlessly.

He collected his cup and offered her another of those devilish smiles. "See you soon, Avery."

Frozen in place with her eyes glued to him, she watched Hunter walk away. A few days ago, she wouldn't have believed any of this could happen to her, especially not with a man like Hunter. But here she was with his number in her phone and the promise of another date on the horizon.

Hunter paused at the door and glanced back at her. She raised her hand and waved. He grinned, flashing his white teeth, and then he was gone.

Avery took in a deep breath and released it slowly. She hadn't realized just how nervous she'd been around him until now. But despite her nerves, she'd been herself, and Hunter had...liked what he'd seen.

Folding the paper bag closed over her lemon bar, she tucked it, along with her phone, into her messenger bag and stood up. She pulled on her coat and drew the strap of her bag over her head before picking up her cup and heading for the door.

She took a sip. The hot cocoa was the perfect temperature now.

The air was still crisp, and her breath came out in a puff of white as she stepped out of the café, but the sun was shining, and the sky was bright blue. She smiled, closing her eyes and tipping her face up to the sunlight.

Avery walked along the Sixteenth Street Mall just as she'd planned, visiting a couple of her favorite shops, and even splurged on a few things—a sensual smelling bottle of bubble bath, a cozy gray long sleeved sweater dress, and a box of gourmet chocolates. The entire time, she radiated happiness.

There were a few moments during which her skin pebbled, the hairs on the back of her neck rose, and a strange, almost an instinctual awareness flared within her. It was as though there were eyes upon her, staring intently. Oddly, the sensation was pleasant sometimes—but other times, it made her skin crawl.

On her way back to her car, she stopped by a pet store and bought a small bag of treats for Beau, who raced to meet her once she'd returned to her apartment and shaken the bag.

While the cat was munching, Avery removed her boots, grabbed her phone, and made her way into her bedroom. She lay on her belly, opened her messages, and nervously bit her finger—the same finger in which Hunter had taken into his mouth.

"The hottest moment of my life," she said with a grin.

Avery tapped on Hunter's name. Would she seem too desperate if she texted him now? Wasn't there some rule about waiting a few days? She didn't know anything about the dating, but she also didn't understand why someone would wait to connect with a person they really liked.

Would he think she was being too...clingy?

She cringed. Maybe she shouldn't text him.

But everything about him and every moment with him felt *right*.

Avery stared at the two messages Hunter had sent—one from his phone and one from hers.

"Okay, I'm doing it."

She hurriedly typed a message and pressed send before she could change her mind again.

Had a wonderful time this morning on our date-date. Thank you. She added the blushing smiley face.

Okay, so maybe she shouldn't have added the emoji.

Her breath caught when the three little dots appeared, and his reply came soon after.

Most delicious thing I've ever tasted. Can't wait to have more.

Another message from him came through immediately after. *Lemon bar and drink were good, too.*

Heat flooded Avery's cheeks, but she couldn't quell the thrill or stop the grin that overtook her face.

Beau jumped up onto the bed and bumped his head against her hand, and she gave into his demand for attention, running her palm along his back.

"I think I might have a boyfriend, Beau. And oh my gosh, he's just..." She let go of her phone and flipped over onto her back, staring up at the ceiling. "He's perfect."

NINE

Fʏʀᴀɴ ʟᴇᴛ the tire iron fall from his grasp. Part of him relished the piercing metallic clang it made when it hit the concrete floor; the sound was loud enough to rise over the music and momentarily pierce his thoughts.

His fingers were already unscrewing the lug nuts. He was inclined to be efficient and remove the nuts two at a time, but he stopped himself from following that inclination. Despite the frantic pace of the guitars and drums blasting through the speakers and reverberating through the garage, he didn't want to finish his task too quickly. Once he was done with this, that was it. There was nothing else to distract him.

And then his thoughts would turn back to Avery, and he wouldn't have any hope of escaping them. He'd think about her dark, shimmering hair, about her eyes, whose gray-blue was as deep and entrancing as the ocean, about the vibrant passion that filled those eyes when she talked, about the soft melody of her voice. About the salty sweetness of her skin.

"*Karak'duun,*" he growled, the curse clawing its way up his throat.

Why the fuck had he thought he could distract himself from a distraction? How many damned layers would he have to wrap around his brain before it was finally insulated from her?

He set the lug nuts on the floor beside his knee, resisting a wild urge to throw them across the garage. Patching some drywall would give him something more to do, but it'd also anger him just enough that he'd risk causing more damage in the process.

Fyran tugged off the tire with a grunt. Another of those impulses rose, this time to throw the tire like it was a...whatever those flying plastic discs were called. A frisbee? But he ignored that impulse, too, and simply laid the tire aside.

Given the way things had been going for him lately, he could just imagine how throwing a tire would work out. His mind's eye presented the scene in perfect detail.

In his imagination, the tire hit the garage door, breaking some of the vinyl panels. Sunlight streamed in through the break as the tire struck the floor and bounced—and he knew it was breaking the law of physics even as he watched it—onto the hood of his car. The metal buckled, and the tire fell over just right for the metal rim to hit the windshield, cracking the glass.

Svesh, sometimes it seemed like it'd be best if his imagination just fucked off.

He grabbed one of the new winter tires and put it in place, sliding the bolts through the holes. Replacing the lug nuts was so mindless a task that of course he was thinking about Avery within a few seconds.

Because the time they'd spent in that café yesterday had been...amazing. Talking with Avery Watson was pleasant, thrilling, comforting, endearing. Arousing. The only other occasions during which he'd felt anything close to that blend of emotions had been the other times he'd spoken to her.

What did that mean? What was happening to him? When he'd been with her the day before, everything else had ceased to be. His reasons for being on Earth, his mission—both the one given by Command and the one he'd assigned himself—had been forgotten. Gregor, his unidentified associates, the vrokars wandering somewhere to the west, all the other aliens on Fyran's list, the Azmus Protectorate; the whole damned universe had vanished.

There'd been only Fyran and Avery.

And that bald *kish'ai* who Fyran should've spotted sooner.

When he'd looked up to see the male who'd been on the corner near the diner outside the café yesterday, he'd barely swallowed his fury. He had no doubt the male was one of Gregor's ilventyrian associates.

Fyran snarled as he moved to the next tire to repeat the process, his hands moving faster in his anger. He wasn't angry at Avery, never at her, but at himself, and the music, with all its speed and build up, was making him feel like he was ready to slay a dragon.

He wasn't even sure what the hell a dragon was. But he did know one thing—he'd fucked up.

Lug nuts clattered on the concrete, followed by the clanging of the tire iron, which bounced from the force with which he'd thrown it down. He'd lost focus yesterday. For the last few days. And even on a relatively harmless planet like Earth, that was a mistake that could've cost him everything.

He didn't know how long Gregor's crew had been on to him, if they actually were at all, but Fyran should've been paying more attention to his surroundings. His chances of uncovering Gregor's plot might've been destroyed now, his life might've been placed in immediate danger, and the whole faloran presence on Earth might've been put at risk.

How stupid was it of Fyran to think metal—whether that of his car or the blaring music—could provide him any sort of respite? Banging drums, galloping guitars, and clanging tools would never be enough to drown out his thoughts.

Changing strategies, he set to his task as fast as he could. As he worked, he recalled the feel of Avery's hand beneath his, its warmth and softness in such stark contrast to the cold metal now against his fingers.

Her taste was still sharp in his memory—but so was the sight and scent of her blood. He was furious with himself for harming her, for not reacting quickly enough.

Karak'duun, *I'm hopeless.*

When he finished getting the final snow tire on, he hurriedly removed the vehicle from its blocks, tightened the lug nuts, and put away his tools. He stacked the old tires in the corner of the garage and stalked into the house, trying to touch as little as possible with his filthy hands.

His hands had *always* been filthy. All the more reason to keep away from Avery. He was a danger to her. Her blood was not at all the first he'd spilled, and it wouldn't be the last. She deserved far better than him.

As he reached the master bathroom, he inhaled deeply. The smells of grease and motor oil lingered in his nostrils, undoubtedly clinging to his clothing, and they only made him long for a very different blend of scents—cinnamon, vanilla, and cloves.

Just the thought of her fragrance produced a deep ache in his groin that crept up to the base of his shaft. He hastily stripped out of his clothing and leapt into a cold shower, hissing as the water hit his skin.

This was all too much, and it was too far outside his knowledge. How could he be so attracted to this tiny human when no other female had ever caught his eye? No one had affected him like this before, not even with a fraction of this power. How could he have developed such an attachment to Avery in so short a time?

Fyran scrubbed himself clean, soaping and rinsing his arms and hands several times before he was satisfied. He refused to acknowledge his lingering arousal, refused to acknowledge the growing notion deep within him—that he was lost, that he was woefully unprepared, that this non-combat operation may well have been the most dangerous undertaking of his life.

"Bullshit," he snapped, spraying water from his lips.

Fyran Voltanix had overcome every other obstacle he'd faced, one way or another. This would be no different. A bit of willpower would overcome this problem; a bit of willpower would recenter his focus.

The best way to begin that process would be to stay out of Denver today.

To stay away from Avery.

After finishing his shower, he dried off, walked into the bedroom, and retrieved a clean pair of sweatpants from the dresser. He pulled them on and was about to tuck his tail inside them when he stopped himself.

Even in the privacy of this residence, where he'd had no visitors but delivery people, he'd rarely left his tail free. For Fyran, it had always been a matter of practicality and preparedness over comfort and convenience—always assume you could be seen at any moment. Always maintain the disguise.

He was vaguely aware of the human concept of a funeral shroud. For an *althicar*, it was the lack of a shroud—a holoshroud —that often led to the funeral.

And though it flew in the face of all his training and of all his recent self-admonishment over his carelessness, Fyran decided to leave his tail free. Perhaps it was another small act of defiance against the mission, or a way to signal to himself that he really wasn't leaving the house today. Perhaps it was a subconscious reclamation of the comfort he'd always denied himself. It didn't really matter. If nothing else, it would remain invisible to the naked eye thanks to his holoshroud.

Tail swinging behind him, Fyran went downstairs into the kitchen, opened the refrigerator, and perused its contents. The tuft of fur on the end of his tail brushed the backs of his calves.

Just need to rethink the Gregor situation. To take it more seriously.

To start treating it like an official operation.

He pulled the jug of raspberry lemonade out of the fridge, twisted off the cap, and took a long drink. The sweet, cold liquid was delicious—like so many human foods and drinks. He helped himself to another swig.

What did Earth have that would be considered a valuable

commodity to non-human beings? What did Jerry's diner have that would be considered valuable?

Avery.

Fyran paused mid-drink, nearly choking on the lemonade as a fluttery, uncomfortably hot sensation rose in his chest. The thought of her being taken from him, of her being harmed, was alarming in ways he'd never imagined possible, and his flare of jealousy over the possibility of another male claiming her was overwhelmingly strong.

Focus, damn it.

He lowered the jug, replaced the cap, and returned it to the fridge. He couldn't let Avery cloud his judgment, couldn't spend every moment thinking about her. Figuring out what Gregor was plotting—what product he was going to move—was far more important. Especially with—

His phone, which was on the nearby counter, chimed with a text message alert.

Fyran walked to it, glancing down at the screen just before it went dark. All he caught was one word—Avery.

Fyran's heart quickened, and a heat wholly unlike the unsettling one of a few moments before spread outward from his belly. His lips curled into a smile as he picked up the phone. That fluttery feeling had moved to his stomach now, but it was no longer unpleasant.

What the fuck is happening to me?

That question faded when he unlocked the phone and read her message.

Good morning! I just wanted to say I hope you have a good day.

As he was reading, another message came through.

And I totally didn't mean for that to rhyme! Sorry!

Ridiculous as it was, he could hear those words in her voice, and his smile stretched into a grin. He typed a quick response. *It just got a whole lot better.*

The three dots appeared, and anticipation flooded Hunter for her next reply.

Maybe a slice of cherry pie could top it off later? she texted.

His thumbs moved without conscious thought. *That an invitation?*

Maybe? Yes? Depends on how crazy you think I am. I'm sorry. Dating is new to me and... Am I coming on too strong? Please tell me if I am. I don't want to scare you away. There was a pause, then another message appeared. *Oh my gosh, even that sounds desperate. I am so sorry.*

Fyran clenched his jaw and let out a long, slow breath, hoping to ground himself. *Svesh*, it would've been so easy to get changed, jump in the car, and race into Denver to see her right now. But he couldn't let himself do that. Could he?

Should he?

I need at least one more taste, one more glimpse.

Let me see you, he sent. He pressed the icon to start a video call.

It rang for a long time, and he feared she wouldn't answer. His hand tightened around his phone. Just as he considered ending the call, the screen switched to video, and Avery appeared. The air fled his lungs at the sight of her. Her eyes lacked the black eyeliner she'd worn the other times he'd seen her, her normally neat hair was tousled, and she was wearing a wide necked sweater that hung off one shoulder, baring it.

"Hi." She smiled bashfully. "You...kind of caught me off guard. I don't start my shift for another four hours, so I haven't even gotten ready yet."

Based on the angle and steadiness of her camera, he guessed she was on her laptop.

"You're beautiful," he said.

She ducked her head, and a flush stained her pale cheeks, but her smile widened. "Thank you." Her gaze flicked over him from behind her glasses. "I, uh, see you're in the middle of getting ready, too?"

Somehow, he managed to maintain his expression even as he dropped his tail in a flash of panic. His holoshroud was up; she couldn't see his tail. Still, how foolish was it for him to have started a video call while it was free?

Yet looking upon her now, he couldn't regret it.

"Just got out of the shower. I was thinking about you when your message came through." His heart still hadn't quite slowed, and that inner warmth hadn't diminished.

"Were you thinking about me while you were *in* the shower?" Her eyes widened and she raised a hand, covering her mouth with her fingertips. Her nails were painted black. "Oh my gosh, don't answer that."

Fyran's cock twitched in response to her question. He'd thought about her in the shower, of course, and had barely managed to resist his arousal. Part of him regretted his restraint. But his willpower wasn't going to last long while he was looking directly at her, even if it was just through video. "You were thinking of me."

Avery dropped her hand and lowered her gaze. "I am. I-I mean, I was." She took in a deep breath, her brow creasing before she met his gaze again. "Actually, I can't seem to stop thinking about you."

Fyran raked his fingers through his hair, grazing his scalp with the tips of his claws. Hearing her say that felt...good. Damned good. His lips stretched into a slow grin. The drive to Avery's apartment was around thirty minutes long under normal circumstances, but he was fairly certain he could make it in twenty...

You're not supposed to know where she lives, Fyran. And you're not supposed to head into Denver today.

Why did his inner voice suddenly sound reminiscent of the *ultricar?*

"I can't stop thinking about you, either," he said.

Avery caught her bottom lip with her teeth.

Fyran nearly groaned. He ran his gaze over her features, settling it on her lips. His tail flicked behind him, ignoring his efforts to keep it still. It was just as disobedient as his cock, which was erect and throbbing, largely unrestricted by his sweatpants.

He wanted to feel those lush lips against his, wanted to feel her skin, her hair. Wanted to fill his lungs with her fragrance and his mouth with her taste. He wanted *her.*

Not going to Denver today.

"You said you're going to be at the diner today?" he asked.

"Yeah. I go in at one."

Karak'duun, I am not going to Denver today!

"You get a break at some point? Don't want to go eat pie by myself."

Her face brightened. "I'll save my break for you."

She was so fucking sweet. One corner of his mouth tilted up. "I'll be there at six."

Ah, fuck. I'm going to Denver.

"I can't wait to see you, Hunter."

My name is Fyran. He wanted to growl it out loud, to tell her so she would say his true name, so he could hear it in her melodic voice, so he could see her lips and tongue shape the sounds. He wanted to tell her who he was, show her what he was...

"Going to feel like a long day until then," he said. Maybe he should've set an earlier time.

Shouldn't have set any time, damn it.

Fyran shook off those thoughts before they could reach their inevitable conclusion, during which he'd tell himself to go fuck... himself. That wouldn't be helpful. There was only one person he wanted to rut.

Avery chuckled. "It will be. Goodbye, Hunter."

"I'll see you soon, *vaerina.*"

The call ended, and the phone returned to the text message thread. His eyes fell on the last message he'd sent to her.

Let me see you.

So much for discipline and willpower. So much for focusing on what was important. He'd never been so out of control, not in his entire life. Not even as a child. When he'd told Avery he was cold and calculating, he hadn't been lying, and yet around her he was anything but.

He told himself there were positives to this situation as he returned his phone to the counter. He'd have a chance to get a feel for the new tires on his car, would get to have another slice of delicious pie, and would get to enjoy Avery's company.

What did it matter if the latter was what he craved more than anything right now?

Fyran growled and dropped a hand to his groin, clutching his cock through his sweatpants as he closed his eyes and let his head fall back.

And fuck, did he crave her.

TEN

If Fyran had wanted to spend his night in the winter cold, he should've done it outside Avery's building. Just knowing she was close would've made the discomfort so much more bearable. But opportunities didn't care about comfort, and they didn't give a shit about Fyran's preferences.

This was the work. Sometimes, as the humans said, it sucked.

The lot around him was dark, and the snow piled around its edges undoubtedly hid all sorts of scrap and trash. Part of an old automobile was jutting up out of the white nearby, its paint having long since flaked away and its metal corroded by untold years of exposure to the merciless elements. The snow and the shadows cast over it were his only shelter from prying eyes.

Well, those and his holoshroud's cloaking function, which was currently rendering Fyran invisible.

He adjusted the angle of the listening device in his hand, grateful that the wind was calm and the street between this lot and the one he was observing was all but deserted. He was especially glad that he'd installed sound dampeners in his car. They'd proven useful tonight. Revving the Hellcat's engine was like coaxing a roar from a mighty beast—as impressive as it sounded, it also alerted everything nearby to its presence.

"How much longer?" the bald male with the fur around his coat collar asked in the Ilventyrian tongue.

Gregor replied in the same language. "As long as it takes, Varketh."

"*Kregvahk.* You said a week or two at most."

The two ilventyrs were in the lot across the street from Fyran, standing a few paces away from a black SUV that was parked in front of a seemingly abandoned warehouse. There'd been two other males with them initially, but both had entered the warehouse without speaking. The only light that hit the ilventyrs and their vehicle was a residual orange glow cast by the floodlights of another building down the street, leaving them largely in the dark.

But it wasn't dark enough to hide them from Fyran's eyes, and it certainly wasn't dark enough to hinder ilventyrian eyesight.

"You know the job," Gregor said. "Plans change, plans stay the same. We do what we must."

Avery crawled back into Fyran's mind. Though it had only been a few hours since he'd last spoken to her, he was desperate to do so again. He'd never planned for her, and he'd attempted to ignore her and forget all about her time and again, to fall back to his original plan, but he'd been failing. Failing miserably.

There's nothing miserable about the time I've spent with her.

No matter how intent he seemed on arguing with himself lately, he couldn't disagree with that notion.

"This job is *jattosh.* Why haven't we made the move?" asked Varketh.

"You know." Gregor slapped a hand over the back of his companion's neck. "Buyer will be spending a lot of money. All needs to be perfect, and we need to be sure we'll get paid before we fulfill our part."

"So when? We're overdue, *drekon.* When do we go to fresh territory?"

Drekon. That was an old Ilventyrian word, popular amongst ilventyrs on the wrong side of the law. It meant boss—though, more accurately, it was closer to what the humans would've considered a lord or a master.

"Soon, Varketh, soon. And much richer when we do."

Varketh pulled something from his pocket and raised it to his mouth. Fyran couldn't make out the device until Varketh turned his head slightly, revealing what appeared to be one of those vaping devices that was so popular amongst humans.

Fyran carefully leaned forward, trying not to disturb the snow pile as he narrowed his eyes to get a clearer look at the device. It looked human-made from this distance, but Fyran couldn't be certain.

The bald ilventyr exhaled, releasing a mouthful of smoke that swirled into the air. "I always follow you, *drekon*. Always will. But either this buyer wants it, or he doesn't. He is wasting our time."

"He'll pay," Gregor said gruffly. "And once this is done, we will relocate, and we will expand."

"We should have moved months ago." Varketh took another puff of his vape inhaler. "And now, we're stuck waiting for this buyer to make up his mind...fuck him, *drekon*. We will find good business without him, as we always have."

"Enough. If you don't trust my judgment, then we have a much bigger problem. The time is coming soon. I'll finish this my fucking self if you won't."

Varketh grunted, turning away from his companion to blow out another cloud of smoke.

"Go get rest," Gregor said with a wave of his hand. "You can go back to watching tomorrow."

"Yeah." After taking a final drag from the device in his hand, Varketh returned it to his coat pocket and walked to the nearby SUV—the vehicle he'd driven to the warehouse.

The vehicle Fyran had followed here.

Gregor watched Varketh climb into the SUV, his expression rigid. The vehicle started, its brake lights flashed red, and its white reverse lights came on. As the vehicle backed up, Gregor turned away and strode to the warehouse. Though the building's exterior was dark and dilapidated, light shone from within when Gregor opened the door and stepped inside.

The SUV swung around, its tires crunching on dirt and snow,

and rolled toward the gate. Once it was on the street, it stopped, and Varketh hopped out to close and lock the gate.

Fyran tensed; he should've already been in motion, whether to return to his own vehicle and continue following Varketh or to cross the street and get a closer look at the warehouse. His work wasn't done, and despite the limited information in the ilventyrs' conversation, Fyran *had* learned something tonight.

By all appearances, this building was a base of operations for Gregor and his crew. This was the most significant lead Fyran had found in a damned long time.

I wonder if Avery is still working...

Perhaps he could surprise her if the diner wasn't closed. He could buy some food to share with Avery when her shift was done, or perhaps take her out to another restaurant that was open later so they could sit and eat somewhere other than her workplace, so they could talk and he could hear her lovely voice, revel in the loosely veiled longing in her eyes, and witness the radiance of her smile.

The SUV's door slammed shut, jarring Fyran from his wandering thoughts. For an instant, he saw Varketh through the vehicle's windshield, illuminated by the interior lighting, but the cab quickly went dark. Within a moment, the vehicle was driving away.

"Ah, *svesh*," Fyran muttered as he deactivated the listening device and tucked it away in his coat. There was little chance of catching up with the departing ilventyr now, even if he wanted to.

Aggaan sin thar, Fyran. You didn't even make mistakes like this as a fucking recruit. You could've been killed ten times over just tonight with how often you've lost your focus.

Fyran swung his gaze to the dark warehouse. He knew Gregor was inside, and some part of him was eager to infiltrate the building.

But that would be stupid for a lot of reasons beyond his current lack of focus. For one, he had no idea of how many people Gregor had in his crew, how they were armed, or what technology they had access to. He also had no idea of the building's internal layout.

Making any move would require a lot more information, and that meant surveilling the building and its grounds over a prolonged period, watching for people coming and going. That meant digging through human records for ownership records and floorplans. That meant investing time. All his time.

Fyran stood upright, stretching his legs and, to a lesser extent, his tail, which was still tucked along his left leg. He couldn't neutralize the deep frown that had claimed his lips.

What was he doing?

He couldn't possibly count the number of times he'd asked himself that question since arriving on Earth, but he'd always had an answer in the past, even if those answers weren't always entirely convincing.

Now, he truly didn't know.

With a low growl, he walked back toward his car, obscuring his tracks in the dirt and snow as he moved.

In his mind's eye, he saw Avery as she'd stepped out of the diner that second night, her features bright with wonder as snow fell all around her. Something clamped around his heart and squeezed without mercy, making his chest achy and hollow. All his time on the streets during his youth, all the training he'd undergone as an *althicar*, all the experience he'd gained in the field—none of it had prepared him for Avery Watson.

He kept the sound dampeners active on his car as he climbed into the driver's seat and slammed the door shut, at once grateful the sound was so muted and irritated to have missed out on the petty satisfaction he would've garnered from the bang.

As distracted as he was, Fyran still remained alert on his drive to his residence, keeping close watch for pursuit all the while and taking a deliberately circuitous route. The long, dark countryside highways were largely devoid of other vehicles, but he resisted the urge to push the car to its limits. He'd not forgotten his encounter with Trooper Sullivan.

Of course, the extra drive time—which he should've used to

plan his next move regarding Gregor—gave him ample opportunity to think about Avery.

He'd seen her every day since he'd followed her into that café, even after deciding to stay out of Denver—and he'd been in Denver on each of those days.

Monday had been the hot chocolate at The Sweet Spot; Tuesday was pie and milkshakes at Jerry's during Avery's break. On Wednesday, they'd gone into the Denver Art Museum to get out of the cold for a few hours after one of her rare early shifts. There'd been many beautiful pieces of art on display, a good portion of which Fyran hadn't understood. More than once, he and Avery had been forced to stifle their laughter as they viewed some of the more absurd works the museum considered art.

Fyran was certainly uncultured by human standards, but he failed to see how mundane objects arranged on a wall could be deemed artwork.

Yesterday, he and Avery had walked up and down Sixteenth Street before her shift—with Fyran keeping his cool despite spotting Varketh more than once. Today was the first time this week he'd not seen her. Telling her that he had business to attend to had been surprisingly difficult, but he'd no longer been able to ignore Varketh. Being in Fyran's company placed Avery in potential danger.

The days he'd spent with his female had been the best of his life.

That realization struck Fyran hard.

Yeah, his past experiences hadn't exactly set a high fucking standard for what comprised a good day, but there was really no comparison to be made here. In all the best ways, Avery was unlike anyone he'd ever known.

She's mine.

Those words echoed in his mind, deep and powerful, and pulsed outward to hang in the air, making the car feel as though it were charged with electricity.

Clenching his jaw, he cranked up the volume on the radio and fought back every thought that arose for the duration of the drive. He found no particular success in that battle.

By the time he'd made it into his living room, he was thrumming with restless energy and knew he couldn't hold back those thoughts any longer. He paced around the room, claws digging into his palms, tail twisted stiffly against his leg, and boots thumping on the floor.

Even amidst this turmoil, he wanted nothing more than to call her just to hear her voice. No, that wasn't all he wanted. That tease couldn't truly satisfy him. He wanted to see her, to smell her, to touch her...to taste her again.

He craved a deeper taste, a *true* taste, not just the sample he'd stolen from her fingers.

But his hands were covered in blood. They did not deserve to touch Avery's pristine, innocent flesh. He could offer her nothing but danger, nothing but lies—the very lies necessary to protect a mission he'd never wanted any part of. And by pursuing her, wouldn't he be doing exactly as he'd been ordered? Wouldn't he be accepting everything he'd fought against?

Wouldn't he just become another one of *Exthurizen's* breeders?

His strides quickened as though to keep time with the blistering rhythm of his heart, and his path expanded into the hallway and kitchen.

No, the *Exthurizen* had no part in this; Command had no authority here. This was about Fyran and Avery and nothing else.

"And what the fuck do I know about any of it?" His voice was ragged in his tight throat.

Karak'duun, he wanted Avery. Wanted her...as his lifemate.

Though he wasn't even certain of what that truly meant, he knew down in the deepest parts of himself that Avery was meant to be his mate—and that he'd settle for nothing less. He would have her. *All* of her.

Yet his desire for her couldn't change the fact that he'd never been with a female. Everything he wanted to do with her, *to* her, was the product of an imagination he'd fed too much.

As he stalked into the hallway, he tugged off his jacket, tossed it aside, and kicked off his boots. He raked his fingers through his hair, grazing his skin with his claws before grasping the strands and pulling until his scalp stung.

He yearned to run his hands over every inch of Avery's body, to caress her skin with his fingertips and tongue, to tease her with the tips of his claws. He yearned to slip his fingers between her thighs and touch her most intimate, sensitive parts.

And what then? He knew the basics, of course, but that wasn't enough for his would-be lifemate. He wanted to overwhelm her with pleasure, wanted to hear her cry out in need, wanted to make her burn with desire.

Fyran returned to the living room, resuming his pacing across the carpeted floor. His thoughts were racing, his blood ablaze, and the ache that suffused his groin whenever he was near Avery had returned in full force, making his cock throb. He clamped a hand over his shaft and squeezed, but it continued to harden, unimpeded by his grip.

A cold shower. That will help, won't it?

He turned toward the stairs, but hadn't made it a single step before answering himself.

It's never helped before.

"Fuck."

Thinking of food couldn't nourish a starving man. Only one thing could satisfy Fyran's appetite. But...how? They'd not progressed that far into their relationship, and he didn't know how to do so in a way that would please her.

He was a full-grown male, one of the most dangerous *althicars* in generations according to Command, and he knew precisely fuck all when it came to pleasing a female. Fyran Voltanix, who'd studied and scrutinized everyone and everything, who'd made sure to learn every detail about each of his targets and every environment in which he'd operated, had no idea how to please the female for whom he longed.

The tightness and heat inside him only intensified as his eyes fell upon his laptop computer, which was set on the end table beside the couch. His cravings mattered little if he couldn't satisfy Avery's. He had to be worthy of her in that way if in no other.

With a growl, he snatched the laptop off the table, opened it, and powered it on.

Should be figuring out the Gregor situation.

Oh, fuck off.

His mission objectives had expanded, his priorities had changed. It was time for a different sort of reconnaissance.

If only he'd paid more attention to the lessons Command had provided regarding female humans and their reproductive anatomy. It figured that the first time he'd rebelled like this in his whole career was coming back to bite him in the ass, especially considering this was also the first time he'd wanted for anything personally.

He dropped onto the couch, laying the laptop over his thighs.

Finding pornography on the internet was staggeringly easy. Far more difficult was determining what would be the most informative. There were so many categories, classifications, and tag words that he didn't know where to begin, especially when he didn't have any context for most of it and so many of the thumbnails looked identical. He'd never seen so many slits, asses, cocks, and breasts.

Frowning, he leaned his face a closer to the screen, scrolling through the listed videos. With more scrutiny, the differences were clear. He never would've guessed that human reproductive anatomy could be so varied. But that didn't make it any easier to find what he was after.

Fyran refined his search, typing in *pleasing a female.*

Amongst the top results were videos like *licking MILF pussy til it squirts* and *Eating Out My Hot Girlfriend.* Perhaps not exactly what he'd envisioned, but with the view counts these videos boasted, they *had* to have valuable information, right?

Though he had no idea what differentiated a MILF pussy from any other, Fyran selected that video.

The humans on screen—a busty blonde female and a relatively fit male—wasted little time in the set up. Within the first fifteen seconds, she was sitting back on a couch with her skirt hiked up and her thighs spread wide, and the male was on his knees before her.

Fyran's eyes widened, and he sat forward as the male in the video dipped his face between the female's legs to drag his tongue along her sex, licking away her moisture.

The fire in Fyran's belly flared, and his cock was instantly hard again, straining desperately against his jeans. That was what he'd yearned for without understanding it—not just another taste of Avery, but a taste of her lust, her arousal, her *essence*. Just the thought of it made his mouth water, his tail curl, and his balls tight.

He watched, enrapt, as the male used his tongue and mouth on the female, who was soon writhing and moaning in pleasure. Everything seemed to center on the little nub at the apex of her slit; she shuddered whenever the male lavished it with his attentions. The clitoris.

Without realizing what he was doing, Fyran stood up, holding the laptop on his open hand, and started walking. His mind was racing again, absorbing the images on the screen and desperately attempting to apply them to what mattered—how would Avery respond to his tongue on her sex? What sounds would she make, how would she move?

How would she *taste*?

He halted abruptly, squeezed his eyes shut, and dropped his free hand to his groin to clamp it over his twitching erection.

Fuuuuck.

Drawing in a harsh breath, he pushed himself forward, staggering up the stairs as though drawn by a deep-buried instinct. His thoughts and body were out of his control; he felt like a spectator, like a passenger, and part of him thrilled in it. After years of discipline and decisiveness, there was something liberating about the thought losing himself in another person.

The female grew increasingly vocal and restless as the male continued his attentions. He'd taken hold of her legs to keep her in place, allowing her no escape from his mouth.

His pace now frantic, Fyran entered his bedroom and went to the dresser. He tugged open the top drawer, and his hand plunged in of its own accord, finding what he sought by feel alone. It emerged with Avery's lacy panties in its clutch.

Fyran moved to the bed in a flash, tossed the laptop onto the blanket, and hopped up. Keeping his grip on the panties, he hurriedly unfastened his belt, opened his jeans, and shoved down his boxer briefs, releasing his throbbing shaft. He growled as he clamped his hand around its base.

It hurt to touch, but he couldn't leave it be, couldn't ignore his needs, his overwhelming arousal.

He lifted Avery's panties to his face and inhaled. The scent of her essence lingered in the fabric, and he took it in greedily. He pumped his fist along his shaft, making himself shudder, and quickened his motions. His breath was soon ragged, emerging through his bared fangs and entering through flared nostrils. He was desperate for more of her perfume, for more of her taste, for more of her touch.

But he could not ignore that it was his hand on his cock. He could not ignore that the sounds of pleasure were not coming from Avery, but an anonymous woman in a video on his computer.

Fyran growled, pumping his hand faster still. The pressure within him was unbearable, the ache having sunken into his bones, and yet the harder he tried, the further away his release seemed.

He closed his eyes and struggled to picture Avery—to picture her thighs open for him, her skirt hiked up, and her legs hooked over his shoulders. To picture her gorgeous little body before him, her blouse open and breasts exposed with their nipples budded. He struggled to imagine the look on her face—pleasure, desperation, passion, adoration. His mind attempted to have her cry out his name, to gasp, to beg for more from him.

But his imagination couldn't go that far; it could never do her justice.

The woman on the video screamed out in pleasure. Something about the sound seemed exaggerated, seemed...fake.

Fyran halted his fist and squeezed it tight around his shaft. The resulting flare of pain made him hiss through his teeth. His pulse—a rapid, rumbling beat—pounded in his cock, and his need roiled on the edge of becoming maddening, but he allowed himself no further movement save to lift a leg and close the laptop's lid with his heel, silencing the video.

He dropped his head back against the headboard, wadded the panties in his fist, and lowered them from his face.

"*Karak'duun,*" he grumbled. His entire body was tense, and his shaft remained hard and throbbing.

He'd taken himself in hand perhaps half a dozen times in his life to ease those rare urges, and while he couldn't say any of those experiences had been pleasurable, they'd offered at least some release. But this...

This was torture. Because now, with his need blazing stronger than he'd ever thought possible, anything short of what he craved would bring him no relief.

Nothing but Avery would slake his desire.

Fyran had no idea how much time had passed before his erection faded. That it had persisted so long despite everything was a wonder, but it was also troubling. This situation had spiraled out of control so quickly that he could barely fathom what had happened. How would he restrain himself going forward? How could he resist?

When he was finally able to do so without causing himself any more pain, he tucked his cock back into his pants and zipped them up, leaving the button and his belt unfastened.

He stared up at the ceiling. Though his arousal had eased, his desires had not. There was so much else he should've been focusing on, but there was only one thing he could bring himself to do.

Fyran lifted his ass off the bed, pulled his phone out of his back pocket, and opened the photo album. He'd never used the phone's camera much, but over the last several days, he'd taken a few pictures—pictures of himself and Avery together...and pictures of her alone. Most had been captured with her knowledge. She was smiling at him in those photos. But he'd taken a few during the candid moments when she'd glanced away from him and that joy had been lingering in her eyes, when she'd looked like she didn't have a worry in the world.

There were also a few he'd taken as he'd followed her to and from work, watching to make sure she reached her destinations safely. Something about seeing her walking in the winter sun with snow sparkling around her was hauntingly beautiful.

His favorite was a photo of her with her face turned upward, eyes closed, as she enjoyed the sunshine on her skin.

He exited the photo album and sent her a text. *You still up?*

He waited, second after excruciating second; by the time five minutes had passed without any sign of a response, he growled and dropped his hand onto the bed.

The phone vibrated.

Fyran scrambled up into a sitting position, heart thumping as he looked at her message.

Yeah, sorry. I just got out of the shower. Everything okay?

His cock leapt the mention of her being in the shower, but he forced his desire down.

Everything's fine. He sent that through and took a moment to consider what to type next. *Just had a long day. Figured it'd be better if I ended it talking to you.*

It was a long day at work for me too. I...missed you.

Something in his chest constricted. It was a surprisingly *good* feeling. Had anyone ever said that to him before? Had anyone ever missed him while he was gone, had anyone ever been waiting for him after a deployment?

Had he ever formed enough of a bond with anyone for them to care about him?

Another message from Avery appeared a moment later.

I'm sorry. It's only been a day, and we just met. I must sound like a clingy girlfriend.

No, you don't, he replied quickly. *And it felt like a lot longer than one day. You don't need to be self-conscious with me, Avery. You're not going to scare me off.*

If anything, she was only drawing him in deeper and deeper.

That...makes me happy to hear, she texted back. *I was worried I might. But what I said was true. I really, really missed seeing you today, Hunter.*

Fyran smiled despite seeing that name; more and more, he longed for her to use his true name. *I missed you too, Avery. We'll have to fix this tomorrow. Will you be working?*

Yeah, a late shift. I'll be working until eight.

I'll be there near the end of your shift. Take you out somewhere.

And where do you plan to take me? There was a wide grinning face included with her question.

He couldn't help a pang of guilt in his chest when he replied. *Can't tell you all my secrets, Avery. It's a surprise.*

Of course, he'd need to figure out just what that surprise was... but there was time for that.

Tall, handsome, and mysterious, she replied. An animated image of woman fanning herself with her hand followed. *I didn't think men like you existed in the real world.*

That guilty pang intensified. He'd tell her the truth eventually. Tell her everything.

Fyran froze, his heart skipping a beat. That desire to be honest with her was like the final piece of a puzzle clicking into place. It was no longer a matter of wanting or hoping; she was his lifemate. He felt it in his core—in what humans would've called his heart. It was woven into his very being as though it were coded in his genes. Avery Watson, this little Earth female, was his.

His thumbs quickly typed a response. *There are no other men like me in this world or any other. I exist only for you, Avery.*

You have no idea how hard my heart is pounding at those words. Does that mean I get to claim you as mine?

As long as I get to claim you, too. Not that he'd be deterred regardless.

I'm yours, Hunter.

Just like that, the arousal he'd fought so hard against resurged. Fyran hissed through his clenched his teeth. He wanted to hear those words from her lips, in her voice, wanted to look into her eyes as she said them. But if he let himself dwell on it too long tonight, he'd get no sleep.

And he'd likely end up driving to her apartment.

Can't wait to hear you say that tomorrow night. Sleep well, Avery.

Goodnight, Hunter.

She sent a picture immediately after her reply—a *selfie*. His female's hair was loose and damp, and she wasn't wearing her glasses. Her eyes were half-lidded, her freckles stood out starkly against her skin, and the silver piercing in her nose glinted with reflected light. Her lips were puckered above her upturned, open palm.

A kiss. She was blowing him a kiss.

Fyran's heart thumped, and his cock pulsed. He groaned, dropping a hand over his erection and pressing down hard. He lay back and stared at that picture even though he knew better, even though he was only torturing himself.

Avery, my beautiful, radiant, delectable mate.

He trailed his thumb just above the phone screen as though stroking her cheek, wishing he could feel her.

It was going to be another long, long night.

ELEVEN

Avery glanced at the clock above the kitchen window as she picked up a pair of food-laden plates and set them on her tray next to the two chocolate shakes. It wasn't the first time she'd checked the clock—she'd been doing so all evening, and the minutes only seemed to pass slower and slower as she neared the end of her shift. Her thrumming anticipation had made a busy Saturday night crawl by at a snail's pace.

She still had twenty minutes until her shift was over. She swept her gaze around the restaurant, searching, but there was no sign of Hunter.

Soon, Avery. He'll be here soon.

She blew the wisps of hair that had escaped her ponytail out of her face, turned, and smiled as she carried the plates to their destination—a booth where a father sat with his little girl on a daddy-daughter date.

He was dressed in a nice shirt and a tie, and his seven-year-old daughter was wearing a beautiful sky-blue dress with sequins, ruffles, and long, sheer sleeves. The little girl had told Avery it was an Elsa dress. Her hair, a mass of thin, dark braids, was pulled up into a bun and had been topped off with a silver tiara. A single long-stemmed pink rose lay on the table near the wall.

It was adorable seeing them coloring the children's menu together.

"All right. I have some homemade meatloaf for dad," Avery said as she set the larger plate down in front of the father. She placed the other plate before the little girl. "And golden chicken nuggets with fries for the princess. And best of all, two chocolate shakes, one with *extra* cherries."

The little girl's eyes widened as they fell on the milkshake, which was topped with no less than five bright red cherries. She turned her excited face up to Avery. "Thank you!"

Avery smiled. "You're so welcome. Is there anything else I can get for either of you?"

The father shook his head, chuckling as his daughter plucked up a cherry and popped it in her mouth. "We're good. Thank you."

"I'll check back soon. Enjoy your meal."

Avery made her way toward one of her other tables—one of the round ones in the middle of the dining area, currently occupied by four rowdy men in their late twenties or early thirties. Their boisterous laughter carried clear across the restaurant.

Her smile, which had come so easily a moment before, felt forced as she neared their table. They were those sorts of customers who made crude remarks and unwanted *compliments*, the sort who looked at her in a way that made her skin crawl. It was clear that they'd been undressing her with their eyes the whole time they'd been here.

Thankfully, they were nearly finished with their meals and would soon be on their way.

"Refills for you guys?" Avery asked.

One of the men grinned as he leaned toward one of his friends. Though he whispered when he spoke, his voice was plenty loud enough for Avery to hear. "I'd sure like to fill that."

Avery clutched her tray to her chest but kept her smile in place.

The other man laughed, meeting Avery's gaze. "Yeah, babe. Fill 'em."

Setting her tray on the edge of the table, she gathered their empty glasses. "I'll be back shortly."

Glad to escape, she hurried away, and was sure to take her time refilling their cups.

Someone nudged her arm, startling her. She turned her head to find Brandy smiling at her.

Brandy dipped her chin and flicked her gaze past Avery. "Loverboy's here."

Avery's heart leapt. She turned her head and her gaze locked with Hunter's. He sat at the counter directly behind her, his hair wild and loose. His dark eyes were smoldering and ravenous, intent upon her and her alone.

"God, you lucky bitch," Brandy said quietly, leaning close to Avery. "I wish I had a man who looked at me like that. Like he couldn't wait to stick his head between my legs and—"

Avery's eyes widened as she snapped her head toward her co-worker. "Brandy!"

The woman laughed. "Well, it's true! He looks like he wants to eat you up." Brandy nudged her elbow against Avery's arm again and grinned. "Let me know if you ever get tired of him. He can play Big Bad Wolf with me any time."

Brandy disappeared into the kitchen, and Avery looked back at Hunter, catching her bottom lip with her teeth.

He'd look pretty damned good with fangs.

All the better to eat me with.

Warmth flooded Avery's cheeks, and a deep, hot ache bloomed within her core. She'd never thought about bedroom roleplay even though she enjoyed roleplaying games, but she suddenly found the idea of naughty roleplay with Hunter *very* appealing.

Avery set the soda-filled glass onto her tray, wiped her hand on her apron, and approached Hunter with a smile. "Hi."

"Evening," he said, lips lifting into a rakish half-grin. "You can let her know it's not going to happen."

Avery's eyes widened, and she covered her mouth, muffling her embarrassed laugh. "Oh my gosh, you *heard* that?"

How could he have picked up that conversation with all the noise in this place?

"I've got pretty sharp hearing." He combed his fingers through his hair to tug it back and tapped his ear.

All the better to hear you with, my dear.

She chuckled. She could imagine those ears of his tapering to points, could imagine tracing their tips with her fingers...or maybe her tongue.

Avery pressed her thighs together. Hunter was insanely hot as it was. If she kept imagining him with features that only made him more enticing, she wouldn't be able to finish her shift without having to change her panties.

She glanced at the clock and nearly groaned.

"I...have ten more minutes until my shift is over. Is there anything you'd like while you wait?" she asked.

Hunter leaned across the counter, hooked her apron with a finger, and drew her closer. "You."

"Sorry, sir. I'm not on the menu." She bent toward him until her mouth was next to his ear. "Yet."

He muttered something, his voice so low and rumbly that she couldn't understand what he'd said, and inhaled deeply. One of his big hands rose, and he ran the tip of his finger along her jaw before capturing her chin in a firm grasp. He guided her face toward his. Their eyes locked.

"Best get to work, *vaerina*," he growled, "or you won't be able to finish your shift."

A thrilling shiver ran through Avery, and her pussy clenched at the promise in his voice. Just like that, she went from Little Red Riding Hood to Alice in Wonderland.

Eat me. Drink me.

"Okay," she whispered. Withdrawing from him was one of the hardest things she'd ever done.

Avery turned back to the soda fountain and finished refilling the glasses she'd left on her tray. The entire time, she could feel Hunter's gaze on her as though it were a physical touch. Whereas the other men's stares had made her feel uncomfortable, Hunter's aroused her.

He made her feel safe.

Picking up the tray, she cast Hunter another a smile as she passed him and walked over to the father and daughter. The dad had worked his way through half of his meal, and the girl's milkshake was nearly gone—though her food had barely been touched except for a few fries and a single nugget. Their water glasses were still mostly full.

"How is everything?" Avery asked.

"So good!" the girl said with a wide grin. There was a dab of whipped cream on the side of her mouth. "Best. Milkshake. Ever."

"Aww, thank you. Jerry might do the cooking here, but I make some amazing milkshakes." Avery looked at the father. "Anything else I can get you?"

"Nope. We're great," the father said.

Avery smiled. "I just wanted to let you know that my shift is just about over, so Brandy will be taking over for me. She'll take good care of you."

"Thank you."

"Have a wonderful night."

One more table and I'm free.

She carried the tray to the rowdy table and distributed their drinks. The men had wiped their plates clean, leaving only a few tiny, hard French fries, smears of ketchup, and a leaf of lettuce. Even the baskets of appetizers were empty.

"How was everything?" Avery asked, setting her tray on the edge of the table to gather the baskets and plates.

"Delicious," one of the men replied, leaning back and folding his hands on his abdomen. "Though not as delicious as you look."

Avery ignored his comment, as she had many others in the past. It meant nothing. "Did you save any room for dessert? We have ice cream sundaes, milkshakes, or pie."

The burly man next to her laughed. "I'd sure like a piece of this."

He smacked her ass.

Avery gasped at the sharp sting, the force shoving her into the table. But it wasn't just a slap—he pressed his palm hard against her flesh and squeezed. She whirled around to face him, accidentally striking one of the cups with her hand as she moved.

The sound of the glass shattering on the floor seemed to silence the rest of the diner.

"Fuck, you spilled that shit all over me!" The man who'd grabbed her shoved his chair back from the table. His shirt and pants were soaked, and his expression was furious.

He turned his face toward Avery and placed his hands on the table as though he meant to stand.

A dark figure appeared behind the man. Before Avery could fully register that the figure was Hunter, he clamped a hand around the back of the man's head and slammed his face on the table. The silverware and dishes rattled, several more items clattering onto the floor.

Avery jumped in startlement.

Hunter caught the man's arm and wrenched it behind the man's back as he leaned down, keeping the man's face pinned on the tabletop.

The man cried out in pain and struggled against Hunter's hold. He managed only to shake the table some more.

"You touch her again," Hunter said in a low, gravelly voice that was barely more than a growl, "and I'll tear off your fucking hand."

Avery's breath hitched. She'd never heard him so furious, so deadly, so savage before. His eyes were so impossibly black, the eyes of a shark who'd scented blood and had closed in for the kill.

Someone grasped Avery by her arms from behind and tugged her back. "Are you okay? What happened?"

Brandy.

"That man groped me, and Hunter..." Avery couldn't take her eyes off Hunter.

"What the fuck?" one of the other men demanded. They were all on their feet now, their expressions conveying strange blends of fury and uncertainty.

One of the men lunged toward Hunter, whose only move was to apply more pressure to his captive's arm. The face-down man screamed, dropping onto his knees as his chair slipped out from under him, and the would-be attacker hesitated.

"You're gonna break his fucking arm," one of the other men shouted.

Hunter's response was simple, guttural, primal. It was colder than the Colorado air. "And?"

"What the hell's going on out here?" Jerry's voice boomed from behind the counter.

Avery looked over to see Jerry approaching, a spatula still in hand, the kitchen door swinging behind him like he'd just burst through it.

"This guy fucking attacked our friend," one of the men said, jabbing a finger toward Hunter.

"Their *friend* got handsy and copped a feel on Avery," Brandy said, glaring at the man.

"That true, Avery?" Jerry asked, though his angry expression remained directed at the men.

Avery knew him well enough to understand that he wasn't doubting Brandy; he was simply giving Avery a chance to speak for herself. She could feel the eyes of all the other customers upon her, could feel the hatred in the glares from these men, who must've thought their uninvited come-ons and groping should've been without consequence.

Avery nodded, flicking her gaze between Hunter and the face-down man. "He slapped me and grabbed my ass, and him and his friends have been making lewd comments since they came in."

"That's bullshit," said one of the men. "You lying—"

"Another word," Hunter snarled, "and you're fucking next."

"All right, son," Jerry said. "Let him go. Him and his friends are about to pay their check and leave. And they're not welcome in here again."

Hunter tensed, lips peeling back to bare his teeth. For an instant, Avery imagined his canines elongated into fangs. Even without big, sharp teeth, he was scarier than the Big Bad Wolf ever could've been.

He was a hell of a lot sexier too.

But he looked like he was about to rip the man's head off, and as much as Avery thought the guy deserved it, she didn't want Hunter to get into any trouble. Especially not because he'd defended her. She flicked her gaze over the people within the restaurant, spotting the seven-year-old girl whose eyes were rounded and uncertain. Avery didn't want that little girl—or anyone else in the diner—to witness more than they'd already seen.

She stepped away from Brandy and touched her palm to Hunter's shoulder. "Hunter?"

He turned his head to meet her gaze. It took her a moment to see through his rage to the man beneath.

"It's okay. I'm okay," she said softly.

The light in Hunter's eyes changed subtly, as though all the heat in them was suddenly directed at her—but none of that fury. Even through his leather jacket, she felt his muscles ease beneath her hand. Slowly but smoothly, he straightened, keeping the red-faced man pinned on the table as easily as he might've held down a small child, or perhaps even an insect.

His gaze shifted to the other men, who were still gathered around the table. "Any of you so much as come near her again, I'll make this look mild." He twisted his hand slightly.

The man with his face on the table cried out in fresh pain.

"Am I fucking understood?" Hunter growled.

"Okay, man," one of the other men said, holding his palms out in front of him and taking a step back. "Just let him go."

Hunter stared at the three men until they'd averted their gazes before finally releasing their companion. He made no show of it; he simply withdrew his hands and took a step back.

The man fell onto the floor, nearly knocking over the table, and cradled his arm against his chest. His friends, casting wary glances at Hunter, hurried over to help their friend to his feet.

Hunter paid them no mind. His eyes were upon Avery, and as

soon as she met his gaze, he took hold of her wrist and tugged her along as he stalked toward the front door.

Avery quickened her steps to keep up. Her heart was racing, and she felt the tension radiating from Hunter through his grip on her wrist. It didn't hurt, and he didn't squeeze, but it was firm.

"Avery?" Jerry called. "You gonna be okay?"

She looked over her shoulder, glimpsing the worried looked on Jerry's face. "I'll be fine!"

Hunter pushed the door open and dragged her outside. The cold night air swept over her skin, making it prickle with goosebumps. He led her along the sidewalk at a rapid pace, his clothing making him look like a big, ominous black figure despite the bright Christmas lights on the nearby trees.

As soon as they reached the opening of the alley that ran through the middle of the block, Hunter turned into it. There in the shadows, he pulled her close to him, backed her against the wall, and pinned her in place with his body. The chill night air was instantly forgotten as Hunter's heat enveloped Avery.

She swore she saw a flash of red in his eyes before he bent down and slammed his mouth over hers.

Avery's eyes flared, and she instinctively grasped his arms. A small, surprised squeak escaped her. For a moment, her mind was blank with shock.

Her heart sped and her clit pulsed when she realized what was happening.

Hunter was kissing her.

His lips were hard, searching, and demanding even as they caressed hers. It was a delicious sensation that had her lashes fluttering shut and her body going pliant; she succumbed to him. She reveled in the feel of his mouth, in his heat, in the solidness of his body. She relished in the feel of his fingers on her waist and hips, in the strange sensation of his nails digging into her flesh as though they were filed to sharp points.

His scent, sandalwood and fir with hints of leather and woodsmoke, enveloped her, and the long strands of his hair brushed her face. Everything fell away, leaving only the two of them. Leaving only Hunter.

But there was just a touch of hesitancy in him, a subtle restraint, an uncertainty that had him bristling with tension.

Avery tipped her head back. She nipped at his bottom lip with her teeth and flicked her tongue over it to soothe it.

Hunter growled against her lips, and the sound rocked Avery to her core. It was the call of a beast about to claim what it desired. With that simple, primal, maddening sound, all his hesitancy and restraint vanished. He ravished her mouth with a savage intensity that stole her breath and left no room for doubt—she was *his*.

His fervency, his hunger, and his passion flowed into her; they became hers. When he dropped his hands to her ass, she was already reaching up to bury her fingers in his hair. Hunter lifted her off her feet and forced his body between her legs, which she wrapped around his waist, drawing him closer still. Avery moaned when she felt the hard press of his erection against her pussy, unmistakable despite the barrier created by their clothing.

Hunter's grip on her ass tightened, pricking her with his nails, and he bared his teeth with a snarl. Touching his forehead to hers, he ground his pelvis against her and shuddered.

"Hunter," she rasped. Pleasure jolted through her, sparking a rush of liquid heat between her thighs. Her nipples ached with the need to be touched. She kissed the corner of his mouth and swept her tongue over his lower lip and teeth and felt...a fang? That couldn't be right.

Panting, Avery drew her head back and looked at him. His eyes opened. She swore she saw another flash of red, but it was there and gone in an instant, leaving only that dark, smoldering stare.

He lifted a hand to her face, grazing his fingertips down her cheek and again creating that sensation of claws running over her skin. His hand halted only when it was around her neck, grasping her jaw and keeping her chin angled up. His voice was raw and guttural when he said, "Say it, *vaerina*. Say you're mine."

Avery's core clenched, and she'd never been so aware that it was clenching around *nothing*. She'd never felt so hollow, so desperate to be filled.

"Say it, Avery." His accent had thickened, turning her name into something exotic, into something beautiful, something saturated with lust, with reverence, with *need*.

"I'm yours," she breathed. "Only yours."

His eyes closed, and his nostrils flared with his deep inhalation. He groaned. Avery felt his cock twitch.

He was smelling her. She knew it, and damn was it a turn on. A shiver raced up her spine and spiraled into her limbs, making her tremble. She released a shuddering breath.

Hunter went still, his whole body suddenly as hard and unmoving as a statue. His eyes snapped open first, impenetrable black pools but for tiny, faint glimmers in their depths. He glanced down at her, brow furrowing, and then to the side—to the alley they were standing in.

When he swung his face back toward her, his expression softened. He shifted his hand back to her face, brushing her skin with his fingertips in a delicate caress, and said in a very low voice, "No. Not here."

He took hold of her wrists and removed her hands from his hair, pausing to place a gentle kiss on each of her palms. Then he guided her legs down, set her on her feet, and backed away from the wall to give her space—more space than she wanted at the moment. Her knees felt wobbly, and the ache in her core was as fierce as ever.

"I owe you a surprise," he rasped.

Avery chuckled as she righted her skirt. "I'd say that was quite a surprise."

Now that his body was no longer pressed against hers, now that he was no longer kissing her, the winter cold wrapped Avery in its icy grasp, biting through her inadequate clothing. She rubbed her hands over her bare arms, seeking relief from the chill.

Hunter's gaze dipped, running over her body slowly before meeting her eyes again. Though that fire remained in his expression, it was tempered by something more solemn.

"You're freezing." He unzipped his jacket and tugged it off, wrapping it around her shoulders. "Let's go back inside so you can get your things."

His jacket was saturated with his tempting scent, and Avery drew it tighter around her, burrowing into the heat left from his body. She looked up at him.

He tucked her hair back behind her ear, searching her face, before he turned and placed a hand on her back to guide her out of the alley. His voice was low and tight when he said, "This isn't where I want to make you mine."

It didn't take a stretch of Avery's imagination to know what he meant. He meant to *take* her—to claim her fully. Part of her wondered if they were moving too fast, but a larger part of her didn't care where or when it happened, as long as she had him.

She'd been kissed by boys in high school, unbeknownst to her mother, but she'd never been kissed like this. Nothing and no one could ever compare to what she felt with Hunter. What would it be like when they came together as one?

A simple stroke of his finger on her hand could send whispers of pleasure through her, and his kiss, his merciless, claiming kiss, had set her soul aflame. Anything more than that would shatter her into so many pieces that she might not ever recover from it, anything more would tear her apart with sheer ecstasy.

And she wanted it more than anything.

Dʀᴇssᴇᴅ in her new sweater dress, black leggings, and knee-high boots—all of which she'd brought to work in anticipation of going out with Hunter—Avery gathered her hair atop her head and tied it into a messy bun, tugging down wisps of it to frame her face. Once she was done, she stuffed her work clothes in her bag and put on her jacket.

When she stepped out of the bathroom, Jerry was waiting for her in the hallway. His eyebrows were low, and his face was pinched in concern. "Are you sure you're okay, Avery?"

It wasn't the first time he'd asked since she and Hunter had walked back into the diner.

"I'm okay," she said. "I promise, Jerry. Hunter dealt with them, and you kicked them out."

He nodded. "Next time, you tell me *any* time a customer says something out of line, and I'll deal with it before it can get out of hand, all right? I'm not doing my job if you guys don't feel safe here."

Avery smiled. "Thank you, Jerry."

He glanced down the hall, toward the door that led into the dining area. "And Hunter? You're...safe with him? He seems pretty intense."

She reached out and touched Jerry's arm, bringing his attention to her. "He is, but I feel safest with him. He'd never hurt me, Jerry. I know it."

Avery wasn't sure how she knew that, especially not when she'd only met him a short while ago, but it was true. She trusted Hunter with her life.

Jerry's kind brown eyes met hers, and he covered her hand with his. It was big, rough, and strong, but it was also gentle. "We're family here, Avery. If you ever need help, you just ask."

He patted her hand and gave it a squeeze. It was such a fatherly gesture that it made her heart clench. Tears stung her eyes, welling until her vision was blurred. Was this what it was like to have a father who cared?

Jerry's brow furrowed deeper, and he frowned, opening his arms. "Come here, Avery girl."

Avery stepped into his embrace and pressed her cheek to his chest. He smelled of cologne and fryer oil, but she didn't care. In that moment, she was a little girl again, longing for a father who gave a damn, a father to comfort her, to care for her, to love her. To hug her like Jerry was doing right now.

He had no blood ties to her, and she'd only known him for a couple years—since the day he'd interviewed her for this job—and yet he'd been more of a father to her in two years than Derek Watson had been in twenty-two.

She blinked, willing the tears away before it could make her mascara run. "Do you think those men will go after Hunter?"

"Nah. They're dumb, but I don't think they're that dumb. And even if they tried to take legal action, there's the matter of the sexual assault to deal with." Jerry let out a heavy sigh. "You tell me what you want to do about that. You want to press charges, I'm behind you all the way."

She shuddered as she recalled the feel of that man groping her ass. What Hunter had done to him wasn't exactly justice, but it felt close enough. It had been justice for Avery. She hoped it would make the man think twice about ever doing it again. "I just want to move on."

"All right."

"Thank you, Jerry. For everything."

He released her and drew back, patting her shoulders and smiling down at her. The wrinkles at the corners of his eyes grew more pronounced. "You ever need anything, we're here for you. Got it?"

She grinned, pushed her glasses up her nose, and nodded. "Got it."

Jerry dropped his hands. "Now get out of here. Your man is waiting for you."

My man.

The thought sent a thrill through her that made her heart flutter.

After bidding Jerry goodnight, Avery hurried to the dining area, where Hunter awaited her. He had put his jacket back on, though he'd left it unzipped, and was leaning against the wall with his hands in his pockets, somehow managing to look indifferent and impatient at once. At least until his eyes fell upon her.

His indifference evaporated, his impatience seemed to flee, and all his attention was directed at Avery and nothing else. The smoldering gleam in his dark gaze had not diminished while they'd been apart. If anything, it had only intensified—and it continued to do so as she walked over to him.

He pushed himself away from the wall, his eyes roving up and down her body slowly. The corner of his mouth tilted up into a rakish, sexy-as-sin smirk before he met her gaze again.

Avery smiled up at him and slipped her arm around his. "I'm ready for this surprise you have to show me."

Hunter glanced down at his arm, which was now firmly in her hold, and his smirk softened into something tender and more intimate. "Wondering if I should just bring you to my place so I can keep you to myself."

She laughed. "So, a surprise kidnapping, huh? Guess that's all right. I've always been more of a Netflix and chill kind of person. But I mean literally chilling, especially when I have ice cream. Always have to keep a blanket on the couch."

But she really, *really* wouldn't mind 'chilling' in another fashion with Hunter. She was almost twenty-three years old. She was damn well ready to turn in her V-card. With him.

Another of those growls sounded in his chest, this one rolling and appreciative, as he turned with her on his arm and opened the door. "I'd be all over that, but I already bought tickets."

She glanced up at him as they stepped outside. "Tickets? To what?"

Hunter chuckled, his long legs setting an easy pace. "Wouldn't be a surprise if I told you."

Avery groaned and pressed against his side, resting her head on his arm. "Boo."

They walked to a parking lot a couple blocks away, and Hunter led her to a sleek black muscle car with tinted windows, the sort of vehicle she'd only ever seen driven by privileged rich kids and men with something to prove. Hunter didn't really fit either of those descriptions, and next to him...the car was just a little more intriguing, just a little more dangerous.

And a whole lot more exciting.

She'd never cared what someone drove, had never been impressed by guys' cars, but this one fit its owner perfectly.

He unlocked the car, brought Avery to the passenger side, and opened the door for her. Avery climbed in. As she settled into the seat, a scent wafted into the air around her, faint but unmistakable—cherry.

Hunter closed her door once she was clear and strode to the driver's side. The vehicle rocked as he lowered himself into the driver's seat.

"Wouldn't have guessed you were a cherry air freshener kind of guy." Grinning, she tucked her bag on the floor between her foot and the console.

He turned his face toward her, nostrils flaring as he sniffed the air. Muttering a curse, he shook his head. "Cleaned that damned seat at least ten times and it still has that smell. Had an unfortunate accident with a slushie a couple weeks ago."

Avery laughed. "I'm surprised you'd allow anything but water in a car like this."

The engine rumbled as he started it. "I'm usually more careful. Got distracted. Though I have to admit"—his eyes locked with hers, and that hungry light in them was suddenly brighter—"someone's made me pretty fond of cherry in the time since."

The cherry pie.

Her smile softened as she held his gaze.

Hunter reached out and brushed the backs of his fingers over her cheek. His gaze dipped to her mouth, and he grazed his thumb over her bottom lip. His features tightened, and, somehow, his black eyes darkened further with lust as he stroked her lip.

He's going to kiss me again. He's going to kiss me and I'm going to pull him closer and we're not going to—

Hunter withdrew his arm abruptly and faced forward. His voice was thick when he said, "Buckle up, *vaerina*."

Avery released a shuddering breath, squeezing her thighs together and curling her hands into fists atop them. Her core pulsed with desire. She didn't know how much longer she could hold out, how much longer she could last before that desire became too much. She wanted Hunter. She'd never wanted anyone as much as she did him, and the kiss they'd shared in the alley had proven he was the one.

He was her passionate forever.

Willing herself into action, she pulled the seatbelt across her body and buckled it. "I've been meaning to ask...what does that word mean? I've tried looking it up, but nothing really comes up."

"*Vaerina?*" He buckled his own seatbelt, keeping his gaze lowered as though in contemplation. "Doesn't really translate directly into English. It's like...morning flower, but that's not exactly right."

"Would you try to explain it for me?"

Hunter's tongue slipped out, wetting his upper lip. "One of my earliest memories is of living in a big city. Everything was concrete, steel, and grime. Everything was...gray. But there was this little garden tucked away amidst all that, the only place I'd ever seen anything growing, and it had these flowers in it. They'd be closed up"—he lifted his hand, the tips of his fingers and thumb squeezed together tight—"pretty much all the time except for this little while in the mornings when the sun was angled just right."

He unfurled his fingers, staring down at his now open hand. "And they were beautiful. I never really understood how...special they were." His gaze rose to Avery's face, and there was something new in his eyes, something much deeper and hotter than the lust that always burned within them. "When I first saw you, I thought of them. Because you were this...this flash of beauty in what was an otherwise gray, shitty day."

A million butterflies took flight within her. No one had ever said anything like that to her before, no one had ever given her such a beautiful, meaningful nickname. It was even more special because it meant something to Hunter. She could tell it was hard for him to talk about it—he was closed off about a lot of his past—but here he was, sharing this with her, giving her a glimpse into his soul.

Once again, she was overcome by that surreal notion that she was in a romance novel. People didn't talk like this in real life... Did they?

But then her thoughts turned toward Mary and Harley, the elderly couple who frequented Jerry's, and all the interactions that Avery had witnessed between them.

"It sounds beautiful," she said. "I'd love to see it."

Hunter lowered his hand to the shifter and put the car into drive. "Don't even remember where it was," he said tightly. "But I'd much rather be looking at you, anyway."

Avery's cheeks flushed, and her lips spread into a wide smile. She studied his profile—his strong jaw, the sensual curves of his lips, the blade of his proud nose, the bold set of his brow. He was just so...*handsome.*

"I'd much rather be looking at you, too."

He flashed her a grin that bordered on outright arrogant as he set the car into motion. "Plenty of time for that, *vaerina.*"

They exited the parking lot, falling into a comfortable silence as Hunter navigated Denver's nighttime streets. While Avery had come to love this city, it had never seemed quite as beautiful as it did right now, sitting beside Hunter. They drove along Fourteenth Avenue, right past the Capitol building, and eventually turned south. Avery's growing anticipation stretched out each second. She hadn't gone on a date in...well, she'd *never* gone on a date, and she couldn't remember the last time anyone had surprised her with anything.

Anything pleasant, anyway. Her mother signing her up for that cycling class without her knowledge a few years ago didn't count, especially when Allison's reasoning had been that Avery had put on a few pounds. She shoved that memory aside. She wasn't going to let her mother taint this.

Where was Hunter taking her? What did he have planned?

Avery didn't have to wait long for an answer. The apartments and residences that had lined the road for most of the drive gave way to something different—far more modern buildings behind which she could see hints of colorful lights. She caught sight of a sign just before Hunter turned into a parking garage.

Denver Botanic Gardens.

There were people walking to and from their vehicles inside the garage—a lot of families with children bundled up in winter clothing, some of whom were bouncing excitedly and tugging their parents along. So many of the couples looked at one another with open love and laughter in their eyes.

Avery smiled, watching them with not a little longing.

I want that kind of family someday.

She wanted her children to tug her and their father's hands in their excitement, wanted the bedtime book readings that ended with the kids begging for just one more story, wanted messy hands and faces as they baked brownies from scratch or nibbled on cookie dough. She wanted a husband who looked at her as though she were his world, a husband who couldn't wait to see her at the end of the day, a husband who could argue with her and make up later when neither of them remembered what they'd been fighting about to begin with. A husband who would pull her close, hold her, kiss her, and dance with her even when there was no music playing.

She wanted...a real, loving family.

Avery looked at Hunter, and her heart thumped. What if he really was the one?

They drove around the entire lower level, but there were no open parking spots. Hunter huffed, exited onto the street, and turned into the outdoor lot farther down the road, where they drove around the loop at a snail's pace. Just as it seemed there was nowhere to park there either, the reverse lights of a vehicle came on up ahead.

As miserable as it was to walk in the cold and snow sometimes, Avery certainly didn't miss the challenges of finding parking.

Avery stepped out of the car. Biting wind struck her immediately, making her shiver. She reached up and tugged the wisps of hair out of her face, tucking them behind her ears as she glanced toward Hunter. He was looking at her from the other side of the car with a concerned frown. But her eyes didn't stay on him long for a change.

From their higher vantage, she could see across the street to the Botanic Gardens. Though much of the grounds were obscured by low buildings and hedge walls, she could see brightly colored lights on the many trees, and the big greenhouse was glowing beautifully. It was just a taste of what must've been waiting, but that taste was enough to get her truly excited.

Movement from Hunter called her attention back to him. He'd walked to the trunk, which he swung open. Avery tucked her hands in her pockets and joined him.

He bent down to dig through a cardboard box full of clothing.

Avery tilted her head, glancing at him before returning her eyes to his hand. "You have a box of spare clothes in your trunk?"

"Told you I still do odd jobs," he replied, plunging his other hand into the box to shift the garments inside with a bit more force. "Sometimes a change of clothing comes in handy."

He tugged out a long, black piece of fabric. Once it was free, he stretched it out and held it up in front of him. Little wool tassels dangled from either end. It was a scarf.

Hunter turned toward Avery, reached over her shoulders, and settled the scarf against the back of her neck. He wrapped it gently, slowly, the pads of his fingers brushing her jawline as he moved. Those dark, tantalizing eyes stared down at her all the while.

The warmth provided by the scarf couldn't compare to the heat of his touch.

Once the scarf was in place, he tucked the loose ends under the collar of her jacket, his thumbs stroking along her collarbone and over her shoulders. A thrill swept through her, making her nipples hard and her core clench. Her body was hyperaware of his touch—and it craved more. She shivered in a way that had nothing to do with the cold.

His breath emerged in a cloud, slow and steamy, as a barely perceptible growl rumbled in his chest.

Avery tipped her face up toward his with a smile and pressed a hand to his chest. "Thank you."

His features were tight, and his eyes blazed with lust. For a moment, Avery was sure he was going to drag her into the shadows, press himself against her, and kiss her as he had in the alley.

Hell, she was tempted to do it herself.

He covered her hand with his, engulfing it almost completely. His palm was rough, and she could feel the muscles of his fingers as they flexed. He spoke in a gruff whisper. "Not here, *vaerina*. You're for no one to see but me."

Avery ducked her head. Could he really read her thoughts so clearly? She grinned. "Am I?"

"Female," he eased closer, slipping his other hand around her throat and tilting her chin up, forcing her gaze back to his, "I'd gouge out the eyes of anyone who saw you."

His voice was barely removed from a bestial growl, and there was a deadly seriousness in it that told Avery that he wasn't being hyperbolic. Her heart quickened, and her eyes widened. Was it wrong for her to be so aroused by his vivid, gruesome words?

His thumb, positioned over the rapidly beating pulse on the underside of her jaw, stroked her skin. His expression gentled.

"No one is going to ever hurt you again, Avery. I'll do anything it takes to ensure that." His heated gaze lingered on her before he withdrew his hand from her throat and closed the trunk. Settling his arm around her shoulders, he drew her against his side.

She naturally slipped her arm around his waist and leaned into him, grateful for his warmth and solidness, especially in contrast to the cold night air. They walked out of the parking lot like that, falling into the steady stream of people moving toward the entrance of the gardens. There was another large sign up that she hadn't noticed before—*Blossoms of Light*.

Hunter produced a pair of tickets from his pocket when they reached the gate. Though most people—especially the younger ones—had their phones out with electronic tickets ready to scan, Avery wasn't surprised that Hunter had physical tickets. Every time he'd come to the diner or paid for something for her, he'd used cash. It was simply one of those little things she'd noticed, another little aspect of his personality—and it meant that he'd likely taken the time to come down here in person to purchase the tickets.

That only endeared him to her more.

She would've been content to simply walk with him like this regardless of their surroundings, relishing his heat, his scent, his presence, thrilling in how she seemed to fit against him so perfectly. But when they finally stepped into the gardens, she knew that this place, at this time, was exactly where she wanted to be with him.

Her steps faltered, and her breath escaped her in a misty cloud that slowly drifted away and dissipated. There were more lights here than she'd ever seen, than she'd ever imagined—it was like she'd stepped into magical world, tucked away in an obscure corner of reality. Christmas lights in more colors than she could name adorned the trees, globes of light lined the walkways, and everything seemed so natural, so fitting, so harmonious.

She'd loved Christmas lights since she was a little girl, but her younger self never could've dreamt of this.

"This is so beautiful," she said.

Avery looked up at Hunter only to find him staring down at her, his eyes aglow with reflected light, his smile soft and warm. It made her heart skip a beat.

"Mmhmm." The sound rumbled from him in a contented but lustful purr, vibrating straight into Avery.

The look on his face was everything she'd ever longed for. It said that she was the brightest star in his universe, that she was the only thing he ever wanted to see, that she was his everything.

It was the way a man looked at the woman he truly wanted—at the woman he wanted to spend his life with.

"Come on, *vaerina*," he said, urging her to resume walking. "Can't see it all from here."

They followed the path at a leisurely pace, and Avery barely noticed the other people present. Between Hunter and the lovely light arrangements, she had no attention to spare for anyone or anything else. Hunter seemed to look at her more than the displays, but his expression was so content, so carefree, that she couldn't complain. If watching her made him happy...then that made her happy, too.

He made her feel beautiful, sexy, and worthy of attention. He made her feel exactly the opposite of how she'd felt growing up, when her mother had always treated her as though she wasn't good enough.

She was determined to cherish every moment of this—every moment with Hunter.

Before long, they reached a place where the lights were blue, teal, and green, bathing the garden in a soothing glow reminiscent of a tropical sea. The lights seemed to cover every branch, arching overhead to create an illuminated tunnel. At the opposite end of the path, dozens of strings of lights ran down to form a big, scintillating cone. The colors coursing over that cone were soft and calming, like gentle waves lapping at the shore.

Avery stopped and took her phone out of her coat pocket. She entered the camera app and flipped the camera to selfie mode. Grinning up at Hunter, she scooted closer, caught the collar of his leather jacket, and gave it a gentle tug. "Take a picture with me."

He offered no resistance, bending down to get into frame with her. She faced forward and raised her phone. She snapped a picture, and, before Hunter could draw away, turned her face and pressed her lips to his cheek, taking another photo. She brushed her lips along his jaw before she pulled away.

She hadn't expected him to follow.

He leaned toward her, eliminating the little distance she'd put between their faces, and slanted his mouth over hers. Avery's breath fled, and Hunter took it into himself as he drew her closer, turning her body toward him.

Compared to their first kiss, this one was surprisingly tender. His lips caressed hers, explored them, coaxing her to do the same. She kissed him back with equal gentleness, savoring every moment.

A thrilling heat pulsed through Avery, pooling low in her belly. She wrapped her arm around the back of his neck and melted against him. The burning desire and aching need she'd experienced earlier reignited, as hot and ravenous as ever. His hand at the base of her spine pressed her closer. Even through their layers of clothing, she felt his erection, hard and thick. The evidence of it made her pussy clench with want.

Avery parted her lips and flicked her tongue over the seam of his mouth. He growled, and his hot, delectable tongue swept along hers, entwining with it. His mouth descended once more, claiming hers as he deepened the kiss with that thrusting tongue.

She whimpered and curled her fingers into his hair. Her knees quivered, weak; had he not been holding her up, she would've collapsed right there.

Someone nearby cleared their throat loudly.

Hunter released a slow, heavy breath and broke the kiss, pulling back just enough to meet Avery's gaze as she opened her eyes.

"Gets better every time," he rumbled. His hold on her tightened, pressing her belly more firmly against his pelvis.

"There are *children* here," a man said from nearby in the sort of exasperated, patronizing tone Avery had heard so much in her youth.

The muscles of Hunter's jaw ticked. He swung his head aside to look at the man and growled, "How the fuck you think they got here?"

The man's eyes widened, and he flinched. The woman beside him—who Avery assumed was his wife—wore an equally shocked expression. Looping his arm around her, the man hurried away. Interestingly enough, there were no children following them. There weren't any children around at all.

As the man left, Avery heard him angrily say something about finding security.

Avery couldn't hold it back anymore. She snorted, then burst out laughing. Pressing her forehead against Hunter's chest, she covered her mouth with her hand. "I can't believe you *said* that!"

He chuckled, his hand stroking up her back. "If we offended him, I feel bad for his female."

"Why's that?"

Hunter hooked a finger under her chin, lifting her face to look at him. Avery lowered her hand, flattening it to his chest, and met his gaze.

"Because he is more concerned with what is proper than showering her with unbridled affection," he said, his voice thick and sultry.

She never, ever would have thought she'd be able to stand in the middle of a crowd and kiss a man as passionately as she'd just kissed Hunter, or that she'd be so unconcerned with other people's judgmental looks and condemnation. When she was with Hunter, nothing else mattered. It was only him. And she refused to feel guilt or shame for what they shared.

Avery grinned. "We should keep going before he really does come back with security."

"It would be a shame to get kicked out before we see everything." He shifted his hold on her again, and she moved with him instinctually, returning to her place at his side.

They continued through the Botanic Gardens at an unhurried pace, as though that little confrontation had never happened. Each section of the gardens was different from the last, and in some places the lighting was so well-done that it seemed as though the trees and shrubs were glowing with their own luminescence and orbs of vibrant color seemed to hover over the partially frozen ponds. The more they saw, the more magical everything seemed.

When they reached the little bistro located deep within the gardens, Hunter insisted on buying her dinner—having undoubtedly noticed the way her eyes had followed the steam wafting from the small building, which wasn't much bigger than a snack stand. The menu was limited during the holiday event, but what was available sounded delicious.

They walked away with hot drinks and grilled cheese sandwiches. Rather than sit on the patio, where so many other people were enjoying their meals and snacks, Hunter led her to a bench beside the nearby pond. It was a little quieter there, and they were surrounded by snow, and lights, and beauty, and the cold didn't bother her in the slightest because she was with him.

"Better eat before it freezes," Hunter said, lifting half his sandwich to take a big bite. He'd ordered several toppings with his sandwich, surprisingly choosing veggies over meat—tomatoes, caramelized onions, and spinach.

Avery chuckled, taking a smaller bite of her own. She'd opted for something plainer and more traditional—just cheddar and provolone cheese. And it was just as delicious as it had sounded.

"Mmm." She held her free hand over her mouth as she chewed, nodding her head. "That's good."

Hunter swallowed his mouthful and looked at her. "With just the cheese?"

"Yep. Sometimes simple is better. Want to try?" Avery held her sandwich toward him. Wisps of steam rose from it, made ethereal in the colored lights.

He grinned and dipped his head, keeping his smoldering eyes locked with hers as he opened his mouth and took a bite off the corner of her sandwich. As she withdrew the sandwich, the gooey cheese stretched, pulling longer and thinner until it finally broke. Strings of it fell to stick to his chin like a dangling orange soul-patch.

His eyes dropped, crossing momentarily as though he could see his own chin, and his tongue slipped out to sweep the rogue strands of cheese into his mouth, having to hook them and pull them in three times before all the cheese was gone.

Avery giggled. "Well, you *tried* to make it look sexy."

He wiped his chin with a napkin. "Didn't quite get there, though?"

She shook her head.

And Hunter laughed. Avery had heard him laugh before, but most of the time it was a chuckle, good humored but a little subdued. This was full blown laughter, deep, rich, and husky, the kind of laughter that shook his broad shoulders and resonated from his chest. But it was also...free. Like this moment was the most joyous of his life, like all his cares had vanished for a short while.

It was the kind of laugh that could make Avery fall in love with this man.

She averted her gaze before her expression could betray those innermost thoughts, but her smile was so wide that her cheeks hurt.

Hunter set his sandwich on the cardboard tray resting upon his lap and reached for his drink. Avery had gone with a chai tea after some internal debate; it was hard to resist hot chocolate, especially when it was cold out, but it just didn't sound right with a grilled cheese. Hunter had opted for the same.

He took a sip from the cup. His features immediately went taut, and he shuddered, holding the drink away from him as though it were tainted.

His was the sort of reaction usually reserved for viral internet videos in which little kids ate lemons or super-sour pickles, but there was no sign that he'd been exaggerating or messing around, and that made Avery laugh again.

"Don't like it, I take it?" she asked.

"I don't understand how anyone enjoys such bitter drinks."

"It's not bitter," she said with mock offense. "It's a balanced blend of spices, intended to caress the palette and soothe the soul."

"It's bitter." He covered the top of the cup with one hand and popped off the lid. She watched as he set the cup and its discarded lid aside, reached into his pocket, and produced several packets of sugar.

"You seriously carry sugar around in your pocket?" she asked incredulously.

"How is it different from you having tissues in your bag?" Hunter tore the packets open and dumped their contents into the cup. "I have a...sweet fang."

"Do you mean a sweet *tooth*?"

"Yeah." Replacing the lid, he picked up the cup, moving it in small, repeated circles to stir the contents. "Get mixed up with those sayings sometimes. There are so many different versions of each one, they're hard to keep straight."

"Mhmm..." This wasn't the first time she'd seen him add sugar to his drinks. "I'm honestly surprised you're not diabetic with the amount of sugar you consume." She paused, brow creasing as she eyed him. "You're...not diabetic, right?"

"I'm not. Guess I just have an otherworldly metabolism."

Avery shook her head and chuckled. "Lucky."

They chatted as they ate their sandwiches, their conversation light and flowing easily, but it wasn't until they'd finished eating and were sipping at their drinks that their talk turned more serious.

"My family never did anything like this," Avery found herself saying, her voice sounding oddly small to her own ears as she watched a young couple and their three kids stroll by. It was strange to talk about this—strange to *want* to talk about it, when she'd moved away so she wouldn't ever have to think about it again. "It was always all work and no play for my parents, and my mother basically forced that on me and my sister, too. They wouldn't have seen the point in all this."

"I spent most of my time as a child alone, fending for myself," Hunter said gruffly.

Avery glanced toward him to see his fingers fidgeting restlessly around his cup.

"You mentioned your family traveling a lot. Did they often leave you home alone?" she asked.

"Yeah." He nodded, but there was something off about the gesture—almost like he was trying to convince himself more than her. "They, uh...they were always busy. Never around. So I had to figure out a lot of things on my own. Got into a lot of trouble along the way."

Hunter turned his head to face her, and the smile that he offered was wistful but hopeful. "I've...never done anything like this until now, either. Until you, Avery. It warms me. Here." He pressed his fist to his chest. "And I'm happy that I'm experiencing this first with you."

Those words and that smile made something stir in Avery's chest—something tender, full, and welcome, as comforting as a good blanket or a cup of hot chocolate but so much deeper and more powerful.

Avery smiled and scooted closer to him, laying her head on his shoulder as she looked out at the glowing display in front of them. She placed one of her hands over his and laced their fingers together. "I hope to have many firsts with you, Hunter."

He tipped his head aside, brushing his cheek on her hair.

Avery was hesitant to leave that spot, but there was still more to see, and her childlike excitement hadn't waned. Hunter kept his arm around her shoulders as they continued along, sharing his heat with her and humoring her when she wanted to take a few more pictures—even the silly ones, like when she positioned herself to make it look like she was holding two of the big glowing globes on the palms of her hands.

And all too soon, it was time to leave. She didn't know if it was

Hunter who slowed their walking pace to a crawl as they went toward the exit or herself, and it didn't really matter—neither of them seemed willing to move any faster.

With him, she finally understood the impossible dream she'd heard described so often, the desperate wish to stretch out a single moment in time and make it last forever. She didn't want this to end. But part of her understood that it was more special because it had to come to an end, and that there'd be more to look forward to —more days, more nights, more moments with him.

Her smile hadn't faded when they got into his car. Neither had Hunter's, which delighted her; he'd been wearing that soft smile for most of the evening. It was an expression that didn't quite mask the lust always present in his eyes, but it spoke of something much stronger behind it. When he smiled at her like that, when he looked at her like that, she felt...loved.

"Thank you for tonight," Avery said when they pulled up in front of her apartment building. "It was a perfect surprise."

He shifted the car into park, but he offered her no reply; there was only the soft, subtle sound of his leather jacket creaking with his movements. Avery turned her face toward him just as he hooked an arm around her, grasped the back of her head with his hand, and pulled her into a kiss.

Avery closed her eyes and gave in. She breathed in his scent, wanting to forever lock it in her memory. Lifting a hand, she cupped his jaw and slid her fingers into his hair, leaning closer as their lips parted and caressed each other.

Heat pooled between her legs. Though he moved slowly, there was undeniable hunger in his kiss, giving her the sense that he was prolonging it, savoring it, taking as much as he could and giving everything in return. She wanted to do the same.

Invite him upstairs.

A shiver of want coursed through her. She longed to move on to that next step, to truly satisfy her cravings for him, to feel his body against hers with no barriers. To feel him *inside* her.

And yet, the words stuck in her throat.

Something was holding her back, and she didn't know what it

was. As much as she wanted him, as much as she trusted him, part of her knew he was hiding something. That there was more to Hunter than what he'd told her. He'd given her glimpses of himself, but there was something more there. Something...important.

Avery broke the kiss and pressed her forehead to his. Her heart was racing, her skin was hot and tingly, and her lips pulsed in the aftermath of their kiss. She wound her fingers deeper into his hair, unwilling to let him go. "You were right. It really does get better every time."

Hunter growled, muscles tensing and grip tightening. "Getting harder and harder to resist, *vaerina*."

Her core clenched at his words. Her tongue slipped out to lick her lips—to sample his lingering taste.

I know.

Releasing a shaky breath, Avery opened her eyes and loosened her hold on him. He resisted when she drew back, fingers flexing as though to keep her in place, but he finally let her go. As her hand slipped out of his hair, the tip of his ear grazed her palm. It felt...longer than normal, somehow sharper.

She met his dark gaze.

His face was framed by his hair, which was now wild, like the unruly mane of a predatory beast. He parted his lips as though to speak, but no sound emerged. Slowly, those lips curled into a gentle smile. His voice was husky as he said, "This was a good night."

Avery smiled, too. "It was." She brushed her fingers over his brow, across his cheek, and along his strong jaw. "Goodnight, Hunter."

Hunter took gentle hold of her hand in his, bringing it to his mouth to kiss her palm. His warm breath flowed over her skin. "Goodnight, Avery."

He released his hold on her, the tips of his fingers stroking her hand as he did so, sending a thrill across her skin. She unbuckled her seatbelt, grabbed her bag, and opened her door, stepping out into the cold night air.

Come on, Avery! Speak up! Say it! Tell him you want him.

More than anything, she wanted to open her mouth, to say those words that would lead him up to her apartment, to her bed, but that unknown *something* blocked them in. She took a step back, smiled at him again, and gently closed the door.

Avery felt his gaze on her as she walked toward the building. At the entrance, she turned and looked at the car. She couldn't see him through the tinted windows, but she waved and blew him a kiss. He only drove away after she'd entered the building.

She lifted her hand to adjust the strap of her bag as she turned into the hallway. Her knuckles brushed the soft wool of the scarf he'd lent her, and she paused, running her fingers over it. She'd forgotten to return it.

Loosening the scarf, she lifted it to her nose and inhaled. It carried his scent. Avery groaned, closing her eyes and burying her face into the material.

"Why couldn't I ask him?" she breathed, tightening her fingers around the scarf.

THIRTEEN

THE STEERING WHEEL groaned as Fyran tightened his fists around it. It added to the cacophony inside the car—the noise of the idling engine, the loud music, his heavy, ragged breaths. But none of it could overcome the thunderous pounding of his heart.

"Fuck."

He'd hoped his erection would ease after Avery exited the car, had hoped his body would cool once the object of his desire was out of sight. But he'd only driven a block and a half before he'd been forced to pull over.

Fyran's nostrils flared with another deep inhalation. His hands twisted, coaxing fresh creaking from the steering wheel, and his tail stiffened along his leg—as though mimicking the stiffness of his cock. This car could provide no escape from his thoughts of Avery, especially not while her cinnamon and vanilla scent saturated the air and clung to his clothing.

Worse, there was just a hint of a far more intimate and feminine fragrance mixed in with her usual scent—the smell of her arousal.

He killed the engine, thrust open the door, and burst out of the vehicle, boots thumping on the pavement. His first lungful of icy air stung not because it was so cold but because her scent was absent from it.

Slamming the door shut, he stalked along the street, raising his hands to grasp fistfuls of his hair. His heartbeat echoed with impossible strength in his cock.

He wanted her so badly that he'd nearly lost control a few minutes ago. He'd nearly succumbed to the animal instincts that had awoken in his core, had nearly claimed her as his mate right in his car, out in public. He was furious with himself; he hadn't lied about his female's body being for no one but him. Fyran didn't want anyone fucking looking at her—and he wouldn't tolerate anyone touching her.

He'd been so fucking close to ending that bastard in the diner. So fucking close to taking a life right in front of his female's eyes. For all the battles he'd fought, for all the combat and bloodshed he'd seen, he'd never wanted so badly to kill—and had never longed to do so as brutally as possible.

That really would've endeared me to Avery, huh?

Svesh, she didn't even know his real name, didn't know his true nature. How could he justify rutting her when he'd not even told her the truth?

Fyran dropped his hands, burying them in his jacket pockets. Spinning on his heel, he strode back toward his car only to halt abruptly when his eyes fell upon Avery's building, which was still visible over the smaller residences.

How could he simply leave after having seen the building she lived in, after observing some of her neighbors and overhearing others? He had to be sure she'd made it safely into her apartment.

It was just a part of keeping her safe.

Go home, Fyran.

That voice in the back of his mind was firm and unwavering, tolerating no argument.

Naturally, Fyran ignored it.

He continued walking past his car, his gaze fixed on that run down brick building, his nose focused on the traces of Avery's scent wafting up from his clothing.

You have no self-control.

You have no idea what you might unleash upon her. No idea if you might hurt her.

You don't even know what you feel for her.

But he did know what he felt for her, at least in part—yearning. Fyran never would've believed it was possible to want anyone so much, but he did. It was real, it was true, and he wanted Avery with everything in him. Holding himself back was for her safety. She'd awoken a new side of him that he'd yet to explore and understand. She'd awoken a beast that had lain in hibernation for his whole life.

He also knew that, regardless of his efforts and intentions, it would eventually become impossible to hold back that beast.

Everything inside Fyran cried out for him to take her, to make her his, to form that irrevocable bond with her—the mating bond, that quirk of his people's biology that he'd only learned about after reaching adulthood, many years after his parents had vanished. He'd been taught that making such a bond, which a faloran could do only once in their lifetime, was a matter of choice.

Why did it feel so inevitable, then? How could he be so sure he would make that bond with Avery when so much remained uncertain?

Fyran crossed into a patch of deep shadow, a no-man's-land untouched by the illumination from the widely spread streetlights. He didn't consciously send the command to activate his cloaking field; something about the embrace of that darkness had him doing so instinctually. The brief hum of the field powering on only deepened the ache in his groin.

He hurried his pace, his strides swallowing the distance between himself and the apartment building. He slowed only to check for witnesses before entering through the front door.

This time, he paid no attention to the multitude of sounds and smells that assailed him in the hallway. Only Avery's scent registered in his mind. He moved to the stairs with silent confidence, drawn as much by the invisible tether binding him to Avery as by his knowledge of the building.

When the stairs groaned beneath his boots, he didn't falter; when voices rose into shouts behind closed doors, he did not stop to listen. Each step up drew him closer to his female, and he *needed* to see her. Their time together thus far had been too short.

His heartbeat was frantic as he reached her floor. The hallway was filled with muffled rock music coming from what Fyran assumed was Ian's apartment, but even his lingering irritation with that human couldn't distract Fyran from his goal. He stopped at apartment eleven.

Turning his head, he tucked his hair behind his ear and pressed it against the door, closing his eyes in concentration—doing his best to ignore how much stronger her scent was right here. He willed his heart to slow so its beating wouldn't affect what he heard, but that music, that fucking music, was too loud, and his damned cock was throbbing so hard that he was tempted to pin it between the door and his body in the hope of gaining even the smallest shred of relief.

Fyran released a slow, measured breath through his nostrils and clenched his jaw.

Water. The sound was faint, but it was from Avery's apartment—water running in the shower, complete with those brief flares and lulls in volume caused by a moving body disrupting the flow.

Though he was familiar with the risks, Fyran didn't hesitate to pull out his omnikey and use it to unlock Avery's door. He stepped into her apartment.

Before he could even close the door, her scent crashed over him in a wave, so full, so pleasant, so maddening that he could do nothing but breathe it in for a few seconds. The pressure in his groin strengthened. His balls were tight, heavy, and pulsing, and his shaft was pressed so firmly against his jeans that he swore he could feel every single cotton and denim fiber against his flesh.

He clamped a hand over his cock, moved clear of the doorway, and quietly shut the door. Only as he set the locks did he realize that he'd failed to check if he was alone.

Fortunately, Avery wasn't in sight. The bathroom door was

slightly ajar, with light shining through the gap, and the sound of the shower was far more distinct than it had been in the hall. But her feline, Beau, was present. The cat was perched atop the back cushion of the couch, head raised, tail dangling low, and eyes wide as he stared toward Fyran. The animal's ears were perked, occasionally twitching and turning.

Now, Fyran had to mind his every step, unwilling to do anything that might spoil his chances of seeing her, of being close to her. He filled his lungs again with that sweetly perfumed air and advanced toward the couch.

Despite Fyran's stealth, Beau's face snapped toward the faloran, and the cat went rigid, its tail stilling. The animal's only movement came in the form of rapid breaths and faint twitches of his whiskers.

Beau maintained his position as Fyran neared, leaning his head forward to sniff the air. He meowed questioningly.

Though almost every bit of Fyran was directed toward Avery, he couldn't ignore her pet. Keeping his movements slow and gentle, he extended his arm, brushing the backs of his fingers along Beau's cheek—while bracing himself for the small creature to react by leaping into the air and yowling.

Instead, Beau squeezed his eyes shut and rubbed his face against Fyran's invisible fingers while producing a low, contented rumbling—purring. Fyran had found humans difficult to figure out; house cats, it seemed, were a close second in that regard.

A new sound from the bathroom claimed Fyran's attention. He withdrew his hand from the cat—who responded with a much more demanding meow—and looked toward the closed bathroom door. His feet carried him to it of their own accord.

Warm steam flowed across Fyran's face as it escaped the bathroom through the opening, carrying the scent of Avery's soap and shampoo—spicy with a floral hint. He inhaled it appreciatively, though it wasn't the scent he truly craved.

The shower was still running, that hadn't changed, but now it was accompanied by Avery's voice. She was humming. Bracing his hands on either side of the doorframe, Fyran bowed his head and listened, leaning as close to the opening as he dared.

He didn't recognize the tune—which wasn't surprising—but he didn't care what it was. He also didn't care that she was a bit flat and probably a touch off-key. She sounded...happy. He'd loved her voice since she'd first spoken to him, and this undiluted display of joy was the most beautiful thing he'd ever heard, even if there were far more talented singers on this world.

My female is naked, and she is just on the other side of this door...

What color were her nipples, what color was the hair between her legs? *Was* there hair between her legs? There were so many little variations in coloring and shape he'd seen amongst human females in the pornography he'd watched that he couldn't begin to guess at Avery's appearance. Her body was a mystery to him, a tantalizing mystery that demanded his attention, that demanded he solve it.

In his imagination, he could almost see her in the shower with hot water running down her bare, pale skin, droplets beading on her nipples, rivulets coursing down her inner thighs. If he moved just a little closer, he'd see. He'd know.

Fyran sucked in a ragged breath, his abdominal muscles going taut as the pressure in his cock became agonizing. He barely suppressed a growl. His fingers had curled against the doorframe, the tips of his claws having sunken into the wood, and he could not get them to ease.

All he had to do was push the door open wider, and he could glimpse his female in her most natural, most beautiful state, and he could solve the mystery of what lay beneath her clothing, and he could...could what?

Rut her?

That was where it would lead. If he entered that bathroom, if he saw his female unclothed, he would take her. There'd be no holding himself back. Instinct roared within him to stake a claim on what was his, to mark his mate. And all the while, he'd know that it was wrong. He'd done so many bad things in his life, had crossed so many lines, but stealing even a glimpse of his female while she was at her most vulnerable was too much. Even if he managed to somehow restrain himself in the process, to curtail his cravings, it would be a step too far.

Karak'duun, he wanted her so badly. Craved her. He longed to take her in a hundred different ways, to learn all the sounds she'd make as she was overtaken by pleasure, to hear her crying out his name—his *real* name—in passion, in desperation.

She doesn't know my real name.

Lips peeling back to bare his fangs, he shoved away from the door and spun around. He needed to leave. He knew she was safe now, and it wouldn't any good if he lingered. The only way he'd find calm was by getting away from her, even if it meant having to fill his fucking bathtub with ice water and submerging himself until his erection gave up.

Beau meowed, though *meow* was a generous term—the sound was more of a chirruping.

Fyran turned his head toward the cat to find Beau sitting atop the coffee table, tail lazily flopping from side to side. Beau's ears twitched, and his slitted pupils expanded as he searched—presumably for Fyran.

No distractions. Just. Leave.

But as he swung his gaze aside, meaning to focus on the door to the hallway, Fyran spotted something else on the coffee table. An open spiral notebook resting atop the closed laptop computer, the visible pages filled with writing in blue ink.

He let out a short, harsh breath, and—despite his better judgment—walked to the table to pick up the notebook.

Avery's handwriting was small and scrawling. Even Fyran, who'd only learned to write in English just before arriving on Earth, had to admit it was sloppy, but it wasn't quite that simple. As he scanned the open pages, he understood exactly why her writing looked that way.

Passion.

It was the same passion he'd seen in her when she'd talked about writing at the café, the same passion that had come through in the kisses they'd shared tonight. He guessed she wrote so small to fit as much on the page as she could, and that her letters were formed so haphazardly because it was the only way to keep up with her thoughts.

Most of what was on the pages seemed to be notes about Trevor and Emma, names he recalled from the story he'd seen on her computer the first time he'd come here. This was something about the characters' backgrounds needing to influence the way they fell in love with each other, to affect the way they saw one another.

Those notes ceased, cut off by a hand drawn line that had yesterday's date written on it, and something different followed.

Having trouble focusing today, she'd written, *so...going to try a writing exercise. Ready to get some work in, self?*

Despite the uncomfortable ache permeating Fyran's groin, despite the tension rippling through his body, despite the urges coursing just under the surface of his mind, Fyran smiled at that. He continued reading.

1ST PERSON POV, Attempt 1

What should I have thought about Trevor Collins when I first laid eyes upon him? That he was dangerous? No good? That he came from a world not compatible with my own? Everything about him told me to run. The way he walked, the way he talked, the expression on his face...it all should've said 'stay away', but all it did was draw me in, especially when our gazes met and I saw that fire in his eyes.

Now he stands before me in all his glory, his sculpted muscles enough to put the finest Greek statue to shame, and that inner fire is burning brighter and hotter than ever. My heart races. The expression on his face steals my breath. And I know, without a doubt, that this man is dangerous. I know he commands not just respect, but fear. I know he is powerful in so many ways.

But I'm not afraid of him. I know he'd never hurt me, even if he looks at me like he wants to devour me. And there's nothing I want more than this big, intimidating, dangerous man who's standing before me like a king about to conquer a new land.

He closes the distance between us, enveloping me in his scent, in his heat, and plunges his fingers into my hair. Gathering the strands in his fist, he tips my head back so I'm staring directly into his eyes as his other hand hooks around my back and pulls me close.

"I'm going to make you mine, ~~Avery~~ Emma," he says, his deep voice resonating into me, making me shiver.

He's not asking my permission, but he doesn't need to. I'm already his, heart and soul, and he knows it. I've been ~~Hunter's~~ Trevor's since the moment I saw him.

Ugh!

Why can't I stop thinking about him?

FYRAN GRINNED, and the fires roaring inside him were slightly more bearable for a short while. Knowing that he wasn't the only one obsessed was heartening in a strange way.

The bottom of the page was filled with his name—or rather, his alias. She'd written *Hunter* in various styles and sizes, her handwriting wildly different for each, though it was all neater than her usual penmanship. Some of the lettering even had little adornments and flourishes.

But there at the very bottom, separated from the rest by today's date, was something else.

Hunter's lips are fire and ice, velvet and steel, and when he kisses me, I am undone.

His expression sobered as he brushed the tip of his finger over those words, feeling the tiny grooves her pen had left in the paper. However overwhelming his lust had become, there was something stronger at its core, something deeper. It was that emotion he couldn't rightly identify or describe—or at least that was what he'd been telling himself.

He had a sneaking suspicion it was...love.

The bathroom door swung open, and there was a click of a switch.

FOURTEEN

Fyran's heart stuttered, and panic seized his chest. He scrambled to return the notebook to its place, but his hands decided to forgo their usual dexterity and control, and the book fell to the floor instead. He snapped his head aside to look over his shoulder.

Avery had emerged from the bathroom, dressed in a light blue, long sleeved shirt and a pair of matching shorts that showed off her lithe legs. She was drying her long hair with a towel when the notebook hit the floor. She started and turned her eyes toward Hunter—looking right at him. Then she chuckled, changing her course to walk toward the coffee table. Hunter hurried out of her way, stepping as lightly on the hardwood floor as possible.

Boots are not the best footwear for sneaking around a small apartment.

"It's that bad, huh, Beau?" she asked, smiling at the cat as she bent to retrieve the notebook. Her scent, mixed with that of her soap, struck Fyran fully.

The feline blinked at her, meowed, and turned its head toward Fyran, its ear twitching. Though the cat didn't look directly at Fyran, the message was clear—Beau did not appreciate taking the blame for what Fyran had done.

Slowly, Fyran turned to face Avery. He was glad she'd put on clothes, but her top was form fitting enough that he could see hints of her nipples through the fabric, and her legs... *Svesh*, he wanted to run his palms along them from her ankle up to her ass, wanted to wrap them around his hips, wanted to dig his fingers into her ass cheeks as he rutted her.

Avery stared down at the notebook, tilted her head, and ran her fingertip over the writing at the bottom of the page. A particularly soft smile spread upon her lips. Then she placed the notebook back on the coffee table.

Fyran gritted his teeth and clenched his fists, pressing his claws into his palms. One big step forward was all it would take to have another taste of her. To feel those lips against his again.

She looked at Beau, who continued to stare in Fyran's direction. Fyran's brows furrowed, and his smile fell. As though it wasn't bad enough that he'd been so distracted he hadn't heard her exit the shower, now he risked being exposed by this small, domesticated animal.

Beau flicked his tail and made a twittering sound.

Avery glanced between the cat and the space Fyran occupied and laughed as she pet the feline along its head and scratched behind its ears. "What are you looking at? There's nothing there, you silly kitty."

How would she react were Fyran to reveal himself? How would she react knowing that he'd been so desperate for another look at her that he'd come here in secret?

His tail coiled around his leg, squeezing tight. Only the pain caused by its constriction kept him from succumbing to that sudden, stupid urge to lower the cloaking field, to tell his female everything here and now, to reveal himself to her.

Twittering replaced by enthusiastic purring, the feline stood and arched its back as Avery ran her hand from its head to its tail. Beau leaned against her, rubbing his side against her leg, only to stumble when she walked to her bedroom. The cat hopped down to follow her. Avery stopped within the doorway and tossed her towel into the basket standing on the other side.

Reaching down, Avery scooped Beau up into her arms, cradled the feline against her chest, and scratched under his chin. "Ready for bed?"

Beau's eyelids drooped, and he purred louder.

A chirping ring sounded from Avery's phone, which was next to her laptop on the coffee table. The screen displayed a call from *Allison.*

Avery frowned and crossed the room to look down at her phone. She groaned, tipping her head back to stare at the ceiling. "Way to ruin a great night."

With a sigh, she set Beau down on the sofa's armrest—next to Fyran—picked up her phone, and flopped down on the cushion, drawing her heels up and pulling her knees to her chest. Fyran repositioned himself to watch from behind the couch as she accepted the call.

A woman appeared on the screen. She had wavy, golden blonde hair, full lips that were painted red, and bright blue eyes framed with thick black lashes and dark eyeliner. Though she was clearly wearing makeup, Fyran could see signs of age in the wrinkles at the corners of her eyes and mouth. He was sure he'd never seen the woman before, but there was something familiar about her features...

"Hello, my daughter!" the woman said, grinning.

Daughter?

Allison was Avery's mother. The familiarity was because of the resemblance between the two females, particularly in the shapes of their eyes, though they were different in most every other way.

There was music playing in the background, and well-dressed humans were milling about behind Allison, some of whom were seated at tables adorned with extravagant flower arrangements and laden with glasses of what must've been alcohol.

Avery frowned. "Are you drunk?"

Allison gasped. "Of course not. Is that any way to greet your mother?" She raised a tall glass filled with a golden, sparkling liquid and smiled. "I'm only on my second, the night is still young, and look! I called before eleven this time."

"Whose party are you at?"

Allison rolled her eyes and shrugged. "Some associate of your father's is having an engagement party. It's all rather boring."

"Where's Dad?"

"Somewhere. You know he likes to...*disappear*." She brought the glass to her lips and took a drink.

Avery tilted her head. "You look pretty."

Allison lowered the glass with a wide smile, her eyes shining. "Why, thank you!" She tilted the camera to show off the rest of her body. She was wearing a sparkling red gown, its skirt nearly touching the floor. The neckline dipped low, stopping at her navel. She brought the camera back to her face. "Isn't the dress lovely? I bought it just this morning."

"It's beautiful."

Fyran could almost hear the withheld sigh in Avery's voice.

Beau leaned forward, his nose tapping against Fyran's chest. The feline flinched, whiskers twitching before it rubbed its head against Fyran again. Fyran frowned. Though it wasn't acting maliciously, this cat certainly seemed intent on exposing Fyran's presence—and on getting its drool on his jacket.

Fyran stepped aside.

When Beau extended his neck for another face rub, he encountered only empty air. He promptly lost his balance and slipped off the cushion. He landed on all fours with a muted but irritated meow.

Avery turned, peered over the armrest, and chuckled. "Clumsy cat."

"Are you home?" Allison asked, her brow creasing.

Avery turned back to her phone. "Yeah. I was actually about to go to bed."

"But it's so early!"

"I have work tomorrow."

"You should be going out and having fun. Partying, dancing, having sex."

"Mom!"

Once again, Fyran found himself with his teeth bared and his jaw clenched. Avery could do any of that she wanted—so long as it was with him.

"What? You're young. Explore a little before you finally come home." Allison took another swig from her glass.

"This coming from you, who never let me have friends as a kid?"

Allison scowled. "Oh, come on, Avery. I let you have friends. You just chose the *wrong* kind of friends."

Avery closed her eyes and pinched the bridge of her nose above her glasses. "They were not the wrong kind. They liked me and didn't talk about me behind my back."

"They were low class trash. They even looked like trash with their piercings and cheap clothing."

Avery dropped her hand and opened her eyes. "Are you serious?"

"Yes! And speaking of...when are you going to remove that thing from your nose?"

Avery touched a fingertip to her silver nose piercing. "I'm not."

"Well, you're going to have to when you come visit for Christmas." Allison's eyes moved as though she were studying Avery's features. "You'll also need to get your eyebrows groomed. I'll make an appointment with my salon. At least that way we know it'll get done correctly."

"There's nothing wrong with my eyebrows, and the piercing stays."

Allison sighed, rolling her eyes. "Why must you be so unreasonable? You never appreciate my efforts to help you look your best. You even refuse to cover your freckles."

"Because there is nothing wrong with them!"

"They are unsightly."

I should have left. It had been near-overwhelming lust that had almost driven Fyran to revealing himself when he'd first arrived, but now it was anger urging him to dropping his cloaking field—not so he could sweep Avery into his arms and taste her again, but to snatch the phone from her hands and tell Allison to fuck off for insulting his female.

Avery pressed her lips into a tight line, took in a deep breath, and slowly let it out. Her body relaxed. "Mom, I had a really good night tonight, and I would rather you not spoil it, so I'm going to say goodnight."

"What—"

Avery tapped the end call icon, cutting off Allison's voice and killing the video feed. She ran her finger through her hair. "*Not going to let her ruin tonight.*"

Fyran had never heard her voice so strained, had never heard her so...upset. Though it would've been foolish to assume she was never anything but happy, Avery always seemed to endeavor to show the world a smile despite everything.

He wanted to place his hand on her shoulder, wanted to assure her through a simple touch that she was safe, that she was not alone, that all was well. That her mother's words held no weight. He wanted to run his lips over her skin, to kiss and lick those cinnamon freckles that Allison had called *unsightly* and show Avery just how desirable he found them.

Lowering her feet to the floor, Avery set her phone to silence, returned it to the coffee table, and stood. She crossed the room, turned off the overhead light—leaving the soft lights of the small Christmas tree as the only source of illumination—and disappeared into her bedroom.

Fyran needed to leave. It was a terrible idea to stay in Avery's apartment, but he couldn't risk opening the front door until he knew she wouldn't hear it. All he had to do was wait in the living room until she was asleep.

He walked to the bedroom door, which she'd left open, and peered inside. Though she had the lights off, he could see clearly.

His eyes widened, and all at once his cock was straining against the confines of his jeans. Avery was bent over, her ass toward him, as she slid off her shorts. For once, it was fortunate that he'd been caught off guard. His shock was all that kept him from going to her right then. The pale skin of her legs hinted at the subtle muscle tone of her calves and thighs as she moved, begging Fyran to run his palms over it, to learn every inch of it by feel. Her shapely little ass looked just right to fit between his hands.

Her panties were the same style as the pair he'd taken, but these were black. He longed to peel them off her. Slowly.

She straightened and stepped out of her shorts, leaving them on the floor. Fyran didn't miss the frown on her face as she turned to the bed, and nor did he miss her soft sigh as she pulled down the corner of the bedding.

His eyes dipped to the spot between her legs where only a patch of lacy black fabric stood between him and her slit.

Fyran braced an arm against the doorframe and covered his groin with his other hand, pressing down on his throbbing erection. He knew it would bring no relief, but he had to do something, *anything*.

She climbed onto her bed, lay down, and tugged the blanket over herself.

Even her body being covered didn't lessen Fyran's arousal. He'd been breathing in her scent this whole time, had briefly been close enough to her to feel her body heat, had finally glimpsed the entirety of those legs that had so intrigued him since the first time he'd seen her, and now she was laid out on her bed half-naked.

His nostrils flared as he released a shaky breath, struggling not to make any sound loud enough for her to hear. Though that voice still screamed in the back of his mind to leave, it was distant, diminished...and he was transfixed.

Avery huffed and rolled onto her side, tugging the blanket to adjust it. She nestled down onto her pillow, shifting it with her arm a few times, and swept the hair out of her face before stilling again. That stillness did not last long; soon enough, she'd rolled onto her other side to lie with one hand on the pillow beside her face.

Her legs moved under the blanket, bending and sliding,

holding each position for no more than a few seconds before shifting again.

Fyran had no idea how long she tossed and turned like that. His growing urge to go and take her in his arms, to draw her against his body and comfort her, was no reliable gauge of the passing time, but it mounted along with his arousal to steadily wear away whatever semblance of self-control he had left.

With another huff, she turned onto her back and flopped her arms to either side of her over the blanket. She lay unmoving, staring up at the ceiling. The room was silent save for the blowing fan.

The stillness was shattered when she shoved the blanket down to her waist. Fyran's fingers flexed, claws extending, as Avery brought her hands to her chest and cupped her breasts through her shirt. She kneaded and squeezed them, her fingers moving slowly, sensually. But it wasn't until she pinched her nipples that her eyelids fluttered shut and her breathing grew heavier.

Fyran's eyes widened when he realized what she was doing. He watched as her hands moved, as her features smoothed, as her frustration vanished.

One of her hands slid down her abdomen, disappearing beneath the blanket. Her breath hitched, her brows creased, and she tilted her head back. She moaned, the sound throaty and erotic.

Fyran's cock twitched in response.

My mate is touching herself. Pleasuring herself.

He'd denied himself a look at her while she'd showered. While this situation seemed similar, he couldn't pry his eyes away. His mate was pleasuring herself, and he was going to fucking watch, and every second of it would be forever emblazoned in his memory.

She kicked at the covers, tossing them off her legs until they were bunched at the foot of the bed. She pushed her shirt up, baring her breasts as she took one in hand again, teasing her dark pink nipple. Her other hand was in her panties, moving rhythmically over her sex.

Fyran drew in a shuddering breath that caught in his lungs when he recognized the new scent in the air—her arousal, her essence. Lured by that smell, by the need to be closer, to see more of her, he stepped through the doorway and into her room. The image before him was more erotic than anything he'd ever witnessed. His gaze trailed over her, from her beautiful face to her delectable breasts, from the hand between her thighs down along her lithe legs to her silver anklet, which glinted as it reflected the dim light.

His hand tightened on his cock. The denim of his pants felt abrasive against his hypersensitive shaft, especially given his vise-like grip, but there was a hint of pleasure beneath that pain.

Avery rolled her hips as her breathing became more ragged and the motions of her hand quickened.

Fyran's hands were moving now, too, trembling as he unfastened his belt and opened his jeans. His gaze remained fixated upon her hand. Was it possible to be jealous of Avery for touching herself? It wasn't rational, perhaps, but Fyran was far beyond caring about that. He longed to know how she felt, how she looked, how she *tasted* beneath that scrap of cloth.

She moaned again, and her scent thickened.

Fyran tugged his cock free. The air felt icy against the pulsing heat of his shaft. He clamped his hand around his base, barely holding in a hiss. He imagined that delicate hand of hers wrapped around his shaft, imagined it pumping up and down, and set his hand into motion, matching the rhythm of her movements.

His rough palm glided over the nodules along the top and bottom of his shaft, spreading the slick seed that had already seeped from his tip before he'd even freed himself. In his mind, it was her essence coating him, easing the pumping of her hand. The pressure within him grew and grew, threatening to reach a bursting point, radiating strengthening pulses of pleasure-pain from his core.

Avery's thighs fell wide open, and she bit her bottom lip as she continued to stroke herself. Her moans escalated, growing higher in pitch while her breath became heavier.

Fuck, he wished it was his hand between his mate's thighs, wished it was his tongue or his cock wringing those sexy sounds from her. She was beautiful, sensual, enticing, and he craved her so fucking much.

A whimper escaped Avery. She squeezed her breast, and her toes curled, digging into the bedding. As she turned her face toward him, her brow creased, and her lips parted. Fyran tightened his grasp on his cock but did not still his hand.

Her movements became suddenly erratic. Her knees snapped together, her body tensed, and she squeezed her eyes shut. "Hunter!" she cried, shuddering with her release.

Hearing her cry out his name, even if it wasn't his real name, was more than Fyran could bear. His body quaked with an explosion of pleasure that forced his own eyes shut. He felt himself come undone in that moment, just as she'd described in her notebook, and as ecstasy engulfed his mind, Avery's name escaped his lips in a ragged growl. His seed, hot and sticky, covered his hand as it spurted from him.

Her startled gasp broke through the pleasure clouding his mind. Fyran opened his eyes to find himself staring directly into Avery's—and her staring right back at him, jaw agape.

Aggann sin thar, *Fyran. You damned fuck up.*

His body tingled as he reactivated the cloaking field just before she yanked her hand out from her panties, scrambled to the side of the bed, and frantically clicked on the lamp atop her nightstand.

Another tremor pulsed through Fyran, an echo of his climax, as he backed toward the doorway with gritted teeth. He squeezed his fist tight, but even that iron grip couldn't stop his cock from twitching, couldn't stem the continued flow of his seed.

Chest heaving, eyes wide, Avery's gaze moved over where he stood. Her hair was in disarray, her cheeks were flushed, and her bottom lip was swollen. She was beautiful.

And he was a fucking fool. How the hell had he let himself

become so lost in the moment that his cloaking field had slipped? That he'd spoken her name aloud? How had he been stupid enough to come here in the first place, knowing how tenuous his self-control had become around Avery?

How could he have been willing to risk everything—his cover, his mission, his relationship with her—just for a chance of spilling his fucking seed?

He'd...spilled his seed.

In all his years, he'd never done that, had never made the conscious decision to do so—and he'd not made the decision now. His desire for her had been so powerful that he'd been unable to hold it back. Her influence on him had been irresistible.

His gaze dipped to the floor. *Spilled* was an understatement. *Svesh*, he'd dumped buckets onto her floor, and if she were to get off that bed, if she were to even look down...

Fuck, fuck, fuck!

Fyran stuffed his cock back into his pants, unable to worry about the mess he'd made of his clothes, and sank into a crouch. He reached to the side blindly.

Avery released a shaky breath and closed her eyes, burying her face in her hand. "It was just my imagination."

He had no time for relief. When his hand felt upon the uppermost item in her hamper, he paused only long enough to let the cloaking field spread over it. He withdrew the item; it was the towel she'd used after her shower, still damp, still smelling of her.

Holding his breath so as not to breathe in any more of her scent, he used the towel to wipe his seed from the floor, eyes darting back and forth to seek out every last drop of it. Once he was done, he wadded the towel, pressed it over his groin, and backed slowly out of her room again.

Avery dropped her hand and opened her eyes. She frowned as she looked down at her hands in her lap. "Damn it, why couldn't I ask him?"

Fyran froze in place, partway through the doorway. His brows furrowed.

Ask me what?

With a sigh, Avery scooted toward the edge of the bed and stood up. Fyran shifted away from the doorway in time to allow her through. Her fragrance was unavoidable as she passed him. He squeezed his eyes shut and swallowed a groan, catching his lower lip between his fangs and biting down to keep himself silent.

"I'm going crazy. God, I can even *smell* him," Avery muttered. A moment later, the bathroom door closed, and the sink came on.

Fyran darted to the front door, unlocked it, and tugged it open, closing it harder than he'd intended once he was through. He froze in the hallway, listening, but all there was to hear was the music from one of the other apartments. With the towel still firm over his pelvis, he pulled out his omnikey and locked her door.

He put little effort into being quiet as he exited the building, taking the stairs three at a time. There was no escape from his foolishness, no excuse for it—and there was no escape from the fact that he still yearned to go back up there even now. That he'd not had nearly enough.

Part of him knew his hunger for her could never be sated, that he'd never be in control around her, and that...that was terrifying.

No. Just...unacceptable.

Fyran didn't release the cloaking field until he was back in his car. Though the towel had wiped away most of his seed from his hand, there were still a few sticky spots on his flesh, and his cock... well, that was going to feel somewhat unpleasant as it dried.

He didn't bother taking it back out; that mess wasn't going to be cleaned by a towel alone. After wiping his hand off as best he could, he fastened his pants, trying to ignore the way his fingers shook.

He threw the towel aside and slammed a fist against the steering wheel, grating out a curse. This...this carelessness couldn't continue. Avery was making him crazy. He couldn't think about anything but her, couldn't get over this obsession with her, couldn't make rational decisions because she was in his head and in his heart, leaving room for nothing else.

"No more," he growled. The words were like fire in his throat, leaving a searing pain in their wake that spread down into his chest.

Whatever she was making him feel, it was too much, it was too big. His life had shaped him into a killer, a soldier, but it had never equipped him to deal with this. With...her. How could he be any good for her if he couldn't even cope with his own emotions? If he was constantly concerned that his passion and lust would overcome him, and he'd harm her because he was so much bigger and stronger and he wanted her too fucking much?

Svesh, he couldn't even control his damned seed from spilling.

Fyran started the engine, clenching the steering wheel with both hands. His cock throbbed within its confines. Despite having come harder than ever, despite having erupted with seed, he was unsatisfied. He knew the fact of the matter hadn't changed—he'd only be satisfied when he had her beneath him, pushing his shaft into her slit.

When he made her *his*.

No.

He'd ignored his sexual urges throughout his life. Surely, he could do so again. He had a purpose on Earth, had a reason, a mission, and Avery wasn't part of it. He had a duty to protect humanity from aliens like Gregor, and he'd ignored it for too long.

Continuing to see her would only leave Gregor and his cronies free to undertake whatever nefarious plot they were engaged in...and if they were aware of Fyran, he was only endangering Avery by being near her.

His throat was tight and dry as he pulled away from the curb, and the sounds and lights around him seemed oddly distant and muted. He just needed...space. He needed to stay away.

Fyran Voltanix was a hunter, an assassin. He was not fit for a mate. And he...he couldn't let himself be ensnared by anyone.

Not even Avery Watson.

FIFTEEN

Avery woke to a heavy weight coming down on her chest, followed by an aggressive, furry headbutt and a blast of the stinkiest breath in the world as Beau licked her chin. She scrunched her nose and turned her face away.

"Ugh, Beau. Rude."

Undeterred, he licked her cheek. His rough, scratchy tongue rasped over her skin.

Avery chuckled, wrapped her arm around him, and rolled onto her side, depositing Beau on the bed beside her. His eyes narrowed, and he looked at her as though *she* was the rude one for disrupting his comfort, but those eyes drifted shut as she scratched the side of his neck and under his jaw.

Beau purred. Just like that, she was forgiven.

"Good morning, Beau," she said, smiling.

And it was a good morning. Apart from the incident in the diner and her mother calling, last night had been wonderful—her date with Hunter had been wonderful. More than that, it had been...perfect.

I kissed Hunter.

Avery grinned. Well, technically he'd kissed her each time, but the fact of the matter was...they'd *kissed*.

She'd cursed herself more than once last night for not inviting him up to her apartment—for not inviting him into her bed. Those kisses had only been a taste of what they could've shared. Nothing had ever felt so good, so thrilling, so...*right*.

But she'd still held back. She'd still denied her desires, even though she craved Hunter so badly that her mind had played tricks on her last night. His scent had haunted her, had followed her into bed, had hung in the air as she'd touched herself, as she'd brought herself to orgasm. Avery had been so lost in her thoughts of him that she'd conjured his image in her room. For an instant, she'd heard him, had seen him there, his face taut with pleasure and his hand wrapped around his cock.

Except...he'd been different. His eyes had glowed red, and his features were sharper, hungrier, and his lips had been drawn back to reveal fangs. She'd even glimpsed black claws on the tips of his fingers. He'd been like a vampire summoned by her deepest, darkest fantasies, there to seduce her in the dead of night.

He can bite me anywhere he pleases.

A pulse of heat raced straight to her core.

Avery dropped her face onto her pillow and groaned. If only it'd been his hand between her legs last night, his fingers delving into her pussy, stroking her flesh, circling her clit. If only it'd been his tongue...

She had only herself to blame.

Lifting her head, Avery ran her fingers through her hair and looked at Beau. He blinked at her, likely wondering why she wasn't petting him.

"Was I just being a coward?" she asked him.

No. She wasn't being a coward. Though she couldn't explain why, she had an intuition, a gut feeling, that something wasn't right. That she wouldn't have been...what? That she wouldn't have been getting *all* of Hunter? It seemed silly when she thought of it that way, but it was the truth. Avery couldn't make that commitment to him if she wasn't sure he was giving her all of himself.

Regardless, she wasn't going to let any of that ruin her time with Hunter. They'd take that next step when the time was right. They'd only just met, everything was still new. What was the rush?

Her pussy clenched in objection.

Avery smirked and squeezed her thighs together, which of course did nothing to alleviate her aching need. She wasn't going to do anything about it, though. As good as touching herself had felt in the moment, she'd been left empty and craving afterward.

With a sigh and one last pet along Beau's back, she withdrew her arm from the cat and lay on her back, glancing at the digital clock on the nightstand. It was seven forty-eight. The alarm was set to go off in twelve minutes. Avery snorted and looked at Beau, who remained on the bed beside her.

"You couldn't have waited just a little longer before waking me up?" she asked.

Beau looked at her, slowly blinked, and yawned.

Avery grinned. "You're such a loaf."

Climbing out of bed, she found her shorts on the floor and pulled them on.

"Are you ready for breakfast?" Avery asked Beau as she stepped out of her bedroom.

He answered with an excited meow before he raced past her to disappear into the kitchen.

She moved to follow but stopped when she spotted her phone on the coffee table. She'd forgotten to plug it in last night. After that conversation with Allison, Avery hadn't wanted anything to do with her phone.

Avery picked it up. No messages. Once her phone was unlocked, she opened the photo album and smiled as she swiped through the pictures she'd taken with Hunter in the Botanic Gardens. She stopped on the selfie they'd taken together. Her heart fluttered as she stared at Hunter. He was so breathtakingly gorgeous. His dark, sensual, intense eyes drew her in, and Avery knew she was lost. Utterly, happily lost.

She swiped to the next picture, which was when she'd turned her head to kiss his cheek. The photo had been taken after his gaze had dipped toward her, capturing the heat in his gaze—right before he'd taken her lips in a passionate kiss.

Desire pooled heavily in her core at the memory of his mouth on hers, of his erection against her.

Avery worried her bottom lip as she opened her messages.

Thinking of you, she sent to Hunter, adding the red lips emoji.

She waited a moment, anticipating those blinking dots. Normally, he was up early, and he'd respond to her messages right away. But as minutes passed with no reply, Avery wondered if he was still asleep.

After hooking her phone up to the charger in the kitchen and feeding Beau, Avery grabbed clean work clothes and stepped into the bathroom to get ready.

By the time she had her boots and coat on and was about to step out the door, there was still no reply.

It's no big deal. He's either still sleeping or he's busy, Avery.

She managed to get through her walk to work without checking her phone again, but when she was placing her messenger bag in her locker, she paused. Brow furrowed, she took out her phone, chewed on her lower lip, and stared at the last text she'd sent Hunter. Still no reply. Though she told herself it was nothing, she still couldn't push aside the terrible anxiousness in the pit of her stomach.

Her thumbs moved over the letters as she typed another message. *Do I get to see you today?*

The door to the breakroom opened, and Avery slipped her phone back in her bag.

"Hey Avery," Noah said as he came to stand beside her, opening his locker. His dark, concerned eyes met hers. "Brandy told me about what happened yesterday. You doing okay?"

Avery closed her locker door and offered him a smile. "I'm fine. Hunter came to my defense and took care of the guy, and Jerry banned them from the diner. I don't think they'll be a problem."

Noah snickered. "Yeah, if Hunter dealt with them, I bet they shit their pants. Dude's scary."

Though Avery had never felt threatened around Hunter, she knew there was a violence lurking within him. She'd seen it when he'd handled the man who'd touched her ass. How far would it have gone if no one had stopped him? If *she* hadn't stopped him?

The darkness that had exuded from Hunter in those moments should've been a warning sign, a red flag to scare Avery away, but she knew he'd never turn that anger on her. It was evident in every heated glance he cast her way, in his every touch, whether possessive or gentle, in each of their passionate kisses.

"Oh, did you see the trailer for that new Infinite City RPG?" Noah asked. "They have a bunch of playable races, and they're hinting at a lot of romance options with all kinds of aliens. Saw some dudes with three eyes and horns in there for a second. I know you prefer the fantasy and paranormal stuff, but this looks *good.*"

"Huh? No, I haven't yet." She'd been so preoccupied lately that she hadn't kept up on gaming news. Usually, she waited with bated breath for word of a game with decent romance involved. There were so few.

"It looks amazing. The kind of stuff that really makes me excited to build up my portfolio and start putting it out there, you know? They always need concept artists for that stuff."

"And you're really good," Avery said, smiling. "You always come up with the coolest designs. But if that game is all next-gen graphics...I doubt my laptop will be able to handle it. I'll just have to watch some let's plays or something when the time comes."

Noah shoved his backpack into his locker. "You have time to save. We'll get a badass setup together for you one of these days." He closed the locker door and grinned at her. "So, let's get out there and make some money."

Avery chuckled and followed him into the dining area.

With it being Sunday morning, the diner was a whirlwind of activity and noise. Normally, time flew by when she was so busy, but every second seemed longer than the last. Her eyes kept drifting to the clock, and she counted down the minutes until her break.

Her thoughts kept returning to Hunter. Had he replied? Would she get to see him again? She wasn't just eager to check her phone, she was anxious to. She didn't understand her unease.

The highlight of her shift was visiting Mary and Harley when they came in for lunch around noon. Mary talked about her knitting group, about their kids and grandkids coming to visit in a couple weeks for Christmas, and about how excited she and Harley were to see them.

"How about you, my dear?" Mary asked, taking Avery's hand. "What are your plans?"

"I don't really have any plans. It's just going to be me and my cat."

"Oh, but you can't be alone on Christmas." Mary frowned. "No family to visit?"

Avery barely suppressed her cringe. "No. Things are...complicated with my family."

"I'm sorry." Mary gently squeezed Avery's hand before she released it.

"Now, I don't want to put any pressure on you, Avery," Harley said, "but we'd love to have you over for Christmas dinner."

Mary gasped. "That's a lovely idea!"

Avery's eyes widened. "Oh, my gosh. I couldn't intrude on you and your family."

"Nonsense! We'd love to have you." Harley reached into his pocket and pulled out pen, jotting something down on a napkin.

"Think about it, dear," Mary said with a smile. "You've always been so good to us. We hate the thought of you being alone for Christmas."

Avery's chest warmed at their gracious offer. "Thank you so much."

"Here." Harley held the napkin out to her. "If you change your mind, give us a call."

She took the napkin from him. He'd written *Harley Brennan* with a phone number below the name.

"Now don't be getting any ideas," Harley said, puffing out his chest and grinning at his wife. "I'm a taken man."

Avery laughed, her heart feeling lighter. "I wouldn't dream of it."

She left them to get their drinks and put in their orders. It wasn't until they'd paid their bill and left that she finally took her break.

She rushed to the breakroom, nearly plowing into Jerry on her way, and tugged opened her locker. She reached into her bag and withdrew her phone. Her heart leapt when she noticed a message waiting for her—only for it to plummet when she realized the message was from Eliza. It was a picture of Eliza's Yorkshire Terrier, Molly, with bows on her ears and her claws painted pink. The picture was captioned *Grooming Day!*

Tears stung Avery's eyes. She...she was just overacting, right? She couldn't expect Hunter to always respond promptly, especially when they'd only started dating last Monday, not even a full week ago.

So why did she feel this sense of dread? Had she...done something wrong? Was he annoyed that she hadn't invited him up to her apartment last night? Was...was sex all he'd wanted from her all along?

No, she couldn't believe that. Not with the connection she'd felt between them. He would have pressed her harder last night if that was what he was after.

Give him time, Avery. Don't jump to conclusions.

Maybe something had happened? Maybe...maybe he was on one of those odd jobs he'd mentioned taking from time to time? But if that were the case, wouldn't he have told her like he had before?

Is everything okay? she typed out and pressed send.

She wasn't surprised when there was no response. Putting her phone away, Avery sat at the table and nibbled on a granola bar that tasted like sawdust on her tongue. She washed it down with a bottle of water and returned to the dining floor.

When her shift was over, there was still no text from Hunter. There wasn't one from him later that night, or the next morning, either. Worse, she'd started her period the night after their date, leaving her an emotional wreck over the following days.

She decided to call him, needing to assure herself that he was okay, needing to hear his voice, to...to hear it from him if what was going on between them was over, but it rang until it went to an automated voicemail.

On the fourth night, Avery sat on the edge of her sofa, knees bouncing restlessly, and eyes blurred with tears as she stared at the unanswered text messages on her phone. Her heart ached; it felt as though it had cracked wide open. She covered her nose and mouth as she sniffled.

She had been so sure that Hunter was it. That he was the one...her passionate forever. Had she subconsciously known that she'd been wrong? Was that why she hadn't pushed things further that night?

She sent him her final message.

Did I say or do something wrong?

When there'd still been no reply by the next morning, Avery came to her own conclusion.

Hunter didn't want her.

SIXTEEN

ADJUSTING his grip on his knife, Fyran pulled the metal door open wider and slipped into the warehouse. He found himself at the end of a long corridor, dark but for the residual light spilling in through an open doorway at the far end. All the doors along the corridor were closed; he counted five, not including the open one. The floor was covered in dirt and dust except for a path straight down the middle, along the edges of which were clear footprints moving in both directions.

It was confirmation that Gregor's people used this rear door regularly.

Holding his breath, Fyran eased the entry door closed behind him. Despite his caution, its soft clang and the click of its latch echoed along the corridor, reverberating off the concrete floors and cinderblock walls.

Fyran sidestepped into the corner beside the doorway, pressing himself into the deepest shadows out of habit even though his cloaking field was active. He listened as the echo faded and silence gripped the place—a silence so complete it seemed unreal. He hadn't experienced such total, consuming silence since he'd come to Earth fourteen months ago.

He heard no signs of movement elsewhere, no footsteps to

mark the approach of any of Gregor's associates, no voices calling out in question or alarm. Just silence. That only made sense; he'd identified seven people in Gregor's crew over the last week, including Gregor and Varketh, and he'd seen them all leave at various points today. The place should've been deserted.

Still, he let the seconds pass. Five. Ten. Thirty. Fyran counted each until a full minute had gone by before pushing himself out of the corner and proceeding along the corridor.

He'd found himself obsessively marking the passage of time as of late. Perhaps it was a way to make up for his carelessness over the last few weeks. Timing, after all, was everything when it came to the completion of his missions.

Fyran had waited in the snowy lot across the street from this warehouse for eight hours and twenty-two minutes, plenty long enough for the cold to sink into his fingers and toes. Twenty minutes ago, Gregor and two of his associates—the only ilventyrs who'd been left in the warehouse—had emerged from the building, climbed into a black car, and driven off.

And it had been seven days, zero hours, and fourteen minutes since he'd last spoken to Avery.

His step faltered, and a harsh breath escaped him. The pain in his chest hadn't subsided over those seven days. If anything, it had only intensified. He wasn't sure how it was possible to feel utterly hollow and as though he were filled with an immense molten weight simultaneously, but he certainly felt that way.

Fucking focus, Fyran, or you're going to get yourself killed.

He drew in a steadying breath and continued forward. He'd check behind each of the closed doors so long as circumstances allowed, but it was best to take the path of least resistance until he confirmed he was alone.

Karak'duun, even that word—alone—hurt. He'd thought he knew what it felt like, that he'd learned to cope with it long ago, that he preferred being by himself, but this week had proven that he hadn't known a damn thing about loneliness.

Fyran positioned himself against the wall beside the open doorway and peered through. He found himself looking into a large loading dock with three big rollup doors, each bay set up so the trailer of a truck would be level with the floor. It was illuminated by several hanging light fixtures with yellowish bulbs that cast an unnatural glow.

His mind shifted back to that night at the Denver Botanic Garden a week ago, where the manmade lights had created an atmosphere of harmony and beauty, where he and Avery—

Damn it, no. Not now.

He would not reminisce about the pretty light display while he was infiltrating a criminal base of operations, and he sure as hell wasn't going to let his mind drift back to the kisses he and Avery had shared, or what he'd seen and done in her apartment...

Gritting his teeth, he turned his attention back to his surroundings.

There were no vehicles parked inside the loading bay, and the room was empty apart from several wooden pallets stacked against the far wall, bits of trash and debris scattered across the floor, and a large plastic crate that looked too new to fit in this dilapidated environment. Inside and out, this warehouse looked as though it had been abandoned for some time. Only the crate, the functioning lights, and the footprints suggested otherwise.

Fyran crept over to the crate. It stood as high as his waist and was at least four feet wide, constructed of heavy-duty plastic. Its design and coloration suggested a military origin. But there were panels on the lid and two of the sides that made him question that inference—the panels had tiny holes, so fine that they were virtually invisible from even a few paces away. There was an electronic lock on the lid, the sort that required a code to operate, but it didn't appear to be engaged.

After another quick check for company, Fyran placed his hands on the lid and lifted it.

The interior of the crate was padded with dark fabric over some sort of foam that gave way under his touch much like a mattress would have. The holes on the exterior panels ran clear through to the inside.

They were air holes.

This crate was purposed to hold a living creature, and that it was large enough to fit an adult human did not put Fyran at ease.

He lowered the lid, grateful that it closed silently, and turned his head toward the blue-painted metal door opposite the rollup doors. There was another rollup door beside it, sized for a forklift or a similar piece of equipment, but that was closed and locked to the floor with heavy padlocks.

A faded sign reading *EMPLOYEES ONLY* hung on the blue door's face. The trails left in the dirt and dust on the floor led directly to that door, and there was an arc of shallow grooves on the concrete left by the door scraping as it opened and closed repeatedly over untold years.

The door was locked. For several seconds, Fyran listened, keeping his breathing slow and soft, but he couldn't hear anything from the other side.

When he removed his omnikey from his pocket, his mind again leapt back to Avery. He inserted the end of the device into the keyhole and activated it, trying to push away his thoughts of the female, of what he'd seen, smelled, and heard in her home.

Of what *he'd* done.

Can't think about her anymore. Can't speak to her, can't see her.

But *can't* hadn't stopped him thus far, had it? Yes, by some exceptional feat of willpower he'd not spoken to her since he'd dropped her off at her apartment a week ago, but he hadn't been able to keep away.

He'd gone to find her several times during the week. He'd told himself to leave as he'd watched her through the diner's windows; he'd told himself return to his dwelling as he'd followed her home, keeping an eye out for any threats to her; he'd told himself it wasn't his problem when a very eager, very inebriated Ian had trapped her in a rambling conversation as she'd tried to get into the building.

He'd also told himself it was necessary when he'd confronted Ian hours later and made it clear to the human that Avery was off limits—and that anything more than a friendly *hello* would be answered with no small degree of unpleasantness.

Fyran had watched her all week. He'd seen her strained smiles, had seen the light in her eyes fade, had seen the way she frowned when she checked her phone for messages that had not—and would not—come.

Despite everything he'd done in his life, Fyran had never hated himself. He'd always been able to justify his actions and hold back the crushing guilt, had always been able to detach himself from the situations just enough to keep from getting swept up in emotion. But cutting off his contact with Avery Watson, seeing those texts she'd sent him for days afterward, *hearing* them in her voice as he read them over and over and over again…

He'd never hated anyone as much as he did himself right now.

Did I say or do something wrong?

His chest seized, and leaden heat sank into his belly, twisting his insides into knots. That had been her final message, three days ago. She'd wondered what *she* had done wrong. His resolve had very nearly crumbled after receiving that message, and it remained tenuous even now.

Of all the wrongs he'd done, hurting her seemed the most heinous, the most unforgivable.

It's to keep her safe.

The omnikey finally found its shape. Fyran swallowed his errant thoughts and unlocked the door, opening it slowly and using it to shield his body as he peered through the opening.

The next room was better lit than the bay, and might've been just as large, but it was far more densely packed—and clearly saw a lot more use. Fyran removed the omnikey, returned it to his pocket, and entered the room slowly.

Old shelves—metal frames with plywood boards—stood along the edges of the room, filled with boxes, bins, and crates of various shapes and sizes. Four more plastic crates identical to the one in the loading bay were against the far wall in a neat line, and there were crates of similar design but smaller dimensions beside them. The table, chairs, couches, and desk arranged amidst all the shelving and crates confirmed what Fyran had observed thus far—Gregor and his cronies spent a lot of time here.

Fyran moved to the smaller crates against the wall. They lacked the ventilation holes of their larger counterparts and seemed more worn. Fyran opened one.

The foam padding inside that crate served on obvious purpose—to keep the firearms laid atop it in place.

Fuck.

Fyran knew those blaster pistols; he had a similar one stashed in his residence back in Westminster. They were faloran blasters—a couple generations behind his weapon, but unmistakable. More of the stolen weapons were in some of the other crates, along with firearms from at least half a dozen civilizations from across the universe. Fyran expanded his search, uncovering stocks of off-world drugs in several of the bins on the shelves and various pieces of alien technology.

He'd seen dozens of rooms like this on many, many planets, had spent several years of his life working from a room like it, and he had no question of what Gregor and his associates were involved in save for one—what did they transport in the crates with airholes?

Something within Fyran stopped him from further speculation; deep down, he knew. And he already had enough information to justify moving against Gregor regardless, damn the *ultricar's* orders. The ilventyrs who operated this warehouse were criminals, they were threats to this planet and all the innocent people inhabiting it. And Fyran could not ignore that.

He could not let it stand.

He couldn't let his feelings for Avery get in the way of this work, especially not when she was one of those innocent people. When her life was one of the billions put at risk by the presence of the ilventyrs and their like on this planet.

It was too easy to lose himself while he was with her, too easy to get swept away in his thoughts of her, in his yearning. She would understand if he explained it to her. She would understand why he needed to stay away.

So why haven't you told her?

You fucking know why you can't tell her.

Fyran clenched his jaw, but he forced his hands to remain open, riding out the fresh wave of tension that gripped his body from head to toe. The last thing he needed to do was draw blood from his palms and leave it for the ilventyrs to detect. They were already suspicious of him, and he'd spotted Varketh a few more times at the mall and around the diner during the week. They couldn't know Fyran had discovered their base of operations. They couldn't know what was going to come for them. As far as Fyran knew, the ilventyrs still thought him nothing more than a human, a nuisance.

Fyran continued his search, moving his focus to the desk—and the laptop computer resting upon it.

He opened the laptop's lid with the tip of a claw and turned the computer on. The building was so quiet that the sound of the computer's hard drive spinning up was thunderous, and his eyes repeatedly darted back to the blue door as though that sound alone would be enough to call back Gregor and his goons.

After an eternity of whirring and clicking, the laptop reached a password screen. Fyran didn't hesitate to link his neural transceiver with the device. Interfacing with human technology that had potentially been modified by aliens undoubtedly posed unique risks, but Fyran had neither the time nor the means to take a subtler approach. It was possible he'd have all night to search and catalog the items in this warehouse—but it was just as likely he'd only have seconds to finish what he was doing.

The neural transceiver made short work of the password. Fyran maintained the link, using the transceiver to sift through the computer's files and programs, seeking patterns, seeking information. Much of the data was encrypted well enough to slow the highly advanced piece of tech in his head.

Fyran's jaw ticked. He felt time melting away, felt it flowing around him, and each second only strengthened his wild instinct to fight back against the passage of time. To reclaim all those lost moments.

The distance he'd placed between himself and Avery...it only heightened his craving for her. He awoke each morning with Avery in his thoughts, was kept awake through the nights by his yearning, and had caught himself so many times with his phone in hand, staring at her contact information with his finger hovering over the call button. The memory of her taste, of her scent, of the feel of her arms around him and her lips against his, had haunted him.

But it went well beyond his sexual hungers; he missed hearing her voice, her laugh. Missed seeing her smile. Missed her talking about her writing, or about her favorite books and games, missed those little glimpses she'd given him of her innermost feelings, her past, her family.

Fyran missed having her look at him like he could be her everything.

He'd not slept more than a few hours any night this week.

Seven days, zero hours, twenty-two minutes. All that time he could've spent *with* Avery rather than staring at her from afar. All that time he could've been experiencing new things with her, amazing things, instead of wallowing in misery. And this was only the start. He had a lifetime ahead of him without her.

He had a lifetime ahead of him without...happiness.

His lips peeled back to bare his fangs as a harsh breath escaped him, forced out by a painful pang in his chest.

I don't deserve happiness. Don't deserve her.

Fyran inhaled deeply. He just needed to finish this business and get out of here. Then he'd be occupied with the real work, the work he'd always excelled at—eliminating dangerous individuals.

He'd yearned for action since he'd come to Earth and had realized the reality of his assignment. Since he'd come to understand that he was on this planet to be removed from active duty, to become a breeder. All he'd wanted was reason to put his skills to use—to shed blood for the greater good. It was the only way he knew how to contribute.

Yet now the chance to utilize his talents felt...empty. He'd spent so many months trying to fill in the gap left in his life by this assignment, obsessing over it, over his *purpose*, and now that he was finally on the cusp of obtaining what he'd wanted...

I only want her.

The neural transceiver's automated search pulled something up on the laptop's screen—some sort of untraceable communication program. Fyran shook himself, casting aside his thoughts as best he could even though he knew they would cling to him forever.

His eyebrows fell as he ran his gaze over the screen. Though most everything else on the computer was in English, the text in this program was Ilventyrian, complete with the alien alphabet. Gregor and his associates had made some modifications to the human tech, it seemed. But it was the contents of the text that made Fyran's stomach churn.

Those big crates were for trafficking humans.

The encrypted messages ran back across months and months. As Fyran dug deeper, the cities mentioned in the messages shifted from Denver to Tampa, Seattle, Kansas City, places scattered all over the country. How long had Gregor and his crew been running alien weaponry, drugs, and living humans?

There's something they want at the diner...

Fyran's throat was suddenly dry. His claws almost gouged the touchpad as he hurriedly went to the most recent communications, which had been logged today.

Buyer is locked in. Advance payment to be collected in person, 21:45 at designated location. Remainder upon delivery, said the first incoming message.

The reply had been sent only moments later. *I will be there for the advance. Varketh will be happy to make a move.*

The person on the other end had asked, *Has the complication been resolved?*

The complication hasn't turned up all week, the outgoing response read. *Timing couldn't be better. I'll have Varketh ready.*

Another message had been sent from this computer about an hour after that one. *Target is occupied until 22:00. Will harvest tonight. Arrange for delivery within the next two days. And start looking for new locations, we're due to move on.*

Twenty-two hundred—ten o'clock. It couldn't be a coincidence that was when Jerry's Diner closed every night. It just so happened to be a few minutes before ten o'clock right now. And this *complication* they'd mentioned having been absent for a week...

No. No, no, no, they couldn't be referring to Avery in those communications, even if they were almost certainly talking about someone from the diner. He'd seen her go in to work this morning, fourteen hours ago, had made sure of it before dedicating the rest of his day to surveilling the ilventyrs.

Pulse pounding in his ears, he plunged deeper into the message chain, sifting back through the weeks until he reached the first message, which had a photo embedded in it.

Buyer lined up. Big sale, huge payout. Looking at this specifically.

The photo was of Avery stepping out of the diner with her coat on over her uniform.

Everything within Fyran froze, and icy, merciless claws clamped around his heart, squeezing it. Their target was Avery. They were after Avery. *His* Avery.

He'd been so stupid. So, so stupid, so blind. For all his concern about endangering her with his presence, he'd completely overlooked the truth of the matter—Varketh had been watching *Avery*, not Fyran. They saw him only as a complication, undoubtedly because his presence had meant Avery wasn't as alone and isolated as they preferred. Things like this were so much easier when the victim didn't have anyone to immediately report them missing.

A torrent of emotions tore through Fyran over the course of a few seconds; terror, despair, self-loathing, all of them cold and crushing, but they were followed by a firestorm of rage that swelled up from his core.

Avery was *his*. He couldn't have tolerated knowing these ilventyrs were kidnapping any humans, but the matter was personal now. They were after Fyran's human. After Fyran's *mate*.

And it was already ten o'clock.

"*Fuck*," Fyran growled. He forced the computer to shut down and slammed the lid closed, racing toward the exit without a backward glance to check if he'd left anything amiss. None of that mattered now.

His phone was already in his hand when he emerged from the building, and he was calling Avery before he was even two steps away from the door. The line rang, over and over, while he darted across the lot. When he peeled back the disconnected portion of chain link fence in the back corner to exit the property, the phone went to voicemail.

"Avery, where are you? Why—*karak'duun!*" He ended the call. What the fuck good would it do to ask her questions in her voicemail?

Hands shaking, he pressed call again as he sprinted toward his car. All he received was that ring tone, over and over, and the tauntingly cheerful snippet of her voice in the greeting of her voicemail.

The moment the warehouse was out of sight, he deactivated his cloaking field and switched to text messages. He didn't allow himself to look at that last message she'd sent; the guilt would be too much for him, especially now. His trembling fingers hurriedly typed messages that were readable only due to autocorrect doing its damned job properly for once.

Where are you?

If you're at home block the door and do not answer it

If you're at the diner stay there

I'm coming to you

Where are you

Please where are you?

Fyran tugged open the car door as soon as he reached it and dropped in, starting the engine and throwing the car into drive before he even had the door shut. The phone was already at his ear again, giving him that maddening ring tone, each repetition of it making his heart beat a little faster, a little harder.

If Avery had started work early this morning, she should've gone home hours ago. But she sometimes worked extra shifts for the money. Had she done so today? It was ten o'clock now; if she'd worked a double shift, she'd just be getting off.

Her voicemail picked up again. "You've reached Avery. I'm either working or have my nose in a book, so leave a message and I'll get to you after the next chapter!"

"*Karak'duun*, there's not going to be a next chapter if you don't answer the phone!" Fyran growled, ending the call to start another.

His other hand was clamped over the steering wheel, guiding the car along the dark streets of Denver with desperate precision, and his foot was heavy on the accelerator. It was a fifteen-minute drive from Gregor's warehouse to Avery's building under normal circumstances. The Hellcat screeched to a halt in front of Avery's apartment at nine minutes after ten o'clock.

Fyran was still trying to call her as he burst through the front door and raced upstairs. He was still trying to call her as he knocked on her door, and the line was still ringing when he used his omnikey to open the door.

The call went to voicemail yet again as he stepped into her apartment, and he immediately forgot about it.

"Avery?" Breath ragged and eyes wide, he swept his gaze around the place.

The lights were off, even the little Christmas tree, and the only movement came from the couch, where Beau, body curled up tight, lifted his head to regard Fyran with glowing feline eyes.

Fyran checked the interior side of the door, the windows, the bedroom and bathroom and kitchen, but there were no signs of forced entry, no signs of a struggle, no signs of Avery. That didn't necessarily mean anything; he'd entered her apartment easily enough, and he had to assume the ilventyrs were capable of the same.

Avery was out there somewhere, and she wasn't answering her

phone. If she left the diner at ten, it'd be another ten minutes before she made it home...but he didn't have ten minutes to waste in wait. She was at her most vulnerable during her walk home.

"*Zorak akai*," he snarled, rushing back to the hallway, "please don't let me be too late."

He'd have to drive along her normal walking routes, and fuck the one-way streets that'd attempt to divert him. Human authorities were the least of his worries right now. Only one thing mattered—only one thing had ever mattered, if only he'd been smart enough to see.

They're trying to take Avery. My female. My lifemate.

He ended the ongoing call and redialed for what felt like the hundredth time as he ran for the stairs. Even though she'd yet to answer any of his calls or texts, he couldn't help the thought that pulsed through his mind with each thunderous thump of his heart.

Please answer. For all that is precious in the universe, vaerina, please answer.

SEVENTEEN

BRANDY LEANED back against the locker, opened a round compact mirror, and held it up to her face. "You should come dancing with me tonight."

Removing her coat from her locker, Avery drew it on and watched as Brandy applied a coat of bright red lipstick to her lips. "I don't really feel like dancing tonight."

"That's the point!" Brandy rubbed her lips together and made a popping sound. "You've been really mopey this past week, and I know why."

Avery sighed. It wasn't like she'd told anyone about Hunter ghosting her, but Brandy had figured it out after a few days of Hunter not showing up at the diner. Well, that and Avery's disposition having been...off. Every one of Avery's smiles over the last several days had been forced, and more than once, she'd found herself on the verge of breaking down and crying.

And Avery would rather forget the day Brandy had caught her actually crying. Avery had abruptly excused herself from the dining area after a customer had ordered a slice of cherry pie, and she'd barely made it into the back before the flood of tears had come.

Stupid period.

She was really glad that was over.

Of course, there'd also been plenty of anger, and she'd used her writing as an outlet for it, but what she'd felt more than anything was hurt and confusion.

It felt like her heart was broken.

It was sometimes hard to breathe when she thought about Hunter and their moments together, and her feelings hadn't lessened over time.

Avery zipped up her coat and grabbed her bag from her locker, pulling the strap on over her head until it rested comfortably on her shoulder. It was bulkier than usual with her uniform stuffed inside, but it was worth it to have some warmer clothing on for the walk home. "Tonight's not a good night, Brandy."

She heard the soft buzz of her phone vibrating inside her bag, but she ignored it. It was probably her mother another one of her random late-night calls—which Avery had been ignoring all week —and Avery was *really* not in the mood.

Brandy closed the lipstick, snapped the compact closed, and dropped them both into her Coach purse. "Oh, come on, Av!" She straightened as Avery closed her locker door. "We could have a few shots, loosen up, pick up a couple hot guys, and you can shake that gorgeous little ass on the dance floor."

The last thing Avery wanted was another man flirting with her, hoping to get into her pants for a night of meaningless sex that wasn't going to happen.

Maybe you should. It isn't like being a virgin is anything special. Why hold out? Get drunk, find some hot guy, get it over with, and enjoy yourself.

But the thought of another man touching her made her skin crawl and her stomach revolt. Avery didn't want some random man inside her, she didn't want his hands on her body, or his mouth on hers.

She wanted Hunter.

No, I don't. He ghosted me. He made me fall for him and then he stomped all over on my heart.

Avery could just imagine every condescending and cruel thing her mother would've said about this. That Avery should have known a man like Hunter would never settle with a woman like her, that she had been reaching too high, that she was so naïve, so childish to believe that Hunter had wanted her for more than a fuck.

She removed her glasses, closed her eyes, and rubbed her them, trying to soothe the dull throb resonating behind them. "I'm really sorry, Brandy, but I just worked a double shift, I'm exhausted, and I'm really, really not up for going out." Avery opened her eyes and put her glasses back on.

Brandy's smile softened. "Okay. I get it, I do, and I know you'd rather not talk about it. What about a movie?"

"Can I raincheck you on that? I just...would *really* like to go home and get some sleep."

"Oh, okay. Go mope by yourself." Brandy reached out and gave Avery a playful nudge. "But if you want to talk, you got my number."

"I do. And thank you, Brandy."

"Yeah, yeah. Just don't tell Noah how soft I am."

Avery chuckled and walked toward the door. Her phone continued its insistent vibrating. She opened the door and paused, looking back at her friend. "So, you really think I have a gorgeous ass?"

Brandy laughed. "Girl, Hunter missed out on the chance of a lifetime when he chose not to pound that." She winked, turned, and smacked her own curvy backside. "It's not as hot as mine, though."

Avery grinned and left the diner in better spirits than she'd been in all week, though that humor faded on her walk home as her exhaustion caught up to her. Though she liked working doubles because it meant extra money, this week had been rough. She would've preferred to stay home, but Noah had really needed the day off, and Avery hadn't had anything else to do, so she'd offered to pick up his shift. It beat sitting at home and wallowing in her own self-pity.

You only knew Hunter for a week, and then he ditched you. This is pathetic.

So why did it hurt so damned much?

Because she'd *known.* She'd known deep down that he was the one. She'd never thought love at first sight really existed, but she swore she'd experienced it. And if it hadn't been real...then why was it so hard to move on? Why couldn't she just delete his phone number, the text messages, the pictures, and carry on as though she'd never met him?

But she knew that erasing all the evidence of him having been in her life wouldn't accomplish anything. Even in his absence, she'd felt that pull toward Hunter, she'd had a sense that he was near, that he was often so close but somehow out of sight. And so many times, she'd caught a hint of his scent on the air only to turn around and find...nothing.

Avery had never realized that being ghosted by Hunter would mean he'd become her personal phantom, haunting her all day, every day, and through every night.

Or maybe you're just going crazy.

Avery crossed her arms over her chest and sniffled as tears blurred her vision. The winter wind blew against her face, making her next inhalation sting and her eyes burn. She tilted her head down and blinked, watching the ground as she walked.

Still, her dang phone continued vibrating.

"Jeez, Allison, get the hint," she muttered.

A gust of wind slammed into her, sending a shudder through her body. It carried a few flakes of snow, one of which landed on her cheek like a tiny, icy kiss. As much as she loved walking everywhere, she was going to have to start driving soon, or one of these days someone was going to find her frozen in a snowdrift on the side of the street.

Tomorrow. I'll start using the car tomorrow.

The insistent vibrating in her bag persisted even as Avery crossed into the residential neighborhood where her apartment building was located—and where everything was darker.

She frowned. What if it was an emergency? Why else would

her mom keep calling like this? As much as she hated being around her family, as crummy as her parents made her feel, she didn't want anything to happen to them.

Stopping, she reached into her bag and pulled out her phone. As the screen flashed on, Avery's breath caught at the number of missed texts and calls—dozens of them. And they were all from one person.

"Hunter..." she rasped.

Don't answer.

She clenched her fingers around the phone and pressed her lips together. Her throat grew tight. Anger and pain collided in her chest, swirling into a maelstrom.

What if he has a reason? What if he's calling to explain himself? What if—

Damn it, Avery, don't make excuses for him!

She wanted to ignore him, to show him she could be as uncaring as he'd been with her. But she...couldn't.

When the next call came, she pressed accept and brought the phone to her ear. "What do you want, Hunter? You have—"

"Avery? *Parax a'tar.*" Hunter's voice, thick with relief, was raised over the roar of an engine, but it quickly hardened. "Where are you?"

Avery's brow creased. "Where I am is no longer any of your business."

"Are you outside?"

"Yes, I am."

"You need to get back into the diner, now. Tell Jerry or Noah to stay with you until I get there."

She frowned. He sounded...frantic, almost panicked. "I'm almost home already. And I don't want to see you right now."

How was it possible for something to be a lie and the truth at the same time? And how could it hurt so damned much to say?

"Where are you?" Hunter demanded. "Exact location."

Avery resumed walking, her pace sped by her indignation. "I'm going to hang up—"

"Avery, don't!"

"—because you're not listening to me at all."

"Don't hang up!"

From somewhere a few blocks away, tires screeched on pavement, the sound diminished by the distance. That same sound came through the phone a fraction of the second later, far louder. When the wind eased, she could hear a car approaching, its engine roaring like a demon unleashed from hell.

Had he gone to her apartment?

Tears stung her eyes, and it was growing harder and harder to hold back her emotions. Her feet slowed to a stop. "I don't know what you want from—"

Her pained cry cut off her words as something grabbed hold of her hair and tugged back hard. She jerked backward, her momentum halted when she hit something large and solid.

"Avery?" Hunter yelled through the phone. "Avery!"

The man behind her clamped a big, strong hand over her mouth before she could utter so much as another syllable, using that hold to keep her against his chest. His other hand released her hair to close around her phone and pry it from her grasp so easily it was though she'd let go on purpose. She heard Hunter's voice frantically calling through the speaker as the phone fell to the ground.

With a vicious yank, the man forced Avery's head back and to the side, exposing her neck.

Her eyes widened; in that moment, she understood what was happening, understood it on the only level that mattered—the primal level. She was being kidnapped.

Avery screamed against the unrelenting hand. She thrashed against the man, reaching back to claw at his face, but he leaned away, leaving her to strike only empty air. She scratched at his hand instead, digging her nails into his thick skin.

The man tightened his grip on her mouth, his fingers pressing painfully into her cheeks, and said in a heavy accent, "Stay still, you little bitch."

Avery swung her arms down, hitting his belly, his thighs, his groin, anything she could find. Her assailant grunted, but his hold remained firm.

A cold, hard object pressed against her neck. There was a faint, anticlimactic click, and something pierced her skin. Searing heat followed by numbing ice radiated from the spot, racing through her every vein and artery to consume her from head to toe. She cried out again, knees buckling.

Desperate, she shoved a hand into her bag, feeling for her pepper spray. She pulled the little can out and fumbled to turn it toward her attacker. Just before she could push the button, he caught her wrist in his hand.

"No, you fucking don't." He shook her arm once, hard; it was enough to break her hold on the pepper spray. The cannister clanged on the sidewalk.

Fresh tears spilled from Avery's eyes, blurring her vision.

No! No, no, no, not like this, not here, not now!

Her heart raced, and the lump of dread in her belly was big enough to make her nauseous, but she refused to go down this easily. She refused to go down without more of a fight.

Avery lifted her foot and slammed it down, the heel of her boot striking the inside of the man's ankle. He grunted again, but this time, he staggered slightly. She repeated her attack again and again, her boot connecting with his calf, his shin, the top of his foot, everywhere around that damned ankle without actually hitting it a second time.

"*Haur vash reithen, gethuk,*" he growled.

Avery didn't have time to wonder what language he'd just spoken. Her breath came in short, sharp bursts through her nostrils, and the spot on her neck throbbed. Her head began to spin. The pain was gone already, leaving a strange sensation behind. She felt like her limbs were growing impossibly heavy, but her head, her mind...well, that was getting all floaty, as though her consciousness was going to soar high into the air and drift away from her body like a lost balloon.

The man shifted his hold on her mouth, trying to get a better grip on her. Avery used that brief leeway to bite down. His flesh was tough, like an overcooked steak, and there was an oddly metallic tang to its taste.

Blood and iron.

What did that mean? What had he injected her with?

Am I...am I a cannibal now?

Spitting another word in that unrecognizable language, the man tore his hand away from her. Avery shoved herself forward, stumbling over the sidewalk, and would've fallen were it not for his viselike grip on her wrist.

That roaring car engine was suddenly very loud—and remarkably close.

Hunter had a car that sounded like that, all powerful and fast. But she didn't want to see him now, he was...was...

The man dragged Avery back toward him, nearly lifting her off her feet in the process. The force of his pull made her turn toward him again just before she crashed into his broad chest.

Bright light bathed the man's face for an instant. Avery glimpsed someone vaguely familiar—a wide, squared jaw, deep set eyes, shaved head, and fur around his collar—and then tires screeched and the light turned sharply away from him.

"Fuck," the man snapped, releasing his hold on her.

Avery fell, hitting the concrete with a jolt—or at least she thought she did. She didn't quite feel it like she should have. It was almost like someone else's body had fallen to the ground, like she wasn't really a part of all this but was just watching.

Except she couldn't really watch. Everything was all blurry and indistinct. She reached up to her face to wipe the tears from her eyes, but there were none.

Her glasses were gone. They'd fallen right off her face without her noticing.

I really need those. They'll be expensive to replace.

Trembling, she pushed onto hands and knees. Her messenger bag slipped down to hang beneath her, bumping her arms and thighs as she crawled in search of her glasses. She knew she should've been running, that she should've been getting away while she could, that her life was in danger. But she couldn't shake the notion that she *needed* her glasses first.

Boots stomped across the pavement rapidly, rising above the rumble of an idling engine. Someone—some*thing*—roared nearby, and Avery swore the sound vibrated the air around her, that it displaced the falling snow, that it pierced straight into her heart because it sounded just like a wild beast roaring in defense of its mate.

She looked up to see two dark figures slam into one another. They moved too fast, too savagely for her to follow, each movement punctuated by a grunt, a growl, the dull *thwap* of a landing punch or kick.

Avery fell onto her hip, coming down partially on her bag. Her hands were freezing, and the chill was coursing up her limbs to assault her core. She'd never been so cold. Never been so tired. What was wrong? What was happening to her?

Was she...was she dying?

Focus, Avery. You need to get out of here.

She tried to push up to her feet, but neither her arms nor her legs seemed strong enough to manage it.

The dark figures snarled in some guttural language. Avery looked up to see one of the figures reel back and release a pained yell. His head whipped aside, and something spattered the ground beneath him. Metal glinted in his hand a second later, and he turned toward his opponent.

The other figure grabbed the first's arm, and there was a bright flash, accompanied by a high-pitched whine—like a laser out of a movie.

A bolt of blue-white light darted past Avery and struck the ground with another flash and a hiss. She jolted away from the blast, breath caught in her throat, as something metal clattered to the ground.

She wasn't sure if it was a sob, a scream, or some combination of the two that came out of her mouth, but she didn't stop it. She couldn't.

"Avery," one of the men called.

One of the figures darted past her and into a nearby yard.

"Fuck," someone growled from nearby.

Avery swung her eyes to the remaining man. He seemed huge in her blurred vision, tall and broad with arms spread and claws on his fingertips. She lifted her gaze to his face. All she could see was shadow and two glowing, crimson eyes.

She had no question as to what sound she made this time—she screamed, and it momentarily chased away the numbness that was spreading through her body. With what little strength she had left, she turned and scrambled away from the red-eyed demon, aware of her hands and knees hitting the pavement only because of the jolts their impact sent up her arms and legs. But every movement sapped more of her waning energy, every movement pushed her closer to that black abyss of exhaustion, and her own damned bag was fighting her, threatening to trip her.

A powerful arm coiled around her middle and plucked her off the ground. She opened her mouth to scream again, but a hand covered it—a big, strong, rough hand with a startlingly gentle touch. She struggled, trying to twist and thrash, but she couldn't tell if her limbs were actually moving, and her eyelids were so, so heavy.

I didn't find my glasses.

I didn't get away.

I'm going to die.

She released a muffled cry.

"Shh, Avery," the man rumbled in her ear, his gritty voice instantly familiar.

Hunter. Hunter came. Hunter's here.

Her eyelids fell shut, her body eased, and her head tipped back to rest on his shoulder. She sagged against Hunter, and she tried to talk to him, to tell him what was happening, to tell him something was wrong, but her lips refused to move.

"I've got you, *vaerina*."

Avery drew in a breath. The air smelled like snow, sandalwood, leather, and fir.

Darkness closed in around her, snuffing out her awareness.

EIGHTEEN

"Avery?" Fyran shook her gently, but she remained limp and unresponsive.

His heart pounded, its beat so fast and strong that it was a wonder it hadn't cracked his ribs. He turned her to face him and quickly looked her over, barely noticing the red glow cast upon her face by his eyes.

She was still breathing; that was most important. Her cheeks were red, her lower lip had split open, and there was a tiny puncture wound on her neck from which a single drop of blood had trickled.

Varketh must've hit her with some sort of tranquilizer. All Fyran could do now was hope it would wear off soon, and that it would have no lasting effect upon her. Her palms were scraped, smeared with blood and dirt, but the wounds looked superficial. Most concerning was the coolness of her skin. It seemed too extreme to be merely from the cold, but he couldn't be sure. Humans were less tolerant to weather extremes than falorans.

Though seeing any damage done to his female stoked the fires of his fury, her wounds were nothing that required immediate attention, which was good.

They needed to leave.

And yet he couldn't stop himself from drawing her into a one-sided embrace as he carefully smoothed back her tousled hair, which was damp from the falling snow, and held her close a little longer.

This was his female, his *mate*, and he'd nearly lost her tonight.

As if I didn't already try to throw her away.

He clamped his jaw shut and released a slow, strained breath through his nostrils as the reminder of what he'd done to her tore at his insides. He'd never understood just how much emotions could physically hurt—not until Avery.

And he never wanted to go back to his ignorance on the matter.

Fyran hefted her up over his shoulder, swallowing his flare of alarm as her head lolled. She was just unconscious, that was all. She'd wake up soon.

She *had* to wake up soon.

He swept his gaze over his surroundings. The street was still dark, and there was no one watching as far as he could see, but that didn't mean the authorities hadn't been alerted.

"Fuck," he rasped. Of all the curses in all the languages he knew, that one seemed to fit this situation the best. It was the perfect word. This was fucked.

Get her home. Figure the rest out later.

Fyran latched onto that thought. The circumstances didn't matter; he was an *althicar*, and he would adapt regardless of what had occurred...or to whom it had occurred.

With his arm banded around Avery's legs to keep her secure on his shoulder, he did all the cleanup he could afford to do, gathering the fallen plasma pistol, her eyeglasses, her phone, powering off the latter so it could not be tracked. The ilventyr blood on the pavement and the hole melted into the sidewalk would have to remain, hopefully to be covered by the snowfall before anyone could discover them.

He dashed back to the car, which was still idling with the driver's side door open, and deposited Avery in the passenger seat.

He turned her head to get her strapped in, and the feel of her too-cool skin under his fingertips made his chest tight and his breaths short.

Once she was secure, he hurried around to the driver's seat, slammed the door shut, and drove. His restless hands squeezed the steering wheel, and his eyes darted repeatedly between the road ahead, the rearview mirror, and the unmoving female beside him.

Cold and methodical. He'd referred to himself that way when Avery had asked if he was secretly a homicidal maniac, playing it as a joke—but it hadn't been a joke. Command had described him using similar words. Always calm, always detached from emotion, always focused on the mission. How had that changed so much since he'd come to Earth?

Fyran's gaze returned to Avery as though in answer to his question.

His grip on the wheel tightened so much that his hands ached. Keeping his thumbs hooked under the wheel, Fyran straightened his fingers and spread them wide, stretching them. The blood coating his claws and fingertips was dark under the orange street-lamp glow pouring in through the windshield.

He couldn't say it was all because of her; these changes in him had been happening well before he'd known she existed. Undoubtedly, it had all been thrown into overdrive after meeting her, but even then, none of this was her fault.

"*Svesh.*" He curled his hands into fists again.

What a fucking mess. He wasn't so foolish as to believe things couldn't have gone worse, but they could've gone a whole lot better. For one, Varketh had escaped. The *Exthurizen's* best assassin had failed to eliminate a lone ilventyr.

As though mocking him, the semiautomatic handgun holstered in his pants seemed to grow in weight, pressing hard against his leg. Even in his rage, he'd avoided using the human firearm, knowing it would've been too loud and potentially easy for human authorities to trace. But the whole thing would've been over a lot faster had he leapt out of the car with pistol in hand.

Of course, he could well have hit his mate by accident had he started shooting.

That risk to Avery violated his unrelenting, instinctual drive to protect her at all costs. It was the same instinct that would've drawn satisfaction from Fyran shredding the ilventyr's flesh with his claws, the instinct that insisted he destroy anyone and anything that threatened her. The damage he'd inflicted upon Varketh hadn't been enough.

Fyran growled and forced his holoshroud back on; he'd not deactivated it on purpose, but there was nothing to be done about it. Just another mistake on a growing list.

Avery's here, and she's alive. That's all that counts.

For the first time in his life, Fyran was carrying a lot of regrets. The latest was that he'd only managed to claw out one of Varketh's eyes before the ilventyr had escaped.

Drawing the blaster had been sheer desperation on Varketh's part. He'd undoubtedly intended to kill Fyran with it, but the wild shot he'd taken before Fyran wrestled the weapon from his hand had succeeded in one way—the cry Avery had released as the bolt struck only feet away from her had distracted Fyran.

The ilventyr had taken the opportunity to kick Fyran away and flee.

Now there was a one-eyed ilventyr trafficker on the loose who was sure to tell his associates that a certain *complication* had resurfaced to thwart their plot. They'd know that Fyran was more than just an inconvenience now. They'd know that he wasn't human—his holoshroud had slipped again during their fight—even if Varketh hadn't properly identified him as a faloran. And there was a good chance they'd take direct action against him.

After all, Gregor would've collected the advanced payment half an hour ago—but he had no product to deliver in exchange.

So much for your big sale, huh, Gregor?

Any petty satisfaction Fyran might've drawn from that small success was snuffed out when he glanced at Avery again.

Fyran's lips peeled back with a snarl, and he tightened his grip on the wheel until the leather cover was creaking in misery. There could be no satisfaction now. Not when she'd been harmed, not while she remained unconscious, not while she remained in danger.

He seized upon his anger, letting it grow well beyond the other tangled emotions at war within him. It was the only emotion he knew how to use, the only one he knew how to repurpose, how to convert into fuel. Everything else could wait.

Priority one remained unchanged—get Avery to safety. Take her home.

Fyran guided his vehicle through the city on a long, intentionally convoluted route meant to reveal any tails and obfuscate the way to his dwelling. He remained tense throughout, battling the urge to slam his foot down on the accelerator and race home at the Hellcat's maximum speed.

Denver's streets were maddeningly quiet despite it being a busy Saturday night. That seemed somehow obscene, like an affront to everything that'd just happened. It was too harsh a reminder that this world—that the entire universe—didn't really care what happened to anyone.

Patience and vigilance. Focused rage.

Get her home.

Finally satisfied he wasn't being followed, he left Denver. Even after he hit the long, dark stretches of highway between the city and the mountains, he resisted the impulse to speed. He didn't think he'd be able to talk his way out of trouble if Trooper Sullivan were to pull him over and find a dirty, pale, unconscious female slumped in the passenger seat.

There was little relief to be had when Fyran turned into his driveway, not even from the familiar crunch of snow, dirt, and gravel under the tires. His fury persisted, but so much else roiled beneath the surface, threatening to break through at any moment. His breaths came harsh and heavy as the car rolled into the garage.

He pressed the garage opener and sat, hands flexing and

relaxing repeatedly on the steering wheel, as he waited for the door to shut. He wouldn't risk anyone getting even the briefest glimpse of him moving Avery out of his car.

The instant the door made the rumbling thump that signaled it was closed, Fyran killed the engine and burst out of his vehicle, barely stopping himself from leaping across the hood in his rush to get to Avery.

He yanked her door open, not caring that he might've torn it off had he used just a little more strength, and forced himself to carefully unbuckle Avery's seatbelt, gather her in his arms, and lift her out of the car.

With one arm behind her back and the other under her knees, he cradled Avery against his chest and carried her into the house. Her bag dangled at her side, swaying as he walked.

Those repressed, volatile emotions battered his mental barriers relentlessly, but he held them at bay as he brought his female upstairs. He wasn't consciously aware of his intentions, but he didn't question himself when he laid her atop his bed.

She was safe there. She *belonged* there, even if these circumstances were less than ideal.

He tried to pretend his hands weren't trembling when he tugged off her boots and socks and tossed them aside, leaving only the delicate anklet around her left ankle. He tried to ignore his gut churning while he maneuvered her body to remove her bag and peel off her dirty coat. And he pretended he didn't notice the faint blue tinge to her skin when he slid off her wet, torn pants.

His little female had never seemed so delicate, so fragile, so... lifeless. The Avery he knew was bright and joyful, ready to laugh and smile freely. So full of life.

But I cast a shadow over her light days ago. I killed her smile.

And hadn't he expected that? Death was all he knew how to give.

Karak'duun, you don't have time for this self-loathing bullshit, Fyran. She needs you.

As minor as they appeared, her wounds required closer examination and tending. He'd paid just enough attention during the pre-mission briefings to know that humans were susceptible to all sorts of infections if they didn't properly treat and care for their injuries. And she needed warmth.

He reached toward her, meaning to move her into a better position, but froze when he saw his hands again—when he saw the dark ilventyrian blood dried to his skin.

He couldn't touch her with these hands. Couldn't mar her flesh with that blood, couldn't risk contaminating her wounds.

Fyran backed away from the bed and glanced down at himself. That same dark blood had dried on his jacket, pants, and shirt. He strode into the bathroom, where he looked at himself in the mirror. More blood had spattered his face. He looked like he'd stepped out of one of those damned horror movies of which humans were so fond.

"No wonder she screamed when she saw me," he muttered as he stripped, piling his soiled clothing on the floor and placing his weapons on the counter.

He turned on the shower, cranking the lever most of the way to hot, and stepped in before the water had even begun to warm up. Using copious amounts of soap and shampoo, he scrubbed himself clean, rinsed, and washed again. His mind remained thankfully blank during the process, even when he stood mostly still for nearly a full minute to let the scalding water burn the lingering feel of filth away from his skin. Even with that delay, he was done within five minutes.

When the shower was off, he stepped out without any regard for how much water he dripped on the floor. He snatched a towel out of the closet, dried off vigorously, and plucked the human-made pistol, holster and all, off the counter before returning to the bedroom.

His heart was still racing, having barely slowed since before his shower.

Though Avery was right there, so close, Fyran didn't allow himself to look upon her until he'd put on a pair of sweatpants.

She lay exactly as he'd left her—the same spot, same position, without a single hair out of place.

The first night he'd entered Avery's apartment, Fyran had seen her sleeping. She'd looked so relaxed, so serene. She'd looked...unburdened, like all the joy she was so quick to share with those around her could never possibly have been faked.

She didn't look that way now. Despite her slack features, she appeared troubled. Vulnerable. She looked...unwell. With her hair in disarray, her cheeks smudged with black streaks from her makeup, her split lip, and the concerning pallor of her skin, she looked like she'd been through hell.

And she still looked so fucking beautiful.

Fyran returned to the bedside and reached down, brushing wild strands of hair out of her face. He'd come so close to losing her tonight. Had he been a few seconds later, his Avery would've been...gone.

Even if she'd been captured, I know where they would've taken her. I could've saved her.

He scoffed at the thought, but the sound that came out of him was far more choked and strained than he'd intended. Avery made no sign that she'd heard him.

Releasing a shaky breath, Fyran stroked the backs of his fingers along her jaw.

The truth remained—he'd almost lost her tonight. Had Fyran not intervened when he had, who knew what sort of further trauma she might've suffered before he could rescue her from the ilventyrs?

He hadn't realized what losing her would really feel like, couldn't have imagined it, even after attempting to discard her as though she'd meant nothing to him. He'd learned little of loss during the last week because he hadn't truly cast her aside. He'd still followed her, had still watched her.

But tonight...tonight he'd almost learned what it would really mean to lose his female, and he knew now that he would not survive it. He'd never felt such *fear*.

And he could feel himself cracking and crumbling at the sight of her current state—at the countless threads of what could have been.

He gritted his teeth as he moved his hand to rest beneath her chin, stroking her jaw with his thumb. He didn't deserve her, perhaps he never would, but he was going to fucking claim her anyway.

Avery was *his*, and no one would take her from him. Not Gregor and his ilventyrian gang, not any of Earth's governments or military forces, not the fucking *Exthurizen*.

Fyran placed the handgun on the nightstand and hurried down to the kitchen to retrieve a pair of bowls, which he filled with hot water in the bathroom after returning upstairs. He grabbed a couple washcloths from the linen closet and set them, along with the filled bowls, on the nightstand before kneeling to open the hidden floor compartment and retrieve the compact medkit stashed with his equipment.

Returning to the bed, he sat on its edge beside Avery. With a damp washcloth, he washed away the tear-streaked makeup that had run down her cheeks, keeping his touch as gentle as possible. As the black smears faded and revealed her pale, smooth skin and its dusting of freckles, that familiar tightness in his chest resurged.

His hand trailed lower, following the contour of her cheek to the corner of her mouth. He cleaned the dried blood from her lip with even greater care. She didn't react even when he dabbed at the cut.

With his free hand, he cupped the side of her face. Her skin was still cool to the touch. He slid his thumb down to brush first beneath her lower lip and then, delicately, directly across it. He remembered how these lips had looked after he'd kissed her, so pink and full, slightly swollen—delicious and begging for more.

"My *vaerina*," Fyran growled as he continued tracing her lip with the pad of his thumb. In his mind's eye, he saw Varketh with his hand clamped over her mouth, the headlights reflected in his inhuman eyes. "Fuck."

Fyran closed his eyes and stilled his thumb. His other hand fell onto his thigh, and he squeezed the washcloth in his fist.

Water trickled out of it and spread along his leg as his sweatpants absorbed it, but he didn't move his hand away, didn't ease his grip. After a deep, steadying breath, he opened his eyes. He wasn't done.

He turned her head aside, granting him a better view of the tiny wound on the side of her neck. Leaning down, he inspected damage more closely. Her fragrance filled his nostrils in its fullness. But he couldn't allow himself to be caught up in it, couldn't allow himself that luxury.

The single, crusted drop of blood on her neck flaked away at the lightest touch of the cloth, leaving behind a miniscule pink dot.

Karak'duun, he wished he knew what she'd been injected with. Given the ilventyrs' business, it was logical to guess it had merely been a powerful sedative, but there was no being sure of it, and he was far, far away from anything that'd be able to run a definitive scan to find out what had been introduced to her system.

He lifted one of her hands next, curling his fingers loosely around the back of her wrist so her palm was facing up.

Fyran washed away the blood, grit, and grime from her hand with a soapy cloth, rinsing it off with clean water when he was done. The abrasions on her skin were small and shallow, just as superficial as he'd thought, and they were no longer bleeding even after his ministrations. That knowledge didn't reverse his frown or erase the crease between his brows.

If he hadn't abandoned her, if he hadn't distanced himself, she wouldn't have gone through any of this. His presence hadn't been bringing danger to her—he'd been her only defense against forces she didn't even know existed.

He swallowed his anger and continued his work, washing and rinsing her other palm. His eyes repeatedly flicked up toward her face, looking for signs of feeling, of movement. None came. He moved on to her left knee, which had been skinned by the concrete sidewalk. Her right knee was the angry red of a potential bruise, but the flesh was unbroken.

When he was finished cleaning her, he dropped the washcloths into the bowls and opened the medkit to remove the healing ointment. He rubbed it over her wounds, starting with her knee and working up to her hands. Finally, he placed a tiny bead of it on his thumb to brush over her split lip.

Karak'duun, he'd yearned to touch her, to explore her body with his fingertips, to learn the feel of her skin inch by inch. But not like this. Never like this.

He forced himself off the bed even though everything inside him demanded he remain beside her—or, even better, that he lie down, draw her into his arms, and hold her against his body. But he would share his body heat with her soon.

Fyran scooped Avery off the bed, balancing her weight on one arm as he pulled the blanket down. When he set her atop the bed again, he positioned her so her head was upon one of the pillows, taking a moment to free her hair from beneath her back and shoulders so it was fanned out around her. He then drew the covers over her body, tucking them under her chin and around her sides to seal in as much warmth as possible.

His legs were loath to move; he could have easily stood there for hours staring at her, memorizing each of the tiny freckles on her cheeks and nose, losing himself in her features, willing her to wake, to smile.

But he forced them into motion after a moment's hesitation. Tucking the holstered pistol into his pocket, he got to work. He was scarcely aware of his actions as he cleaned up, dumping out the bowls and placing them in the dishwasher downstairs, stuffing his bloodied clothing into a trash bag, getting her clothes in the washing machine, scrubbing his hands clean again, double-checking all the containment fields on the doors and windows and ensuring the sound dampeners were active. He tucked her phone away in the garage so he could deal with it later; he'd need to ensure it couldn't be traced by human means before he returned it to her.

All that done, he returned to the bedroom. He placed her glasses on the nightstand beside her. Fortunately, they'd not suffered any damage despite falling off her face, and she'd prob-ably want them whenever she woke. With another fleeting glance at his mate, he picked up the medkit, fetched the ilventyr's blaster pistol from the bathroom, and knelt beside the still open floor compartment. He placed the blaster and the medkit inside before fishing out the communication disc.

Holding the disc on his palm, Fyran huffed through his nostrils. This was about the last thing he wanted to do, but...he needed to report. For all his anger, he could still recognize that this situation risked spiraling further out of control. Command needed to know.

He glanced at Avery over his shoulder—she still hadn't moved, damn it—before closing the compartment, standing up, and exiting the room. He closed the door softly behind him.

Fyran activated the comm disc and walked down the hallway. The blue light atop the disc flickered on, scanning his identity. It had finished the process by the time he stepped into one of the spare bedrooms. He paced along the room's perimeter as he awaited a connection.

After what felt like years—but which couldn't have been more than a minute or two—the disc flashed, and a hologram of *Ultricar* Khelvar Bathiras's face materialized in the air over it.

There was an infinitesimal downward shift of the *ultricar's* eyebrows. "*Althicar* Voltanix. Didn't expect to hear from you so soon."

"I didn't expect to have anything to report," Fyran replied, combing back his long hair with his free hand. "Yet here we both are."

Khelvar dipped his chin in a shallow nod. "Proceed."

"I've discovered the ilventyrian base of operations and have confirmation that they are involved in illicit activity. They're moving weapons, some of faloran make, drugs—"

"You were ordered to focus only on your assignment, *althicar*, and nothing else. I don't care how much of a mistake you think we made in this, Fyran, you—"

"And humans, sir," Fyran snapped. "They are kidnapping

humans and selling them to unknown, presumably alien buyers. I haven't uncovered whether they are keeping them on-planet or not."

"And that may warrant further investigation, but it is *not* your mission." A dark crease had formed between Khelvar's eyebrows now, and the slight downturn of the corners of his mouth had somehow resulted in one of the most severe frowns Fyran had ever seen.

Fyran ground his teeth together, jaw muscles bulging, and dropped his hand to his side, where he curled it into a tight fist.

Khelvar released a harsh sigh. "What do you not understand, Fyran? Your pursuit of these aliens endangers our entire mission, it threatens what's left of our species. If our operations on Earth are discovered prematurely, the repercussions could be dire. And that's not to mention that I don't want one of my best throwing his life away for no damned good reason."

"Protecting these people *is* a damned good reason," Fyran snarled.

"We're not in a position to—"

Fyran's fingers trembled around the comm disc, squeezing its edge, and the claws of his other hand lengthened to press into the heel of his palm. "*Karak'duun*, Khelvar, they tried to take her!"

The *ultricar* narrowed his eyes. "Tried to take who, Fyran?"

Fyran turned his face away, baring his teeth to draw in a ragged breath. "*Her*. My...my female. My mate. She was their latest target, and I only realized it tonight. They tried to take her, and I wounded one of the ilventyrs to get her back."

For a time, Khelvar was silent. When he finally spoke, the edge had left his voice. "Have you made a mating bond with her?"

Tension rippled through Fyran, and he felt that constriction in his chest, felt it coiling around his heart and lungs. "Not yet. But" —he turned his face back toward Khelvar and bared his teeth—"I will. She is *mine*, and I'm not going to lose her. I will bind her to me in every way possible."

"Send in any intel you have on the ilventyrian operation," Khelvar said. "We'll start looking into it. Earth is the future of our race. It needs to be safe. But *you*, Fyran...you need to focus on your mission. On your female. She is your concern, not the defense of her entire species. Am I clear?"

He and Khelvar held one another's gazes. For a little while, it was almost as though they were standing together in person again. Fyran could still remember clearly the first time he'd met the *ultricar*, years before...could still remember how different their stares had been, how different the circumstances. They hadn't been on the same side back then.

But it was foolish for Fyran to have convinced himself they were on opposing sides now.

Fyran nodded. "I understand, *ultricar*."

"Good. Are you safe? Has your cover been compromised?"

"I believe we're safe. Even if the ilventyrs have uncovered my human alias, my records on this planet are obscured enough that they won't be able to tie it back to this residence or my vehicle."

"If you feel it becomes necessary, I will have other *althicars* relocated to your area." When Fyran only shook his head, Khelvar continued, "Contact me if the situation changes. Be careful, and tend to your mate, Fyran. Check regularly for communications in the coming weeks."

"I will, *ultricar*."

The hologram vanished as the connection was severed, leaving Fyran alone in a dark, quiet room. He curled his fingers around the comm disc. Gregor and his ilventyrian gang would be impossible to ignore, but Fyran knew how to lie low, knew how to avoid attention. If only he'd put those skills to better use lately.

Thinking like that's just a waste of fucking time now.

He couldn't change what had already happened, but he could control what he did with the future—and all he truly wanted to do was make everything right with Avery. All he wanted to do was make her his.

This was the chance he'd craved. This was his opportunity to be with Avery without any secrets, without any lies. During his career, he'd demonstrated time and again the ability to focus on his mission with unwavering intensity.

Avery was his sole mission now. Avery was his target, and there were no more excuses, no more distractions. She was going to receive *all* his attention. And Fyran would have her again say those words that had driven him mad before—*I'm yours. Only yours.*

NINETEEN

IN ALL HER LIFE, Avery had never woken up feeling as miserable as she did right now. Every part of her body was sore and heavy—her limbs, her head, her eyes and eyelids, her fingers and toes. Even her hair seemed to be weighing her down. It was a surreal sensation, and she might've questioned whether she was truly awake at all if it weren't for the other discomforts.

There was a dull, slow throbbing in her head, centered just above her eyes. Her mouth and throat were so dry they would've made a desert seem humid in comparison. When she swallowed, pain radiated from her throat.

I'm dehydrated. Just need some water.

How overboard had she and Brandy gone last night? Though she didn't drink very often, Avery had overdone it a time or two, and she'd suffered the following mornings. She was such a lightweight when it came to alcohol. But this...

I...didn't go out with Brandy.

Avery's brow creased, and she grasped the sheet in her fists. The air was suddenly too thick, and it was too hard to breathe. Her heart raced, its pounding permeating her body as her skin prickled with unease.

I didn't go out with Brandy.

Flashes of memory flickered through her mind—screeching tires, Hunter speaking to her on the phone with panic in his voice, a cruel hand clamping over her mouth...

The pain as something pierced her neck.

Glowing red eyes.

Avery's eyes snapped open. Her chest rose and fell with her rapid, wheezing breaths as she raised a hand to her neck, touching where she'd been stabbed. Though she felt no evidence of a wound, the spot was tender.

Her eyes darted across the ceiling and over the walls, taking in the sparsely furnished room. She didn't need her glasses to tell this wasn't her bedroom. This wasn't anywhere she knew.

She'd been taken. Kidnapped.

Can't breathe.

Avery sat up and clawed at her shirt with desperate, trembling hands, as though pulling it away from her skin would somehow ease the constriction in her chest.

A hand settled on the center of her back; it was big, warm, and totally unexpected. "You're okay, Avery."

That voice.

Hunter.

A wave of calm washed over her. Hunter had been there during her attack. He'd...he'd saved her. He was here.

With tears stinging her eyes, she took in a deep, shuddering breath and turned to face him. Except it wasn't Avery's Hunter who was sitting on the bed beside her. This man had Hunter's face, but his features were sharper and more defined. He had Hunter's long, wild hair, but the colors were more pronounced— the gold streaks even more golden, the brown darker than before— and one side of it was tucked behind his ear. His *pointed* ear. Just like that of an elf.

And his eyes...these weren't the twin black pools in which she'd lost herself so many times. They were red as blood and shone with their own light, making his stare even more intense than normal. He wasn't wearing a shirt, revealing his broad shoulders and toned torso, and all those ridges of muscle she'd dreamed of running her hands over. Tattoos ringed both his biceps, their strange, flowing, intricate symbols and patterns glowing the same color as his eyes.

She met this stranger's gaze. One corner of his mouth tilted up in Hunter's smile, but his canines were elongated. He had fangs.

All the better to eat you with.

Avery screamed. She scrambled backward in a frantic retreat only to be reminded of a simple fact—beds were finite. They had edges.

Rather than the mattress, her hand met empty air, which was unfortunately ill suited to supporting her body weight. She tumbled off the bed with a cry. The hardwood floor knocked the breath out of her when her back struck it. The throbbing pain in her head intensified. It felt as though she'd split her skull open.

That quickly, she found herself staring up at the ceiling again, her legs tangled in the blanket and one foot still up on the bed.

"*Karak'duun*," the Hunter-impostor muttered. "Should've waited to show her."

The bed rocked, and he appeared above her, braced on his hands as he leaned over the edge. "Are you all right, *vaerina?*"

Her eyes widened, and another scream built in her chest, but her throat was too tight to let it out.

"Calm down, Avery," he said, giving her another glimpse of those wicked fangs.

Avery tried to scoot back, tried to put distance between her and this Hunter look-alike, but her legs were caught in the blanket. "I am calm!"

He chuckled. It was the same laugh she'd heard so many times, that she'd come to love. "No, you're not."

She tugged on her legs again, but the bedding was twisted around them too tight to escape, and every movement seemed to sap more and more strength from her. Her heart was pumping so fast that she swore it was about to burst out of her chest. "I am perfectly calm."

Oh my God, why can't I get my legs out?

"Mmhmm."

That sound rolled up from his chest and resonated in Avery. How could such a simple sound have such a huge effect on her?

Not-Hunter shifted so he was only on his knees. Avery watched, breathing raggedly, as he reached down to peel back the blanket. His inhuman eyes caught her gaze and held it captive. Her breath caught in her throat when he cupped the back of her calf with one hand. His touch was firm, confident, and heated, and it sent a thrill across her skin that she could not ignore. When his thumb stroked the side of her leg, fire flared in her core.

She wanted that hand to slide up, wanted those fingers to curl around her thighs, wanted them to brush the sensitive flesh of her sex before delving deeper.

With his other hand, he slowly unraveled the blanket that had bound her. Why did that feel so much like he was peeling off her clothing? Why was he looking at her like that was exactly what he was doing?

Why don't I have any pants on?

Brow furrowing, Avery dropped her gaze to the hand cupping her calf. It was the same hand she'd held, the same hand that had touched her cheek and curled around her shoulder to keep her close, the same hand that had delved into her hair as he kissed her. It was Hunter's hand.

But even through her blurred vision, she could make out the long black claws on the tips of his fingers.

"W-what are you?" Avery asked, voice quiet as she stared at those deadly claws. She dared not move for fear they'd shred her flesh. Though her heart was still pounding as fast as a terrified rabbit's, that heaviness was spreading through her again. It felt like she was sinking into the floor.

The faintest frown settled on his lips as he slid his hand down to stroke the pad of his thumb across her skin just beneath her anklet. That touch felt so good despite those dangerous claws, despite those predatory eyes, despite...all of it.

Hunter released her leg, lowering it gently. Though free, Avery no longer had the energy to run—or perhaps she no longer had the urge. All she could do was watch him as he moved.

He braced himself on one arm, swinging his legs over the edge of the bed. His toes were also tipped with black claws, shorter than those on his fingers but looking no less sharp. Yet as he planted his feet on the floor, it was something else that caught her attention, something else that made her eyes widen further.

Something flicked behind his back. She didn't see it fully until he stood up, and that something skimmed across the top of the bed, curling to hang beside his leg.

A tail. Hunter-but-not-Hunter had a tail, its short fur a soft brown that was a few shades darker than the golden highlights in his hair. But the tuft of longer fur at its tip was dark.

How would it feel for him to run that over my skin?

Avery squeezed her eyes shut.

What was wrong with her? She'd nearly been kidnapped—or maybe she *was* kidnapped—had been injected with who-knew-what drug, was sore everywhere, and the man she'd wanted more than anything or anyone, the man who she'd thought had broken up with her, wasn't human. Why the hell was she wondering what his tail would feel like on her body?

He had a freaking tail! Why wasn't she racing for the door?

And why am I acting like the tail is the part that should make me run?

Though she hadn't heard him move, she felt his presence beside her suddenly, felt it as surely as she had every time they'd been close to one another before. His familiar sandalwood and fir scent filled her nostrils when she breathed in.

"Look at me, *vaerina*," he said, his voice low, smooth, commanding.

Avery opened her eyes to find him crouched beside her. The glow of his eyes softened as his gaze met hers, and, despite all those differences, she *knew* he was her Hunter. Only he had ever looked at her like that. Only he *could* ever look at her like that.

She didn't recoil when he slipped his arms beneath her and lifted her off the floor. He was warm, and solid, and he smelled so, so good. His hold on her was steady as he sat down right there on the floor and drew her onto his lap, keeping his arm around her back for support.

He grasped her chin and angled her face up toward his. His thumb trailed along her jaw slowly, soothingly. "You have nothing to fear from me, Avery. I will never hurt you."

Avery gazed into his eyes. Her skin came alive beneath his touch, her chest tightened with emotion, and tears blurred her vision further. Now that she knew this really was her Hunter, she no longer feared him...but he was wrong.

"You did hurt me," she said.

His expression grew strained, a crease forming between his brows and his lips turning down. "I know. And it was the biggest mistake I have ever made."

"Why?" She blinked, and the tears spilled down her cheeks. "Was it me—"

"No," he growled, eyes flaring brighter. He released a heavy breath through his nostrils. "I can't stop thinking about you, *vaerina*." Tenderly, he wiped away her tears, never once scratching her with his claws. "Every moment of every day, you're in my thoughts, and all I can do is yearn for my next taste of you. And that was making things very dangerous for me. I thought it was endangering you, too. Thought they were after *me*, and that you'd get caught in the crossfire."

Avery couldn't deny the warmth flooding her at his admission. All those days without hearing from him, all those days of hurting, of wondering if she'd been the problem, if she hadn't been good enough, just as she'd never measured up in her family...had been because he was trying to protect her?

She brought her hand up and touched her fingertips to her mouth as she recalled the rough, unforgiving palm that had covered it and the merciless fingers that had dug into her cheeks. "Who...are they?"

He clutched her closer as a low growl rumbled in his chest. "Criminals. They traffic drugs, weapons, and people. They also happen to be aliens."

Aliens.

But aliens didn't exist...right? Except...

"And...you?" Avery asked, her hand falling from her mouth to rest on her chest.

"Also an alien, but not a criminal. Well, not technically. Anymore. Sort of." Hunter shook his head and glanced up at the ceiling. "I've wanted to tell you the truth for so long now, but my mission, the circumstances...I couldn't. Couldn't risk it. Until now."

He looked back down at her. "My name is Fyran Voltanix. I'm a faloran *althicar*. Faloran is my species, and *althicar* is my rank, I guess you'd say. I'm a soldier specializing in covert operations and...assassination."

Fyran Voltanix. His name had never been Hunter. He'd never been who she thought he was. He wasn't born in Wyoming—wasn't even from Earth at all—and he'd never worked in private security, at least in the way she thought. Instead, he was an...

Avery's palms grew clammy, and her skin tingled with anxiety. "An assassin?"

"I've killed people, Avery. A lot of people, all over the universe. That was my duty as an *althicar*—to defend my species and keep my people safe by showing our enemies they had nowhere to hide."

Something brushed her leg. She dropped her gaze to see his tail curl around her ankle. It made her all the more aware that she was sitting in his lap wearing nothing but a long-sleeved shirt and panties, with her legs completely bare.

Hunter—*Fyran*—again wiped the moisture from her cheek, bringing her attention back up to him before he combed his fingers through her hair, grazing his claws lightly over her scalp. Avery's lips parted. The sensations he evoked were thrilling and calming. Though the latter effect, combined with the ache in her head and the heaviness in her body, made her want to simply close her eyes and let him continue until she fell asleep.

He brought his face closer to hers, and the long strands of his hair brushed her chest and the back of her hand. "You will always be safe with me, *vaerina*. I'll kill anyone who means to harm you. Just have a bit of a backlist to work through on that front."

Deep down, she'd known he was keeping part of himself from her. He was so guarded about himself, had rarely spoken of his professional life or his childhood, giving her only tiny glimpses of who he was. She'd thought perhaps he had some dark past, a criminal record that he didn't want her to know about.

But she'd never dreamed he was hiding fangs, claws, and a tail from her. She'd never imagined that he was an assassin. An *alien* assassin.

That he wasn't human.

"So you're...not from Earth?" she asked.

"No."

"Why are you here? Why are...*they* here?"

"They're either in hiding or they smelled a chance to make money. Maybe both. There are a lot of aliens on this planet. But these just happened to fuck with the wrong human." Fyran dropped his hand to her leg, grasping it just above her knee. His touch had that firm, possessive quality that drove her mad, especially paired with the fire that had reignited in his eyes. Her blood warmed, flowing down to pool between her legs. It didn't matter that he wasn't human, her body still wanted him.

"As for me," he continued, "I'm here on an assignment that I've been avoiding by identifying other aliens hidden amongst your people."

"Wait...you're a highly trained assassin sent from who-knows-where to conduct a mission on Earth, and you've just been...procrastinating?"

"Spent some time dating you. I wouldn't call that procrastinating."

Despite everything, a small smile curled her lips. "What would you call it, then? It's not like you were sent here to seduce and breed with a human woman, right?"

His eyebrows rose, and his lips parted as though to reply, but only a soft huff came out. His fingers on her leg flexed. For several seconds, he just stared at her.

Avery's smile faded, and uncertainty trickled into her chest. "*Right?*"

Fyran pressed his lips tightly together, drew in a deep breath that made his chest swell, and said, "I *was* sent here to take a human mate and breed with her."

"What?" she breathed. She'd...she'd just been joking when she'd said that. She hadn't thought... That panic she'd felt when she woke up returned, like a fist squeezing around her heart.

"Easy, *vaerina*," Fyran whispered, tipping his cheek against her forehead and stroking her leg.

"Y-you were using me? To...to..."

"No. Never." His voice rumbled into her. "Hear me when I say that, Avery. I wanted nothing to do with that mission. I did all I could to avoid it. When I met you, I didn't even realize what was happening. I fought it, but I couldn't stay away. And by the time I realized that being with you would fulfill that mission...I didn't care. So long as I had you."

Avery stared at the glowing markings around his bicep. So many questions flitted through her mind, but all she could bring herself to ask was, "Why?"

That question could've had a million answers, but he seemed to know exactly what she'd meant by it.

"Because my species has few females left. We're on the verge of extinction, and the bond we must form with our mates in order to reproduce...it can't be artificially replicated. Humans are the only race we've found that are compatible."

Her brow furrowed. "What happened?"

"A virus. It hit my people a few generations ago, disproportionately affecting the female population. Killed most of them outright, but those who remained exhibited very low fertility rates. We've only dwindled in the time since."

"And you want me to...to...have your...your baby?"

He lifted his head and again captured her chin, turning her face toward his. Those crimson eyes bored into hers. "I want *you*, Avery."

Avery's breath hitched at the vehemence in his tone and the

intensity of his gaze. The heat that had coiled between her legs bloomed within her core, filling her belly and making her pussy clench.

Fyran inhaled, and a low groan sounded in his chest. His body heat increased, his hold on her tightened, and, thanks to their current states of dress, she felt his hard cock twitch under her ass.

He closed his eyes and tipped his head forward, pressing his forehead to hers. His hair fell around her, ticking her skin and filling her senses with his scent, as he slipped his fingers into her hair. Avery lifted her hand, which still felt heavy and clumsy, and flattened it on his chest. His strong, steady heartbeat pulsed under her palm.

A shudder coursed through him, making his muscles tense around her.

There was such a small amount of cloth separating them. She wouldn't even have to take her panties off if she didn't want to. It'd be so easy to ask him to pull that scrap of fabric aside and take her right here, right now, but...

But she couldn't forget the last week so quickly. She couldn't let go of the hurt he'd caused her, couldn't forget how insignificant he'd made her feel by lifting her so high and then dropping her cold on her ass. And her mind, fuzzy from whatever she'd been drugged with, was still trying to come to terms with everything he'd told her. With the truth of what he was and what had happened to her last night. Her whole world had been turned upside down, and as crazy as it was, the thing that had her reeling the most was his reaffirmation that he wanted her as his.

And she'd only just learned his *real* name.

She just...she needed time to think. And she couldn't do that while sitting on Fyran's lap with his thick cock pressed against her, while his strong arms were around her, and his tantalizing scent was filling her senses, making her want to forget everything else and just *feel*. Making her want to tip her face up until their mouths met and she could lose herself in his kiss.

"I have to pee," Avery blurted, cheeks flushing.

Well, it wasn't a lie. Her full bladder just so happened to be the perfect excuse to get some space from him so she could think straight.

Fyran grunted and, with noticeable reluctance, drew back from her. His lips curled to flash his fangs for an instant before he shifted his hold on her, leaning back against the bed. His shoulders heaved with his deep breaths.

He remained that way for a short while, and his pulse slowly eased—though his erection didn't seem to falter in the slightest.

Finally, he reached aside, stretching his long arm to snatch something off the nightstand. Her glasses. A flick of his wrist unfolded the arms, and she reached up to take hold of them, examining them for damage. Somehow, they'd survived unscathed. She slipped them on.

When Fyran dropped his arm and unwound his tail from her ankle, Avery moved her leaden legs, expecting him to place her on the floor, but he had no such intention. He slipped that arm beneath her knees and stood up smoothly, lifting her along with him as though she weighed no more than a feather.

So why did it feel like each of her limbs was as heavy as an anvil?

He carried her into the adjoined bathroom, flicked on the light with his tail, and set her on her feet in front of the toilet. She wobbled, reaching out to catch herself by holding onto Fyran's waist, but his big, steady hands caught her hips, keeping her upright.

"You going to be okay?" he asked gently.

"Yeah. I'll...take it slow." She looked up at him. The heat in his eyes had dimmed, leaving only concern.

After a moment of scrutiny, he nodded. "We'll talk more later. I'm going to grab you something to eat and some water. Need anything else?"

You.

Avery bit down on her lip and shook her head.

"All right. I'll be back shortly." But he stood there a little longer, fingers tense on her hips as though he was afraid to release his hold on her.

The soft tuft of his tail swept along her outer calf, but she couldn't look away from his eyes. When he removed his hands from her, he did so slowly, like a man who'd just built a house of cards and was terrified it would collapse if he moved too suddenly.

Avery locked her knees and managed to remain surprisingly steady. "I'm okay."

Fyran nodded. He raised a hand, brushing his fingers across her cheek to tuck her hair behind her ear. He grazed his claws along her jaw as he withdrew his touch. "You're mine, *vaerina*. I was a fool to think I could live without you."

He turned and strode out of the room, glancing back at her just before he closed the door.

Avery counted slowly in her head once Fyran was gone, her heart beating so erratically in response to his parting words that she wondered if she might faint. When she'd reached twenty and he hadn't returned, her trembling knees gave out, and she caught herself on the toilet.

You're mine, vaerina. *I was a fool to think I could live without you.*

A shiver raced along her spine. Avery knew she shouldn't forgive him so easily for the emotional hell he'd put her through the entire week, but...she didn't know if she could stay mad at him. She didn't know if she even wanted to be mad at him. If it weren't for him, who knew where she'd be right now?

Brutal, unforgiving hands, rough skin, blood in her mouth...

Don't, Avery. Don't even think about it.

She closed her eyes and let out a long exhalation.

I'm safe.

And she knew it was true. No matter what happened, Fyran would keep her safe. Despite the secrets, despite everything he'd kept from her, she trusted him wholly.

Avery opened her eyes and looked down at her open palms. Their skin was red, but there was no sign of damage. She checked her knees and saw the same—unbroken skin, free of scabs, cuts, and scrapes. She could have sworn she'd fallen on the pavement...

Let it go.

Pushing away her questions, she moved her hands to the waistband of her panties and pushed them down, wiggling and working them lower until they were around her knees. She relieved herself, nearly groaning as the pressure on her bladder faded.

After she wiped herself clean and worked her underwear back up the same way she'd moved them down, Avery was all but exhausted. She grasped the counter and used it as support to stand. Her legs were unstable, feeling like they'd give out again at any moment. She hated this feeling of helplessness. Hated that there was some drug in her system that was sapping her strength and trying to drag her back into the abyss.

Leaning against the counter, Avery washed her hands, putting all her concentration into keeping herself upright. Once she was done, she glanced up and caught sight of her reflection. She frowned. Her freckles stood out against her pale, pale skin, and there were dark circles beneath her eyes, making them appear both a bit sunken and larger than normal. What little makeup she'd worn yesterday was gone, and her hair was a tangled mess around her shoulders.

And Fyran still wanted her.

Avery smiled. He'd seen her at her worst, and he hadn't recoiled. The fire in his eyes had been just as intense as ever, if not more so now that they weren't hidden behind a false face.

But even maintaining a small smile was too much for Avery right now. The weakness and unnatural heaviness of her limbs increased with every passing second, and she knew that she wouldn't be able to keep herself upright for much longer despite the counter supporting most of her weight.

The process of waking up had reminded her of a hangover, but this was reminiscent of the time she'd taken a muscle relaxer—just multiplied by one hundred. She hadn't touched them or anything similar ever again.

How easy would it be to just slump to the floor and go back to sleep?

Avery wasn't dumb. There was no way she was going to be

able to walk out of this bathroom, not without falling and cracking her head open on the floor.

And my head already feels like it's been split open, so I'll pass on any actual *head trauma, thank you very much.*

Clutching at the counter, she unlocked her knees and slowly lowered herself to the floor. The gray vinyl floorboards were cold against her legs and near-bare ass. She turned onto her hands and knees and crawled toward the door. Though the bathroom wasn't huge, it felt as wide as a football field, leaving her trembling by the time she arrived at the door. She wasn't sure how she managed to reach the knob and open the door, especially considering it opened into the bathroom and she had to hang onto it for support, but she sure as heck was aware when her hands slipped off the knob and she fell through the open doorway. At that point, she didn't want to move any farther. She also *couldn't.* So she lay there with her head resting atop her folded arms and her ass sticking up in the air.

Apparently, there really was a point when dignity became entirely unimportant.

That was how Fyran found her.

He called her name, coaxing her eyes open—not that she recalled having closed them. She saw him standing in the bedroom doorway, his expression a perfect mix of bewilderment and concern, with a bowl in one hand and a bottle of water in the other.

Fyran strode out of her view, placing the bowl and bottle on the nightstand before walking to her. He made no comment as he gathered her off the floor and carried her back toward the bed.

"Thought I'd take a nap," Avery said, resting her head on his shoulder. She tilted her face up, brushing his neck with the tip of her nose, and inhaled. He smelled *so* good.

"Probably more comfortable on the bed," he rumbled just before he sat her down atop said bed with her back against the headboard. Once she was out of his hold, he swept the rogue strands of her hair out of her face. "You need to eat and drink before you sleep, *vaerina.*"

Avery pursed her lips and wrinkled her nose in protest.

Fyran laughed and brushed the tip of her nose with the pad of his thumb. "You've slept for quite a while. You need sustenance, female."

She released a long, resigned sigh and glanced at the nightstand. The bowl appeared to be filled with some kind of chicken noodle soup. "I'm sure I'd make a mess of your bed if I tried eating right now."

He sat on the edge of the bed and picked up the bowl. With his other hand, he grasped the spoon, bringing a spoonful of soup toward her lips. He kept the bowl under the spoon to catch the dripping broth.

Avery stared at the spoon with a frown. "I...could just wait. I'm not hungry."

She was starving.

"Bullshit."

She flicked her gaze up at him and arched a brow. "Can't a girl keep *some* dignity? I'm not going to waste away skipping a meal."

His expression was hard, unwavering. "Firstly, the drug is still in your system, and your body needs to be at full strength to flush it out. Secondly, you've missed more than one meal. I found you just after ten o'clock last night. It's almost four in the afternoon right now. And thirdly"—he leaned his face closer to her, the red in his eyes suddenly brighter and his voice dropping into a growl— "my mate will *not* go hungry."

Unbidden warmth spread through her because of his closeness, because of the gleam in his eyes, because of his words. But those same words made her tense. She'd been unconscious for almost an entire day, and she still felt like this? She turned her face toward the clock on the nightstand. Sure enough, the glowing blue numbers said three fifty-six.

"What...what did they put in me?" she asked.

"Don't know for sure. Something to keep you easily manageable and make sure you didn't have a chance of fighting back or escaping even after you woke. It will pass, Avery."

She nodded and looked back at him. When he lifted the spoon

again, she parted her lips, allowing him to feed her. The soup was hot, but not painfully so—and it couldn't compare to the heat in his eyes as he watched her eat, spoonful after spoonful, his gaze fixated on her lips. Her self-consciousness quickly lost out to her hunger; she ate every single bite until Fyran had scraped the last drops of broth from the bottom of the bowl.

"Thank you," she said.

Fyran set the spoon in the bowl and raised his hand, resting the pads of his fingers upon her cheek. He stroked his thumb along her lower lip, wiping away the moisture left by the broth. Her tongue slipped out reflexively to lap at his thumb.

His hand froze. Eyes wide, Avery met his gaze only to find renewed heat burning in it and a slow grin spreading across his lips.

Cheeks burning, she drew her head back, breaking all contact with him. "So...what now?"

He lowered his hand, his movements slow and hesitant. "You drink some water and rest."

"I mean after."

His nostrils flared with a deep breath. "You remain here with me."

Avery lowered her brows. "I can stay until this drug wears off some more, but I need to get back home tonight."

"No."

"No? What do you mean no?"

Fyran placed the bowl atop the nightstand, picked up the water bottle, and unscrewed the cap. "I mean no. You're staying here. This is your home now."

Avery stared at him in disbelief. "I...I have work, bills, my cat —who is possibly dying of starvation right now." Beau wasn't starving; she'd filled his food dispenser yesterday morning since she knew she'd be working a double shift, but that was beside the point. "I can't just disappear and leave everything behind, Fyran."

"That's exactly what you're going to do, *vaerina*."

"You can't be serious!"

His eyebrows fell low over those predatory eyes. "I'm very

serious. You're still a target. They weren't after a human female, they were after *you*. And if they fail to deliver you to their buyer, it's going to be a blow to both their income and their reputation—not to mention they'll likely end up with a price on their heads. I've dealt with their type enough to know they won't tolerate any of that. You'll be staying with me from now on. And this is exactly where you belong, Avery. My mate should be at my side."

My mate.

He had called her that earlier, but she'd been too caught up in the revelation that she'd been unconscious for seventeen hours to understand what he'd meant by that word. This...this was all moving too fast. It'd only been a week since their last date, since she'd wanted to invite him up to her apartment, since she'd wanted him to make love to her—and she'd resisted that desire because she'd had the sense he was hiding something.

Well, she'd been right, and that something had been revealed now. It turned out she'd known nothing about the man sitting in front of her. The man she'd craved was an alien assassin.

An alien assassin who wanted her to have his *baby*.

"People usually date and get to know one another before they get married and start having babies," Avery said.

"We have come to know each other," Fyran placed his hand on her thigh, fingers curling around it. "We've dated. We've spent time together. I've met no one in the universe like you, Avery."

Her skin came alive beneath his touch, sending a thrill through her that coalesced low in her belly. She stared at his hand with its long, claw-tipped fingers. It should've frightened her. That hand was lethal, capable of shredding the flesh from bone, capable of killing, but it only inflamed her further. She willed it to slide farther up her leg, to touch her far more intimately.

Stop it, Avery! Now is not the time.

She understood what Fyran was saying. That it was too dangerous for her to go home, that whoever—or whatever—had tried to take her was still out there searching for her. She'd be safest with Fyran. But that...that didn't make them *mates*.

"We...we broke up for a week," she said, meeting his gaze,

"and I didn't even know your real name. I feel like I just met you, Fyran."

He closed his eyes, and a low groan sounded in his chest as his fingers flexed around her thigh. The end of his tail curled atop the bed. "I feel like I have waited eternity to hear you say my true name."

The flames in her core expanded in response to his groan, to the exciting prick of his claws, to the look upon his face. If he was this turned on by her saying his name, what would he look like when he was seized by pleasure? Despite everything, Avery wanted to know.

She still wanted him.

Fyran's nostrils flared with a deep inhalation, and his eyes opened, smoldering with that crimson light. "It doesn't matter if we just met, *vaerina*. You told me yourself—you are *mine*. And even now, your body recognizes it. I can smell your desire, Avery."

Avery's eyes widened. "You...you can..." She ducked her head as her cheeks grew hotter. Her hair fell forward, partially shielding her from his heated stare, but there was no escaping him or the realization that he could smell...*that*.

Had he been able to all this time?

His hand shifted higher up her leg and tensed. He released a long, slow breath and removed that hand, but not before a faint tremor coursed through it. "We'll discuss this further another time. You need to drink"—he raised the open water bottle—"and get more rest."

She was thankful that he was allowing her this respite, that he wasn't pushing her for more. At least not yet. She needed time to examine what she was feeling and thinking without this fuzziness and pain in her head, needed time to understand the enormity of Fyran's revelations and what they meant for her, to consider what her place in all this would be.

Avery reached out with both hands for the water bottle, and Fyran helped her drink. Surprisingly, she drank deep and fast, guzzling the entire bottle down. That weariness beat down on her again immediately afterward, threatening to drag her own. Even something as simple as drinking was exhausting.

"Thank you," she said as he set the empty bottle on the nightstand.

She slid her butt forward, meaning to wiggle and scoot herself down, but Fyran acted before she could move far. He slipped his arms around her, lifted her smoothly, and laid her down with her head on the pillow.

Avery smirked up at him, fighting the heaviness in her eyes. "You like manhandling me, don't you?"

With both hands, Fyran took gentle hold of her glasses and drew them off her face. He grinned, flashing his fangs at her. "I'll take any chance to have my hands all over you, Avery."

Warmth suffused Avery as her eyelids fluttered. She imagined Fyran's hands on her, roaming across her bare skin. She curled her fingers, grasping at the sheet to either side of her, as that inner heat steadily grew.

Fyran growled. Fabric rustled, and a moment later he drew the blanket over her, locking in that heat. The fabric settled on Avery with exaggerated, comforting weight, and she felt like she was sinking, like she was melting into the soft mattress, cocooned in his scent. She struggled to hold on to the images forming in her imagination, but they were soon lost in a haze.

The last thing she heard before everything faded away was Fyran's voice, barely more than a mutter.

"*Karak'duun*, this female drives me mad."

TWENTY

A sweet, spicy aroma—cinnamon, vanilla, and cloves—lured Fyran out of his slumber. His awareness emerged from the oblivion of sleep slowly, like a diver ascending from the lightless depths of the ocean. At any other time, such a gradual awakening would've been cause for concern, even for alarm. The circumstances of his childhood had trained him to wake instantly, fully alert and ready to act. That had served him well in his career as an *althicar*.

He drew in another lungful of that fragrance and hummed in appreciation. He was already surrounded by warmth—from the blanket draped over him, the small body tucked against his side, the soft, deep breaths fanning across his chest—but that scent sparked heat inside him.

He'd slept with strangers in hovels where he'd kept a weapon in hand through the night, had slept beside comrades outdoors in mud, dirt, and muck, had weathered cold nights in dank alleyways with only vermin to keep him company. But even in those brief periods during which he'd been at an *Exthurizen* base or on one of their spacecraft, when he'd had a bed, he'd never slept with his guard down in all his memory. It wasn't a luxury he'd been able to afford.

With Avery in his bed, he'd slept more deeply and soundly than ever.

He opened his eyes, blinking away the grogginess and letting them focus slowly. Avery's face was before him, angled down toward his chest—upon which rested one of her hands.

Fyran smiled. The first hints of daylight were filtering through the blinds, bathing the room in a surreal grayish glow that made his female look ethereal. Hers was a haunting beauty, the sort that would always linger with him, the sort that he could've searched for on a thousand worlds but would never have found anywhere but right here, right now.

His eyes flowed over her features, taking in the downward sweep of her dark lashes, the tousled locks of hair around her pale-skinned face, the dusting of freckles across her cheeks and nose. His gaze followed the curves of her pink lips, danced across the glinting ring that adorned her nose, dipped to her delicate chin.

He'd slept beside her. It was a dream he never would've dared consider not that long ago, something he couldn't have fathomed before Avery. To have lowered his defenses so fully and left himself so vulnerable with anyone should've been unthinkable.

But what was there to question? He trusted her. She had every reason to be furious with him, every reason to feel betrayed, every reason to attempt an escape. He'd shattered Avery's heart when he'd cut off communication with her, and he'd shattered her world with the information he'd given her yesterday.

Were she anyone else, he would've reviewed a thousand scenarios before he'd lain down for sleep last night. He would've identified all the weapons she might've used to achieve her revenge, all the different methods by which she could've enacted her escape, and he would've planned a response to each.

Yet when he'd finally succumbed to his overwhelming need to be near her last night, he'd simply climbed onto the bed and drawn her into his arms. His trust for her was complete. He had no idea what she'd done to earn it, but it was undeniable, it was instinctual.

Avery was his mate, and he trusted her more than he did anyone in the entire universe.

Why had he resisted his mission for so long? Why had he been so stubborn, so insubordinate, so foolish? To know that she'd been so close all along, that he could've found her so much sooner...

If I had been looking, I might never have found her at all.

He'd never had reason to believe in mysterious forces like fate, but his chance meeting with Avery certainly felt like it had been meant to occur.

Holding his breath, he lifted a hand to her face and, as gently as possible, trailed the pad of his finger down the bridge of her nose.

She shook her head, wriggling and scrunching her nose, before snuggling even closer to him and going still again. Something constricted in Fyran's chest, and the breath he'd held came out shakily.

Words like cute and adorable had never had much effect on him. He wasn't even sure that he'd used them—or similar words in any language—in all his life. But they applied perfectly to her, and *svesh*, it made him *feel*. It was that fire deep down in his gut, yes, and it was also that tightness in his chest. It was that sense of fullness that overcame him when she talked to him—when she said his true name. It was the cold fear that had seized him when she was in danger, and it was the fiery passion that raged through his blood whenever he thought about her.

My mate.

He wasn't sure how those two simple words could encapsulate so much, but they did. All that and so much more.

He *needed* to make that bond with her. His cock pulsed in response to that need, making him aware of what he'd somehow missed—that it had been fully erect since he'd woken up.

Karak'duun, how he wanted her. That desire permeated every inch of him, making his claws lengthen, his tail wind farther up her leg, his heart race, and his balls tight and heavy. He could almost taste her skin on his tongue, and he could still smell a hint of her arousal mixed in with her normal scent.

Fyran squeezed his eyes shut and withdrew his hand from Avery's face, pressing it down on his thigh and digging his claws in. The pricks of pain didn't ease his desire, but they gave him just enough to focus on to suppress the growl that had threatened to sound in his chest. It was just enough to prevent him from putting his hands on her in places far more intimate than her nose.

She's not ready.

Difficult as it had been to accurately gauge her state of mind while she was still suffering the effects of the mystery drug, Fyran knew that much. Avery wasn't ready to move that far so soon. All his lust, all his need, didn't mean a damned thing until she made that choice. It didn't matter how much she clearly wanted it. She'd not crossed the line.

She'd not fully accepted that she was his mate.

And while he wasn't averse to tempting her, he would not take what she wasn't ready to give. Not until she asked him to. For now, he'd have to be content with knowing it was inevitable. Avery was his; time would ensure it.

He'd just have to endure the torture of self-restraint until the inevitable came to pass.

After taking a few steadying breaths, Fyran carefully unraveled his tail from around Avery's leg and extracted himself from the bed. The fact that they hadn't been otherwise entangled made his escape easier, but he couldn't bring himself to see that as a positive; he still yearned for more closeness than they'd so far shared.

Avery moved only to nestle herself tighter in the blanket. Her breaths were slow, steady, deep, and her expression remained untroubled.

As soon as he was on his feet, Fyran pressed a hand over his cock, forcing the damned thing down. His shaft was pulsing, molten steel against his thigh, and his touch only brought it discomfort.

He inhaled again. Though he was no longer beside her,

Avery's scent struck him anew, and his cock twitched. He squeezed his hand tight around it and hissed through his teeth as seed leaked from its tip.

Self-control had never been easy for him to maintain when it came to Avery. He'd learned that lesson repeatedly over the last couple weeks, and he always seemed to forget it shortly afterward. But now, with her in his bed, self-control was almost impossible. His instincts were roaring to take her, to claim her. She was right there. Right *fucking* there…

Need something to do. Need to let her rest.

Keeping his hand firmly in place, he glanced back to ensure she was still sleeping and exited the bedroom. Perhaps if he went and worked himself to exhaustion, he'd find some of that elusive restraint.

***

AVERY WOKE WITH A STRETCH, arching her back and raising her arms above her head. It felt so dang good that she didn't want it to end. As her body relaxed, she sighed and rolled onto her belly, hugging the pillow beneath her cheek. The delicious aromas of sandalwood, fir, and leather filled her senses. A soft moan escaped her, and she turned her face, burrowing her nose deep into the pillow. It smelled like…

Hunter.

No, *Fyran.*

She gasped, her eyes snapping open as she lifted her head. Dragging her tangled hair back from her face, she looked around the big bed with its black sheets and rumpled gray blanket.

He wasn't here.

Perhaps it had been a dream, but she could have sworn he'd been right here in this bed with his arms around her, holding her as she slept.

She squinted, looking around the room. "Fyran?"

There was no answer.

Turning her head, she glanced at the clock, squinting to make out the numbers through her blurry vision—nine thirty-six. With sunlight streaming in through the blinds and curtains and brightening the room, there was no question that the night had passed. She'd just slept another seventeen freaking hours.

She dropped her face onto the pillow and groaned. So many hours gone. Thankfully, her head no longer hurt, and it seemed as though she had full use of her limbs. She was also starving—and she *really* had to pee.

But where was Fyran?

Pushing herself up, she turned and swung her legs over the side of the bed to sit on the edge. The movement—and her new position—only made her more aware of just how full her bladder was. After rubbing the grit from her eyes, she plucked up her glasses and slipped them on, bringing her surroundings into focus.

She'd been too out of it to pay much attention to this room while she'd been awake before, and to her disappointment, she hadn't missed much. The same gray vinyl flooring from the bathroom, the kind that looked like hardwood, covered the floor of this bedroom. The white walls were completely unadorned—no pictures, no paintings, no indication that the occupant of this room had a personality. The bedframe, nightstand, and dresser were black, plain, and practical, all part of the same set. Even the bed set was all grays and blacks.

It was so...simple, which seemed totally at odds with Fyran. If it said anything about him, it was that he was dull and unimaginative, and she knew that wasn't true.

Avery stood and cautiously stepped forward. When her legs didn't wobble and she wasn't overcome by a wave of weakness, she took another step, then another, and she breathed a sigh of relief as she walked into the bathroom. She shut the door behind her.

After using the toilet and washing her hands, she examined the counter and peeked in the drawers and cabinets. Perhaps some part of her had expected—maybe even hoped—to find strange alien devices hidden everywhere, or maybe clothing made from some otherworldly fabric, or something with indecipherable symbols printed on it. But everything in Fyran's bathroom appeared perfectly normal.

Okay, so maybe not *perfectly* normal. All the items in the drawers and cabinets were arranged with deliberate neatness—each item, no matter how small, had a precise place. The drawers had little dividers to keep their contents in place; the towels and washcloths in the closet were folded and stacked meticulously; even the spare rolls of toilet paper under the sink were stacked in neat rows. Everything in the medicine cabinet was spaced evenly, labels facing directly outward.

Smirking, Avery turned a few of the items in the medicine cabinet so they were just slightly askew or backward and dropped a couple floss sticks into the drawer compartment that held the replacement razor heads.

"Oops."

She didn't know if it would bother him, but she was interested to find out just how deep his need for order ran.

With that bit of mischief concluded, Avery decided it was time to tend to herself. She took out one of the spare toothbrushes from another drawer—he had half a dozen of them in various colors, all new—and removed it from the package. She scrubbed her teeth, rinsed, and scrubbed them again. Getting rid of her nasty breath was one step closer to feeling human again.

She snorted. "Human...which Fyran is not."

Staring at the shower, she debated whether or not to take to one. Other than the clothes she was wearing, all she had was her dirty work uniform to change into—and that was in her bag, which may or may not have currently been lying on a sidewalk a few blocks from her apartment building. But it had been two days since she'd last bathed. Her skin felt sticky, like she'd been sweating out whatever drug she'd been injected with, and her hair had that annoying oily feel to it.

"Shower it is," she said, pushing away from the counter. She turned the water on to let it heat up and grabbed one of the neatly folded towels from the linen closet.

Once the bathroom was warm and steamy, Avery removed her

glasses and clothes and stepped into the shower. She moaned when the hot water hit her, and for a time, she just stood there, eyes closed, letting the water drum upon her back.

She washed her hair and body, using Fyran's shampoo and soap. The spicy fragrance smelled wonderful, but it was nothing compared to Fyran's scent. Whatever pheromones that man emitted put these products to shame.

Turning off the water, she took her towel from the rack and dried herself, getting rid of as much of the moisture in her hair as possible. She wrapped the towel around her body and stepped out. It didn't take long for the air temperature to drop as the steam dissipated. The cool air teased her skin, making it pebble.

It was at that moment that her stomach growled, and she was struck by a hollow ache in her belly that made her slightly nauseous. She swallowed thickly and stood still until the feeling passed.

At the sink, she combed her hair with Fyran's comb, wincing when it caught on the tangles, and returned it to its place when she was done. She slipped her glasses on and glanced at her dirty shirt, bra, and underwear on the floor. There was no way she was putting them back on after getting clean.

Avery smirked. "Fyran did say this was my home now."

She cracked open the bathroom door and peeked out into the bedroom. It was still empty. Avery rushed to Fyran's dresser, opened the top drawer, and took out a pair of folded black boxer briefs. She caught her bottom lip between her teeth, and her body warmed as she imagined what Fyran would look like in these— and *only* these.

Or in nothing at all.

"You're only torturing yourself, Avery," she muttered as she bent, stepped into the boxer briefs, and drew them up her legs.

His socks were in the same drawer. They were neatly folded and tucked in straight rows, all the same color—black. She grabbed a pair and pulled them onto her feet. She found a pair of gray sweatpants and a plain black t-shirt in the lower drawers.

Keeping her eyes on the door, she dropped the towel onto the floor and hurriedly dressed. The sweatpants were unsurprisingly long and loose, so she rolled up the hems and cinched the waist as much as possible to keep them from falling off. As for the shirt, she simply tied it into a knot at the bottom.

Now to find her alien man and demand he feed his starving human.

Avery walked to the door and reached for the handle. She half expected to find it locked as she closed her fingers around it, but it opened without difficulty.

She poked her head out into the hallway and glanced both ways. There were no lights on, but she could see the closed doors on either side of the hall and a stairway leading down in the relative gloom. She eased the door open wider and stepped out. For a moment, she just stood there and listened. The house was so quiet it almost seemed unnatural.

Avery made her way to the stairs and followed them down, her hand gliding along the banister. Walking through this silent, still house, the home of an alien in disguise, was yet another reminder of how surreal this whole situation was.

Yesterday, she was just a waitress and an aspiring writer going about her business despite heartbreak. Today she was...was what? Roommates with an alien assassin?

Or was she his prisoner?

As she neared the bottom of the stairs, a faint, droning sound drifted up to meet her. She slowed her pace and turned her head to try to hear better. Though it was impossible to tell the song or even the genre, that sound *had* to be music. It had that muffled, far away quality to it, just like the music she'd sometimes hear in the quiet of night coming from Ian's apartment.

Avery turned at the base of the staircase to find herself in a large living room. It had the same gray flooring and white walls as his bedroom, and the furniture was also darkly colored, but there was at least a little more fullness here.

She walked over to the large wraparound couch, running her palm over the back cushions. For some reason, her first thought was of just how much Beau's shed fur would stand out against the dark microfiber upholstery. She paused there. A large flat-screen TV stood on a wide, black glass TV stand straight ahead. The black coffee table was positioned atop a large white rug that had gray patterns run through it. The couch was flanked by end tables that matched the coffee table, with a pair of remotes resting atop one of them. There was a large marble fireplace on one wall, complete with a pair of tall black vases that had dried flowers standing within them, providing little splashes of reds and purples.

There were some pictures on the walls here—a couple black and white photos of cityscapes and landscapes, a few of the generic sorts of paintings you'd find in a department store. The blinds and dark gray curtains were closed.

Avery frowned. She supposed this was better than the bedroom, but it still said nothing about Fyran. This was his house, but it wasn't a home.

She continued onward into the kitchen, which shared a space with the dining room. The music was a little louder from in here, but she still couldn't tell what it was. Like everywhere else, the room was sparsely adorned and exceptionally tidy. Lots of counter space, dark granite countertops, a big refrigerator. All this place needed was some stuff to bring it all together, to make it appear lived in.

Her gaze fell on the dining table, and her eyes widened. Her messenger bag was resting atop the table, appearing no worse for wear. Beside it was her coat, leggings, and work clothes, all clean and set in a neatly folded pile, and her boots were on the floor nearby. She hurried to her bag and opened it. The rest of her things were inside—her wallet, her keys, her notebook, her pens, all the miscellaneous junk she carried around with her for *just in case.*

The only thing missing was her cellphone.

Avery let out a long, slow breath, blowing a strand of damp hair from her face. She refused to think about how that alien had pried it from her hand as Fyran called her name through the speaker.

It's replaceable. You are not.

But damn, that was going to be a costly replacement.

Leaving her bag on the table, she wandered over to an open door on the other side of the kitchen. The laundry room was dark, but the music was undeniably louder within, if only by a teeny, tiny bit. She pressed her palm to the closed door inside the room. The wood vibrated and thumped against her hand to the sound of the music.

She smiled.

Well, I found my alien.

She pulled the door open. The big garage on the other side was lit with fluorescent bulbs, their pure white light almost intense enough to make her squint after walking through the dim house.

Fyran's car was parked near the center, its black body gleaming as though freshly polished. She wasn't sure how anyone could keep a car so clean during winter in Colorado, but it wasn't surprising after seeing the rest of Fyran's house. Along the far wall was a workbench, a huge, rolling toolbox, and a pegboard with dozens more tools neatly arranged on it.

She shifted her gaze aside, and that was when she spotted Fyran. He was at the back wall, lying on a workout bench with a barbell in his hands and his tail hanging off to one side, its tip brushing the black mat beneath him. Her eyes rounded again as she noted just how many weights were attached to that bar.

The muscles of his arms and chest flexed as he pushed the barbell up and let it back down, over and over, pumping as though it were no heavier than a pillow to him. She leaned against the doorframe and bit her lip as she watched, her eyes running over those bulging muscles and rippling abs. Heat curled low in her belly.

Her brow furrowed when she realized something strange— though the door was open, the music was no louder than before. Was it coming from outside?

Avery stepped across the threshold.

A wall of sound blasted her, pounding drums and blistering

guitars, so sudden and overwhelming that she recoiled reflexively. The instant she crossed back into the laundry room, the music receded to that far-away droning.

What. The. Heck.

Heart thumping, she eased back into the garage. As soon as she was through the doorway, the music erupted to full volume again, like someone had cranked the dial all the way up.

He's alien, Avery. What did you expect?

Shiny laser guns that go pew-pew? Fishbowl space helmets? The illudium Q-36 explosive space modulator?

She turned her gaze upward, searching for something out of place, some sci-fi gadget that could've been creating the effect, but nothing stood out. Just another white wall over a perfectly normal doorframe. Bracing her hands on the sides of that doorframe, she eased back into the laundry room, reducing the music to that distant drone as she checked that side for any weird devices.

When she stood up straight, shifting back into the garage fully, the music had stopped. Her brows furrowed. She crossed the threshold again, but there was only silence in the laundry room.

"What are you doing?" Fyran's voice shattered that silence, coming from right behind her.

Avery started, whirling around and bumping her back against the doorframe. Her wide eyes met Fyran's. He stood only a few feet away. His hair was pulled back in a messy bun, revealing his elflike pointed ears, and a sheen of sweat glistened on his tan skin. Her gaze trekked down his mouth-watering body to where his sweatpants hung low on his hips, revealing that delicious, prominent V of his Adonis belt. And there, outlined in his pants, was his cock. His long, *thick* cock.

That heat in her belly descended to pool heavily between her legs. Her pussy clenched, and her pulse quickened as whispers of desire filled her.

"I...I was... The music?" she said.

For someone who wants to be a writer, I sure have a way with words, huh?

"It was loud," he replied, calling her attention back up to his face. A knowing smirk tilted up one corner of his mouth. "Turned it off so I could hear you."

Avery's gaze shifted to one of his pointed ears. *All the better to—*

No more Big Bad Wolf references, dang it!

"How...could I not hear it out there?" She pointed to the laundry room.

His red eyes flicked past her, following her gesture. "Sound dampeners. They create a barrier that can diminish or silence any sound waves that hit it. Didn't want to disturb you while you were asleep." When he looked at her again, his gaze dipped, trailing slowly over her body. His smirk spread into a grin. "You look good in my clothes, *vaerina*."

Heat flooded her face. "I showered and didn't have any other clothes. I also used one of your toothbrushes. I...hope you don't mind."

Fyran stepped closer, eyes smoldering. His scent was even stronger now, and she knew it was *all* him. "Would've preferred to take a shower with you, but it's all right." He settled a hand on her shoulder, trailing it slowly down to her arm. "Feeling better?"

A thrill raced through her in the wake of his touch. "Yeah. I...uh, I was looking for you." Her gaze dipped again to his chest and all those muscles. "So strong..."

His hand changed direction, sliding back up to catch the damp, dangling locks of her hair between his fingers, twirling them slowly.

How did those claws make his hands even sexier?

"Yes, I am." Fyran leaned closer still, drawing in a deep breath through his nose and producing a low rumble in his chest. "And I will not hesitate to use that strength to protect what is mine." His tail brushed along her thigh, sliding higher until it reached her middle and coiled snugly around her waist.

Avery's breath hitched. There was no question as to what—or who—he considered his.

Her clit pulsed, and her nipples hardened as a needy ache

suffused her. She stared up into his eyes, into those inhuman, glowing orbs, and she understood that one more step would mean she'd be lost forever, swallowed up in his crimson stare, that she'd forsake everything just to feel his lips against hers again.

Distance, Avery. You need distance.

Swallowing thickly, Avery reached up, plucked her hair from his fingers, and dropped her hands to his tail. They fumbled for a moment as she unwound it from her waist. Once she was free, she took a stumbling step away from him.

She cleared her throat, which suddenly felt very, very dry. "I need to go back to my apartment."

"You will stay here, where you're safe." And damn him, but that lust didn't leave his eyes even though she'd withdrawn from him.

"I need my stuff, Fyran. And my cat. I will *not* leave my cat." Her hands moved of their own accord, stroking the velvety-furred thing in her hands as though seeking the same comfort she would've received from Beau.

The thing in her hand twitched. Fyran's gaze dropped. Avery's brows furrowed as she looked down, quickly realizing that it was Fyran's tail she was petting. She hurriedly released it.

Fyran lowered his tail, and Avery had no doubts that he very deliberately brushed it along her leg as he did so. He was putting off so much heat, and that delectable scent, and there were so many muscles right in front of her. It wasn't fair that he had such an effect on her! She eased farther back, crossing into the laundry room.

"It's too dangerous," he said, voice husky and raw. "You're staying."

Those words pushed away some of the desire clouding her mind. "Look, I know it's dangerous out there, and I understand what you're trying to do. And I'll agree to stay here with you, I won't even fight you about it, but you can't keep me here like a prisoner."

He stepped forward, closing that bit of distance she'd only just created, and braced his forearms on the doorframe. He bent toward her, his big, broad body filling her vision, and his nostrils flared with a deep inhalation.

"Mmm. You're not my prisoner, *vaerina*"—his eyes roved over her again, hungry, playful, leisurely—"but you are mine."

Avery's eyes widened. His cock, clearly outlined in his sweatpants, had grown into a full erection. She could see vague hints of something more along his shaft, like it wasn't quite as smooth as human's would've been.

She squeezed her thighs together. "We'll, uh, come back to that subject another time."

"Oh, we'll be *coming*. A lot."

Heat shot through her body, making her skin flush. "Oh, my God. Can we just...get my things? You can come with me—"

His grinned widened, turning absolutely wicked.

"Okay, bad choice of words." Avery left him there and walked into the kitchen. Distance. She needed distance. "I mean, I'd prefer it if you came along after what happened, and if that... man...alien is still out there..."

Though he didn't make a sound, she felt Fyran following her.

"Let me take a shower," he said, "and I'll bring you over there."

Avery stopped and turned to face Fyran, intending to thank him. But her words were cut off by a gasp as he came to an immediate halt only inches away from her, having been following her more closely than she'd imagined possible. Though his eyes still burned with that lustful fire, there was a more dangerous light in them now, something cold and unrelenting.

"One trip, in and out. If you can't carry it, it's not coming." He lifted a hand to brush his finger along her jaw, starting it just below her ear and trailing down until he took hold of her chin. "I'm not going to risk you, Avery."

A shiver ran through her. She reached up and curled her fingers around his wrist to draw his hand away, but she couldn't bring herself to.

Fortunately, her stomach saved her by producing another loud growl that shattered the brief but palpable silence between them.

Avery pulled her lips inward, trying to hold back her laughter as Fyran's brow creased and his eyes dropped to her stomach.

"I guess you better feed this human before you risk her dying of starvation," she said.

Fyran's concerned frown was almost enough to make Avery lose the struggle against her laughter.

"Will you live until we can pick something up on the way, female?"

"As long as my stomach doesn't decide to eat itself."

His eyes rounded in horror. "That's not something that can really happen, is it? I think there's more soup in the pantry." He walked past her, striding toward the cabinets with his tail flicking urgently behind him. He threw open cabinet after cabinet, many of which were empty, until he found a single can of soup.

Did he...believe her?

Avery couldn't fight it any longer; she laughed. Probably a lot harder than was warranted, but it felt good after everything that had happened.

Fyran turned to look at her, the crease between his brows deepening. He set the can on the counter and flattened his palms to either side of it. "So, it's not something that can actually happen."

"Well, I mean, it *could.*"

He narrowed his eyes on her.

She snickered. "I'll be fine waiting, Fyran."

Fyran released a huff through his nose, pressed his lips into a tight line, and shook his head. "You're going to pay for that, female."

"What, are you going to spank me?" Avery's eyes widened, and she slapped her hands over her mouth, shocked at her own words. Had she really just said that aloud?

His smirk curled back into place. He pushed away from the counter and approached her slowly, muscles rippling, that devilish gleam having returned to his eyes. Breath catching in her throat, Avery tipped her head back, held by that gaze as he drew close. Her skin tingled with anticipation.

But he just kept walking, moving right past her. She released that breath, and her body sagged.

Fyran's hand swatted her ass, making her jump in surprise not because it was painful, but because it had been so unexpected—and oh God, it felt good. How had she not seen that coming?

"I mean to give my mate everything she desires," Fyran purred, not even missing a step.

Avery faced him, rubbing her backside, and watched him retreat into the living room. At the foot the stairway, he paused, giving her another meaningful, heated look, and then he vanished upstairs.

TWENTY-ONE

FYRAN TURNED his head to look down the intersecting street as he drove past it. His gaze fell immediately on a black SUV parked across from the big brick building.

There was a strange phenomenon he'd recognized here on Earth—once you were looking for a certain make and color automobile, you tended to notice them *everywhere*. Maybe that vehicle was just one of hundreds or thousands of black SUVs in the Denver area. But maybe it was the same vehicle he'd seen Varketh drive to the warehouse.

He continued past the intersection.

"That was my street," Avery said, twisting in her seat to look back.

"Not safe to go in the front," Fyran replied, glancing in the rearview mirror. No SUV pulling out behind them; that was good, but it didn't mean they'd passed unnoticed.

As much as he'd come to appreciate this car, he had to acknowledge in hindsight that it was probably more recognizable than was ideal—and Varketh had likely seen enough of it to be able to identify its make and model.

If the bastard hadn't been holding her, I would've hit him with the fucking car.

Avery faced forward again, one of her hands fiddling with the strap of her seatbelt. "There's a back door out in the parking lot."

I know.

He'd spent a lot of time familiarizing himself with this building, though he'd never imagined that familiarity would be useful in quite this way.

"Good," he said, turning down the street after Avery's. He would've preferred to park farther away, but he wasn't keen on transporting an unknown amount of her belongings—and a live cat—across several city blocks.

Fyran parked in a spot where the apartment building was out of view and, after a quick scan of their surroundings, turned off the engine. He knew coming here wasn't a smart move, that Gregor's crew definitely knew where Avery lived, that they'd be watching even if that black SUV wasn't theirs...but he couldn't deny his mate, and he couldn't just leave her feline to die.

He'd killed without hesitation for years, but he'd never been cruel—at least not to those who didn't deserve it.

Avery unbuckled her seatbelt and reached for the doorhandle. Fyran placed his hand on her thigh, and she stopped, turning to look at him.

"Let me get out first, *vaerina*. I'll come open your door."

She offered him a smile that only hinted at her underlying nervousness and nodded. He couldn't help but be impressed by her resolve. She knew this was dangerous, she knew she was putting herself at risk, but she cared enough about this—about Beau—to accept that risk.

Hers was the true face of courage.

He gave her thigh a squeeze before unbuckling his seatbelt, opening his door, and climbing out of the car. The sky was clear today, and the late morning sun was bright. Ilventyr weren't necessarily fans of daylight, but it was only the threat of witnesses that would stop them from taking any overt actions during the day. That wasn't enough to put Fyran at ease.

He closed the door and kept his gaze moving, scanning for anyone or anything amiss as he rounded the car. Now that they were here, now that they were so close, he couldn't hold back his doubts, couldn't ignore his instincts. He'd willingly brought Avery here. He was knowingly endangering his mate.

Infiltration and extraction. You've done this more times than you can count; it's no different than any other operation.

Fyran opened the passenger door and offered Avery his free hand. She took it, and he helped her out of the car, guiding her aside so he could close the door.

Their eyes met for an instant. That was all it took for the fires deep within him to rekindle, for his chest to swell with overwhelming, tangled emotions.

This *was* different from all those other missions. The stakes were higher than ever—because Avery was involved. She was more important than anything he'd ever done, than anyone he'd ever known, and he'd never cared so much for anything as he did for her. He couldn't even fathom how much he cared. His instincts were in overdrive when it came to her; he needed to protect her, to be near her, to touch her, to smell her, to see her smile, to know she was happy, to provide for her, to mark her as his.

He'd always been able to focus in on his target, to pursue his quarry with ruthless efficiency. But those hunts always ended. There'd always been a final thrust of a blade, a final shot fired, an explosive detonated—and there'd always been another mission waiting. Another target.

Avery had become his target the moment he'd met her. He'd pursued her, he'd stalked and prowled. He'd made his moves. And now he had her. Not in every way, not yet, but she was his, and everything else would come eventually. Fyran couldn't imagine another mission, another target. He couldn't imagine dedicating himself to anything after her—to anything *but* her.

She wasn't a target, not really. She was...his obsession. His thoughts were consumed by her, his every breath was taken for her, his entire body yearned for her. And yet, obsession didn't seem the right word.

This wasn't merely a fixation. He wasn't merely intrigued or lustful, this wasn't merely a matter of wanting. He *needed* this female with every fiber of his being. She was his other half. It was frightening, but it was true. He'd go to any lengths to keep her safe, would sacrifice anything for her—and he'd do so gladly.

His gaze dipped. She was still wearing his clothes. Though they didn't necessarily flatter her tiny frame, there was just something right about it, something arousing...especially when he thought of slipping those pants off her lithe legs. She was marking his things with her scent, and that thrilled him. To be surrounded by her fragrance all the time would be a sort of bliss of which he never could've dreamed. And the mental image of Avery wearing nothing but one of his shirts...

Svesh, we're not here to rut. In and out, remember?

He clenched his jaw as he realized that *in and out* could imply something totally unrelated to going into her apartment. A dull ache blossomed low in his belly, threatening to spread into his cock. This was certainly not the time—and it wouldn't be helped by what he was about to do.

Fyran drew Avery close. She gasped, grasping his shoulders as he dropped his hands to her ass, pulled her against him, and lifted her off the ground. Her knees went to either side of his hips, opening her to him. Even with clothes on, he couldn't ignore how soft and warm she felt, how perfectly she fit against him.

His claws could make short work of the fabric separating them...

Avery breathed, "Fyran, what are you—"

He cradled the back of her head with his hand, guided it onto his shoulder, and activated his cloaking field. That faint tingling sensation raced across his skin, enveloping him. The field expanded, covering Avery, reducing her to a vague outline he could see only through the neural transmitter.

Avery shivered. "W-what's happening?"

"Hold on to me, *vaerina*," he rumbled. "Nice and tight."

Body tense, she slipped her arms behind his neck and locked her legs around his waist. "I can't see myself. Can't see you. What is this?"

He smoothed down her hair, and the fingers of the hand still on her ass flexed. This was new for her; he had to keep that in mind. He had to cast aside the effects of her closeness, her heat, her scent. All he had to do was get into the building. He could last that long, right?

"A cloaking field," he said softly. "It's designed to expand so it can hide objects I'm holding, but it can only stretch so far. I want you to cling to me tight as you can until I set you down, all right?"

"Okay." She tightened her hold, pressing her body more firmly against his, squeezing her thighs around his hips and digging her heels into the backs of his thighs.

Again, the thought flitted through his mind—his claws could shred the barrier between them so he could push her up against his car and rut her right here, hidden from prying eyes.

Fuck.

Fyran forced his legs into motion, tension rippling through his body as his strides jostled her just enough to make her sex bounce against his erection. Her breath hitched, and her fingers dug into his back. Despite the clothing separating them, that friction was intense and torturous. Why hadn't he just lifted her a little higher? Why wasn't he making the adjustment now?

He already knew the answer—he couldn't. Though barely noticeable through the ache of his desire, the little whispers of pleasure caused by that friction were too thrilling to give up.

He walked along the street, scanning his surroundings constantly despite his powerful urge to look down. When they reached the entrance to the apartment building's parking lot, he turned into it, slowing his pace to follow the already existing tracks through the snow.

The reduced speed didn't ease the friction between their bodies.

Just need to get inside...

The door, unsurprisingly, was unlocked. Fyran had to open it wide to fit through with Avery clinging to him like this, and he had to turn sideways to avoid bumping into the doorframe with his arms and shoulders. He closed the door quietly behind him.

This was the time to set her down, to break this contact before it drove him wild. They were alone, unseen, and it was quiet. But instead, Fyran found himself holding her tighter, closer, as he strode down the hallway. He took the stairs quickly, ignoring their creaks and groans beneath his boots.

How could he be concerned with the sounds when every step he took bounced Avery upon him, creating more friction, more pressure in him? How could he care about anything while her breath was quickening, while her scent was being colored by her growing arousal, when her blunt little nails were clawing at his back?

Much too soon—and quite fortunately—they were in the third-floor hallway, standing in front of apartment eleven. Fyran kept his breathing deep and even, but his control was tenuous. Rutting her against the wall was as good as doing it against his car, wasn't it?

Not here, not now, not like this! My mate deserves better.

He grasped her thigh, trying not to feel anything as he slid his trembling hand to the back of her knee. That she resisted as he guided her leg down did not help; she wanted him just as much as he wanted her, he could smell it, he could feel it in the heat emanating from her core.

Fyran forced himself to pry her other leg off, combating his hesitance by abruptly dropping the cloaking field. She slid down his body but did not remove her arms from around his neck until he reached back and separated them. Her soft breasts were pressed to his chest.

Avery swayed as he stepped back from her. She wore a dazed expression, eyes half-lidded and lips parted. A pink flush colored her cheeks, and a smoldering light burned in her eyes.

If he looked at her for another moment, his resistance would end.

Fyran turned his full attention to the door, pretending that his body wasn't thrumming and throbbing with need as he pulled Avery's keys out of his pocket.

Focus, althicar. *You're stepping into an unknown situation.*

He drew his human-made pistol from its hidden holster, switched off the safety, and slid the key into the keyhole. In his peripheral vision, Avery blinked as though emerging from a daze, turning her head to watch him with curious expression.

Fyran unlocked the door and opened it, weapon at the ready.

He opened the door wider, sweeping his gaze across his expanding line of sight. The living room was clear. A drawn-out half-yawn, half-meow came from the couch. A moment later, Beau hopped onto the floor, extended his front legs, and dipped with his ass in the air as he stretched.

Taking the pistol in both hands, Fyran advanced into the small apartment, quickly checking every room—kitchen, bedroom, bathroom. There was neither visual nor olfactory sign that anyone else had been here.

Avery was standing in the entrance doorway as he emerged from the bathroom, staring at him. A crease had formed between her eyebrows, deep and troubled, and her pink lips were downturned.

Fyran strode over to her, took hold of her arm, and pulled her into the apartment, closing and locking the door once she was inside. For a moment, he stood facing the door, hand flattened on its surface and head bowed. They were away from prying eyes again. They were alone. And she smelled so fucking good...

"All right, let's get your things," he said as he returned the pistol to its holster, unable to keep some of the strain from his voice. He turned to face her only to find her still staring at him, her confusion now bordering on suspicion. "What's wrong, Avery?"

"How did you know which apartment was mine?"

Fuck.

He gritted his teeth and released a huff through his nostrils. He'd messed up, plain and simple. Of course she wouldn't question that he knew of where her building was—she'd had him drop her off here after their date. But she'd never given him her apartment number.

They didn't have time for the truth right now, but he couldn't keep anything more from her.

This would've been so much easier if I'd been able to confess on my own terms.

Aggaan sin thar, you could've done that any time, Fyran.

Fyran ran a hand through his hair, tugging the strands back hard. "I, uh...might've followed you home a couple times."

Her eyes flared. "You... You followed me? A couple times?"

Beau brushed his body against Avery's leg, but she ignored him, keeping her eyes on Fyran.

"Well, couple might not be the right word," he said.

"What do you mean?"

"Over the last few weeks, I've followed you home"—he drew in a sharp breath through his teeth as he performed the mental tally—"thirteen times."

"I... You... Wait, why did you specify *home?*"

"Because I've followed you other places, too. Mostly just when you went to work. And for the sake of honesty, Avery...I've been in here a couple times, too."

"*What?* You were in here, in my apartment? When were you —" Her eyes widened further. "The cloaking field. Oh, my God. You *were* here after our date that night. You were here when I...when I..."

"I had to see you again," he growled. "I couldn't stay away. And when you started touching yourself..."

Karak'duun, just recalling that night was making him hard, and he didn't think sporting an erection right now was going to calm the situation. But his cock didn't care much for thinking, did it?

"I saw you! I saw you, I even smelled you, and I told myself it was all my imagination, but you were here." She glared at him, her blue-gray eyes flashing with anger. "You...you *watched* me! Do you know how wrong that is?"

Fyran scratched his cheek. He knew the next words to come out of his mouth would not help anything, but he couldn't stop them. "If it makes you feel better, you can watch me later."

Avery gaped at him, but Fyran didn't miss the blush coloring her cheeks. She threw hands up. "I can't believe you. You want a...a...a mate, yet you break my trust like this? Invade my privacy? You...watch me doing...that..."

She turned and walked away from him, eyebrows falling as she crossed her arms over her chest. Her voice was softer, filled with hurt, when she looked at him and asked, "Did you follow me to the café that morning, too?"

If there was anything he could've said to ease the unmasked pain in her voice, he would've said it. But Fyran didn't know any words that could soothe her now, didn't know enough about the boundaries he'd crossed. He'd been involved in work like this—following people, surveilling them, learning their daily routines and inner lives—for almost as long as he could remember. All he had to offer her was the truth.

"Yes. Because I wasn't content with just...following you. I wanted more. I wanted to speak to you. To hear you laugh, to see your smile and know it was for *me*." He strode over to her, caught her chin between his fingers, and tilted her face up toward his. "I wanted *you, vaerina*. All of you. And I will never stop wanting you."

Her eyes glistened with gathering tears; it was like a knife through Fyran's heart.

"*Vaerina?* Was that whole story a lie, too?"

The rawness in her voice was nearly his undoing; it threatened to steal his breath, to stop his heart, to crush him beneath its immense weight.

"No," he rasped, throat suddenly dry. "That was the truth. The other things about my life were a cover, made up to make me seem like a real human, but the flowers... Those were real. I was born in a huge city, surrounded by dozens of different species, and my parents disappeared when I was very young. Looking at those flowers...that was the only good thing I had in my life for a long time, Avery. Everything else was struggle and shit, but it was okay because I'd get to see those sometimes, and they'd get me through.

"And you...you mean so much fucking more to me than those

flowers ever could." He stroked his thumb over the hollow of her chin, just beneath her lip. "I can tell you more about my past, tell you everything I remember, anything you want to know, but now is not the time, and this is not the place. Get your things, and we'll talk later."

Avery jerked her chin out of his grasp and took a step back. She tucked her hair behind her ear as she looked away from him. "No."

Fyran curled the fingers of his now empty hand into a lose fist, dropping it to his side. "No?"

"I'm not going back with you."

He clenched his jaw. He'd brought her into this situation knowing the danger, and now she was trying to prolong her exposure to that danger?

"Avery, it's dangerous for us to stay here even a few minutes longer than necessary. The building is being watched, and half the tenants probably heard when you raised your voice. We need to grab what we came for and get out of here."

"You can leave, but I'm not going with you. I'll just...stay at a hotel and call the cops."

"Like hell you will, female," he growled, stepping toward her again. She retreated from him until her back was against the wall, where he caged in her with his arms, leaning down.

Grunting, she pushed against his chest with all her strength. "Leave me alone, you...you...peeping Tom!"

"I don't know who the fuck Tom is, but if he takes a single look at you, I will kill him," Fyran snarled.

"You're Tom! Because you're a voyeuristic jerk!"

"My name is Fyran Voltanix"—his fingers curled, claws digging into the drywall—"and you are my *mate*. The police aren't going to fucking save you from an alien trafficking ring, a hotel is not going to shield you from the people that are after you, and you are not going anywhere without *me*. I am the only one on this whole fucking world, in this whole fucking universe, who will keep you safe, and that is what I am damned well going to do whether you want it or not."

He ducked down and wrapped his arms around her, lifting her over his shoulder. He was only distantly aware of her hitting his back, of her legs swinging, of her angry shrieks; he was too focused on what needed to happen. He was too focused on saving her, even if he had to do so despite her efforts.

Fyran carried her into her bedroom, heat roiling through his body—the worst of it in his belly. He paused at the foot of her bed, staring down at it. Still unmade, likely from when she'd woken two days ago, still saturated with her scent—with her truest scent.

A growl tore out of him as so much of that heat flowed to his cock, making it instantly hard. He could toss her on that bed, tear off his pants—both the ones he was wearing and the ones she had on—and bury himself inside her within a couple seconds. He could feel her all around him, could taste her essence directly, could lose himself as their bodies moved together in a tangle of limbs and passion.

And even in her anger, he sensed that she wouldn't put up much resistance to it. That she still wanted him even now.

But he would not take her. Not yet. Not while the pain he'd caused her was so raw, not while the invisible wounds he'd inflicted were so fresh. He wanted all of her—and that included her trust. Even if he'd not had a second thought about coming into her apartment without her knowledge or watching her as she touched herself, he knew that he had a long way to go to regain her trust after this.

He bent forward, muscles tensing as he sat her on the edge of the bed as gently as he could manage while she was struggling against his hold. He stepped back, turned away from her furious glare, and walked to her closet, his stride stiff. Tugging open the door, he looked inside. What he sought was in plain sight, on a shelf above the hanging clothing. He pulled down the suitcase and dropped it onto the bed beside her.

"Pack your things, female," he commanded.

Avery bared her teeth at him and growled.

The sound flowed straight to his cock; he barely suppressed a groan. His tail twitched within his pants. "Growl at me all you want later. I'll fucking welcome it."

She leapt off the bed, grabbed the suitcase, and yanked the zipper open. "Fine! But you can forget all about me being your mate and the...the *coming*!"

"Oh, we'll fucking see about that," he said with a humorless laugh. "You're mine, *vaerina*, and you'll be begging for it before I'm through."

He walked out of the bedroom, leaving her to her work, and dropped a hand to his shaft the moment he'd crossed the threshold. He squeezed, tilted his head back, and hissed.

Karak'duun, how the hell had he managed to hold himself back for this long? Even when she was furious with him, he found her captivating—maybe even more so, with that fire in her gaze.

When he opened his eyes and lowered his chin, he found himself with an audience.

Beau was sitting on the floor a few feet in front of Fyran, staring with slitted, slightly narrowed eyes. The animal's furry tail flopped from one side to the other, coming to rest on the floor.

Seconds passed. Hangers rattled in the bedroom, clothing rustled, and Avery muttered under her breath, using the sorts of words Fyran had never heard from her mouth before, and the faloran and the feline simply stared at one another.

Though Beau's expression did not change, it seemed to grow increasingly judgmental. Fyran's brows fell low.

"You could've fucking told her I was here, too," Fyran grumbled, "but you chose to lick your own asshole instead. So who's really at fault here?"

The cat blinked.

"*Svesh*." Fyran ran a hand through his hair, scraping his scalp with the tips of his claws. "You're right. Still me."

TWENTY-TWO

In his time on Earth, Fyran had done a lot of driving. His time behind the wheel had been mostly mundane and uneventful, but he'd experienced his share of tense drives, frustrating drives, and relaxing drives. He'd had a few thrilling drives, and a couple recently that had been frantic and panicked.

But this drive... He wasn't sure how to categorize it. Uneasy? Uncomfortable? Soul-crushing? He was more restless than he'd ever been, even during rush hour traffic or while stuck behind a slow-moving vehicle, and it had nothing to do with impatience.

The tip of his tail curled against the side of his leg. One of his hands twitched on the steering wheel, while the fingers of the other drummed the shifter. There was a persistent hollowness in his stomach, but it wasn't hunger—it was closer to nausea, though even that wasn't quite right.

He glanced at Avery from the corner of his eye. She sat with the plastic cat crate on her lap, and her head was still turned away from him. She'd changed out of his clothes while she'd been packing at her apartment, and now wore a pair of skinny jeans and a sweater.

He didn't understand why seeing Avery in her own clothing

bothered him so much. She looked as amazing as ever, but it felt like a rejection—especially considering that when she'd first emerged from her bedroom after she'd changed, she'd thrown his wadded-up clothes in his face.

Fyran hadn't been certain, but he'd guessed that she wasn't going to just get over their argument.

He clenched his jaw, brows falling low, and let out a heavy breath.

"Talking to me won't kill you, female," he said.

Avery angled herself more toward the window, leaning so close to it that her head was nearly touching the glass.

Fyran's uneasy restlessness, his sick feeling, only intensified.

Fyran swallowed thickly, forcing his attention forward. "I don't know what this is, but whatever you're doing, Avery, you need to stop."

Seconds passed, each one like a blade slowly sinking into Fyran's back, and the only sound was the continued rumbling of the car's engine. Fyran tightened his grip on the steering wheel to support his weight while he lifted his backside off the seat and adjusted his position. The change offered no relief. His tail felt confined; it always felt that way when it was hidden, but this was somehow worse than usual.

His gaze flicked between the road ahead and the dashboard clock repeatedly. They'd be back at his dwelling within ten minutes, and maybe then they'd restore some semblance of normalcy in their relationship. He just had to make it through the rest of the trip.

An eternity passed. Universes were born, expanded, and contracted, collapsing upon themselves and vanishing from existence.

The minute number on the clock ticked up by one.

"Damn it, Avery, talk to me!"

Beau made a sad, tortured yowl—as though he were tired of hearing Fyran's voice.

Fyran turned his head toward his female as she finally looked away from the window. She bent over the cat carrier, slipped a finger through one of the holes, and whispered, "Shh. It's okay, Beau. You're doing fine."

Those were the first words she'd spoken since leaving her apartment, and she'd spoken them to her *cat*.

I am not jealous of that animal right now.

Fyran's teeth ground together, and his jaw muscles bulged. He didn't realize how much more strength he was putting into his grip on the steering wheel until he heard that now familiar creaking of leather.

How had the day taken such a drastic turn? Only a couple hours ago, he'd been flirting with Avery, getting them both worked up and hungry for one another. Now she refused to even acknowledge his existence.

"I wasn't going to say anything, but I won't sit here and listen to you comfort that cat while you make me suffer. He knew I was in your apartment both times. So *he* betrayed you, too. Maybe some of your anger's misplaced, isn't it?"

Avery paused, turned her head, and shot Fyran a glare before returning her attention to Beau. "You'd never betray me, huh, Beau? You're just a big ole softy. You're the cutest little kitty, aren't you? And there's no way I could be mad at you, because you're not a grown-ass man who has the ability to recognize the difference between right and wrong and act accordingly."

Fyran growled. "Yeah, well, he also licks his own asshole."

"But that's okay, Beau, because you're a *kitty*, and you don't pretend to be anything else, do you?" She leaned closer to the cage as the cat pressed his face to one of the holes, rubbing her nose against his. "I'd rather have you lick your asshole than be an asshole."

In case her meaning hadn't been clear, she shot Fyran another brief glare.

Karak-fucking-duun.

Althicar down. Need immediate extraction.

Beau meowed. His fur stuck out through several of the little openings on the cat carrier, making it look like he were about to burst out of it.

"You're doing so good, Beau," Avery said. She turned her face back toward the window.

"Well, fuck me I guess," Fyran grumbled.

Avery snorted dismissively.

"That's a direct response." Fyran lifted his right hand off the shifter, wagging a finger in the air. "That counts as a response, so you might as well start talking to me now."

She responded to him again—with stone cold silence.

That silence expanded, growing thicker and heavier with each passing moment, with each passing mile, until Fyran swore it was pressing against his skin and making his throat tight. He didn't like this. Didn't like how it made him feel, didn't like how it was making him act.

He'd conducted missions during which he'd been alone for weeks, missions during which he'd not spoken a single word or had anything said to him. It had never bothered him. Fyran and Avery had shared companionable quiet before, had found comfort and warmth in simply being near one another. But this silence...

To have her so close he could touch her by shifting his hand only a few inches aside, to have her scent filling the car and teasing his nose, to have her here and yet to feel like she was so damned far away was a torture unlike any he could've devised. This was worse than the ache that so often pulsed in his groin, worse than the torment of his unfulfilled desires.

And all she was doing was not talking to him. How could something so simple be so effective?

He glanced at her again; her position remained unchanged.

Fyran ran his tongue over his teeth. All he wanted to do was slip his fingers into her hair, cup the back of her head, drag her close to eliminate this damned gap between them, and kiss her.

Would that help anything? It seemed unlikely to improve her mood, but he couldn't know. He'd never dealt with an angry female. Fyran had been recruited as an *althicar* for his combat abilities, not because he was some masterful negotiator or diplomat. His solution to most of the problems he'd faced in life had been violence.

And that wasn't even up for consideration. He'd *never* do anything to hurt his mate.

He was certain of only one thing—though revealing the truth had created the current dynamic in their relationship, it remained the only way he could gain her trust.

But that didn't mean he wasn't irritated that she'd spoken to her cat instead of him.

Fyran tried to focus on the task at hand instead of the thoughts and emotions tumbling through his head as he drove the rest of the way. Regardless of Avery's attitude toward him, his current objective was unchanged—get her back to his dwelling where she would be safe.

She could be angry with him all she wanted so long as she was somewhere he could protect her. That'd be one less worry, at least. Then he could work on softening his female toward him again and getting her in his bed.

When he pulled the car into the garage, Avery had her door open almost before the vehicle was fully stopped. She unbuckled her seatbelt, grasped the handle on the top of the cat carrier, and reached down blindly to pluck her laptop case off the floor.

She didn't so much as glance at Fyran as she climbed out of the car.

He turned off the engine, popped the trunk, and exited the vehicle, walking around the back to grab her bulging suitcase. He reactivated the garage's security field as he proceeded into the house. She was already at the top of the stairs by the time he reached them, gently hushing her yowling cat.

Fyran took the steps three at a time, devouring the distance between himself and his mate. He caught up to her just as she stepped into his bedroom.

"Avery."

She turned toward him, met his gaze with narrowed eyes and pursed lips, and closed the door in his face.

A second later, the lock clicked.

Fyran scowled, brow furrowing. "Avery, open the door."

The only sound that came from the other side was the faint squeak of the cat carrier's latch being released.

Fyran clenched the handle of her suitcase, claws extending to dig into his palm. *Svesh*, his palms were going to be covered in fucking scars at this rate. He tried—with limited success—to keep his voice calm and even as he said, "You can't lock me out of my own room, Avery."

Her continued silence conveyed her message clearly enough —*I just did.*

He growled through his teeth, squeezing his fist even tighter. The lock would've been simple to pick from this side. Not that the door would've stood up to even a single blow from his boot, but...

Just give her time. She can't keep this up forever.

As confident as he was that they'd work through this, he couldn't ignore the sting of her purposely putting this barrier between them.

For most of his stay on Earth, he'd felt lost, directionless, purposeless. His bitterness over this assignment had threatened to consume him time and again, and he'd found few outlets for his frustration. That had been his daily life for more than a year. That had been his life until Avery changed everything.

This rift torn open between them felt worse than any of that. He hadn't wanted a mate when he'd first come to Earth. He'd ignored his orders in protest, had pursued leads on totally unrelated matters despite admonishment from Command, had done everything he could but search for a female to make his own. But now that he'd found his female, he couldn't imagine life without her.

Body stiff, he set down her suitcase in front of the door. It took a considerable amount of effort to open his hand and release the handle. For a time, he simply stood there, breathing as deeply and evenly as he could while listening for any evidence of movement from the bedroom.

"Your suitcase is here," he said. "I'll be downstairs if you need anything."

He shifted his weight, meaning to walk away, but his feet refused to move. He only realized then that he'd been holding his breath to ensure he'd hear if she responded.

But there was nothing.

Fyran huffed, turned away from the door, strode downstairs. There were still a few things in the car, including Beau's food and litter box. Bringing them in and getting them set up would occupy him for a few minutes, and that was a hell of a lot better than standing in front of the closed bedroom door.

And what the fuck am I going to do when that's done?

The answer was a simple as it was daunting.

Figure out a way to fix this.

***

Avery sat on Fyran's bed with Beau cradled in her arms, absently scratching the cat behind his ears and staring at the door as Fyran's footsteps receded. She'd half expected Fyran to break the door down, storm into the room, and demand she speak to him. More than once, she'd been tempted to respond to him—to curse at him, to rage at him, to...to...

To what?

She was angry, and rightfully so. Tears burned her eyes. Beau meowed and wiggled, ducking his head in his attempt to escape. Avery opened her arms and released him.

Beau leapt onto the floor and began to explore the room, pausing to cautiously sniff at every object he encountered.

Had everything with Fyran been a ploy? Had their first meeting at Jerry's been a chance occurrence, or had he planned it? How long had he been following her, stalking her, spying on her? How much did he already know about her?

The deceit hurt Avery's heart. Her tears, which she'd been holding back since they'd left her apartment, spilled down her cheeks. She wiped them away with the back of her hand. She felt like a fool. He was an alien who'd come to Earth to impregnant a human. *She* was his mission. There she'd been, thinking their first date must've been fate only to discover that he'd orchestrated the whole thing.

Now...she didn't know what to believe or how to feel. She was angry, hurt, and confused, but she had to believe Fyran felt more for her, that it went beyond his duty. Everything they'd done together, everything she'd experienced—every look, every touch, every kiss—had all felt so real.

I wasn't content with just...following you. I wanted more. I wanted to speak to you. To hear you laugh, to see your smile and know it was for me. I wanted you, vaerina. All of you. And I will never stop wanting you.

Those words... She had to mean more to him than a mission to accomplish, right? How else could he have echoed her feelings so perfectly? She missed him when they were apart, longed to see him, to hear his voice, to feel his touch. And though she'd held back, she'd yearned for more with him—more time, more connection, more intimacy.

Fyran sneaking into her apartment and watching her had been wrong. It was a violation, it was criminal.

And yet now that she was over her initial shock and anger... she was aroused by the idea. It turned her on to know Fyran had been so desperate to see her, that he'd watched as she touched herself, that he'd seen her utterly vulnerable, her inhibitions forgotten.

Avery pressed her hands to her cheeks, which had warmed at the memory of what she'd done. She had cried out his name, and he'd been there to hear it, an unseen audience to her pleasure, to her release.

But she had *seen* him. She'd thought he was a figment of her imagination, a red-eyed vision, a vampire visiting her in the night that had been inspired by one of the many romance novels she'd read, but it had been him.

What he'd done was wrong—so, so wrong— but dang it...she *liked* it. There was something thrilling about being watched, about being the object of someone's obsession—of being *Fyran's* obsession. Even now, despite everything, her body warmed and her core clenched. What had Fyran thought as her body had shuddered in pleasure, as she'd called his name?

Beau jumped up onto the bed and stretched, extending his claws and snagging them on the comforter.

"No, Beau," Avery said as she freed his claws.

He flopped over, exposing his belly, and purred. She smiled and gently brushed her fingers over his stomach.

"Just because it turns me on doesn't mean he gets off easy after everything he's done. It was still wrong of him. I'm just... God, I'm so confused. There are too many unknowns, too many secrets, Beau." She frowned and withdrew her hand from the cat. "I don't know what to think or do."

Beau turned his head to look at her and meowed.

Avery narrowed her eyes. "So, did you know Fyran was there?"

He simply blinked at her.

She snorted. "Some guard kitty you are."

Apparently, Beau wasn't going to accept her criticism if she wasn't petting him; he stood up and jumped down to the floor again, rubbing his face against the corner of the bed.

With a sigh, Avery slipped off the bed and walked to the door. She unlocked it and quietly eased it open. The hallway was empty save for her suitcase, which stood in front of her, but she did hear faint sounds coming from downstairs.

She crouched, grabbed her suitcase, and rolled it into the bedroom before closing and relocking the door. She didn't know what to do with her clothes, didn't know if he'd want her to stay in this room after all this—or if *she* wanted to stay in here—so she set the suitcase next to his dresser.

Returning to the bed, she crawled onto it, lay on her stomach, and dragged her laptop case closer. After removing the laptop from the bag, she flipped open the lid. The screen came to life. Out of curiosity, she clicked on the network connections. There were only two wi-fi networks in range. The first was a secured network with a name that made her eyes round. *FuckYourMission.*

Well, that's obviously Fyran's.

But she didn't have much time to dwell on Fyran's interesting choice in network name, as her eyes fell upon the second network.

Avery's Phone.

Her brow furrowed. She had her hotspot set up for instances when she was away from home and wanted to get some writing or research in—the wi-fi at Jerry's wasn't exactly fast or reliable—but it would only have come up if she was within range of her phone.

Maybe the list just needed to be refreshed? She clicked on the *Avery's Phone*, expecting the computer to tell her there was no connection available—but, to her surprise, it connected.

"That...that...*asshole!*"

Her phone was here, and he hadn't returned it to her. Why? What else was he keeping from her?

Stewing, she opened the document for her work-in-progress novel. Perhaps some writing would keep her occupied for a little while.

She could introduce a new character named Hunter and have him killed off in a car accident—or in a duel with Trevor. Never mind that her book was set in the modern day...

But as the minutes passed, Avery found she was too distracted to do any meaningful work—by thoughts of Fyran. She hadn't even managed a single complete sentence before she closed the file in frustration.

"All right," she muttered. "Maybe some mindless social media instead?"

She opened the web browser and was scrolling through local news when her eyes caught on the headline *Missing Denver Women.* Everything within Avery went cold. Her palms became clammy, and her pulse raced. She clicked on the link.

The article cited nine different missing persons cases from the Denver area over the last year, none of which were considered related by the authorities, but the author seemed unconvinced of that. The oldest of the women had been twenty-five, the youngest just days shy of her nineteenth birthday. All nine were believed to have disappeared at night—and five had left work after their shifts only to never be seen or heard from again.

There was no real, concrete evidence tying the cases together, and the author made it clear that this was all merely speculation, but Avery's heart only quickened further as she continued reading.

Most of the women had been transplants from out of state. All of them either had no family in the Denver area or were estranged from local family members, and all of them had small lists of acquaintances and friends for the police to interview. The author speculated that these women had been targeted because they were people who would've fallen through the cracks; one of the women was believed to have been missing for over a month before a missing persons report had been filed by her employer.

That could have been me. I could have been one of those missing women.

Avery's fear from that night returned. Her throat constricted, and her breath grew heavy. She touched the spot on her neck where she'd been injected.

Fyran had been the only reason she'd escaped. He was the only reason that she wasn't one of the names on this list, that she hadn't been taken who knows where, hadn't suffered whatever horrors had awaited her. He'd saved her, and he was continuing to protect her.

As though sensing her need for comfort, Beau nudged her shoulder with his head and rubbed his body against her. She wrapped her arm around him, rolled onto her side, and drew him close.

When Avery had left California, all she'd wanted was to create a life for herself—a fulfilling, simple life, away from the drama, the judgment, the superficiality. And for a while, she'd had what she wanted, or at least a taste of it.

Then she'd become the apparent target of an alien kidnapper and the object of an alien assassin's lustful fixation, leaving her... adrift. What could her future hold now? How could she ever look at the world the same way?

All she knew was that, despite everything that had happened, despite everything Fyran had kept from her, she could no longer imagine her future without him in it.

But she could still be mad at him.

For a little longer, at least.

TWENTY-THREE

Avery was just beginning to doze off after a couple hours of aimless scrolling and failed attempts at writing when a knock on the door startled her. She groaned, grabbed the pillow, and buried her face in it.

"Go away," she grumbled. She inhaled deeply, and barely held in a moan as the potent scents of sandalwood, fir, and everything male—everything Fyran—flooded her nose.

Ugh, why does his pillow have to smell so good?

Fyran growled.

And why does he have to sound so sexy when I'm still supposed to be mad at him?

"This is *my* house, female, and that's *my* bedroom."

Avery shifted the pillow, turned her head, and glared at the door. "Oh, and here I was thinking I was your mate and that this was my home now, too. Guess you better take me back to *my* apartment."

"You are my mate, damn it, and this is your home," he said, and Avery could just imagine him raking his hand through his hair in frustration. "Enough of...of *this, vaerina.* Open the door."

"No."

Something scraped against the other side of the door. His claws?

"I prepared food for you. A gourmet meal. Come and eat with me, Avery."

"I'm not hungry, and I'm still mad at you." At least one of those statements was a lie.

"You haven't had anything since this morning. You can be mad at me while you eat, just open the door and come downstairs." There was a pause. "Please."

Avery's lips twitched into a smile. She couldn't help but compare this to the scene from *Beauty and the Beast* when Belle refused to join the Beast for dinner. Still, Avery wasn't ready to face Fyran. Her emotions were a tangled mess she hadn't yet unraveled.

She could almost understand Fyran's position, could almost understand that in his eyes, he'd done nothing wrong. The deception, the stalking, breaking into her apartment, it was all normal for the life he'd lived.

Though she was pretty damn sure watching his targets masturbate wasn't part of his job.

But even were she to reach that understanding, it wouldn't invalidate the damage done to her trust in him. He'd kept so many things from her.

She couldn't let herself trust him again until she knew the truth of his heart. Was she just a target for him, a means of completing a mission he resented, or were his feelings for her genuine? Did he desire her beyond the obsession he'd developed?

Avery hated to admit it, but she was weak when it came to Fyran. He had a way of clouding her judgment, of consuming her thoughts, of making her want to do nothing but sigh dreamily and stare at his ass. Or his chest, his shoulders, his face, his hands, his arms and legs and hypnotic crimson eyes...

Ugh. Everything about him, every darned part of him, was tantalizing, sexy, seductive. And now that she'd seen the *real* him...those alien attributes had only amplified his appeal.

Avery flopped onto her back. Beau flinched next to her, but he recovered smoothly, lifting his head and stretching his front legs. He spread those adorable little pink toe beans and yawned.

"Avery?" Another pause. "I searched the internet. I will not tolerate this *silent treatment* any longer."

She grinned. She could picture him frowning over a computer, typing *why won't my female speak to me* into a search bar with the tips of his claws.

"I was just speaking to you," she said, running her fingers through Beau's fur. "So this is obviously no longer the silent treatment. But I can get back to it now, if you want."

"No," he replied quickly. "Just come out. Come eat. The food will get cold."

"I'm fine where I'm at in *your* bed."

He growled again, but this time it was far deeper and more bestial. "Open the door."

"No."

The silence from the other side of the door was deafening. She knew he was still there, she could feel him there, but she felt something else, too. Something...powerful.

The door burst open with a bang, spraying several splintered bits of wood and slamming into the wall. Hackles rising, Beau yowled and scrabbled off the bed, disappearing from sight. Avery sat up with a gasp.

Fyran stormed into the bedroom, his tail whipping behind him, and locked his blazing red eyes on Avery. "Done asking."

She crawled back on the bed, a hint of fear sparking within her. Had she pushed him too far? "Fyran..."

He caught her by her ankle and dragged her toward him.

She fought to find purchase with her hands, but all she managed to do was to pull the blanket along with her. "I'm not hungry!"

"But I am," he snarled, baring his fangs. His hands moved faster than she could react to, one hooking behind her knee and the other snaking under her back.

Avery squeaked as he scooped her off the bed and tossed her over his shoulder, trapping her in place with one arm banded around her thighs. Her hair fell around her face, obscuring her view of everything but his ass below her. She caught her glasses before they could fall, holding them in place with one hand while she pressed the other to his back.

Fyran turned and strode toward the door. "Been hungry for you since I first saw you."

Avery clutched his shirt and grunted as his shoulder dug into her belly. "Dang it, Fyran, put me down!"

"No." His voice rumbled into her, as strong and unrelenting as his hold. They entered the hallway.

"Just because you're bigger and stronger than me doesn't mean you can just cart me around like this whenever you want."

There was a sharp *slap* on her ass. Avery's breath hitched, and she jolted at the sting. But that flash of pain was accompanied by something deeper, something pleasurable, something that thrummed in her clit and made her pussy clench.

"You spanked me," she said, shocked.

His big hand remained on her ass, rubbing to soothe away the lingering sting as he moved down the stairs. "You can have more after you eat."

She sputtered, unable to believe what he'd just said and done. Unable to believe that she...*wanted* more. "You—you big jerk! You don't get to do anything after everything you kept from me."

"Not keeping anything from you anymore."

"Oh yeah? Then where's my phone? I know you have it."

He grunted and flexed his fingers on her ass, his claws pricking her through her jeans. "I'll return it to you, *vaerina*. Just had to make a few modifications."

"What modifications?"

"Needed to make sure it can't be tracked."

"Wait, who would track my—"

Before she could utter another word, her world was again upended as he sat her down on a chair at the kitchen table. Avery pushed her glasses back up her nose and combed her hair back out of her face. Fyran pushed her chair in and loomed behind her as though waiting for her to try to run. Heat poured off him, sinking into her skin. When he finally withdrew, she wasn't sure whether to be disappointed or grateful.

She shifted her eyes to the table, and they stopped on...a TV dinner? Brow furrowed, she stared at the tray. The largest of the four compartments contained a brown slab of what Avery assumed was meat smothered in brown gravy. The other three held cut green beans, an overcooked chunk of chocolate brownie—or maybe cake?—and mashed potatoes.

"This...is what you call gourmet food?" she asked. It wasn't like she was above eating a TV dinner—she'd lived off food like this for the last couple years—but this wasn't what she'd envisioned when he said he'd prepared a gourmet meal for her.

Fyran sat down on the opposite side of the table in front of an identical tray of food. He frowned. "Don't you? It said gourmet food on the box."

Avery pressed her lips together to hold in her laughter, but he looked so earnest and confused that a snicker escaped. "That's just...misleading branding, I guess. Kind of like when you say you *prepared* a meal, people naturally think you cooked it yourself."

"I did cook it myself. Who do you think put these in the microwave and pressed the buttons?" His eyebrows had fallen low, but there was a ghost of a smile on his face, and the light in his eyes had softened.

"Hmm." She pushed her chair back, stood, and walked to the cabinets, checking inside each one. They were all empty but for a single can of chicken soup and a box of cereal. She stepped to the refrigerator and opened the freezer. There were more TV dinners stacked inside. The fridge contained a couple take out containers, a few dozen cans of soda, and three bottles of juice.

"Is this really all you eat and drink? TV dinners, fast food, and soda?" She looked back at him.

Fyran had remained in his seat, watching her. He tilted his head. "Is that wrong? I don't usually spend much time here. Easier to have things that can be prepared quickly."

"It's all...junk. How do you stay like that"—she waved her hand at him—"eating all this?"

Oh God, now I'm starting to sound like my mother.

I'm going to be sick.

She could just hear Allison now, talking about how all this crap would just go right to Avery's ass and thighs.

Fyran shrugged, one corner of his mouth tilting into a smirk. "I exercise a lot. Also, I'm not human, so that might help. My metabolism favors a lot of that sweet, sugary food you humans have so much trouble with.

"And really"—he leaned back in his chair—"after so many years of having to scrounge for food on alien worlds or rely on nutrition capsules to survive, this planet's food is like...an awakening. You'd think a species that has mastered intergalactic travel would've learned how to make those capsules taste like something other than shit. Now," he said, softening his voice, "come and eat, Avery."

Avery returned to her chair and sat down, a smile playing on her lips. She found it funny that Fyran, an alien soldier, was living the bachelor life just like any human guy—his fridge was just packed with soda instead of beer.

She picked up her fork, cut into the meat, and ate a bite. It wasn't bad, but it was incredibly salty. "I...can cook you a real meal if we go to the grocery store and get some real food."

He hadn't touched his food yet; his eyes were intent upon her. Thankfully, their usual intensity was eased by his smile. "I bought these meals at the grocery store. Wasn't aware that some of the food there was fake."

She chuckled, shaking her head. "This is real food, it's just... not healthy to eat every day."

Fyran scooped a forkful of mashed potatoes into his mouth. "So you're concerned about my health, then?"

"Well, if I have to stay here, isn't it about my health, too?"

He narrowed his eyes, and his smile widened. "Yes, it is. But going out...it may be too risky."

"There's hardly any food here, Fyran. Just one trip, we get whatever groceries we need, and then you can keep me cooped up here for a while if that's what you want."

His smile faltered, and some of that intensity faded from his gaze. "It's not what I *want*, Avery. Just what's safest." He looked down at his meal for a few moments, pushing around the meat with his fork. "I'll take you to the store tomorrow. And...I'd like it if you cooked for me."

Avery's lips stretched into a grin, but she hurriedly smothered it with a bite of food. She was excited about the prospect of cooking for him. She'd only ever done so for herself, and the idea of making dinner for the two of them felt...intimate.

Did you forget what he did?

Oh shush. I'm still conflicted on that.

"Thank you," Avery said. She took a bite of her green beans. "So, what was your home like? And...do you plan to go back?"

Fyran kept his gaze on the freezer meal, fiddling with the food without taking another bite. Despite him being a big, strong, dangerous alien assassin, there was something endearingly child-like about him right now.

Only when his hand had stilled did he speak. "I don't have a home."

Avery frowned. "What do you mean?"

"It's...complicated, Avery. The place where I was born isn't anywhere I ever want to see again."

"Well, my schedule is free. If you're willing to tell me."

She saw his fingers tighten on his fork just before he laid it down.

"Told you my parents vanished when I was young. Maybe... six or seven years old. I had to fend for myself after that. Slept in the safest, driest, warmest places I could find, but I couldn't always meet all those criteria. Tried to work when I could, but more and more often I had to steal to get by, and I had to learn to fight to protect what I stole. That escalated. I got involved in what you'd probably call a...gang.

"I was just a child, so they treated me like shit. Constant insults and threats, sometimes a kick, a slap, a punch. They only gave me and the other kids the jobs they didn't want to do. Begging, sorting through people's garbage, running messages from one side of the city to another. But I had to do it, had to deal with it, because as long as I delivered, they gave me a safe place to sleep, kept me fed, and protected me from anyone who wasn't part of the gang.

Fyran folded his forearms on the edge of the table. "And that bothered me. It was a lot fucking better than sleeping under trash in an alley every night, but it ate at me. I knew already that I was smarter and more capable than a lot of the older members. I had to be. For a lot of them, it was about money, status, power. For me, it was fucking survival.

"So I pushed harder and harder. I wasn't as big or as strong as most of them, so I made sure I was more skilled. I fought back. Usually wound up just getting my ass kicked, but slowly I earned a little respect. Just a little. But I was still just a kid to them. Sometimes useful, usually a nuisance.

"I was about fourteen when I really started to push for more. Had a growth spurt, and when one of the bigger guys hit me one day, well...I fucking hit him back. Can't say I didn't come close to having my brains bashed out in the process, but I knocked him out eventually. After that, I demanded to be recognized for my abilities. To be allowed to contribute in the ways I knew I could.

"They still didn't want to indulge that. They didn't want this scrappy faloran kid showing them up, didn't want their reputations to be damaged by being outdone by me. But they finally gave in, and gave me a way to prove myself—though they knew it was most likely a way to get myself killed. One less annoyance for them to deal with. And honestly, it was probably retaliation, too, for fucking up a senior member.

"They told me to kill a lieutenant from a rival gang we'd been clashing with over territory. Kill him and bring back proof. A trophy. I knew what they were trying to do, knew that they just wanted me gone, and it just hardened my determination. I was going to show them who the fuck I was.

"So I went to the other gang's territory. I slipped in, and I watched. To them, I was just another kid on the streets. I found the place they were operating from, and I waited, and I learned who was usually there, when they came and went, where they gathered. Where the lieutenant spent most of his time. And after a few days..."

He turned his hands palms-up, spreading his fingers. His black claws extended before Avery's eyes. "I went inside in the middle of the night and killed my target. Stabbed him to death in his own bed, cut off his ear so they could see the earring he always wore still attached to it, and went back to my gang. The looks on their faces when I dropped that on the table..."

Despite the hunger Avery had felt earlier, her stomach revolted at the idea of taking another bite.

Fyran released a heavy breath and flattened his hands on the table. His tongue slipped out briefly to wet his lips. "I vomited as soon as I was alone again. Felt sick that whole night, and most of the next day. I was disgusted with myself, but I was also...proud. I was proud to have done it, to have put all those skills to use, to have accomplished what they all thought was impossible. And once that disgust passed, I didn't feel much of anything. Just...empty.

"But I got what I wanted. The gang brought me into the real business. All the things they had the children doing, that was petty, unimportant. Meant more as a distraction for the authorities than anything else. Drugs were the real money, though they moved a lot of stolen goods, too. And that was a dangerous game. A lot of rivalries, a lot of enemies. But now they had a new weapon."

"You?" Avery asked quietly.

Fyran nodded. "They made good use of me from then on. I assassinated six more gang leaders over the next couple years, and killed a lot more than that in open fighting. I just kept getting better at it, and our gang was gaining a reputation—you fuck with us, and there was nowhere to hide. I had a reputation, too. Killing had become what I did. Didn't bother me anymore. Part of me thrilled in it, at least a little. But the gang started to look at me differently. I wasn't much of a kid anymore at sixteen...I was a potential threat.

"Overheard them a couple times talking about me like I was a problem they'd need to solve. Because what if I decided to turn on them? What if I decided my cut wasn't big enough, or I wasn't appreciated enough? And I..."

He chuckled. There was bitterness in the sound, but it was subtle—like the scar of a small wound that had long ago healed. "I started to wonder about that myself. The way they operated seemed sloppy to me sometimes, seemed unnecessarily risky. And I wasn't getting a big enough cut. For all I was doing, didn't I deserve more in return? I won't lie and say I didn't feel betrayed. Those people weren't my family, weren't even really my friends, but I'd shown them loyalty. I'd shed blood for them. And they were prepared to discard me on a whim?"

Fyran's fingers curled atop the table, his claws carving shallow grooves in the wood. "When my parents disappeared, I didn't know what happened. Maybe they were taken. More likely they were killed. But I never once even considered that they'd abandoned me. I *knew* that then, and I know it now. I couldn't say the same about my comrades."

Avery placed her hand over his, stroking her thumb up and down across his finger, feeling the smoothness of the claw. The tension eased from him as he turned his face toward her hand, and his claws retracted. Her heart broke for him, for the boy he'd once been, alone with no one to watch over him, to care for him. For the boy who had no idea of his parents' fates.

"What happened?" she asked.

"I kept my mouth shut, and I watched. Did what I was told and little more. I could feel things changing, could feel them planning. I knew it was just a matter of time. That was until they brought in a big shipment of stolen faloran weapons. We'd moved that stuff before, but only when there was little heat. Only older shit no one would miss. I didn't know a whole lot about my own people, but everyone knew the falorans didn't take kindly to their military tech being stolen and sold on the black market.

"This stuff...it was fresh. We'd never seen anything so new, so advanced. And I told them to ditch it. Fuck the profit, they needed to get rid of it immediately, because holding onto that shit for any amount of time was not going to go well for us. The leaders didn't like me speaking out like that. They told me to fuck off, that there was going to be hell to pay if I didn't just keep my mouth shut from now on.

"That night, I overheard them talking again. They said they couldn't let it go on much longer. They had to take care of their *problem* before it caused them real issues. There was no objection voiced. Just one stipulation—they didn't want it to happen in our base of operations. They needed to get me away somewhere first."

The muscles in his hand tightened again. "So I did what I always do. I waited. For days, I stayed in our headquarters, waiting for that order to head out with some other people on some obscure job elsewhere in the city. Most of them seemed to know it was going to happen soon, and they weren't very good at hiding it...at least not from me.

"Finally, the order came. They told me I'd be going out the next day with a group to deal with rivals trying to push into our territory again. That night, I sat in my room, unable to sleep. Even now, I don't know exactly what I felt. Anger, absolutely. They'd betrayed me. I paced back and forth, getting myself angrier and angrier. Everything I'd done had come down to that? To being murdered in an alleyway by the people I'd fought for?

"I think part of me recognized even then that I deserved it. I'd done terrible things. But I wasn't going to just let them make their move. I knew I'd be outnumbered, that as good as I was, they had most every advantage. But as long as I took a few of them out with me...that would've been enough. I remember thinking that it would've been enough for it to end, as long as it ended with a fight. I just wished it had all been for...for something."

Fyran met her gaze and held it, his eyes brighter red than she'd ever seen. "I was too young to have known it, but I understood that I had no real purpose. That my years had been spent by spiting a universe that wanted me dead. That I had done wrong, and that my lack of remorse made it all the worse.

"That was the night the falorans came to retrieve their property. I was still in my room when the attack began. I heard the explosions, heard the shouting, heard the blasters firing...and I just stayed there, sitting on the edge of my bed, waiting. I didn't know what the *Exthurizen* was then, didn't know their reputation or their capabilities, but I didn't need to know. Everyone in the gang was being killed. I would be amongst them.

"An *althicar* breeched my room a few minutes after it all began, and he swung his blaster toward me, already squeezing the trigger...but our eyes met. It was the first time I'd seen another faloran in a decade. And I guess the last thing he'd expected to find was one of his people in that place. He could've fired. Maybe should have. But something stopped him.

"And he, uh...he had me extracted with his team. There were a lot of questions. I was technically an enemy combatant in the eyes of the *Exthurizen*, a criminal who'd dealt with stolen faloran weaponry, but given my circumstances, they chose to be lenient with me. They tried to have me settled on a planet controlled by the Azmus Protectorate, but I didn't want that. How could I live a normal life amongst my own kind when I barely knew anything about them but their language? How could I live a normal life *anywhere* after everything I'd done?

"So I pushed to join them. The soldiers. The *althicar* who found me, he tried to convince me to give up on it. Said I was young, that I deserved"—Fyran's brow furrowed, and a wistful light crept into his gaze—"a better life, but I wouldn't hear it. He was on his way up through the ranks, and he used that to get me a chance. After a lot more evaluation, a lot of hard work, and a lot of learning, I became one of them. I became an *althicar*. After all that time, my skills had a real purpose, and I could put them to use to protect something.

"And that's what I've always told myself. Every time I killed on a mission, I told myself it was for something bigger, for something better. For something good. That every target I eliminated meant countless innocent lives saved. It wasn't because of greed or power, wasn't to boost someone's reputation on the streets. It was because that target had been deemed a threat by my people and their allies.

"That was...eighteen years ago. The *Exthurizen* gave me structure, gave me purpose, gave me comrades I could trust to have my back even if I could never fully connect with them. My whole adult life has been spent in service. I've been to so many places that I can't remember most of the names. And I've taken so many lives that I lost count long ago.

"I always thought I'd die in the field. And that was fine. That was better than I deserved, but it was fine. It was the only future I could imagine for myself. Retirement and honors...that didn't suit me. So when they sent me here, gave me this mission... To borrow a human phrase, I was fucking pissed. I'm not lifemate material. I don't know how to...how to have a relationship, how to...live."

Fyran turned his hand over, laying it over hers and squeezing it. His eyes were bright again, locked with hers. "But you make me want those things. You make me want to learn. You make me want to live, *vaerina*. I don't have a home, but *karak'duun*, I want nothing more than to make one with *you*."

TWENTY-FOUR

Avery's eyes flared, and her heart quickened at Fyran's words.

And oh God, were they the *right* words.

Tears stung her eyes, and she pressed her lips together to prevent them from trembling. Though her and Fyran's circumstances and backgrounds were vastly different, Avery felt the same way. The place she'd grown up had never been a home to her. It had always felt like a prison, one from which she'd had to escape—and her mother had been the warden.

Avery had been eaten alive by anxiety and uncertainty in the weeks before she moved out of her parents' house, and those feelings had lingered long afterward. She still hadn't fully shaken them. But she'd built enough courage, at least, to do it, to finally act. Fyran was showing similar courage now. What she thought of as a *normal life* was as alien to him as he was to her, and Avery's experiences helped her understand how hard it was for him to adapt.

His fingers flexed around her hand, and a faint tremor coursed through them, gone as quickly as it had come. "I've never shared all that with anyone."

Avery dropped her gaze to their hands. His was so large it engulfed hers completely.

"Thank you for sharing your story with me, Fyran."

Silence stretched between them. For that little while, Avery felt more connected to him—the *real* him—than ever. Though he'd kept his voice relatively steady throughout his story, there'd been moments during which it had wavered just enough for her to notice, when it had brimmed with emotion, when his cool demeanor had cracked to show the pain he must've carried beneath. She had no doubt he was being honest when he said he hadn't shared his story with anyone else.

That meant something. It meant...a lot.

Fyran made the first move, withdrawing his hands and picking up his fork. "Came down here to eat, not listen to me talk."

Avery snorted. "It wasn't like I came by choice."

He chuckled, flashing a grin that showed off his fangs—the sight of which made her feel all kinds of wicked things between her legs.

"My female needs to eat." He broke off a piece of meat with his fork, slipped it between his lips, and frowned. "Almost as cold as it was before I heated it up."

He stood, grabbed both trays, and carried them to the microwave. Avery crossed her arms atop the table, clasping her hands together loosely as she listened to the microwave door open and close, the beeps of the buttons being pressed, the sound of it running. Fyran returned to the table a short while later, holding a steaming TV dinner in each hand.

He placed Avery's meal on the table in front of her. "Now I can say I've cooked for you twice."

She laughed, and it set the tone for the rest of their meal. For the fifteen or twenty minutes they spent eating and talking, she almost forgot everything else that had happened, almost forgot that she had been nearly kidnapped by aliens or that the man she was so enamored with was an alien himself.

After they finished and Fyran had cleaned up, he went out into the garage. He returned with her phone in hand. The look in his eyes—solemn but oddly vulnerable—said everything for him. This was an extension of his trust. He was handing her a way to call for help, to report him, to make things very difficult for him if she wanted to. And no matter what Fyran had done, no matter how wrong it had been, Avery knew she wouldn't betray that trust.

She brushed her thumb over the small crack on the corner of the phone screen. The screen lit up under her touch, displaying several missed calls and text messages. Some were from Jerry, Noah, and Brandy, likely wondering why she hadn't come into work and if everything was all right. The other calls, along with many of the text messages, were from Allison.

"Where are Beau's things?" she asked, looking up at Fyran.

"I set them up in the laundry room," he replied.

"Thank you." She wiggled her phone. "I, uh...should call work."

If he had any misgivings about Avery having her phone back, Fyran didn't reveal them in his expression. He simply nodded.

Avery turned and wandered into the living room, feeling his gaze on her the entire time; it was a sizzling caress that sent tingles down her spine. Attempting to ignore the sensation, she tapped in her pin to unlock her phone. What greeted her wasn't the picture of a starry night sky she'd changed her background to when she'd though her and Fyran were through, but the selfie they'd taken together at the Denver Botanic Gardens.

She fought hard to contain her giddy grin as she scowled and shot an unsuccessful glare at Fyran over her shoulder. "Hacking into my phone is *also* invading my privacy."

"Happened before our talk, so it doesn't count," he replied with a shrug.

"Doesn't count? Of course it still counts!"

"You won't be mad about it after you check your photos."

Brows furrowed, she looked down at her phone and tapped on her photo album. Sure enough, all the recent pictures were of Fyran. There were selfies, there were shots taken of him standing in front of the mirror, and a couple from his point of view, looking down his body over the muscles of his broad chest and defined abs. His chest was bare in all the pictures.

A total thirst trap—and oh, was Avery parched. He was grinning in some, more serious in others, and in a few he was giving her what could only be described as puppy dog eyes, but his gaze smoldered in almost every photo. His human disguise was active in each, but that didn't matter. The man was irresistible either way.

The last series of photos was of Fyran slowly running his free hand down—over his chest, along his abs, dipping lower and lower until the final image, in which it had slipped beneath the waistband of his sweatpants. The bulge in his pants could not possibly have been caused only by his hand.

Avery bit down on her bottom lip as heat coiled in her belly. She'd had her fair share of dick pics in the past, all of which had been unsolicited and all of which she wished she could unsee. But for the first time, she desperately craved one—from him.

"You're looking, aren't you?" Fyran asked.

She started and hurriedly exited the photo album. "No!"

He laughed. "So the no lies rule only applies to me, female?"

Avery growled and walked farther into the living room, plopping down on the sofa. "I'm not talking to you. I have a call to make."

"I'm not stopping you."

"Don't you have something better to do?"

Fyran placed his hands high on the sides of the archway dividing the kitchen and living room and leaned in, grinning wide as his tail flicked behind him. "You."

Had Avery been standing, she was sure her panties would have dropped to the floor in that instant.

Fire blazed through her, and she squeezed her thighs together as her pussy pulsed. He looked so damn good standing there like that, as though he were about to stalk toward her and make his response to her question a reality.

Ignore him. Stop looking—no, don't look toward his cock!—and ignore him.

Avery forced her face away and her eyes down to her phone. She opened her text messages. Fortunately, nothing killed her libido faster than her mother. Allison had sent more than a dozen texts. One was to tell Avery that she had an appointment at Allison's salon to get her eyebrows done—which absolutely wasn't happening—and most of the rest were pictures of various dresses, asking Avery what she thought of them. Only one of those was a dress Allison was suggesting Avery should wear to the Christmas party.

There wasn't a single text asking Avery how she was or if everything was okay.

Those messages had come from Brandy, Noah, and Jerry instead.

Yo avery where u at? U ok? Noah had written.

Jerry said you were no call no show twice. Everything okay? Brandy had texted, followed by another. *Bitch you better be okay. Call me.*

Avery switched to her voicemail, deleting all three of Allison's voicemails. She stopped when she reached Jerry's message, reading the transcription.

Avery, it's Jerry. Just wanted to check up on you. You haven't come in for work yet and we haven't heard from you. Call me when you can.

There were two more voicemails from him after that.

Avery, Jerry again. This is the second day you haven't shown up or called. You okay? Don't worry about the missed work, all right? We all just want to make sure you're okay. Please, Avery, if there's something wrong call us. If you need to talk, or you need help with anything, anything at all, call.

She moved on to the final message.

Jerry again, Avery. I know I'm not supposed to do this, but I'm gonna have Noah come by your apartment tonight to check on you. It's probably nothing, I know, and maybe...maybe you need some time. We know you've been hurting lately. But we're all really worried. We know you're pretty down about that guy right now, but you need to know you got a whole bunch of people right here who care about you. Please, when you get this, call me back.

Tears filled her eyes, and she covered her mouth, unable to

hold back a sniffle. Avery knew they had reason to worry. During the two years she'd worked at Jerry's, she'd only ever called in once.

How was it that the people she worked with had become more like a family to Avery than her actual flesh-and-blood relatives were? How had her co-workers come to care about her so much more than her own parents did?

She also had Fyran, who wanted her to be his. To be his *mate*.

Avery lifted her gaze to look at him, but he was no longer standing there. He wasn't anywhere she in sight. She hadn't even heard him leave.

Wait.

Her breath caught when something in Jerry's messaged clicked. He was sending Noah to her apartment? She checked the time the message was sent. Three hours ago. There was still time.

She found the diner's number, knowing Jerry was working and wouldn't have his cell, and called. Thankfully, it was him who answered.

"Jerry's Diner, how can I help you?" he asked, raising his voice over the din of conversation and the clank of silverware, plates, and glasses behind him.

"Jerry, it's Avery."

"Avery! Are you all right? Please—" the audio became muffled, but Avery was pretty sure she heard Jerry tell someone he'd be right with them before the sound rushed back again. "Please don't tell me there was an accident or anything. You're okay, kid, right?"

Her heart constricted hearing the worry in his voice, and she hated herself for having to lie to him. "Yeah, I'm fine. I'm so, so sorry for worrying everyone and not calling in. There was a...uh... family emergency and I had to leave in a rush. Things have been really hectic, and I'm, uh...I'm still trying to wrap my head around everything."

Jerry let out a relieved sigh. "You don't need to apologize, Avery. I'm just glad you're okay. Tell me what you need to help you through this, and I'll do what I—sir, I told you I'd be with you in a minute—I'll do what I can to make it happen."

"I'm just going to need some time off, but I don't know how long yet. I hate asking, and I totally understand if you need to replace me—"

"Kid, you'll always have a place here whether you just want to pop in for a coffee or you need a job. Always. Take all the time you need, and just give me a call to check in soon, okay?"

Avery wiped the tears from her cheeks and smiled. Her throat was tight when she said, "Okay. Thank you, Jerry."

"I'll let Brandy and Noah know you're doing fine. Have a good night, Avery."

"Goodnight, Jerry."

She hung up and sniffed, removing her glasses to wipe her eyes. She'd never realized just how much she meant to her co-workers—or how much they meant to her. Her only hope was that they'd be left out of whatever that alien had wanted for Avery.

Once her glasses were back in place, she took a deep breath and stood, slipping her phone into her back pocket. She entered the kitchen and glanced around. Fyran wasn't anywhere to be seen, but there was a faint, familiar sound in the air—the dull rumbling of music muted by sound dampeners, once again coming from the garage.

She walked into the laundry room and flicked on the light. She smiled seeing how neatly Beau's litter box, food, and water dish were arranged, tucked beneath a waist-high counter, though it all looked untouched.

Well, there was one way to lure that cat down.

She picked up the bag of cat food from the shelf and shook it.

Within moments, cat feet pounded down the stairs and across the hardwood floor. Beau appeared in the laundry room, saw Avery with the bag, and meowed excitedly. He circled her legs like the fluffiest, cutest little shark, brushing against her shins and calves repeatedly. She returned the bag to the shelf and bent down to show him his food, water, and litter box. He went for the food immediately and started chowing down.

Avery stared at the garage door, wondering whether she should enter or not, but ultimately decided to leave Fyran be. She went back into the living room and turned on the TV.

For the longest time, she flipped through the channels, not really registering what was on and, in part, not really caring. What was Fyran doing in there? Did he have his long hair pulled back again? Were those tantalizing pointed ears showing? Was he working out, and were beads of sweat dripping down that mouthwatering body, trailing over his every muscle just like she longed to do with her fingers—or her tongue?

"Ugh, stop it, Avery. Focus."

She stopped her channel surfing on the movie *The Phantom of the Opera* starring Gerard Butler, one of her favorites. She'd watched it over and over, loving it a smidgen more with each viewing, but her attention kept straying now. With night having fallen a while ago, the room was dark save for the light creeping in from the kitchen and the TV's glow.

Beau joined her shortly after she'd chosen the movie, cuddling next to her. He promptly fell asleep as she petted him.

When the movie was over and Fyran still hadn't emerged from the garage, Avery carefully extracted herself from Beau and headed upstairs to get ready for bed.

She stopped just outside Fyran's bedroom and stared at the splintered doorframe. She worried her bottom lip as indecision seized her. Should she find another room to sleep in, or was she supposed to sleep in his room? In his bed? Fyran had slept with her last night, she was sure of it. And after the way he'd kicked the door in earlier... Avery knew he'd do the same no matter what room she was in. If his bedroom was where he wanted her, she wasn't going to be able to stop him.

He was determined to have no walls—or doors—between them.

She entered his bedroom, turned on the light, and closed the door behind her. It wouldn't latch shut, but it at least stayed in place. Walking to the bed, she pulled her cellphone out of her pocket and set it on the nightstand, along with her laptop. She made the bed, retrieved her toiletries from her suitcase, and hurried into the bathroom.

Curious, Avery opened the top cabinet drawer.

"I knew it," she said with a grin. Everything she'd moved had been returned to its rightful place.

She opened the medicine cabinet. Every bottle inside was facing forward again. With a smirk, she turned several of them askew and scattered a few more items about in the drawers. She added her belongings to the drawers and cabinet, as well, and even put an open box of tampons on the counter in the corner. She could have tucked them in the cabinet below, but it was much more fun to have them out in the open for him to find.

"Wonder if he even knows what those are for. I'm sure if he reads the instructions, he'll figure it out."

When Avery was done messing with Fyran's perfectly ordered bathroom, she brushed her teeth, changed into her pajamas, flicked off the light, and made her way into the bedroom. She turned off the lights, walked blindly to the bed, and climbed on, slipping under the covers. She glanced at the clock. It wasn't late, but she was tired all the same. She removed her glasses and set them next to her phone.

As soon as she lay down on her side, everything that had happened today fell upon her with a great weight. It felt like she'd lived a lifetime since she'd awoken this morning. *Emotional roller coaster* wasn't strong enough to describe what she'd been through today.

Avery took in a deep breath, one spiced with sandalwood and fir, and exhaled in a soft sigh as she closed her eyes. Today had been equal parts draining, frustrating, and thrilling, but she couldn't help feeling content here in Fyran's bed, surrounded by his scent.

That sense of heaviness spread through her body, and she felt herself sinking into the mattress. She didn't fight as her consciousness faded.

Gentle movement—the slightest rocking of the bed—roused her. Her eyelids, still so heavy, fluttered open as a strong arm banded over her middle and drew her backward. Through her blurred vision, she was just able to make out the numbers on the clock—more than an hour had passed since she'd lain down.

Avery let her eyelids fall shut again and used what little energy she had to roll over, placing her hand on Fyran's bare chest. He hummed, the vibrations running through her palm, and drew her closer still, guiding her head to rest on his shoulder. His skin was even warmer than usual.

She breathed in his scent again; the smells of his bodywash and shampoo were fresh and pronounced. "What were you doing?"

"Exercising," he rumbled.

"Again?" she murmured. "For so long?"

"Had a lot on my mind. And it's the only way to hold back my desire for you, Avery."

"Pfft." She rubbed her cheek against his shoulder. She was more comfortable than she'd ever been. "I'm still mad at you."

Fyran chuckled. He covered her hand with his and turned his head, brushing his lips across her forehead and his nose over her hair. "You can be mad all you want as long as you're in my arms."

Avery smiled, and just as she felt herself dropping back into sleep, she heard Fyran speak again. His voice was more subdued, more solemn, his usual cockiness having been replaced by something deeper, something firmer.

"You're mine, *vaerina*. And I am yours. All that I am, for better or worse...I belong to you."

TWENTY-FIVE

THE CROWDS of holiday shoppers that had flooded the Sixteenth Street Mall over the last few weeks had not prepared Fyran for this—grocery shopping nine days before Christmas. It seemed as though half of Colorado's population had been crammed into this building. Many of the humans were pushing metal carts laden with foodstuffs, and a good number of those displayed blatant disregard for the other shoppers around them.

Normally, crowds didn't bother Fyran. He knew how to move through them, knew how to fade into them and how to use them to his advantage, but this was something entirely different.

He tightened his grip on the cart's handle, fighting back the instinct to use it as a weapon. He'd been cut off and nearly collided with more times than he could count in the twenty minutes he and Avery had spent in the store so far, and he couldn't stop himself from perceiving this as a hostile environment.

Worse, Avery regularly moved away from the cart to flit through the crowd and pluck items off the shelves, putting herself at risk of being trampled by the inconsiderate assholes all around. Fyran could ignore the threats to his person, but when those threats were directed at his mate?

He clenched his jaw and followed her around the corner, slowing his speed to watch for cross traffic.

Fyran brought his cart to an abrupt halt as a woman darted out of the next aisle, pushing her cart through the space Fyran's would've occupied in another moment. And, of course, she glared at him as she passed.

Murder bad.

But maybe I can figure out which car is hers and shred a tire or two...

Or, maybe, it would be best to finish shopping so he and Avery could get the hell out of this place before he did anything he'd later regret.

He turned into the aisle Avery had gone down, weaving between two shoppers who were positioned almost perfectly to block the entrance. Each had nearly identical items in their hands and were looking down at those items with bewilderment and concentration.

Though the faces changed, Fyran swore there were some of those shoppers in every damned aisle, and they were all completely oblivious to the world around them.

His eyes fell on Avery; she was already halfway down the aisle, standing on her toes with her arm extended high over her head as she struggled to reach something on a high shelf. But her fingers were just several inches shy of it, and she couldn't get any more height, even when she put her foot on the lowest shelf.

A tall human male walked over to Avery, smiled down at her, and grabbed the jar she'd been reaching for. He held it out to her. When she placed her hand upon it and thanked him, he didn't immediately let it go.

"No problem," the man said, leaning a shoulder against the shelves. "I, uh, wouldn't mind helping you with the rest of your shopping. Maybe we can get a coffee afterward?"

Rage flared in Fyran's chest like an exploding star, flooding his veins with fire. His claws lengthened, and his tail snaked around his leg, squeezing as tightly as his hands were squeezing the cart handle.

Time to do a fucking murder after all.

Fyran released his hold on the cart and strode forward, driven by the need to reach his mate, to claim her, to face this challenger. He stopped immediately behind Avery, close enough that his chest touched her back and her scent filled his nostrils, and reached over her head to snatch another jar off the shelf.

"This female is mine," he growled as he lowered the jar for her to take, keeping his glare fixed on the other male.

Avery released the stranger's jar and took Fyran's offering.

The male's eyes widened, and he raised his hands, one still holding the jar, and took a step back. "Ooookay. I, uh, I can see that." He looked back at Avery. "Are you okay?"

"I am, thanks," Avery said.

His brows dropped, and he briefly flicked his gaze from Avery to Fyran. "You sure? You don't need any...help?"

If Avery weren't in front of him, Fyran would have already attacked; he knew it down to his bones, and that knowledge gave him no pleasure. "She doesn't. But you will, if you don't move on."

"Miss?" the man asked Avery, ignoring Fyran.

Avery smiled at the man; that alone made Fyran want to gut him.

"Thank you, but truly, I am fine." She turned toward Fyran and wrapped her arms around him, resting her cheek on his chest. "My boyfriend just gets a little jealous sometimes."

Fyran slipped an arm around her, smoothing his palm down her back. The gesture was meant to soothe him more than Avery. She grounded him, and her presence was the only thing keeping him from committing an act that would undoubtedly add Westminster law enforcement to his list of problems.

The male watched Avery for a moment longer before nodding and setting the jar he held on a random shelf. "Okay. Well...have a good day."

Fyran watched until the male was out of sight before returning his attention to Avery, who was looking up at him with her chin on his chest and her lips stretched into a wide grin. He released a huff through his nostrils.

"What's amusing? And why did he keep asking if you were okay?" Fyran shot a brief glare in the direction the man had gone. "I made my claim on you quite clear."

She grazed her nails down his back, sending a shiver of delight through him. He dropped his hands to her hips and pulled her closer.

"You came off kind of...intense. He was making sure you weren't abusive to me," she said.

"What? Why the fuck would I—"

Those words died on his lips. Avery was his mate. He couldn't imagine harming her; just the thought of it was almost enough to make his gut twist into knots. Even had she not accepted his claim, she was his, and he'd do anything to protect her, would shield her from harm no matter how much damage was done to his own body.

But he'd seen enough of the universe to know that not every male treated his mate with equal reverence and care. Not every male viewed his mate as someone to be cared for, to be pampered, to be worshipped.

And he knew, also, that not every male was brave enough to say something when witnessing such abuses.

"Not going to apologize," Fyran muttered.

She chuckled. "He meant well."

"Yeah, well...he can go mean well somewhere else. I've got you covered." He leaned his head down, placing a kiss on her forehead. "Next time I'll just run over any elderly humans who get in my way so I can keep up with you."

Avery gasped, looking affronted. "The elderly? Really, Fyran? They're harmless!"

His eyebrows rose high. "Harmless? What was it your friend Noah said about me? That I looked at him like I wanted to murder him for suggesting the specials?"

She laughed. "You heard that? Oh my gosh, how good is your hearing?"

"As exceptional as everything else about me," Fyran replied with a smirk. "I've had more old people look at me like they want to stab me in the last twenty minutes than I can count, Avery. At some point I'll have to make a move just to scare the rest of them off."

"A lot of people just get frustrated around this time of the year, especially with Christmas coming up." She set the jar on the shelf, reached up, and cupped his jaw, placing her thumbs at the corners of his mouth and lifting his lips into a forced smile. She giggled, her eyes shining bright with mirth. "Smile. Kill them with *kindness*."

"Kindnesh ish not a weapon," he replied, staring at her blankly.

"Of course, it is."

"Oh, don't you two make such a cute couple."

Fyran and Avery looked toward the speaker—a short, white-haired elderly woman standing nearby.

Smiling, Avery flattened her palms on Fyran's cheeks, smushing them together and making his lips pucker. "Aww, thank you! He's just so cute, I can't help myself."

The woman chuckled and leaned closer, lowering her voice. "You better keep an eye on that one. Someone might just steal him away."

"Oh, I don't think I have to worry." Avery met Fyran's gaze. Her eyes were still sparkling.

The woman wandered off with her cart, and Avery eased her hold on Fyran's cheeks, patting them gently.

The grin that formed on his lips came without her help this time. "Hope you have all your affairs in order, female, because there's going to be a whole lot of kindness coming your way later."

Avery pulled away from him and grabbed the two jars—both the one Fyran had given her and the one the man had set down. "I'm still supposed to be mad at you."

Fyran followed her back to their cart. "Oh? How could you still be mad at someone so *cute*?"

She placed the jars in the cart. Her saccharine smile, while exaggerated, wasn't fake when she asked, "Do you really need me to recap all the reasons?"

Frowning, he took hold of the cart and set it into motion again. "No."

They continued their slow journey, snaking through the aisles as Avery scratched items off her handwritten list. Their cart was full by the time she'd marked off the last item. Fyran ran his gaze over the chaos inside the cart. Though it had been in some ways unavoidable, everything had been set inside so haphazardly that he couldn't help but feel an impulse to move them into a more orderly arrangement.

This time, she hadn't done it on purpose, but he'd certainly noticed her rearranging things in his bathroom—though *disarranging* was probably the better word. Had any other person done it, including his comrades in arms, he would've been irritated. But he'd only smiled when he'd first discovered that she'd moved things around, and the warmth that had lingered in his chest since he'd first met her blossomed further.

Just wait until I put away all her things and she doesn't know where any of them are...

As they made their way toward the check lanes at the front of the store, they passed a big section of Christmas items. Wreaths and lights, abnormally large candy canes, unsettling anthropomorphic gingerbread cookies, fake pine trees and so much more. Fyran had seen such things before. Christmas seemed unavoidable, at least in this part of Earth.

"So why all this?" he asked, lifting his chin toward the decorations. "Why is this one day out of the whole year such a big deal that they sell things for it months in advance?"

Avery stopped, glanced at him, and turned her attention to the display. "A lot of people just really get into the spirit of the holiday. They put up decorations inside and out, set up Christmas trees and decorate them, flavor everything with cinnamon and peppermint, have parties, buy gifts for the people they love. Kids write letters to Santa to tell him what they want for Christmas and then spend weeks anticipating it, hoping they've been good enough to earn what they asked for."

Fyran tilted his head. "So...what is it about?"

"Well... That really depends on who you ask," Avery said, shrugging.

"I'm asking you, *vaerina*."

Avery frowned, her gaze moving over the lighted trees. "I think it's about...hope. And selflessness. About being close to the people you love and giving them gifts not because you want something in return, but because you want to see them happy. About making traditions that you share with the people closest to you."

The sorrow in her expression seemed at odds with what she'd said, but Fyran already had an idea of why. But still, she'd had a little tree set up in her living room, her tiny beacon of hope. Fyran stepped over to the trees and pulled down one of the boxes—a twenty-four-inch tree with lights built into it.

Avery looked surprised as he slid the box onto the rack on the underside of the cart. "We don't have to get that."

"No, we don't. But I want to. Would've taken yours home, had I known."

Her mouth curved into a tender, trembling smile as her eyes met his. "Thank you."

She turned her gaze back to the displays, smile remaining in place until Fyran spoke again.

"And what of your family?" he asked. "Your traditions?"

"We...didn't have any. None that matter, anyway. Christmas in my family is about who throws the grandest, most decadent party. To my mom, it's always about looking good and impressing others, right down to the gifts she gave us. And if we didn't show *exactly* the amount of gratitude she expected... It was about taking the perfect Christmas picture for social media and then ignoring me and my sister the rest of the day until she had company to show us off to."

She glanced at him and cringed. "Sorry. Didn't mean to unload all that on you. If you haven't already guessed, I have mom issues."

Fyran cupped her cheek and brushed his thumb over her skin. "I'd guessed. I was in your apartment after the Botanic Gardens, Avery. When she called you."

Her cheeks turned red, and he felt the heat emanating from them against his palm. Avery reached up, grasped his hand, and pulled it down from her face. She gave him a pointed look, though there was a smile teasing her lips. "You know, you're not supposed to bring up your misdeeds."

"I'm being truthful with you, Avery," he said, shifting his hand to take hold of hers. "Then and now, all I wanted to do was take away your pain." His lips spread in a wide grin. "Well, that and rut you."

"*Fyran!*" Avery glanced around, her cheeks darkening. There was clear desire in her eyes when her gaze returned to him.

His expression sobered, and he brushed his thumb over the top of hers. "I saw the change in you when you talked to her. I would've dragged her through that phone and ripped her head off right then were it possible."

Avery cringed. "I can't tell if that's the most romantic thing I've heard or the most gruesome." She sighed and laced their fingers together. "As much as I can't stand to be around my mom, I don't hate her, and I don't want anything bad to happen to her. She's still my mother. She's just... I don't know. Too shallow and self-centered to have ever been a mother? Having kids was just another way for her to show off and get attention. We were like... her favorite dolls. We were just supposed to sit on her shelf, looking pretty and keeping quiet. But once we got old enough to have minds of our own, she realized that she really didn't like to play with us because we couldn't be controlled."

Avery was trying to put this all behind her, he could tell, but she still carried so much of the pain in herself—too much for her to fully hide.

"Fine, then. I won't kill your mother. But I will point out yet another of my admirable qualities that fits you perfectly."

She arched a brow. "Oh, and what's that?"

"I *hate* it when you keep quiet."

She laughed and leaned toward him, tilting her head back. "So now I know how to punish you. The cold shoulder and silent treatment."

Fyran's eyebrows drooped, and he narrowed his eyes. "I'm familiar with the silent treatment, but what is this *cold shoulder* nonsense?"

Avery smirked and lifted a single shoulder in a shrug as she turned away from him without answering.

"Female, I already don't like this. Stop. Please?"

She giggled and reached for the cart, but stopped when three human children, none of whom could've been older than eight or nine, ran up to the Christmas trees, calling excitedly to their parents. They pointed out the tree they wanted, and the smallest of the kids bounced up and down with a ridiculous grin on his face. They'd selected the most colorful tree—one covered in flashing lights and glowing pinecones.

When Fyran looked back at Avery, there was a soft smile on her lips and a gleam of longing in her gray-blue eyes. There was so much in that simple expression, so much feeling, so much hope.

Despite all her negative experiences with her own family, his Avery wanted children of her own. She...she wanted a family, wanted to be able to make those traditions she'd spoken about, wanted to have people to love and shower with gifts—people who would give back because they loved her, too.

She wanted children through whom she could see the wonder and joy that so often sparkled in her eyes, with whom she could share it.

Never before had he read so much on a human's face or in a human's eyes, but he knew all that as surely as if she'd told him. And, for the first time, he found himself wondering.

His eyes dipped, taking in her body. What would she look like, belly rounded with child? *His* child? How would it feel to know his baby was growing inside her? How would it feel to be there when that child was born, to hold the baby in his hands and, along with his beloved mate, vow that he would be there always, that he would protect them always?

What would it be like to have children racing through the house, laughing, jumping, and playing, their noses dusted with freckles and their tails flicking in the air behind them? What would it be like to *live*, to be free from the cycle of death and violence that had imprisoned Fyran since he was young? To know joy, and love, and togetherness? To be at peace?

Avery turned her head toward him.

When his eyes met hers, fire swept through his veins anew. He knew now what the emotions swirling within him were, knew what they meant—Avery was his, and he loved her.

He slipped a hand into her hair, cupped the back of her head, and bent down to capture her lips in a scalding kiss, branding her with his essence. She melted against him. He groaned. It had been too fucking long since he'd tasted her mouth—since he tasted her.

Fyran would protect Avery. He would provide for her. He would give her all she wanted, all she needed, all of himself. And he would plant his seed in her. He would father her child, and together they would make a family.

The family neither of them had ever had.

He would fucking make sure of it.

TWENTY-SIX

Avery wrung her hands as she inspected the plates of steaming food on the counter. Though she'd filled in as a cook at Jerry's on several occasions and had prepared and served meals for more customers than she could count, she'd never felt such trepidation. But then, Fyran wasn't a customer, and she wanted everything to be...perfect. That was why she'd gone with her strength—she wasn't an amazing cook, but she knew how to cook a steak. Adding mushrooms, potatoes, and a salad had turned this into a simple and delicious meal to share with him.

Well, hopefully delicious.

She picked up the plates, walked to the table, and smiled as she set Fyran's food in front of him. *"Bon appétit!"*

His nostrils flared with a deep inhalation, and his eyes closed. An appreciative hum rumbled in his chest. He opened his eyes again to watch her as she sat down with her own plate. "Didn't know you speak French, *vaerina*."

"What? Oh, no, I don't," she said with a laugh. "That's just a French phrase that was kind of...adopted by English speakers. It makes us feel like we're a little more cultured, I guess." She picked up the bottle of Moscato wine and poured them each a glass. "Should we make a toast?"

A small crease formed between Fyran's brows. "You've made enough food already, Avery. We can do without slightly burned bread."

Avery laughed. "No, no. Not that kind of toast." She lifted her wine glass and chewed on her bottom lip as she thought of way to explain.

Fyran's eyes didn't leave her mouth for an instant.

"It's, um, when you drink to celebrate or honor something," Avery said, trying to ignore the heat building in her cheeks under the intensity of his gaze. "So...let's drink to delicious food and..."

Fyran lifted his glass, mimicking her. "To a delicious female."

She grinned. "And to a handsome alien. To...us."

His lips stretched into an answering grin, displaying his fangs. "To us, then."

Avery stared at his mouth, and her core tightened as she brought her glass to her lips and took a drink, enjoying the crisp, cool sweetness and the warmth that pooled in her belly afterward.

He followed her lead again, holding her gaze as he tipped back his glass—at least until he actually drank some of the wine, anyway. His features contorted, and he withdrew the glass quickly. His expression as he swallowed was that of a child who'd just eaten the foulest vegetable known to man.

"Humans *like* this?" he asked. "*You* like this?"

Avery touched her fingers to her mouth and chuckled as she set her glass down. "You've never had alcohol?"

"I have"—Fyran shook his head sharply and set the glass down—"and it's all been foul." A shudder coursed through him, making him curl his fingers and peel back his upper lip. "This sets a new standard. Humans have ruined grapes."

Avery couldn't hold in her laughter. It flowed freely, and tears gathered in her eyes. She removed her glasses briefly to wipe away the gathering moisture. "I guess it's an acquired taste."

His expression smoothed, and his lips tilted up into that familiar smirk. "So glad you could find amusement in my suffering, female."

"I wasn't laughing at you."

Smirk holding firm, he raised his eyebrows high.

That only made her laugh more. "Well, maybe I was."

"You're the only one in the universe who's allowed to. Anyone else would get stabbed."

Fyran picked up his fork and knife—after sliding the wine glass farther away—and cut into the steak. Avery dropped her hands to her lap, wringing her fingers as she watched him lift a piece of juicy meat to his mouth and slip it between his lips, torn between a flare of desire and her lingering anxiety.

"Fuck," he growled.

Before she could ask if that was a good fuck or a bad fuck, he sawed off another chunk of steak and stuffed it into his mouth.

"Good?" she asked.

"The best."

Avery released a sigh, expelling her nervousness with it, and set to her own food. Conversation was limited as they ate; Fyran devoured the food like he hadn't eaten in weeks, barely seeming to give himself a moment to breathe between bites. And though his table manners were the sort that would've made her mother blanch—or, perhaps, because of it—her inhibitions fell away. She was hungry.

Even then, Fyran was nearly done with his second plateful of food before Avery finished her first. She drank the last drops of the wine in her glass just as Fyran ate the last piece of baked potato on his plate. She set her glass down just as he placed his fork atop his empty plate.

Fyran sat back in his chair. "That was the best food I've ever had."

"How do you feel about those TV dinners now?"

"Fuck 'em. I'm keeping you."

She giggled and stood to gather the dirty plates. Her body was warm and relaxed thanks to the wine. "I might be convinced."

Despite having eaten what must've been two or three pounds of food, Fyran was on his feet in an instant, snatching the plates up before her fingertips could so much as brush them. "You cooked, female. I can manage this part."

"Well, that's it," she said, tossing her hands in the air. "I've been convinced. A man who cleans and does the dishes is too rare to pass up."

He chuckled and brushed his tail along her leg as his crimson eyes swept over her, smoldering with that passion he never seemed to try to hide. "I'm sure there are still other ways by which I could convince you, *vaerina*. It would be a shame not to explore them all before you decide."

Lust burned in Fyran's gaze, hotter than the surface of the sun.

Avery's pulse quickened. She released a soft, shaky breath and took a step toward the stairway. "I'm just going to go...take a shower."

His laugh was deep, rolling, sinful. "You can only run for so long, female."

"I'm not running. I'm walking, see?" She took a few more steps. "Just to take a shower while you clean. Which, thank you, by the way."

Though his hands were full of dirty dishes, he remained in place, watching her. The predatory glint in his eyes pierced straight to Avery's core. "Thank you, Avery, for the first of many" —his gaze dipped slowly along her body once more—"delicious meals."

Avery squeezed her thighs together for a few moments before realizing that she couldn't very well walk up the stairs that way. She forced herself to take a couple more hurried steps backward before turning and running up the stairs.

Maybe he hadn't known what a toast was, but Fyran was well versed in double entendre—and his delivery was unmatched.

In the master bathroom, Avery flattened her hands on the counter and leaned forward, staring at herself in the mirror. She was flushed after her encounter with Fyran. Though she knew the alcohol was partly to blame, she was also aroused. Her core ached, her breasts felt heavy, and there was a restless energy flowing through her.

She'd wanted Fyran from the moment she'd first seen him,

and she'd been tempted to give in so many times since then. And now there was nothing left to hold her back. The secrets had been revealed. She was ready.

She was *more* than ready.

Avery glanced at the door and caught her bottom lip with her teeth as something crossed her mind. So Fyran liked to watch her? Perhaps she'd give him something to watch—but this time, it would be on her terms. She wanted to relive that feeling, wanted to sense his presence, to know his eyes were upon her, that he was helpless but to stare. She wanted to feel the desire radiating from him even if she couldn't see him, wanted to know he was as enthralled as she.

Pushing away from the counter, Avery started the water in the bathtub. Once it was the right temperature, she grabbed her bottle of bodywash and set it on the edge of the tub. She was thankful now more than ever that she didn't have to worry about shaving. Gathering her hair, she pulled it up and used a hair clip to hold it in place.

As steam rose from the thigh-high garden tub, she walked to the bathroom door, cracked it open, and peeked out. The bedroom was empty.

"Okay," she whispered, pushing the door fully open and taking a step back. She reached for the hem of her shirt. "Come for me, Fyran."

She turned her back to the doorway. Anxiety rippled in her stomach, but she quickly stamped it down; she wouldn't let shyness get the best of her. She *wanted* this. She wanted Fyran.

Avery removed her clothes, tossed them on the floor, and stepped into the tub. She nearly moaned as she sank down into the hot water. Though it was a struggle, she kept herself from looking toward the open doorway as she cleaned herself.

How many times had she bathed and showered in her apartment with the bathroom door open? Living alone, she'd never thought twice about it, but she couldn't ignore it now, not while Fyran could walk in at any moment and see her. There was something thrilling about the thought of being caught in such a vulnerable state, and it was even more exciting imagining what he'd do to do her afterward—because she knew he wouldn't settle for simply watching this time.

Neither would she.

Avery lay back, closed her eyes, and breathed in the berry and flowers scent filling the air. The heat from the water soaked into her, loosening her muscles and easing her lingering tension. It had been so long since she'd just...relaxed. That she was able to do so now, knowing what she wanted to happen, knowing what she wanted to do, only further convinced her that this was the right thing, that this was the right time.

That Fyran was the one.

The only sounds were that of her own breathing, her slowly thumping heart, and the rippling of water with her little movements. She knew that didn't mean anything—she'd only hear Fyran's approach if he wanted her to—but she didn't feel him yet.

Avery bent her will toward him, sending out thought waves in the hope of drawing him in—in the hope of making the predator become her prey, if only for a little while. If aliens were real, why not psychic powers, too?

Of course, if all else failed, there was one way sure to catch his attention—one scent that he was certain to detect no matter where he was in the house. Her hand shifted under water, sliding just an inch or two toward her pelvis, but she dared not move it any farther. Though she was already aroused by her anticipation, it wasn't the time to give in yet.

The quality of the surrounding silence changed subtly. Avery fought to keep her face neutral, to keep herself from betraying anything in her expression even as her heartbeat quickened. There was a charge in the air, electric, thrilling, and mysterious.

No, not mysterious...she knew exactly what it was. The bathroom felt suddenly smaller, fuller. Her skin tingled, as though the electricity in the air was coursing over its surface, spreading from head to toe and everywhere in between—centering at her core.

Fyran was here.

Avery's skin prickled in awareness. She'd felt this before, in the bedroom of her apartment. She hadn't realized what it was then, hadn't even thought about it as she'd touched herself, but she knew what it was now. A small smile curled at the corner of her lips.

Opening her eyes, she sat up. The cool air caressed her skin, and her nipples hardened—but that was in response to Fyran's gaze more so than the cold. She slowly ran her hands along the lengths of her arms, wiping away the bubbles, before bracing them on the sides of the tub and standing up. Water sluiced down her body.

She turned toward the door, but she kept herself from looking that way as she reached for the towel hanging on the rack. Her breasts were achy and swollen, and there was a heaviness in her core. She quickly dried herself, wrapped the towel around her body, and stepped out of the tub onto the gray rug.

Sitting on the edge of the bathtub, Avery removed the hair clip and shook her hair out. Her hair tumbled down around her bare shoulders and back. She brought her hand up an traced the edge of the towel back and forth across her chest. Finally, she released the towel, and it fell apart to pool around her hips.

"I know you're there, Fyran," Avery said, skimming her fingers over her breast and circling her nipple. She shivered. Though it was her own touch, the sensation was enhanced by his presence, by the feel of his gaze following her movements. She glanced at the doorway before closing her eyes. "Do you like watching me?"

Avery trailed her fingers between her breasts and down her belly, parting her thighs. Cool air kissed her sex. When her fingers slipped between her folds, she found herself hot and slick.

Despite her lingering shreds of inhibition, she was aroused by this. The thought of Fyran watching her, whether he was really there or not, excited her, emboldened her, drove her to behave in a way she'd never dreamed. He'd awoken desires within her that she'd never imagined possible.

She spread her legs wider and cupped one of her breasts as she touched a finger to her clit. Catching her bottom lip with her teeth, she circled that tiny bud leisurely, teasingly, winding herself up tighter and tighter. Her breath quickened as pleasure spread through her. But it wasn't enough. It wasn't her own touch that she wanted.

Avery wanted him.

Opening her eyes, she looked toward the doorway. "Do you want to touch me, Fyran?" She stilled her finger, leaned back, and braced her hands to either side, leaving herself completely open to him. "Do you want to taste me?"

Everything was quiet. Avery wondered if she'd imagined those sensations, if he wasn't here at all. If he was still downstairs washing dishes or punishing himself in the garage.

A puff of warm air swept across her inner thigh. Avery's breath hitched, and a shiver raced up her spine. Fyran's touch began as a whisper, the pads of his fingers brushing her calves, barely making contact. That touch grew firmer as it crept higher, and his palms were pressed fully against her skin when he reached her knees.

Avery watched the faint depressions move along her skin as his invisible hands trailed up her thighs. She knew his touch well by now, knew its heat, its roughness, its confidence, but experiencing it like this was impossibly thrilling.

His hands stopped high on her thighs but were still maddeningly far from her sex, his thumbs curling down the insides of her legs. He squeezed possessively. She could see the imprint of each of his fingers in her flesh, could feel the slight prick of his claws.

"*Vaerina*," he growled, "you're mine."

Avery gasped as he pressed his mouth to her sex. Before she could fully register the feel of his lips against her sensitive flesh, his tongue dragged along her pussy from bottom to top, flicking over her clit. She jolted, one of her hands flying up to delve into his long hair. His grip on her tightened.

"*Karak'duun*. You taste so fucking good." His deep, rough voice thrummed against her pussy.

"Fyran," she breathed, clenching his hair.

"Let me hear you, Avery." He licked her again and again, his tongue spreading her and gathering her slick as it swept up to tease her clit with its tip. His growls and grunts punctuated each stroke, sharpening Avery's pleasure and wringing throaty moans from her.

But it wasn't just his tongue and those sounds that were making her blood sizzle and her body burn. It was every bit of contact between them—the heat radiating off his skin, his rough palms and fingers, his claws, the scratch of his stubble against her inner thighs, his hot breath, the brush of his hair over her legs. It was his sandalwood and fir scent filling the air, mixing with the lingering scent of her bodywash. It was the energy crackling all around them and coursing through them.

Avery's belly contracted with every ripple of sensation, and she spread her thighs wider, wanting more. *Needing* more.

Fyran responded by sliding his hands to her outer thighs and back to her ass, dragging her closer to trap her against his mouth. He devoured her with all the ravenousness of the desires they'd both denied themselves for what had felt like a thousand years. His mouth and tongue were forceful and demanding—and yet there was a reverence to his ministrations. He was treating her as though she were a rare, delectable treat, one to be savored, but he was helpless to hold himself back after starving for so long.

His fingers curled, pressing his claws against her ass. Avery moaned, her body rocking against his mouth and ruthless tongue of its own accord as the torrent of need within her coiled tighter and tighter.

Panting, she looked down. She could see the places her skin was depressed by his touch, could see her sex moving with the rhythm of his tongue, could even see the indentations caused by his knees on the plush throw rug, but she couldn't see him.

She was being pleasured by a ghost, by the invisible man, by her hidden alien. But that wasn't what she wanted. He wasn't a figment, wasn't just a fantasy. She wanted to look into those blazing red eyes as he made love to her.

Avery held back the sensations building inside her and gentled her hold on his hair. "Let me see you, Fyran." Her lashes fluttered, and a ragged moan escaped her he thrust his tongue into her channel and stroked her in *that* spot. Her toes curled, and she rasped, "Please, let me see you."

The air before her flickered with a faint, hexagonal pattern in the shape of a man, and then Fyran was there, staring up at her. His crimson eyes were brighter than she'd ever seen, so bright that they were casting light on her belly, and his wild hair was draped over his shoulders.

He pulled his head back slightly, and Avery saw her essence glistening upon his lips. He licked it away, giving her a glimpse of his fangs.

"Now let me see you, Avery." He kissed her inner thigh, grazing her flesh with a fang, his eyes never leaving hers. "I want to see you come undone."

His lips latched onto her clit, and he sucked.

Ecstasy unfurled within her, an inferno blazing through her veins. Avery squeezed her eyes shut and cried out, curling her legs around him as she undulated against his mouth, greedy for more. And he gave it to her with every lash of his wicked tongue. The pleasure consumed her, its delicious heat burning her to ash and leaving room in her mind for nothing else.

Fyran snarled and released her clit, dipping his mouth to lap at her essence as it flowed from her. Each movement of his tongue and lips coaxed out a little more and prolonged the pleasure radiating through her.

Once the maelstrom within Avery had subsided and her awareness returned, she found herself hunched over Fyran, clinging to him, with her fingers tangled in his hair. Her pussy pulsed, her clit throbbed, and her thighs quivered in the aftermath of her climax. But there was still an unbearable pressure within her core, totally at odds with the sense of emptiness there.

She'd had a taste of what he could make her feel, and she needed more. More of him, more of this, more of everything.

Avery sat back, untangling her fingers from his hair to brace her hand on the edge of the tub. When she shifted her pelvis, meaning to pull away from him, Fyran growled, tightened his grip on her ass, and pressed her sex more firmly against his mouth. She felt his hard teeth against her soft flesh, felt the tips of his fangs graze her, and it sent another spike of pleasure through her. His tail coiled around her leg, starting at her ankle and winding upward along her calf until the furry tuft brushed the back of her knee.

He pulled his head back and snarled, "This is mine." Sliding a hand over her thigh, he used his fingers to spread her sex, which he again probed with that strong, talented tongue, licking her essence straight from its source. "*You* are mine."

Avery's hips bucked with the pleasure that speared her as he flicked her clit.

"Fyran."

"So responsive...and all from this tiny bud." He twirled his tongue around her clit, eliciting another cry from her. "Say my name again, *vaerina*. Scream it."

Avery stared down at him, her brows creasing as he teased her in slow strokes. She panted, her toes curling against his back, and reached up to grasp her breast. She squeezed it and pinched her nipple, desperate for something to hold onto. She wished it were his hand there instead of hers. Fresh heat pooled between her legs, and her skin tingled, coming alive with every delicious swipe of his tongue.

That pressure in her core grew and grew, becoming something immense, impossible, too much to bear. It wasn't quite pleasure, wasn't quite pain, but something in between, something fragile.

And when Fyran took her clit between his lips again, Avery shattered. Her cry was a hitched, broken sound. Her body tensed as though it could somehow resist the onslaught of ecstasy assailing her from all sides, but there was no escape, there was no holding it off. It ravaged her and tore her asunder.

"*Fyran!*"

She didn't know if he growled or roared, aware only of the sound rumbling into her and pushing her climax that much higher. Avery clenched a fistful of his hair and clamped her fingers down on her nipple as she struggled to draw in a breath, or to make a sound, or to even move, but the sensations were so strong, were so good, that she couldn't do anything but feel.

And then, too soon, she was sinking. Her body hummed as that overwhelming pleasure released her from its grasp and eased her back down, dissipating slowly.

She was only vaguely aware of Fyran moving, of his arms wrapping around her and his hands palming her ass. She leaned against him and put her arms around his neck when he lifted her from her perch on the tub. Her thighs naturally fit around his waist, and her pussy pressed against his stomach. Her lips skimmed along his neck, and she nearly purred, grinding her sex against him as she inhaled his spicy scent.

"Fuck," he grated. His fingers curled, claws pricking her backside. "Need to claim you, female. Now."

Before she even realized he was walking, Fyran had carried her into the bedroom. He lifted a hand, slipped his fingers into her hair, and slanted his mouth over hers in a crushing, ravenous kiss. His tongue demanded entry, and she parted her lips for him, melting against his body. She tasted herself on his lips, but more, she tasted *him*.

She wished he didn't have a shirt on. Wished it was his skin against her sex, wished his cock was—

Fyran ended the kiss suddenly. He removed his hand from her hair, unraveled his tail from her leg, broke her hold on him, and tossed her onto the bed. She gasped and bounced, disoriented. Pushing herself up on her elbow, she swiped her hair out of her face and looked up at Fyran.

Though her vision was blurry without her glasses and he'd backed away from the bed, he was close enough for her to see his muscles straining against the fabric of his shirt, to see the outline of his erection through his jeans, to see the hungry red light of his eyes and the predatory set of his features. His tail swung behind in with stiff, powerful motions.

"Need to be inside you," he rasped, "right fucking now."

Fyran grabbed his shirt by the collar with both hands and tore it off, shredding it down the middle and thrusting the tattered garment off his arms. He was no gentler with his jeans. The sound of the zipper breaking and the denim ripping as he opened them was stunningly erotic, reverberating through Avery to pulse in her nipples and tease at her core.

He shoved the pants down, kicked them aside, and rose to his full height again.

Avery's eyes began on his face and worked their way down, dragging over his broad shoulders and sculpted muscles and flicking briefly to the glowing tattoos on his arms before stopping on the part of him she'd anticipated most—his cock.

Her breath caught. It was long and thick, with a prominent crown and veins. It might've appeared perfectly human were it not for the raised nubs which ran along the top and bottom of its shaft.

Avery's pussy clenched. She was eager to feel to him inside her.

"I claim you, Avery," he said as he stalked closer to the bed. He dropped a hand to his cock, wrapped his fingers around its base, and groaned. A drop of seed beaded at its tip.

She lifted her gaze to meet his.

Fyran's crimson eyes looked straight into her, right into her heart, and held her as he reached the bed. He crawled onto it, his golden streaked hair framing his face like a mane. Her lion, finally cornering his prey. Finally ready to mate. He drew himself over her, and she laid back, parting her knees and placing her palms upon his chest.

Avery's heart thundered within her breast, and fire flowed through her veins to coalesce in her core. His scent enveloped her, his heat blanketed her.

Fyran braced himself on one hand, grasped her leg with the other, and wedged his body between her thighs. Avery gasped as his shaft, a rod of molten steel, settled over her sex, pulsing strongly enough to deepen the ache at her core.

"In every fucking way, *vaerina*"—he dipped his head low, until his nose was nearly touching hers—"you're mine."

Whether she had a response or not made no difference; Fyran

captured her mouth with his, and her eyelids fell shut as delightful tingles spread outward from her lips.

Avery slid her hands up over his shoulders until she locked her arms around his neck, pulling him closer. She arched her back, brushing her nipples against his chest, and undulated her hips, moaning as his cock stroked along her slick folds and dragged over her clit. She shivered.

"I'm yours," she rasped against his mouth. "I've always been yours."

Fyran growled and caught her chin, capturing her eyes with his. "Damn right you fucking are, *vaerina*."

Releasing her chin, he pulled away from her and pushing her legs wider open. He looked down between their bodies, took hold of his shaft, and angled its tip toward her entrance. He rolled his hips forward. There was a feral, possessive gleam in his eyes as he watched his length disappear inside her.

Avery's breath hitched, but her eyes remained locked on where her body was connected to Fyran's. Despite how aroused and wet she was, despite having used toys on occasion to pleasure herself, she was small, and his cock was stretching her more than any toy could have.

She whimpered at the burning sensation, at how thoroughly he filled her, but she still wanted more. She felt every nub on his shaft as he entered, and she was only more aware of them when he withdrew and pushed forward again, sinking even deeper inside her. Slowly, that tinge of burning pain turned into something else, something carnal.

"*Fuck*, Avery."

Avery's gaze flicked up to Fyran. His eyes were focused, his brow was furrowed, and his lips were drawn back, baring his fangs. He trembled with restraint.

But she didn't want his restraint. She wanted him wild and untamed, wanted him to let go and use her body, to take her, to stake his claim on her in the most savage way possible—to leave his mark on her very soul. She wanted everything he had to give.

Capturing his face between her hands, she turned him toward her and pulled him down into a kiss.

FYRAN RELEASED his hold on his cock to slam his hand atop the bed. He curled his fingers, digging his claws into the blanket, and clutched it as tremors of pleasure radiated from his groin.

Avery dominated his senses—he was drowning in her heat, her scent, her taste. She was in his every breath; she was the fire in his veins and the thumping of his heart. She was his universe.

And *karak'duun,* her sex was so hot, so wet, and so fucking tight that he was already on the verge of spilling even though he hadn't yet fully entered her.

Avery broke their kiss and met his gaze. "Fucking love me, Fyran."

The instant she'd spoken those words, he knew he was lost. There was no further hope for self-control. No more holding himself back. Everything he could ever want, everything he could ever need, was right here.

Fyran Voltanix, highly trained *althicar,* dedicated soldier, unmatched assassin, succumbed to primal instinct.

He drew his hips back, growled, and thrust into Avery, burying himself to the hilt. Avery's lips parted to let out a silent cry, and her thighs squeezed his hips. The rush of pleasure that blasted through him threatened to make his elbows and knees give out, but he had no patience for weakness.

Fucking love me...

He pulled back and hammered into her again, and again, sinking deeper and deeper each time, his grip on the blanket only tightening. Fyran quickened his pace, baring his teeth and pumping wildly, his desperation growing along with the over-whelming sensations inside him. Avery writhed beneath him, her blunt nails clawing at his sides and back. Those scratches only drove him harder.

This was his female. His lifemate. His future, his world, his everything, and this was the moment when he was finally claiming her. This was the moment when he was finally making her indisputably his. She would bear his mark forever.

Her womb will take my seed. She will bear my children.

With a snarl, Fyran reared back on his knees, grasped Avery's hips with both hands, and used his new hold on her to piston into her with increasing force. His tail wrapped around one of her legs, its tip brushing up to the back of her knee.

Avery grabbed fistfuls of the bedding as though seeking something, anything, to hold onto. She stared up at him with half-lidded, lust-glazed eyes, panting through her kiss-swollen lips.

"You're fucking mine, *vaerina*," he said through his teeth, punctuating each word by slamming her against him. Her hair fanned around her head, and her breasts bounced with every forceful thrust.

Her slick, hot sex fluttered around his shaft, caressing every one of the nodules along it to assault him with pure, unrelenting pleasure. But he would not close his eyes. He would not miss even an instant of this.

Fyran needed to see every change in her expression, no matter how minute. He needed to see her reactions, needed to see her giving herself over to him. Needed to see the moment it happened.

"My mate." He grunted as his muscles tensed. He teetered for an instant on the edge of oblivion before pushing even harder and faster. "My forever."

"Fyran... I—" She shut her eyes and thrust a hand into her hair, squeezing it. "*Oh, God.*" Avery's back arched off the bed as she cried out, her sex seizing around his cock, her heels digging into his calves.

Fyran clenched his teeth tighter, refusing to let his rhythm be disrupted. Liquid heat flowed around his shaft.

"*Karak'duun,*" he snarled. That pressure was too great, the ache was too immense. He couldn't hold it back any longer. His appetite for her was insatiable, and she fit him so fucking perfectly it was as though her body had been designed just to be paired with his.

His sweet, intelligent, compassionate female. His mate.

My mate.

A roar built in his gut. He shifted an arm beneath her and lifted her off the bed so she was straddling his lap. Avery's eyes flashed open to look down at him as she reflexively threw her arms over his shoulders, nails scratching his back. Her cheeks were flushed, her hair was tousled, and her gaze was bright with lust.

"So fucking beautiful." Fyran slammed her down onto his shaft again and again. He lifted a hand, curling his forefinger and thumb under her jaw to keep her face toward his. "So fucking beautiful, and all fucking mine."

A shudder wracked his body, making his fingers twitch and his claws dig into her skin.

Avery's sex convulsed again. She raked her nails over his shoulders and breathed, *"Please."*

Fyran fought back the fire about to erupt from his core. "Who do you belong to, female?"

Avery moaned and sagged forward, ducking her head. He forced her chin back up, forced her to meet his gaze, and tipped his forehead against hers.

"Who do you belong to, Avery?"

"You."

He ground himself inside her and against her clit. "Say my fucking name, *vaerina.*"

"Fyran. I belong—*mmph*—to Fyran!" Her eyelids fluttered shut and her sex clamped around his shaft tighter than ever before as another rush of liquid heat flooded her. Her essence flowed out to make his thighs slick.

That roar tore out of his throat, and every muscle in his body tensed simultaneously. The pressure in his groin broke, blasting out with force enough to annihilate Fyran's awareness of everything but Avery, obliterating his consciousness in an explosion of ecstasy that made it impossible to draw breath.

He never would've believed it possible to feel so close to anyone, even in the throes of passion, even during this most intimate of acts. In that moment, Avery felt like more than his universe—she was a part of him, as vital as his heart and infinitely more irreplaceable.

His seed erupted, pouring into Avery in powerful spurts that were each accompanied by a fresh blast of pleasure. She moaned and trembled against him, her body consumed by spasms, and Fyran erratically pumped his hips to seek out every sliver of sensation he could obtain. The tiny contractions of her sex milked every drop of seed from his throbbing cock until he clutched her down upon him.

They remained like that for a while, slowly descending from their climaxes and finding little peaks to share on the way down, neither of them willing to move away. Fyran put his arm around her, holding her steady.

He drew in a deep breath through his nostrils and produced a rolling hum in his chest. Her scent had changed. It was richer, fuller, even more alluring than before—and it bore a familiar hint now. A hint of him. Somehow, he knew it wasn't merely a matter of their scents mingling during their mating. This was something more fundamental. Something more permanent.

Warmth spread through Fyran, filling his chest, and his muscles slowly relaxed under that soothing heat. He'd never felt so satisfied, so content, so...whole in his entire life. He'd never realized everything that he'd been missing.

Avery let out a soft, happy sigh. Her lashes fluttered, and her eyelids opened.

A grin stretched across Fyran's lips. Within the lovely blue-gray of Avery's irises were tiny, glowing flecks of crimson. The contrast between the colors only added to the allure of her eyes.

Their mating bond had been made. They were connected in a way he'd never considered, in a way he'd never wanted before her.

"Ah, my Avery," he purred, stroking his thumb along her jaw. "I will never let you go."

TWENTY-SEVEN

Fyran entered the bedroom, closed the door, and paused. His gaze fell upon the bed, and the corner of his mouth quirked up. The bedding was still rumpled, the pillows scattered and askew, and the fitted sheet had come off one corner to reveal the mattress pad beneath. Normally, he made the bed every morning after waking. His routine had been pleasantly disrupted as of late.

He walked to the bed, closed his eyes, and smoothed his hand over the spot that had become Avery's. He inhaled. Avery's essence had infused the bedding, but more than that, the bed smelled of their mating bond—that perfect blend of his scent and hers, that fragrance that roused a swelling of pride and possessiveness in his chest.

His cock throbbed, hardening rapidly, and his sweatpants offered it scant resistance. Fyran clenched his jaw and curled his fingers, dragging his claws over the sheet.

He was tempted to go back downstairs, throw Avery over his shoulder, and carry her up here so he could toss her onto the bed and rut her again just like he had this morning. Or he could take her right there on the couch—or against the wall, or on the counter...

Over the four days since they'd forged their mating bond, they'd only just begun to explore the possibilities.

Opening his eyes, Fyran shifted his hand up to Avery's pillow, trailing his fingertips along the indentation she'd left in it. The night they'd forged their bond would forever be his fondest memory, but the morning after wasn't far behind. They'd awoken together in the early morning light, their naked bodies intertwined, their hair wild. Her smile had been shy, delighted, and endearing; it had been for Fyran alone.

The edges of Avery's hair had glowed golden in the sunlight streaming through the blinds, and there'd been a radiant pink to her skin. And those flecks of red in her eyes...they had spread and brightened. By the light of day, they were even more stunning, making her irises seem bluer in comparison.

She'd been languid, sore, and uninhibited by her nakedness, even when he'd peeled the blanket off them and explored her body with his eyes and hands.

Discovering the damage he'd done to his delicate little mate had been like a blow to the gut. Her pale skin had been marked with several tiny scratches left by his claws, and the bruises on her hips and thighs couldn't have been from anything other than his overenthusiastic grip during their mating. But those marks had also instilled him with a degree of pride, because they were just more evidence that she was his—and that she'd been well-loved.

His conflicted feelings had been eased when Avery brushed her fingers over one of the bruises and grinned. She'd worn them like marks of honor. Neither those superficial wounds nor her soreness had stopped her from rolling atop him and mating with him with even greater fervor than the first time. She'd been beautiful with her head thrown back, eyes closed, breasts bouncing, and her blunt nails digging into his chest as she rode him to release.

They'd rutted more than he could count in the days since, and each time left him even more ravenous for her. He'd already wanted her so badly that it had hurt, but that apparently hadn't been the limit of his want.

Letting out a low growl, Fyran shoved the pillows up to the head of the bed, grabbed the untucked corner of the sheet, and stripped the bedding off the mattress. Reluctant as he was to wash away those scents, it was overdue—and it wasn't like those delicious smells would be absent for long.

But he hadn't come up here to deal with the laundry—or to reminisce about the bliss he'd enjoyed over the last four days.

Fyran tossed the wadded bedding onto the floor near the door before stepping over to the hidden compartment and kneeling. He opened the compartment and plucked out the comm disc, laying it on his open palm.

The last thing he wanted to do was sacrifice time with Avery, but he couldn't continue neglecting his duties. He had to make his report.

Allowing himself no further hesitance, he activated the disc.

The identification scan felt like it took twice as long as usual, and it seemed as though a thousand years had crawled by before the *ultricar's* holographic visage materialized.

For an instant, Khelvar's brows rose, and his eyes widened. "*Althicar* Voltanix. What's happened?"

Fyran frowned. "Why do you ask as though there must've been some sort of disaster?"

"Because there's no other reason you'd be contacting me again so soon. In all the years you've reported to me, Fyran, you've never once made back-to-back, voluntary reports without at least three weeks between them."

Fyran chuckled, his frown giving way to a smirk. The *ultricar's* voice was, as usual, largely neutral and devoid of emotion, but Fyran swore there was just a hint of good-natured sarcasm in it.

Of course, the words were only more amusing given their similarity to an exchange from one of the movies Fyran had watched with Avery a couple days before, a scene in which a woman had scolded her adult son for not calling her often enough. Avery had related to that scene rather strongly.

The movie had been a comedy; the genre had become one of

Fyran's favorites because he loved Avery's laughter, loved her smiles, loved the light that danced in her eyes when she was amused. But those movies also made him feel...lighter. They'd provided him an escape from his worries and stress for a little while. They'd given him reason to laugh freely—which he'd never done much before Avery.

"The mating bond has been forged," Fyran said.

Another crack formed in the *ultricar's* normally stoic mask—Khelvar smiled. "That's excellent news, Fyran."

Fyran couldn't help but agree. As much as he'd enjoyed his time with Avery before the bond, everything seemed so much richer and fuller now. Every moment had become infinitely more precious. The act of mating was beyond his ability to describe, but the depth of their new bond was so, so much greater than that.

And it was liberating to be open with her. To have shared his secrets with her.

"I have news to pass on, also," Khelvar continued. "We raided the warehouse three days ago. No sign of the ilventyrs, but we recovered the stolen weapons and the drugs, just as you'd described. Field reports indicate the ilventyrs were prepping for a big move."

Mention of that place only reminded Fyran of what Gregor and his associates had intended for Avery—it reminded him of the fate she'd only narrowly avoided. Anger flared in his gut, sizzling up into his chest and throat. Until he knew without a doubt that Gregor, Varketh, and their comrades were dead, Fyran considered them a threat to his mate.

"None of them were accounted for?" Fyran asked.

"None. But we're on their trails. We managed to uncover more evidence of their operations in several other Earth cities, and we're in the process of identifying the wider trafficking ring. Their whole business is in its final days."

Fyran's fingers tightened around the edges of the comm disc. "Command authorized that big an operation?"

Khelvar huffed through his nostrils. "Would it make a difference?"

Fyran snickered and shook his head. "You already know my answer."

"Of course I do. You're not nearly as unpredictable as you think, *althicar*."

Though that brought a smile to Fyran's face, his mind turned away from Khelvar's jest to something more important—Avery.

"What now, Khelvar? We've made the bond, we're bound, but I have no idea what comes next. What is the plan? How the fuck does the *Exthurizen* intend to deal with this situation?"

"Our research team will want to examine the female should—"

A ragged growl tore out of Fyran's throat. "Let me make one thing perfectly clear before you go on—no one will lay so much as a finger on my mate without my consent or I will bite that finger off and use it to fuck whoever is stupid enough to think they can touch my female."

The *ultricar's* unreadable expression made its grand return. "That's one lesson already learned, *althicar*. The scientists will be involved only if your mate ends up with child."

Child.

That word, that notion, struck Fyran differently now than it had only a few days before. He'd thought about it every time he'd filled his mate with his seed. He'd thought about it as they'd shared meals, had thought about it as they'd watched movies on the couch, whether those movies were comedies or sappy romances. Oddly enough, he'd especially thought about it while they'd watched a couple horror movies—not because parenthood frightened him, but because those movies had frightened his mate.

Avery wasn't a fan of scares and gore. Her squeaks had been adorable, but every time she'd curled against him, every time she'd buried her face against his chest and clung to him, that protective instinct within Fyran had surged. It felt damned good to be the one she turned to when she was afraid. It felt good to be the one she turned to for strength and security.

Would he be able to provide that to a child, to *his* child?

Would he be able to grant his son or daughter the stability and peace he'd never known in his youth?

For the first time in his life, Fyran wanted to try.

He couldn't quite keep his voice steady when he asked, "Where will we have to go?"

"Nowhere. And, after your eventual release from service...anywhere."

Not long ago, the prospect of having a whole world, a whole universe, open to him had been daunting. What life could he have had without the *Exthurizen* providing him with a purpose?

That question was no longer relevant; it was being answered every day he spent with Avery.

"And...when will I be released?" Fyran asked.

"The mission is to produce a child."

"If that doesn't happen? How long before I'm torn away from her, Khelvar?"

The ultricar was silent, staring at Fyran through the holographic projector from some unfathomable distance across the universe. And, briefly, Fyran felt just as he had the first time he and Khelvar had met—like a child, lost, alone, and more afraid than he would ever let on.

He'd gone from hating this assignment, this planet, to being unable to imagine himself anywhere else. To being unwilling to go anywhere else. He'd kill anyone who meant to take him from his Avery.

"You will not be separated," Khelvar finally said. "I swear that to you."

Fyran couldn't bring himself to do anything but nod.

When Khelvar spoke again, his voice was lower but softer. "You've changed, Fyran."

"I was wrong about this fucking planet, okay? I've realized my error."

"No, it's not that...even if I can't help a bit of smug satisfaction over it." Now Khelvar's expression softened, too. "You're more balanced. More...grounded. Calmer."

"My conduct through much of this mission has been...regrettable."

"It was insubordination, *althicar*. But it's also in the past. Your mate has inspired this change in you, I'm sure. She's given you something more."

Fyran's heart thumped. He'd always known that Khelvar had a talent for seeing into even the most guarded individuals, but this...had Fyran given away so much?

"There's no shame in it, Fyran. I'd..." Khelvar sighed, brow furrowing. "I'd hoped you would find something like this. Hoped you'd find someone. When I took you out of that shitty life on Vabos, I never intended to thrust you into a different kind of shit."

A leaden lump formed in Fyran's gut, swirling and twisting. He'd never seen the *ultricar* like this. He'd never felt like this—like his entire life had been boiled down to his unresolved, emotional bullshit. "Khelvar, you... I chose this. I pushed for it."

"You were never given a choice, Fyran. Not really. No one ever worked hard enough to show you a different way. I didn't work hard enough."

A few weeks ago, Fyran would've ended the communication right then. He wouldn't have had patience for this. What the fuck was he supposed to say? How was he meant to react, how was he meant to *feel*? He'd known anger, bitterness, and loneliness. They'd aided him as an *althicar* at various points. But those had been the extent of his emotional range.

Maybe...he really had changed.

"*Karak'duun*, Khelvar, what did you know about a different life back then?" Fyran asked. "And it wasn't your place to show me, regardless. You're not my father. You had no obligation to me."

The *ultricar* averted his gaze, features uncharacteristically tight. "I know, Fyran, but—"

"But you've been like a father to me regardless." The words came out of Fyran's mouth with surprising ease, like water through an opened floodgate. Fyran couldn't understand it. He'd never articulated any of this, whether out loud or in his head, had never even allowed himself to reflect upon it. "You never had any obligation to me, but you've always been there. Even when I seemed determined to destroy myself.

"So...thank you. For all the things I've never acknowledged, all the things I never realized. For assigning me to this mission."

Because the truth was apparent—without Khelvar, Fyran would never have met Avery. He would never have found the person who made him feel complete.

He would never have survived his time on Vabos.

Khelvar met Fyran's gaze and gave a single, firm nod. That unreadable mask fell back into place slowly, though it did not return to the *ultricar's* eyes. "Keep me informed, *althicar*. About the ilventyr...and about your mate. Keep her safe."

"At all fucking costs," Fyran growled.

The holographic projection flickered out, and the comm disc went dark.

As Fyran returned the device to the compartment, his gaze fell upon the pistol he'd taken from Varketh.

The emotions of that night—when he'd nearly lost his female —had not yet fully faded. He doubted they ever would, but he refused to let them weigh him down. Gregor and his crew remained at large, but Fyran had learned an important lesson from the ordeal—to cherish every moment with Avery. There would always be some battle on the horizon, some challenge to overcome, but he didn't have to spend all the time between those struggles doing nothing but anticipating the next fight.

He closed the compartment and stood. He'd spent the last four days making love to his mate, talking with her, learning all he could about her. They'd watched movies and shows, he'd assisted her as she cooked their meals, and he'd witnessed her face light up and her fingers fly as she lost herself in her writing. If this was the life he'd feared, the life he'd railed against so much and fought so hard to avoid...well, he'd been a damned fool.

With Avery, with their mating bond, he felt lighter. Unburdened. *Alive.* He had a purpose. And that purpose was to protect what was his—his mate. His...family.

And he'd already spent too much time away from her.

He walked to the door, bent down, and gathered the wad of bedding off the floor. He lifted it to his nose and inhaled, groaning at that lingering scent. Yes, he'd be cleaning that tantalizing smell off the sheets, but the couch was still a viable option...

Grinning to himself, Fyran opened the door and went to find his lifemate.

TWENTY-EIGHT

AVERY REMOVED her glasses and leaned over the bathroom counter to peer at her eyes in the mirror. The speckles of red in her irises had become more prominent. When she'd seen them in her eyes the morning after she and Fyran had first made love, she'd been startled. It looked like red glitter amidst the blue-gray, a subtle dusting initially, but as the days had passed, the crimson had multiplied and grown more vibrant.

She hadn't been sure how far the change would go, if her irises would become fully red like Fyran's, but he'd assured her that wouldn't be the case—this was the full extent of the change. These red flecks were his mark upon her, signifying their mating bond.

A bond that was a far deeper and more permanent than a marriage certificate.

I'm mated to Fyran.

Avery's lips spread into a giddy grin as she straightened and put her glasses back on. It was still hard to believe that she was basically married to an alien. She'd always hoped she would meet a man like the ones in her romance books. Of course, that had been an unrealistic expectation, but a woman could dream, couldn't she? In truth, she'd simply wanted someone unlike her father—someone who was kind, caring, loyal, and passionate.

Someone who *loved* her.

While Fyran hadn't said those words, he displayed them in everything he did—the way he looked at her, the way he touched her, the way he made love to her. The way he spoke to her and the way he listened to her. Even when she talked about subjects he undoubtedly knew nothing about, he'd never once seemed disinterested or unengaged, and some of the passion she felt for the things she enjoyed was always reflected in his eyes. He was eager to learn everything about her.

And oh, was Fyran *very* eager to learn her body and every way he could give her pleasure.

She touched her fingers to her lips, which were slightly swollen from his kisses this morning, and trailed them down her chin and neck to her chest, where she brushed her nipple through her shirt. Her breath hitched. The well-loved bud hardened immediately. She lightly circled it, feeling whispers of pleasure as warmth spread through her and pooled in her core. Her clit pulsed with the memory of Fyran sucking her nipples into his hot mouth, of his lashing tongue and the press of his fangs against her tender flesh. He'd sucked on them long after she'd begun writhing beneath him, long after she'd begun begging for more, begging for an end to the torment he was subjecting her to, until, finally, he'd thrust his cock inside her.

Avery released a shaky breath and dropped her hand. "No more of that. Fyran's busy in a meeting with his boss upstairs, so there's no point in getting worked up now."

She gripped the hem of her shirt and brushed her fingers across the waistline of her pajama pants, contemplating whether she should slip her hand into her panties and pleasure herself while she waited for Fyran. It wouldn't take long. She was already aroused, so a few strokes of her clit would do the—

She groaned and tilted her head back, staring up at the ceiling with a scowl. "Oh my God, what has he turned me into? I'm a freaking sex addict."

And touching herself would only leave her dissatisfied and hollow when all she really wanted was *him*. Fyran, her mate.

Turning toward the door, Avery opened it, flicked off the bathroom light, and stepped out into the small hallway connecting the downstairs bathroom to the living room. She'd just have to get her mind off sex by working on her book.

She snorted.

Yeah, because writing romance is a great way to stop thinking about sex.

Avery crossed the living room, stopping in front of the sofa and smiling when she found Beau all balled up on the cushion with his paws curled in and his head upside down. It was too much to resist.

She lightly tapped his adorable little pink nose with her fingertip. "Boop."

Rather than wake, Beau simply tucked his face down and covered it with his paws.

"You're just too dang cute," Avery said, running her hand through the soft fur along his side.

Picking up her laptop from the end table, she plopped down on the opposite side of the couch from Beau and drew her legs up, crossing them. She placed the laptop on her lap and lifted the lid. She entered her password to wake the laptop up, and the screen switched her book document, which she'd left open.

She'd been riding a burst of inspiration for days now, and since she couldn't go to work at Jerry's, she'd used her spare time to write. Fyran's long workout sessions were prime writing time for her, though there'd been other occasions when he'd been in the room as she worked. The latter times were notably less productive, as she was all too aware of his heated crimson gaze and his nearness, and they'd soon find themselves acting out passionate scenes of their own.

Avery grinned. Sex with Fyran was amazing. Better than amazing, it was mind-blowing. Of course, they'd done other things while they'd been cooped up in this house, but the sex...

"What has you smiling like that, *vaerina*?"

Avery started, her eyes going wide as they flew toward Fyran, who now stood at the base of the stairs. He was wearing nothing but a pair of gray sweatpants and a knowing grin, and his golden streaked hair was loose around his shoulders. His tail lazily swayed behind him. Unfortunately, most of his bare torso was hidden behind the large bundle of bedlinens in his arms.

Avery grabbed one of the decorative pillows off the sofa and chucked it at him. "Stop using your alien stealth magic to sneak up on me like that!"

Despite his arms being full, Fyran swayed, freed a hand, and caught the pillow before it could hit his face. His grin stretched, becoming all fangs and wickedness. "I seem to recall you enjoying that stealth magic not so long ago, female."

"I lured you there. I *knew* you were there. This is just plain sneaking up on me to scare me. Walk a little louder."

"I didn't want to disturb you." He sauntered to the couch, dropped the pillow onto it, and brushed the tuft of his tail over her knee as he continued past her. "You're so fucking tempting when you're focused on your writing."

Beau raised his head, looked at the pillow, and narrowed his eyes as though it offended him.

Avery smiled and caught the end of Fyran's tail above the tuft, giving it a tug and bringing Fyran to a stop. "And you're pretty dang hot when you're doing house chores."

He glanced back at her. "Mmm. Keep that up and neither of us will get any work done."

Drawing Fyran closer, Avery tilted her head and peered up at him as she brushed the tip of his tail over her neck and down toward her chest. "I wouldn't mind..."

A chime rang from Avery's laptop. She looked at the incoming FaceTime call and groaned.

Talk about a mood killer.

Fyran's tail curled, pressing more firmly to her skin. "You can ignore it, *vaerina*."

"I've already ignored a bunch of her calls this week. She'll just keep calling until I answer." She met his gaze. "As much as I dislike talking to her, she's still my mother."

"So do what most of your kind does and communicate with

her only through text messages. It would be far less stressful for you."

Avery chuckled. "Have you seen the text messages from her? I've had to put my phone on silent with how much she blows it up. It's better to just talk to her, let her get it out of her system, and then she'll leave me be for a little while."

Fyran withdrew his tail, offering her a smirk before walking away. "So you choose punishment. Noted, female."

"You can punish me later if you want," she offered, grinning as her eyes focused on his ass and swaying tail. "I think I'd prefer yours."

"You'll have to earn it, *vaerina*." He turned for the laundry room, leaving her line of sight.

Still smiling, Avery looked down at her laptop and accepted the call. Allison appeared on the screen. She was wearing an airy white blouse, and her hair was slicked back and pulled into a perfect bun atop her head. Her red lips stretched into a wide smile.

"Happy birthday, Avery dear!"

Avery's brows rose. Birthday? She glanced at the corner of the screen and clicked on the calendar. It was December twentieth. Her birthday.

Over the top of the laptop, Avery saw Fyran lean back into her field of view to regard her with lowered eyebrows and narrowed eyes. She knew that look—it was the expression he wore when he was puzzling something out, when he was trying to place a detail he might've missed.

"Why do you look so shocked?" Allison asked. "You didn't think I'd forget my own daughter's birthday, did you?"

Fyran scowled before he exited Avery's vision again.

"Ye—uh, no. It's just that I forgot it myself." Avery hadn't been paying attention to the days, hadn't realized how fast time had passed. Not that she'd really been thinking about her birthday, anyway. She'd just...spaced it.

"Apparently. Your hair is an absolute mess."

"It's called a messy bun, Mom. It's on purpose."

"It makes you look unkempt. And are you still in your pajamas? Really, Avery, it's nearly noon!"

Technically, it was after noon, but Avery didn't correct her. "It's my day off, and I'm spending the day relaxing and writing."

"You should still take some more pride in your appearance. I tried to teach you that, and I don't know where I went wrong. You should fix your hair and put on some make up as soon as you wake up so you look your best no matter what. You shouldn't strive to look like...like *this*." Allison waved her hand toward Avery. "And you really must stop reading and writing so much. It's making your eyes red."

Oops.

Avery had let that little detail slip her mind, too, even though she'd just been looking at those crimson flecks a couple minutes ago.

Beau nudged his head against her arm. Avery lifted it to allow him to walk onto her lap, shifting the laptop to give him more room before running her hand down his back and tail. He arched into her touch, purring.

"It's just eye strain." Avery was grateful Allison didn't realize that the redness would've been in her sclera instead of her irises were it just eye strain.

"Why don't you get dressed and go out with your little friends from your work? It's your birthday, Avery! This is...pitiful. You only turn twenty-three once."

You only turn any age once, Mother.

"Mom, I'm fine. I've just never really been the going out type."

Beau lay down, his tail curling and his eyelids drooping as Avery continued to pet him.

Allison humphed. "Well, we're just going to have to rectify that. I'm buying you a plane ticket so you can come visit for Christmas, and we'll throw a huge Christmas-birthday bash. It'll be beautiful!"

Avery sighed. All that meant was an even more extravagant party than normal—a party she still wanted nothing to do with. "I already told you I'm not visiting this year."

"Nonsense! It'll be a gift, so you have to come."

"Mom, I'm not going back to LA." Avery said firmly, but not unkindly. "I've already been over this with you."

Allison rolled her eyes. "Honestly, Avery, this is ridiculous. I am your *mother*. I gave birth to you."

"And I'm grateful for existing, Mom, but—"

"Do you know how many hours I spent in labor? How much work it was to bring you into this world? All the stretch marks I obtained? My body will never be the same. And all I ask is for my daughter to come visit her parents for the holidays. Everyone is going to be here. Britney, Charles Anderson's daughter, is coming from England. *England.* Do you know how far that is?"

No, Allison. I have no concept of distance whatsoever.

Britney was coming all the way from England? Well, Avery's mate had come from just a bit farther away than that. So, by her mother's logic, didn't that mean it was only right that Avery remained here, with Fyran? Not that she could tell her mother that.

And Britney had always been a stuck-up snob, anyway, who'd liked to tease and call Avery names when they were younger.

Avery glanced up to see Fyran standing in front of her, arms folded over his chest, muscles bulging, and one eyebrow arched. Though his expression looked rather stern, she couldn't deny that he was pretty damn hot glaring down at her like that.

She met his gaze. "Mom, I'm not going. I'm...spending the holiday with my boyfriend."

"What? Your boyfriend?" Allison asked.

Avery returned her attention to the screen.

Allison's eyes were narrowed, and there was a deep crease between her eyebrows as she stared past Avery. She looked like she'd just noticed the unfamiliar background. "Where are you?"

"I'm at his place. I've...been staying here for a while now. It's pretty serious." Avery's eyes flicked up to Fyran.

He tilted his chin down, and his crimson eyes smoldered. His sensual lips curled into a smile that revealed his fangs and reminded her just how dangerous he truly was.

That was all it took for heat to pool between Avery's thighs. Her sex clenched in anticipation. "*Very* serious."

"Then bring him with you," Allison said. "You've never had a boyfriend before. Your father and I would...love to meet him."

Avery frowned at the predatory gleam in her mother's eyes, but she knew exactly what was going on in Allison's mind—*We're going to judge the shit out of him.*

"Mom, I'm sorry, but no. We're staying here. We already have plans, and I'd rather not scare him off by having him meet you and Dad."

Allison scowled. "What? Your father—"

"Thanks for wishing me happy birthday. Bye, Mom." Avery tapped the *End Call* button. Releasing a long, slow breath, she closed her laptop and set it on the side table.

Fyran sat down on the couch beside her, placing a hand on her knee with his fingers spread wide. He gave it a possessive, though comforting, squeeze. "I'm not afraid of your parents, Avery."

She petted Beau and scratched the top of his head. "I know. They're just...*ugh*." She sat back, arms flopping onto the couch cushions, and looked up at the ceiling. Her movement disturbed Beau enough that he stood and jumped off her lap onto the floor.

"All my mother does is judge," Avery said. "She judges every-thing and everyone, especially me. And my father couldn't care less about anything until it makes him appear weak. I just...hated it there. I'm more comfortable in my tiny, rundown apartment, barely scraping by, than I ever was in that big house with all the money I wanted at my fingertips."

Fyran hummed and slid his hand up to her thigh before leaning toward her and capturing her chin with his other hand, turning her face toward him. "And now? Here, with me?"

Avery smiled softly. "I'm happy. Happier than I've ever been in my whole life."

He released a satisfied growl and teasingly stroked her bottom lip with the pad of his thumb. Desire brightened his eyes, but there was still something else in his features, in the set of his brow

—that hint of sternness, laced with salacious promise. "And this birthday, *vaerina*... It's something your people consider important, isn't it?"

God, the way he was touching her made it difficult to think. "Well, kind of, yeah."

"And you"—the tip of his claw grazed her upper lip briefly—"didn't deign to tell me?"

Avery smiled sheepishly as she reached up and took hold of his hand. She drew it away and lifted her head, looking down as she ran a finger over one of his claws. "I completely forgot about it."

His fingers curled, dragging that claw lightly across her fingertip as they did so. "Ah. Well, female, I'll have to make sure you never forget to share such information with me again."

Before she could ask what he meant, Fyran withdrew his hand from hers, looped his arm around her back, and dragged her toward him, laying her on her belly across his lap.

Avery braced her hands on the cushion to push herself up. "Fyran, what—"

He flattened his hand on her back and shoved her down again, pinning her in place. His other hand moved up her thigh, over her ass, and hooked the waistbands of her pajama pants and underwear. He drew them down with a swift tug.

His palm came down with a sharp *smack* on her bare ass.

Avery gasped at the painful sting and the heat that followed it. That heat seeped into her to pool like lava in her core.

"What are you doing?" she asked, still recovering from her shock as Fyran gently rubbed her right butt cheek, where he'd struck her.

"You asked for punishment, *vaerina*," he replied, voice low and husky. His hand left her, only to come back down with equal force on the left side of her ass.

Avery jolted and dug her fingers into the cushion. She'd felt that strike clear to her clit, and it only left her wanting more. "Look, I know birthdays sometimes involve spankings, but—"

His hand came down again, and Avery's breath hitched. Blood

rushed to the surface of her skin. Her pussy thrummed with desire as Fyran soothed her backside, and she hummed and arched into his touch.

He drew in a slow, deep breath, and a growl rumbled in his chest. "My female enjoys this, doesn't she?"

"She does," Avery breathed.

"Well, merry birthday, *vaerina*."

"It's happy birthday."

His palm cracked down on her ass again. "Do not correct me, female."

Avery squeezed her thighs together and raked her nails over the couch cushion, certain that her slick would be running freely any moment. "Just the...writer in me."

He smoothed his hand over her flesh, but this time it dipped lower, forcing her to part her thighs. She did obediently. His hand delved between them, and his fingers slid through her pussy.

"So wet for me," he said huskily.

Fyran stroked her clit, and Avery moaned. He circled the little bud gently, leisurely, as his other hand slipped beneath her shirt to palm her breast. Softly panting, she undulated her hips and strained into his touch, needing more.

"Fyran..." Avery rasped.

"I think my female is ready for her male."

He hooked his arm under her belly and stood up, lifting her as he moved and yanking her pants and panties off the rest of the way. Avery swung her knees beneath her and braced her hands on the armrest when he put her down again. She looked over her shoulder to find him behind her, one leg bent on the sofa with his other foot on the floor, his eyes twin orbs of swirling fire.

His tail brushed the back of one of her thighs. Fyran caught the other in his hand and tugged it aside, forcing her legs wider apart. The cool air flowing across her heated flesh made her shiver.

Fyran shoved down his sweatpants, and his cock sprang free, hard and thick. He grasped it, baring his fangs as a growl rumbled in his chest. Seed seeped from its tip and trickled down his shaft.

Avery licked her lips, longing to catch that seed with her tongue and taste him.

Curling one hand around her hip, he pulled her ass backward and pressed the head of his erection against her opening. Avery whimpered, pushing back against him, desperate to have him inside her.

Fyran didn't hesitate. With a deft yank, he thrust his hips forward.

His cock plunged into her slick sex all the way to its base, stealing her breath and making her elbows buckle. She fell forward, but Fyran's firm hold on her hips kept her backside raised. He snarled, claws pricking her skin, and held her ass against his pelvis for several moments.

Avery's pussy clenched around him. In this position, he felt larger, thicker. She felt so full of him. She could even feel his heartbeat through his shaft.

Grinding against him, she moaned as he sank deeper still. The blissful burn of his entry as he stretched her swiftly turned to pure pleasure.

"*Fuck*, Avery," Fyran groaned, withdrawing his shaft the barest amount and shoving back inside her. "I will never have enough of you. I will never be satisfied. I'll hunger for you always, female."

This time, Fyran pulled his hips back slowly, letting her feel the drag of every single one of the nubs lining his cock before thrusting inside her again. He kept his strokes long and deep, kept his pace deliberate and steady, his ministrations as pleasurable as they were torturous.

Avery clutched the armrest, her breasts swaying as she rocked against him, and no matter how much she tried to quicken the pace, he simply tightened his grip on her hips and kept her moving with his rhythm, ever in control. Her thighs quivered, and her core ached with the blossoming pleasure.

"Please, Fyran," she begged.

"Remove your shirt, *vaerina*," he commanded.

Grasping the hem of her shirt, Avery quickly pulled it up and over her head, tossing it aside.

One of his hands loosened on her hip and smoothed up along her spine, gently grazing her flesh with his claws. His pace didn't falter as he slid that hand around her and cupped her breast. He squeezed the soft mound, caught her sensitive nipple between his thumb and finger, and pinched, wringing a cry from her.

He lifted her, forcing her to straighten so her back was against his chest, and Avery moaned in response to the new angle at which he thrust into her.

His tail brushed over her outer thigh and wound around her waist. Its hold was tight, possessive, unyielding, a silent but clear statement—she was his, and he would not let her go.

Fyran's hand trailed up from her chest to grasp her jaw. He turned her face toward him, and she opened her eyes. The reverence in his gaze made her heart quicken. His crimson stare said the words he'd not spoken aloud—it expressed his deep, powerful love for her.

His head dipped, and he captured her mouth with his own. His tongue swept across her lips, which she parted. Growling, Fyran kissing her deeper, harder, his tongue like velvet as it stroked hers. Avery reached up and cupped his jaw, returning the kiss in full.

She trembled in his embrace. Each thrust of his hips sent a wave of heat through her, feeding the flames at her core but holding her right on the verge, dangling her over the edge but refusing to let her fall. The sensations were so strong, so overwhelming, but they weren't enough.

Fyran nipped her bottom lip with a fang. He didn't break the skin, but it sent a jolt through her, making her clit pulse as liquid heat flooded her anew. Avery whimpered. She was so wet it was dripping down her inner thighs.

Desperately needing more, Avery growled and caught his lower lip with her teeth, biting down.

His rhythm faltered, his hips bucking erratically, and he let out a bestial snarl that sent a shiver of delight through Avery.

Breaking the kiss abruptly, he shifted his hand to the back of her head and grasped a fistful of her hair before shoving her back down so her cheek was against the armrest.

"Ah, female. You want it rough?" Fyran's other hand clutched her hip as he drew his pelvis back. "Then I will do as my mate pleases."

With a fierce snap of his hips, he slammed into her. Avery gasped and clawed at the couch as that feeling of fullness, of pressure, of ecstasy, rocketed through her, but Fyran allowed her no time to recover.

He pounded into her with the speed and ferocity of a lust-maddened beast. His grip was bruising, his claws digging into her flesh, and his guttural grunts combined with the sound of his balls slapping her pussy created a punishing, frantic beat to their mating.

And Avery reveled in it. She *craved* it all.

"Yes," Fyran hissed. "Just like that. Take all of me, my mate."

Her pleasure swirled into a firestorm and unfurling in her veins, building and building—but it still had nowhere to go, had no means of release. She gritted her teeth and squeezed her eyes shut, tilting her pelvis as she pushed back against him. She just needed...needed...

Fyran's tail coiled tighter around her waist, and its tip pressed against her clit and thrummed.

The climax that had eluded her this entire time, that had driven her mad with its closeness, that had tormented her, finally came—and Avery shattered. Pleasure surged through her, so intense that her thoughts fragmented, and her vision went white. Every inch of her body seized simultaneously. Her ecstasy burst from her in a scream.

She writhed, her cries escalating until they became utterly soundless and breathless, as she was wracked with wave upon wave of pleasure.

Fyran filled in that silence with a roar that would've put the mightiest lion to shame. His shaft swelled inside her, growing impossibly larger, and his grip on her tightened as he slammed into her one final time. Heat erupted inside her as his seed spouted from him in molten jets. With a growl, he shuddered and ground against her, pushing deeper as another spurt filled her. Avery's pussy contracted as though eager to suck him dry.

She trembled as she came down from her climax. Her heavy panting blew hair from her face, a sheen of perspiration coated her skin, and her body felt weighed down and weak. She didn't know if she'd even be able to open her eyes. Fyran's tail remained secure around her, its fluffy tip lightly brushing over her sex, petting her, soothing her. Her core felt full, and their combined essences were dripping down her thighs.

Fyran's hands and tail eased their hold, and he gently smoothed her hair back. The gentleness in his touch now was nothing like the feral energy he'd unleashed upon her moments before; Avery relished in the dichotomy.

Moving slowly, he leaned over her, covering her with his body, and nuzzled her hair. His chest vibrated with what could only be described as a satisfied purr. "Happy birthday, *vaerina*."

Avery smiled and hummed contently. "Best damned birthday ever."

Fyran chuckled. He remained in that position, over her but not putting his weight upon her, brushing his lips over her hair, her cheek, and her shoulder as the tuft of his tail stroked her inner thigh. Avery hummed in contentment. She would've been perfectly happy remaining like that for the rest of the night—heck, maybe for the rest of her life.

But Fyran rose after a short while, unraveling his tail from around her waist and withdrawing his cock. He and Avery both groaned at the loss. Looping his arm around her, he drew her upright briefly—long enough to hook his other arm under her legs and cradle her against his chest. He lifted her off the couch, his hold rock solid despite the exertion of their lovemaking, and walked toward the stairs.

When she turned her head to rest it on his shoulder, he rubbed his cheek on her hair and clutched her tighter, wrapping his tail around her ankle and calf. Avery sighed and placed her hand on his chest, feeling his heart pounding against her palm.

"I've never been this happy before either," Fyran rumbled, pressing his lips to her temple. "And it's because I have you, Avery."

TWENTY-NINE

As much as Avery loved the time she'd spent with Fyran in his home, she hadn't been able to hold back her excitement when he'd told her to get dressed—in actual going-outside clothes—and get ready to go.

She understood the situation they were in, but all the same, she'd missed being outdoors, even in the brisk weather. She hadn't been stuck inside for particularly long, but she hadn't realized just how much she'd enjoyed her daily walks to and from work until they'd been abruptly stopped.

And though she was anxious, though her skin crawled with the memory of what had happened that night, she felt safe knowing Fyran would be nearby. That he'd do everything in his power to protect her.

Her excitement had kept her from asking the one question simmering in her mind as she changed her clothes and wove her hair into a side braid, which she lay over her shoulder. She'd managed not to ask it as Fyran activated his human disguise, or as they climbed into his car and drove out onto the open road, had managed not to ask as they'd cruised through the foothills on a meandering, southward path. She'd just been content to be out, to be moving. To be with Fyran.

But when they merged onto the freeway and she saw Denver far ahead and realized they were headed directly for it, she couldn't hold that question in any longer.

"Where are we going, Fyran?"

He glanced at her and grinned. It was so strange seeing him so...*human* again. His fangs, pointed ears, and claws were gone, his eyes were once again so dark they were nearly black, and his features were just a little less sharp, a little less...*him*.

"Out," he said.

Avery laughed. "Well, that's obvious. But where?"

"You will see, *vaerina*."

She brought the back of her hand to her forehead and slumped in her seat. "The suspense is killing me. I don't know how much longer I can take it."

Fyran's grin took on a mischievous slant. "I could pull over if you want me to make the journey more interesting."

Avery dropped her hand and curled her fingers on her thighs, snagging her leggings, as a sudden spark of desire lit within her core. She recalled what he'd done when they'd returned to her apartment, how he'd held her against him, her legs around his waist, and made them invisible. Could he do that again as they made love?

Fyran glanced at her, and his seductive expression gave way to something closer to surprise and delight. "Fuck, Avery. I know that look. You're considering it." His left hand wandered toward the turn indicator as though he were considering it himself.

Heat blossomed on her cheeks, and she smiled sheepishly. She'd never dreamed of having sex in public before, still didn't honestly, but the thrill was there. "Well, you do have some alien tech that would make us unseen..."

He growled raggedly and dropped his right hand to his groin, clamping it over his cock—but not before she glimpsed its outline through his jeans. "My mate is insatiable."

Avery chuckled. "So is mine."

The tendons on the back of his hand stood out as he squeezed, and he released a heavy breath. His grip relaxed gradually. "But we're not stopping. Not yet."

She huffed and stuck out her bottom lip. "Apparently, my mate is also a big tease."

Fyran's laughter was deep and rolling. "Ah, I see. When you do it, it's *building anticipation*, but when I do it, it's just teasing?" He moved his hand to her thigh and slid it up high, grazing a claw along the seam between her legs and making her breath hitch. "I'll make up for it later, *vaerina*." He squeezed her leg.

I can't wait.

Avery placed her hand over his as they continued along the freeway. Fyran's finger occasionally stroked her inner thigh, drawing teasingly close to her sex. She knew what he was doing—*building anticipation*.

At this rate, she'd soon be more eager to get home than to reach their surprise destination.

Fortunately, Fyran turned off the freeway only a few minutes later, turning into an area she knew—and driving toward one she knew even better still. The tall buildings with their shining windows came into view again, far closer and more towering than before. After days away, it was strange to be back in downtown Denver, where there were so many cars, so many people, so many sounds.

Avery gave Fyran's hand a gentle squeeze and looked at him again. He flashed her a smile.

They crossed through the Sixteenth Street Mall, which was bustling with shoppers. Was it really only four days until Christmas? It seemed like Thanksgiving had only just passed.

But that didn't make sense, did it? She'd met Fyran only a couple days after Thanksgiving, and it felt like she'd known him her entire life.

He pulled into one of the many public parking lots near Sixteenth, paid at the machine, and retrieved the receipt, which he placed on the dashboard as he parked in an open spot. After turning off the engine, he unbuckled his seatbelt, smiled at her, and reached for the door. "Let's go, *vaerina*."

Fyran was out of the car and his door was shut before Avery could speak.

She unbuckled her own seatbelt and grabbed her jacket before stepping out of the vehicle. The cold, wintery air sent a shiver through her as it swept beneath her long, loose shirt and over her exposed neck and face.

Avery closed the door and pulled on her coat, looking at Fyran as he rounded the car and stalked toward her. He was dressed in a pair of black jeans, boots, and leather jacket, his long hair loose around his shoulders, and looking so dang sexy.

"Is it a good idea to be here after...you know?" she asked.

"No," he replied, stopping in front of her. "But my people have them on the run, and they won't do anything where there are so many witnesses. If we're out of the house, crowded places like this are the safest."

"Why would that stop them? They're not human, they're not beholden to our laws or anything. And I'd guess they have disguises on, just like you, right?"

"Yes, they do have disguises, and they're not beholden to your laws, but it's not that simple. That tech can only change so much about a person's appearance before things start to seem...off. Works best when it's kept as close as possible to what's underneath. Changing faces doesn't hold up for long. And these ilventyrs have business to conduct. If they gain the attention of human authorities *and* the *Exthurizen*, they're effectively unable to operate. For people like them, that trumps everything."

"So, do you think they left?" she asked.

He bent down slightly and caught the bottom corners of her coat, zipping it up. It was such a simple gesture, but it warmed Avery more than any hot cocoa or crackling fire ever could.

He brushed his finger over her chin, and she felt the light scrape of his claw along her bottom lip. "Not sure they're that smart, but if they value their lives and their livelihoods they'd be long gone by now. Their best move would've been to cut their losses and set up somewhere else. We'll be safe, *vaerina*."

Avery smiled and reached up, wrapping her hands around his.

Tilting her face down, she pressed a kiss to his knuckles. "Are you going to tell me why we're here now?"

"I did some more research. Seems this birthday thing is a more important matter than you implied, Avery, especially when it's the birthday of one's mate. And I failed to make it...special."

Heat blasted into Avery as she thought of her birthday *punishment*—which had really been more of a reward in her opinion—the day before. The aftercare he'd provided had been just as pleasing; he'd taken her into the bath and moved his hands all over her body as she'd reclined against his chest.

"You did make it special, Fyran. I liked it. *A lot.*"

He raised her hands to his lips, kissing her fingers. "I'm unfamiliar with most human customs, Avery. Because I resented being deployed here, I never allowed myself to learn. But that's no excuse. Today, I'm making up for my ignorance, and you will have a birthday gift. As many as you'd like."

Avery's heart melted. She stepped closer to him and pulled her hands free to wrap her arms around his neck. His hands dropped to her hips. She looked into his eyes, wishing they were unmasked so she could see the glowing crimson that matched the glittering flecks in her own eyes.

"Oh, Fyran. I don't want you to spend money on me. I grew up with money, I could have had any material thing I wanted, whenever I wanted it. But none of that mattered. I don't care about things. I just want you. All I *need* is you."

Fyran lifted a hand to cup her cheek, brushing the pad of his thumb back and forth just beneath her bottom lip. "Ah, my Avery. You have me." He angled her face up toward his and slanted his mouth over hers in a slow, sensual kiss.

She tangled her fingers in his hair, moaned softly, and leaned into the kiss.

When he pulled back from her with a pleased hum, his tongue slipped out to trail across his upper lip. "If you want nothing more for yourself, *vaerina*...what about for us? For our dwelling. So it feels more like a home. *Our* home."

Tears welled in her eyes, their sting made sharper by the cold, but she didn't care. She grinned up at him. "Fyran, are you asking me to move in with you?"

"Female, I already moved you in. Already told you I'm never letting you go."

Avery laughed and scraped her nails lightly over the back of his neck. "So you really were keeping me prisoner, huh?"

He slid his hand from her hip to her ass, giving it a firm squeeze. "Anything to have you." He grazed her cheek with his nose. "Now come, before I throw you back in the car and test your invisibility idea."

She arched a brow. "Is that supposed to be a threat? 'Cause I'm far more tempted than afraid."

Fyran buried his face against the side of her neck and growled as he backed up against the car. The vibrations thrummed through her, hardening her nipples and making her clit pulse. She giggled, and gasped when she felt the scalding slide of his tongue behind her ear.

"You are far too tempting for your own good, Avery," he rumbled.

FYRAN'S TIME at the Sixteenth Street Mall with Avery began as torture. It had nothing to do with the crowds or how busy the stores were; with everything spread out over so many establishments and such a wide area, it could never compare to the frustration of their last trip to the grocery store. And it had nothing to do with the items they chose, or that he insisted on carrying them.

It had everything to do with that maddening little phrase —*building anticipation*. Fyran loved teasing his mate, loved getting her excited, loved inhaling the delectable scent she produced. He loved turning her on, especially when he did so without even touching her.

But it always came at a price.

He couldn't tease and tempt his female without making himself wildly fucking horny in return.

Their first few stops were fraught with instances of Fyran finding discreet corners in the stores where he could adjust himself without drawing attention. Avery, to her immense amusement, caught on to it fairly quickly. She offered once to help shield him from view, positioning herself in front of him with her back turned.

The moment Fyran had lowered his guard to handle his business, Avery had *accidentally* backed into him, standing on her toes to rub her ass against his throbbing cock.

He wished he'd brought a spare sound dampener along; then he could've taken her back into a dressing room and made her scream with pleasure in penance for her teasing.

Thankfully, his excitement soon eased enough to no longer be quite so visible, especially as the number of items he carried increased. He took the small glare Avery gave him when he refused to let her carry anything as a taste of revenge.

In all his years, Fyran had never done anything like this. He'd bought food for himself here on Earth, had bought his own clothing, but the furnishings in his residence had already been in place for him—and he'd ignored the suggestion to add more furniture and décor himself. He didn't know the first thing about decorating, didn't know how to express himself through the items he kept in his home, didn't know what humans—or, more importantly, *his* human—considered aesthetically pleasing.

He didn't even truly know why humans and so many other species were drawn to such displays, especially when the objects in one's home were so often private, rarely seen by anyone else. And what purpose did such things serve? All his life, he'd determined the value of items based purely on their functionality and usefulness, even if that meant how practical they would be if he ever needed to use them to kill someone.

But none of that mattered with Avery. It wasn't exactly that he was coming to understand why, but he'd learned the joy of the process. What they chose wasn't really the important part—it was how they chose it, how they worked together, how they used the process to explore one another's tastes. Seeing the things that made her smile, like the aisle of wall art from video games he'd never heard of in one of the stores, brought Fyran more happiness than he could've ever imagined.

And even if he never would've picked up a video game or a romance book on his own, he wanted so much to share in the things his mate enjoyed, if only to grow a little closer to her.

By the time they decided to end their shopping spree, they had bags full of decorative knickknacks to add character to the house, a couple paintings for the walls, a pair of bathrobes—a blue-gray one for him and a crimson one for her—a foot-tall statue of a human couple involved in an intimate embrace, some more Christmas decorations, and a few board and card games.

Thanks to the bulky bags in Fyran's hands, the other shoppers gave him, and by proxy, Avery, much a much wider berth than they would have otherwise.

They decided to stop in one of the many cafés along the mall for some food before heading back to the car. As they walked to the place Avery had suggested, Fyran couldn't help but reflect on their time here. He'd enjoyed himself. Why were so many human males averse to shopping with their females? Wasn't every moment with one's mate a precious thing?

Sometimes it seemed that the more he learned about humankind, the less he understood.

Avery rushed ahead and opened the door for him at the café, waving him through with a flourish. A sparkle danced in her eye and a mischievous smile played upon her lips as he passed.

"I'm supposed to open it for you," he said.

"Guess you should've let me carry some then, huh?"

Karak'duun, he could've taken her right then and there. Playfulness was not a quality he'd been particularly familiar with before meeting her. How had he gone so long without it in his life? Of course, it didn't hurt that her playfulness was fucking hot.

He suddenly remembered his promise to make up for teasing her once they went home, and he was grateful to have the big bags hiding the evidence of his rekindled arousal.

Food first, Fyran. Then fucking.

He'd come to favor Avery's term for their mating—*lovemaking* —but he could not deny that no small portion of what they'd done had been straight up fucking. Hard, passionate, desperate, thrilling. English speaking humans had really outdone themselves when it came to that word.

They stood in line together, surrounded by the soft murmur of the nearby conversations and the clinking of glasses, plates, and silverware. Though this wasn't the same café as the one where he and Avery had shared their first official date, the atmosphere was similar, and he couldn't help but smile.

So much had changed in the few short weeks since that morning. Despite the challenges that they'd face in that time, Fyran wouldn't have changed anything.

Avery spotted an open table after they'd put in their order. She hurried over to it, weaving between the other tables and avoiding the other patrons with the grace he'd first spied as she'd navigated the diner. Fyran took a few moments to appreciate the sight of her from behind, relishing that subtle sway to her hips, before following in her path.

More than once, he had to raise his arms high to avoid hitting people seated at the tables, several of whom cast him disapproving glares even though he'd missed them by wide margins.

Avery was smirking when he sat down across from her. "Tough crowd, huh?"

One brow arched, Fyran lowered the bags to the floor on either side of his chair and glanced around the café. "No. They all look like untried civilians to me."

She chuckled. "I mean some of them seem unnecessarily judgmental. That one guy looked at you like you'd poured a drink over his head when all you did was walk past."

"Ah." Fyran returned his gaze to Avery. "Nothing new there, right? Not like I give a shit what any of them think. Your opinion is the only one that matters."

Her smirk softened into a warm smile. "I've never known anyone who could be so vulgar and romantic at the same time."

Fyran grinned. "Would you have me any other way, female?"

"Heck no."

Their food came not long after—a chicken salad sandwich for Avery, and a steak sandwich for Fyran. His meal was accompanied by the drink he'd ordered, a vanilla milkshake topped with whipped cream and a cherry. As soon as the waiter was gone, Avery plucked the cherry off the shake and put it in her mouth, pulling it off the stem with her teeth. She grinned at him.

Narrowing his eyes, Fyran flattened his hands on the table and stood. Avery watched, eyes rounding, as he leaned toward her. He caught hold of her jaw, keeping her face angled toward his, and slanted his mouth over hers.

He barely restrained a groan when her lips parted for his tongue. He explored her mouth with unabashed greed, unable to get enough of her. She tasted of cherries, sunshine, and sweet rain, tasted unlike anything else in the universe.

She tasted like she was *his*.

Avery placed a hand on his cheek and released a soft moan that made his cock twitch, leaving him once again precariously balanced on the edge of succumbing to his lust.

The hand upon which he was supporting himself shifted, and his fingers curled over the edge of the table so his claws scraped the underside of the wood. He could toss the table aside in a flash and be upon her, feeding his hunger, slaking his thirst.

Need to wait. Not here.

Even the voice of reason in his mind sounded strained, as though it were on the verge of giving in to the powerful desires burning within him. But the thought was correct regardless—now was not the time; this was not the place.

Somehow, he summoned enough willpower to break the kiss, though he couldn't stop himself from flicking her bottom lip with his tongue as he withdrew. She moved toward him as though to chase his mouth.

He hastened his retreat, dropping into his chair more heavily than he'd intended. The jolt of his landing cleared some of the lingering haze from his mind—but it also sent a twinge of pleasure-pain through his shaft, which was once again locked in a desperate battle for freedom with his jeans.

It was all worth it to see the dazed expression on Avery's face. His mate was beautiful as she sat there with her braid hanging over one shoulder, face tilted up, lips pink from his kiss, and cheeks flushed. Her lashes fluttered, and she opened her eyes. They sparkled behind her glasses, a mixture of red and blue that made his chest swell, his heart thump, and his cock pulse.

So. Fucking. Beautiful.

And mine.

"You can steal my cherries any time, *vaerina*, as long as I get a taste of you in exchange."

Avery blinked, and awareness struck her. Her eyes widened and her cheeks reddened further as she ducked her head. She glanced around, likely at all the humans who were staring at them, but he didn't give a shit about them.

"Fyran, you are wicked!" she whispered.

"Mmhmm." He grinned and plucked a chip off his plate, slipping it into his mouth. He bit down, producing a satisfying crunch. "What's that saying? Turning around is fair play? You know, like what you did to me with your delectable little ass in that store earlier."

Avery chuckled. "It's *turnabout* is fair play." She picked up her sandwich. "And what are you talking about? I lost my balance."

"Is my mate lying to me?"

She took a bite of her sandwich, looked away, and gave him a hesitant, muffled, "No."

Fyran's grin tilted to one side as he selected another chip. "Good. I'm sure she wouldn't want to face the consequences, would she?"

Her brows rose as her eyes met his. She swallowed. "I lied. It was a total lie. I did it on purpose. When do I get my punishment?"

Fyran laughed at the earnestness and eagerness in her voice and her expression, grateful that his amusement could mask the flare of heat inside him. Every time he thought it wasn't possible, that he surely must've exhausted her, Avery proved that she craved their matings just as much as he did.

"And you call me the wicked one?" He put the chip in his mouth and chewed slowly, thoughtfully, keeping his eyes upon her. Once he'd swallowed, he licked the salt from his fingertips with that same deliberate slowness.

Karak'duun, the fires in her eyes as she watched him were nearly his undoing.

Keep building that fucking anticipation, Fyran. Until you can't take any more.

THIRTY

THE BRISK WINTER air that swept over Fyran as he stepped out of the café couldn't affect the fires burning at his core. He stood aside, holding the door open with his foot, and turned his head toward Avery as she exited the building.

She beamed up at him. With that bright smile, the flecks of crimson in her eyes, and the pink on her cheeks, she was absolutely radiant.

Bel'ar asai kitharen nal virae—*by all the light in the universe—she's beautiful.*

He still wasn't sure how he'd made it through their meal without kissing her again, without moving his chair next to hers so he could place his hand on her thigh and tease her with his fingers, without grabbing her hand and leading her away to some out of sight nook so he could sate their mutual desires.

She shivered, releasing a breath that drifted away in a cloud.

Mindful of the bags in his hand, Fyran put his arm around her shoulders and drew her against his body. His restless tail twitched within his pantleg. She wrapped her arm around his lower back and flattened her other palm on his chest. Fyran dipped his head; she stood on her toes.

Their lips met in the middle, sparking heat that immediately banished the winter chill. Fyran's eyelids fell shut, and the world slipped away from him like it could only do when he was with her. He made no effort to suppress the needy growl that rumbled in his chest as he and Avery leaned into each other. Her fingers curled, grasping the fabric of his shirt.

Can't get home fast enough.

Karak'duun, if only his hands were free...

His aching cock throbbed, seeping seed from its tip. If he truly meant what he'd said to her—that her body was for his eyes only—he needed to get her back home. Because even with an audience, it was getting terrifyingly difficult to restrain himself.

He pulled back from her, pressing his lips together. They felt as though they'd iced over the instant they were no longer in contact with hers. "The sweetest dessert."

Fyran opened his eyes to find her looking up at him. Her eyes were half-lidded and gleaming behind her glasses.

· "Mmm, yes you are," she said, a hint of huskiness in her voice.

He chuckled, which only exacerbated the ache in his groin and made his perpetually erect cock rub against the fabric of his underwear. Right now, that fabric felt more like a fucking cheese grater than cotton.

"Come along, *vaerina*," he rumbled. "Before I spill in my damned pants."

Avery's smile took on a mischievous curl at its corners. Her hand slid down to his abdomen. "That'd be a good test of your willpower, right?"

"*Svesh*, you have no idea what it does to me when you talk like that, female."

"Oh, I think I do..." She halted her hand's downward movement and traced the waistband of his jeans with a finger. "This female is burning with need for her male."

Fyran gritted his teeth and walked forward, trying to ignore just how close her hand was to the source of his discomfort. He lifted his gaze to scan his surroundings. The mall was busier than it had been before they'd stopped to eat, but these crowds were still nothing like they'd been on the day he'd met Avery.

His eyes fell on the man up ahead, and Fyran came to an abrupt halt.

Avery stopped alongside him, swaying slightly with the sudden loss of forward momentum.

The man was tall and solidly built, with a squared jaw and his head shaved bald. Angry red scars extended past the frame of his sunglasses on one side—the kind of scars left by claw wounds.

"Fuck," Fyran growled.

"What is it?" Avery asked, tilting her head back to look up at him. "What's wrong?"

"Uninvited guest." He dipped his chin toward the man —Varketh.

Avery turned her head to look at the ilventyr. "He's one of them, isn't he? T-the one who..."

"Yeah."

Her hold on Fyran tightened.

Even if the ilventyrs had no idea that they were being targeted by *Exthurizen* agents, why the fuck would they have remained in Denver after their entire stockpile of illicit goods had been wiped out? Surely, they understood that anyone who could manage such a feat was a formidable foe.

There were only two scenarios that made sense to Fyran— either Varketh had stayed behind alone to seek revenge for his disfigurement, or the ilventyrs had been so angered by the blows to their business dealings that they would not leave the city until they'd recovered their *product* and made their new enemies pay.

The former possibility would've explained why Varketh was revealing himself in broad daylight; it was a vendetta. But the latter seemed more likely.

Probably a bit of both.

"What do we do, Fyran?" Avery asked.

Kill him, like I should have the last fucking time.

"Just walk with me, *vaerina*." Fyran forced his legs into motion.

Avery stumbled, leaning on him more heavily for a moment. Then she was walking alongside him, matching his leisurely pace as he altered their course to avoid Varketh. They paused to check for oncoming buses and crossed to the other side of the street.

"He's going to follow us," she said.

Fyran glanced over his shoulder. "Already is. But we're okay, Avery. I've got you."

"I know."

Her response, though brief, was brimming with confidence and trust. Despite the situation, that felt good. Really good. And it helped him focus past the tumultuous emotions swirling within him—past the dread, the anger, the worry, the unfulfilled desire. The only thing that mattered right now was getting her to safety. That was the priority.

However much he wanted to turn around and kill Varketh— and however capable he was of accomplishing it quickly and efficiently—it wouldn't do his mate any good right now. He couldn't very well protect her if he had to fight off human law enforcement in addition to a gang of ilventyrian traffickers.

Varketh kept about a hundred feet back, matching Fyran's unhurried pace, his stare so intense that Fyran could feel it on his back like it were a physical thing.

The humans all around continued their business, still unaware of the aliens prowling in their midst.

When they turned onto the side street where they'd parked, Fyran swept his gaze along the surrounding buildings to confirm what he'd already known—there were security cameras, most of which were hidden within darkened glass globes, positioned along the buildings' exteriors.

He assumed the ilventyrs were aware of the surveillance, as they'd waited until Avery was well into a dark residential neighborhood before attempting to take her.

Without the crowds of shoppers to hamper his path, Fyran increased his pace. Avery clung to him. He knew she was struggling to keep up with her shorter legs, but Fyran couldn't shake his awareness of time—and how little of it they might've had to reach their vehicle and go.

When they reached the parking lot, Fyran scanned it carefully, keeping a healthy distance between the cars and himself and Avery. There didn't seem to be anyone else present—at least not in sight.

"Your turn to run?" Varketh called in accented English.

Fyran looked over his shoulder again to see the ilventyr enter the parking lot, still a hundred or so feet behind. Fyran moved faster still, practically carrying Avery despite his hands already being full. A hundred feet of open space meant little; falorans and ilventyrs alike could cross that space in the blink of an eye.

As they drew near to the Hellcat, Fyran quickly checked the vehicles to either side for any surprise visitors. Seeing nothing, he strode forward, unlocking the doors with a touch.

He released his hold on Avery and opened the trunk. "Get into your seat, *vaerina*. Quickly."

Avery didn't hesitate; she darted around the car as Fyran stuffed the bags into the trunk, pulled the passenger side door open, and jumped into the vehicle. She slammed the door shut so quickly that it was a wonder she hadn't caught any appendages in it.

"You afraid, *jettosh*?" Varketh shouted.

Fyran gritted his teeth, shut the trunk, and clenched his fists, tail twisting against his leg. His fingers itched, and his muscles tensed, anticipating action. Another glance revealed that Varketh was still keeping back, having slowed his approach considerably.

Fyran could draw his pistol, aim, and fire before the ilventyr could even react. One bullet could end this confrontation. One bullet could mean one less ilventyr threatening Fyran's mate.

He wouldn't feel remorse for such a kill. Varketh deserved death for trying to take Fyran's female. Deserved it for ruining what had been an otherwise perfect day, for endangering the most precious person in the entire universe.

But Fyran knew the same thing Varketh did—this wasn't the endgame. Whatever Gregor's gang intended to do, they wouldn't do it here, in the open, with cameras and witnesses all around. This was a delaying tactic.

Get her to safety. This fucker isn't worth it right now.

Fyran dropped onto his belly beside the car. His skin went hot, tingles pulsing across it in waves—a physical reaction to having made himself so vulnerable with an enemy so close by. He quickly checked the underside of the car for anything out of place—tracking devices, explosives, leaking fuel or brake fluid. Nothing seemed out of place.

He had to hope the ilventyrs hadn't tampered with the vehicle in any way—that they hadn't known it was here.

Fyran pushed himself to his feet and grabbed the driver's side door handle.

"We'll find you and your little bitch," Varketh said. "Be seeing you soon, *jettosh.*"

"Only if I'm to your right, you piece of shit," Fyran snarled. He opened the door and dropped into the seat, starting the engine before he'd even fully closed the door again.

The Hellcat's roar as it came to life poured fresh fire into Fyran's veins; the car sounded as eager for a fight as he was. Releasing a huff through his nostrils, Fyran glanced at Avery. Her eyes were wide, her expression was tight, and she looked paler than usual, but she relaxed some when her gaze met his. He shifted into reverse and backed out of the spot, only reaching across himself to pull on his seatbelt when the car was in drive.

Varketh was a solitary figure in the rearview mirror, slowly shrinking as Fyran drove for the parking lot's exit. Just before he turned out onto the road, another vehicle entered the lot through an entrance far behind Fyran. The black SUV stopped beside Varketh. He opened the front passenger side door and climbed in.

"Fuck." Fyran squeezed the steering wheel in his fists as he turned onto the street.

"What's wrong?" Avery asked, voice small but admirably steady.

"He's in a vehicle now."

Avery twisted in her seat to face Fyran. "He's following us?"

"He's not alone." Fyran checked the mirror again to see the SUV pull out of the parking lot and turn toward the Hellcat. "An SUV picked him up."

Fyran merged into another lane and took a sudden turn onto a side street, prompting a startled yelp from Avery. "Need you to keep an eye out, *vaerina*."

She lifted a hand to tuck loose strands of hair behind her ear. "For what?"

"Police."

The SUV reappeared behind them.

"So...I guess your people didn't scare them away?" Avery asked, brows knitted.

"Guess not. But we'll be fine, Avery." He reached aside and placed his hand on her leg, giving her thigh a squeeze.

Avery clutched his hand with both of hers. Her fingers were cold, but warmth slowly returned to them. "What if they use your license plate to figure out who you are and where we live?"

Fyran's mind pounced on that last bit—*where we live*. Hearing her say that was exhilarating, no matter what else was happening.

"They'll try, and they'll fail. I made sure my Earth documentation is almost impossible to connect. False identities and addresses layered around each other. Old habit." He took the car down another side street.

The SUV followed, inching closer and closer.

"That makes sense." Avery gripped his hand tighter as they reached a more open road and Fyran depressed the accelerator. "Hunter Coleman is a pretty mysterious man."

Fyran smiled, but the expression faded quickly. He didn't remove his hand from her leg as he wound through the city streets, giving as little indication as possible of where he intended to go. But the ilventyrs were persistent—and they had no reason for subtlety. The few times Fyran managed to gain a wider lead, it was swallowed up by red lights and stop signs.

This wasn't going to fucking work, and he'd known it the moment Varketh had climbed into the SUV. The small risks he was taking—and these city roads—wouldn't allow Fyran to accomplish what he needed to, at least not for a very long while. But he had no intentions of driving around the city all damned night, hoping the ilventyrs' fuel tank ran empty before his did.

He turned south, heading for the freeway.

Avery maintained her hold on his hand, but she'd turned her head and slouched down on her seat to stare into the side mirror, her eyes intent on the SUV.

Fyran only withdrew his hand from hers when he turned onto the freeway onramp. Limited by the speed of the vehicle in front of him, he could only watch as the SUV crept closer and closer—close enough for him to see Varketh and the other ilventyr in the front seats.

He'd seen just enough action movies here on Earth to be tempted to have Avery take the wheel while he hung out the window to unload his firearm into the SUV's windshield.

The car ahead merged onto the freeway. Fyran glanced over his shoulder, slammed down on the accelerator, and darted across the solid line to get around the slower vehicle.

His heart quickened, and heat spiraled through him. The world outside the Hellcat seemed suddenly brighter, sharper, and just a touch slower. He couldn't deny the thrill of this.

Avery braced one hand on the upper door frame and the other on the dashboard, visibly stiffening. "Oh my gosh, you're not supposed to do that!"

"Law enforcement, Avery." Fyran looked into the mirror to see the ilventyrs keeping close. He guided the Hellcat into the leftmost lane, passing another car with mere feet between their bumpers.

"Wha-what? Where?"

"Watch for them, remember?" Fyran glanced at her.

She was wide-eyed and tense, her glasses having slipped down to rest on the tip of her nose. Those delectable pink lips were parted, and some color had returned to her cheeks.

Fucking gorgeous.

Fyran reached toward her, hooked a claw beneath the bridge of her glasses, and pushed them back up. "You're fine, *vaerina.*"

"Please, *please* keep your eyes on the road," she rasped.

"Much rather keep my eyes on you."

His grin didn't seem to reassure her much.

The SUV grew larger in the rearview mirror, putting on a burst of speed. Fyran urged his car faster and guided it through the gap between two vehicles in the center lane. The maneuver bought them some space, but it wouldn't last.

The freeway was too crowded for him to open a real lead—not without seriously endangering a lot of innocent humans. And he couldn't ignore the fact that his mate was inside this four-wheeled death machine. They were well beyond the velocity at which vehicular accidents became fatal for humans.

He wove through the traffic like he would've traversed a crowd, taking what openings arose and sliding through them with finesse. He tried not to slow down when possible, tried to keep his eyes everywhere at once.

The ilventyrs persisted; even when Fyran managed to jump several vehicles ahead, they always caught up again, pulling closer to the Hellcat's rear bumper every time.

"Cop," Avery called.

"Where?"

"Up ahead. Right side," she said, leaning forward. "State trooper, I think."

Fyran couldn't see the righthand shoulder from his position, but he didn't question her. He released the accelerator and eased onto the brake, dropping the Hellcat's speed to seven miles per hour over the speed limit. The SUV drew so close for a moment that Fyran's guts twisted into a knot and his balls shriveled up.

We're going to get hit, and my Avery will get hurt...

The SUV abruptly dropped back, opening a couple car lengths of distance behind Fyran's car.

With a *whoosh*, Fyran sped past the black and silver state police car that was parked on the shoulder.

"Good job, Avery," he said, blindly patting her leg.

But the ilventyrs were not long deterred. They were soon on Fyran's ass again—another of those lovely human phrases that wasn't usually used for its literal meaning.

As soon as he could, Fyran exited onto one of the smaller, less crowded highways that led along and into the mountains. The

SUV came closer than ever as they rounded the exit ramp—close enough that Fyran could've counted the fucking hairs in either of the ilventyrs' holographic eyebrows had he been so inclined.

"I swear, if you fuckers scuff my fucking car…"

But he didn't give a shit about the car, at least not compared to what—to *who*—was inside it.

"What's the plan, Fyran?" Avery asked.

Fyran saw her look at him from the corner of his eye. Though she seemed a bit less tense, she was breathing quickly, and the pink on her cheeks was more pronounced than before.

"Same as it's been," he replied.

They merged onto the two-lane highway. Fyran didn't restrain himself now, welcoming the sinking feeling in his gut and the rumbling of the engine as he pressed down on the gas pedal.

As he caught up to the cars ahead, he darted into the left lane, jumping in front of the other vehicles one by one. The ilventyrs followed, their SUV keeping pace while the Hellcat was hindered by the other vehicles. Fyran saw his chance as he came up behind the lead vehicle in the chain—the right lane was open as far ahead as he could see in front of the next car.

But there was a long line of vehicles approaching in the left lane.

Fyran clutched the steering wheel, watching as the oncoming vehicles drew closer and closer, as his window to pass the car in front of him dwindled, as the black SUV gained…

"Fyran, just go," Avery urged, glancing back.

"Trust me, *vaerina*."

The pounding of his heart grew to an almost deafening volume, and his skin itched. This risk wouldn't have mattered if Avery wasn't in the car with him. None of this would've mattered. But he wouldn't harm his mate.

And this wasn't going to be the end.

He was putting her in danger to keep her safe. If only he could ignore the way that made him feel—like he was tearing his mind, his heart, in two.

He pushed the Hellcat forward in a surge of speed, darting

into the left lane. The SUV swung out behind him. The oncoming vehicle's horn blared, and the driver swerved. Avery grasped Fyran's thigh tightly enough that he felt the bite of her blunt nails even through his jeans.

Fyran guided the Hellcat back into the right lane, missing the vehicles both in front of and behind him by mere feet.

The ilventyrs' vehicle jerked back into the right lane before they could pass that last vehicle, narrowly avoiding a head-on collision. The ilventyrs inside the SUV—particularly Varketh—were suddenly quite animated.

With no more obstacles in his path, Fyran unleashed the Hellcat's true capabilities. The SUV, stuck behind the slower car, shrank in the mirrors. Avery didn't ease her grip on his leg.

The pain she was causing felt so fucking good.

The Hellcat tore along the road faster than Fyran had ever pushed it. He slowed only when they neared the junction to another highway, where he cut west into the mountains. After a while, he turned north again, working along a roundabout route to return to Westminster. Both Fyran and Avery checked behind the car every few seconds, their tension lingering in the air even though the SUV never came back into sight.

Though he wasn't usually one to dwell on what might've been, Fyran couldn't stop his thoughts from sticking on a simple fact—he and Avery could've died. The slightest complication could've meant their ends during this journey. Just a tap on the rear bumper from the SUV at the right angle could've caused a catastrophic accident.

And he'd rarely felt so fucking alive.

When they finally reached home after what must've been two extra hours of driving, Fyran's heart hadn't slowed, and his blood hadn't cooled. He pulled into the garage and closed the garage door, unable to ignore the burgeoning fire in his chest. His breaths were suddenly short and ragged, and tingles crackled across his too-sensitive skin. His clothing felt restrictive, hot, abrasive...

He turned his head to look at Avery, and she met his gaze. A maelstrom of fear and desperate longing raged within the depths of her eyes, culminating in a fiery, tantalizing gleam that pierced him to his core.

As one, they lunged for one another, only to get caught by their seatbelts.

"Fuck!" With a snarl, Fyran slapped his hand down to press the release on the seatbelt, tossing it aside and barely noticing the clack of it striking the window.

Avery freed herself in the same instant. She was already moving toward him when he hooked a hand under her ass and dragged her onto his lap, grasping her hair at the base of her braid. He pulled her down into a searing kiss, and she opened to him, returning the kiss with equal fervor. Her hands slid over his shoulders and neck to cup his jaw as their tongues danced. Their kiss was bruising and hungry, charged not only with their built-up passion from earlier in the day but with the fear and adrenaline of the chase.

They kissed each other like it could've been their last.

Avery ground her sex against his shaft. Fyran gritted his teeth, hissing through them as torturous pleasure flowed through him. His fingers flexed, digging into her hip, and his cock pulsed, straining against his jeans. Seed leaked from his slit. He groaned. Even through their fucking clothes, it was too much.

And it wasn't nearly enough.

"Fyran," she rasped against his mouth. "I need you."

"Feeling's fucking mutual," he growled.

Pressing his lips to hers again, he moved his hands to her coat, wrestling the zipper down. He tore the coat open and tugged it down her shoulders. In a tangle of limbs, they fought the sleeves off her arms, bumping into the door, the dashboard, the steering wheel, and pressing the horn in their struggle.

Once her coat was off and thrown aside, Fyran sat back and dropped his hands to his waist. He unbuckled his belt and unfastened his jeans as Avery pulled her shirt off over her head and reached back, bumping the horn again as she unclasped her bra. It joined her coat somewhere on the floor of the passenger seat.

He tipped his head toward her, caught her nipple between his lips, and sucked it into his mouth just as he freed his cock. Avery sighed, thrusting her hands into his hair to hold him to her as she arched into his mouth. Wrapping his fingers around his cock, he twirled his tongue around her delectable pink bud and scraped his fangs over the delicate skin of her breast.

His mate's breath hitched, and she rolled her hips, grinding her pelvis along his shaft. "Fyran..."

Fyran shuddered at another wave of pleasure, squeezing his cock tighter to try to hold back that building pressure. He refused to spill—not until he was where he fucking belonged.

Inside his beautiful mate.

With a final suck on her nipple, he pulled his head back. "Lift up, *vaerina*."

Avery looked down at him, settled her hands on his shoulders, and rose on her knees. Releasing his hold on his cock, he grabbed the fabric of her leggings in both hands, pierced it with his claws, and tore it open to expose her panties. He hooked a claw beneath those and pulled them aside to bare her sex.

With his other hand, he dragged the back of his knuckle between her folds. She bit her lip, her lashes fluttering as a soft moan escaped her. She was hot and wet, already dripping with desire, and his cock twitched in response. He brought his knuckle to his mouth and licked her essence away with a long swipe of his tongue. Her fingers curled, gripping his shoulders.

"You taste so fucking good, Avery. But right now"—he flicked his finger and sliced through her panties before framing her hips with his hands and positioning her above the head of his cock—"I need to be inside you."

Fyran slammed her down upon his shaft with a force that stretched her pussy around him. Avery gasped, her fingers biting into his shoulders as she hunched forward, resting her forehead against his.

He gritted his teeth and growled at the strong, wet suction of her sex, raking her with his claws. The pressure in his groin spread through his body. His chest constricted, heat blazed just beneath the surface of his skin, and pleasure and torment thrummed through his veins in maddening, alternating currents.

He bucked his hips reflexively, driving his shaft deeper.

Avery moaned. "I love how you feel inside me."

"*Karak'duun,*" he rasped. "You were made for me."

Locking his gaze with hers, Fyran bounced her on his cock, up and down, again and again, his hold on her strengthening as the sensations in him intensified.

Her scent—*their* scent—bloomed around him, filling his senses, and their shared body heat made the air thick. There was no holding back. Not this time. Not when he'd again come so close to losing her. Baring his teeth, he drove into his mate, thrusting hard and bringing her down upon him with matching ferocity.

Avery's moans became gasps, and her eyes closed as she tilted her head back. Her breasts bounced tantalizingly, but he couldn't look away from her face, which was flushed and strained with pleasure. She slid her fingers into his hair, tugging the strands and scratching his scalp. That only drove him to fuck her harder.

Avery tensed, brow creasing, and came with a choked cry. His name spilled from her lips as she fell over Fyran. She quaked around him, her sex contracting and inner walls fluttering with a rush of liquid heat. Burying her face against his neck, she moaned in pleasure.

Fyran snarled as her sex clamped down on him. His muscles seized as he fought back the inevitable explosion, as he battled to prolong this pleasure, to keep himself in motion and pump into her body over and over. But it was too much; he succumbed to the rapture, to the bliss, and let himself be torn asunder.

He slammed her down atop him, pushing as deep into his mate as she could take. His roar sounded distant as his seed blasted into her in a torrent of blinding ecstasy. Tremors rocked his body, and his hips bucked erratically as he grinded her against him, catapulting himself beyond oblivion. Fyran slid his arms around her, clutching her close as jet after jet of his seed filled his mate. The pleasure was so intense that it was all he could perceive, it was all he could think about, it was everything.

She was everything.

His awareness of the surrounding world returned slowly. Avery was lying upon him, brushing her lips over his neck as occasional shudders coursed through her, each of which triggered rousing tinges of euphoria in his cock. Her breathing was quick and heavy, and her racing heart matched the pace of his.

He smoothed his hand up and down her back and breathed her in, letting his eyes fall shut. She clung to him, cupping his head with one hand and slipping an arm around his neck. They remained like that for a long while, silent and languid, but the emotions that had fueled their lovemaking—and the situation that had driven it to such intensity and desperation—didn't fade from Fyran's memory.

He held her a little closer, a little tighter.

The ilventyrs had to know by now that they were being hunted. They might not have known who was after them, but they knew they'd made a dangerous enemy somewhere—one capable of locating and cleaning out their warehouse. But they were still here. They were still looking for Avery and Fyran.

Most criminals would've simply left town in such a situation, cut their losses and moved on to rebuild their operation elsewhere. But this whole thing...this had become personal now. And it was personal for Fyran, too. He wouldn't tolerate anyone threatening his mate.

Fyran kissed the side of her head and inhaled her scent. She truly was everything to him, and he'd never imagined how simple and utterly complicated that could be. The ilventyrs knew his face, knew his vehicle, and though it was small, there was a chance that they'd locate this place. The only true solution was to hunt down Gregor and his crew and kill them all. But Fyran couldn't bring Avery along as he prowled Denver, searching for the aliens that were hunting him. He couldn't bring her back into that danger.

But he couldn't leave her here, alone and unprotected, either. He would not leave his mate—his heart—vulnerable.

Fuck.

THIRTY-ONE

THE CRACKLING flames in the fireplace bathed the living room in a orange glow that, along with the twinkling lights on the little Christmas tree, made the otherwise dark room feel cozy and secure. Night had fallen hours ago. Soon, Christmas would be over.

Avery smiled as she flattened her palm on Fyran's chest and smoothed it up to rest over his heart, which beat strong and steady. They lay naked together upon the sofa, with Avery on her belly atop Fyran and a blanket draped over her backside and legs.

With his eyes closed, Fyran idly combed his claws through her hair with one hand and stroked her lower back with the other, his fingertips drawing teasingly close to her ass, just above the blanket's edge. His touch sent tingles of delight across her skin. Beneath the blanket, Fyran's tail was coiled around her thigh, its tuft lazily sweeping back and forth along the inside of her knee.

In some ways, today hadn't been much different than most of the others she'd spent with Fyran. Yet in many ways, he'd made it one of the most memorable. She'd awoken to breakfast in bed. Despite his many *skills*—particularly with his hands—Fyran wasn't the most confident cook, but he'd managed to prepare eggs over easy without breaking the yolks, hadn't burned the toast, and the bacon was just crispy enough.

But what had made the meal were the pair of maraschino cherries he'd placed on the plate as garnish.

Once she'd eaten, he had his meal. After half an hour of being lavished by his tongue, she might easily have gone back to sleep, but Fyran had carried her to the shower—where she told him she was eager to lick his candy cane. He hadn't understood her play on words at first, but he picked up the meaning as soon as she'd lowered herself onto her knees in front of him.

When they were dressed and dried, Fyran had revealed his Christmas gift to her—himself. She'd furrowed her brow and tilted her head in confusion; he'd frowned and huffed.

"You told me you don't want things," he'd said, "just me. And you have me, *vaerina*, always...but today, we'll do everything and anything you want to do. We will make your Christmas memories together."

She'd burst into tears at that, which had greatly alarmed Fyran. He couldn't have known just how much his words and his gift had meant to her.

So they'd spent the day together, first making a batch of extra chocolatey brownies, followed by a few rounds of board games— one of which frustrated Fyran. Avery didn't understand why so many people despised Monopoly. She loved it. And, because Fyran's irritation had fed into his aggressive and reckless playstyle, Avery had claimed the title of Monopoly champion in their house.

All hail Queen Avery, Bastion of the Boardwalk, Protector of Park Place, Regent of the Railroads. long may she reign!

He'd thankfully shaken his bad mood within minutes of handing Avery the card for his last property and admitted that she'd outplayed him. And damn, that admission had been *hot*.

For lunch, they'd made peanut butter and hazelnut spread sandwiches. Avery hadn't eaten one since she was a kid, when she'd traded lunch with another student. She'd felt so guilty after-ward—and had been so terrified that her mother would somehow find out—that she'd never risked it again.

Today, she had two and a giant glass of whole milk, and it was *delicious*.

Fyran thought so, too, considering he ate twice as much as her and claimed he could've gone for more when he was done.

Avery had called her sister and talked to her after lunch. Their conversation had been just a bit awkward, but it was nice—especially since neither of them brought up their parents. It almost felt like those rare times in the past when they'd just been sisters enjoying one another's company not because of shared trauma but because of their love for one another. Hopefully, it was just the first of many such calls.

After getting off with Eliza, Avery had sent texts to Brandy, Noah, and Jerry, wishing each a Merry Christmas and letting them know how much she missed them. She exchanged a few more messages with Brandy and Noah before her phone rang with an incoming call.

The caller ID said Allison Watson. Avery had been tempted to ignore it, but it was Christmas, so she answered. She regretted her choice immediately.

Allison appeared on screen, clearly drunk at a party, to wish Avery a Merry Christmas and berate her for being a shitty daughter because she hadn't come to visit. Allison's attention had then veered toward a younger man who seemed all too eager to have it. Avery had hung up after that. Allison didn't matter. All that mattered was Fyran, who been there with arms open for her to fall into.

Okay, so maybe Allison mattered a little. Was it too much to ask for a mother who genuinely cared? Who loved her daughter without conditions, without judgment?

For dinner, they'd cooked roast chicken with mashed potatoes and peas—giving Beau some of the chicken broth and meat—and once everything had been cleaned up, Fyran had lit the fire, and they'd watched a movie... Not that they'd quite made it through the film.

Sitting together with the fire warming the air, they'd been all too aware of each other's bodies. It had begun with Fyran putting his arm around her, and had escalated when Avery cuddled increasingly close, and breathing in his scent and absorbing his heat. He'd slipped his tail behind her and curled it over her lap. She'd reacted in the only reasonable fashion and placed her hand over his groin because at that point, she hadn't given a damn about the movie. All she wanted was him.

So they'd made love. They'd made love through the end credits, made love until the TV had shut itself off for inactivity, had made love well into the night until they were both left blissfully exhausted.

Despite the call from Avery's mother and the lingering threat of the ilventyrs, she couldn't recall having ever had a better Christmas.

"Thank you," Avery said, savoring the pounding of his heart beneath her hand. "For today. For your gift."

"I owe you as much thanks, *vaerina*," he rumbled sleepily.

"Even though I didn't get you anything?"

He scoffed, winding his tail more snugly around her leg. "That a joke, Avery?" He caught her by her chin and tilted her face up, forcing her to meet his crimson eyes. "You've given me everything."

Smiling at him, she cupped his cheek and stroked her thumb just beneath his eye. She still couldn't get over how strikingly handsome he was. She'd been drawn to him from the beginning, when she'd thought he was human, but having seen him in his true form, she couldn't imagine Fyran any other way. The few times he'd donned that human disguise since revealing himself had been strange. She'd caught herself looking at him often, searching for hints of his pointed ears and glowing eyes, looking for signs of his tail moving under his pants. Hunter Coleman seemed unnatural.

But Fyran Voltanix was real, and God was he sexy.

And he was hers.

Whenever he touched her and looked at her with that impossible blend of intensity, possessiveness, tenderness, and desire, when he looked at her like she was the most important thing in the world, the *only* thing in the world, it made her heart quicken and her belly flutter. And he was looking at her that way right now, was touching her in that way now.

She felt so...full. Like he'd poured every ounce of himself into her to ensure there were no holes left behind in her heart.

"Is it possible to love someone when you've only known them for a month?" she asked softly.

His brow smoothed, and the corner of his mouth tipped up into a small but powerful smile. "Yes, *vaerina*. It is."

"Because I do. I love you, Fyran." She shifted, lifting herself to face him completely. Her hair fell around her shoulders and pooled on his chest. "I never thought love at first sight was real, as much as I wanted it to be. I never thought it could strike so fast, so hard, but how else could my heart have been so broken when you left me?"

Fyran's thumb swept up to brush beneath her lower lip. His voice was low and husky when he spoke, barely more than a murmur. "Ah, Avery. Walking away from you is my one regret. I didn't understand at the time, but I loved you from the instant my eyes fell upon you.

"I fought this assignment hard, did everything I could to ignore it, and I was miserable. But seeing you, *being* with you, changed everything. And I want everything, Avery...with you."

Tears gathered in her eyes, blurring her vision. "Everything?"

Fyran wiped the tears away as they ran down her cheeks. "Every-fucking-thing." He slid his hands down to her waist and slipped his thumbs under her, stroking them over her lower belly. "Everything...and more."

Avery's breath hitched. All the times they'd made love, all the times he'd released inside her...

Was it possible? She wasn't on birth control because it made her nauseous and elevated her blood pressure, and neither she nor Fyran had used any protection. There was a chance...

She'd dreamed of having a family of her own, of having children, of giving them all the love and support she'd never had, but somehow, she hadn't considered it during her most intimate moments with him. Even though Fyran had said he'd been sent to Earth for a specific purpose—to mate with a human woman and produce a child—Avery's thoughts had been too focused on the present, which had been too chaotic, perfect, and uncertain for her to have planned that far ahead.

Could she be pregnant even now?

"Would you...still want a baby even if it weren't for your people?" she asked.

Faster than she could perceive, he flipped her over, and her back was atop the couch cushions. Fyran parted her thighs with his hands and wedged himself between them, pressing his cock to her entrance. He caught the underside of her jaw with one hand as he leaned over her, tipping her face toward his. His eyes provided the only light in the shadow cast by his powerful body.

"I will fill you with my seed again and again, *vaerina*," he said as he slowly pushed his shaft into her.

Avery moaned and wrapped her legs around him. She felt every nodule on his cock as they dragged along her inner walls. She curled her fingers around his biceps, right below his glowing tattoos. "Fyran..."

His tail wrapped around her calf. "I'll fill you even after my seed takes root, and I will watch your belly grow with my child." He withdrew his cock just as slowly as he'd entered her, only to push back in. "I will watch you blossom and glow, watch you shine brighter than any star."

Fyran angled her head to the side and dipped his face, brushing his lips over her neck and drawing in her scent. He growled. "Not because of my people. Not because of my orders." He lifted his head and met her gaze again, holding it with that fiery intensity she craved. "I want it because I want you, Avery. Because I love you. Because you are my future, and I cannot imagine creating a family without you."

Once more, tears filled her eyes, and she smiled up at him. Capturing his face, she brought it down and pressed her lips to his. She kissed him tenderly, lovingly, caressing his lips with her own, and he did the same, flooding her with a heat that spread outward from her heart and built in her core as he made love to her.

"I love you," she rasped against his mouth as pleasure hummed within her.

Fyran growled. "Merry Christmas, my Avery."

THIRTY-TWO

Fyran frowned down at the tiny plastic top hat. Its silvery surface reflected the light with an exaggerated sheen, and the words printed on it—*Happy New Year*—glittered with flecks of gold.

He stretched the elastic string attached to the hat's brim. "Will I really have to wear this, *vaerina?*"

Avery chuckled, took the hat from him, and rose on her tip toes to place it upon his head. She was gentle with the elastic band, making sure it didn't snap as she tucked it behind his ears and extracted his hair from it.

"Yes. Tomorrow is New Year's Eve, and we're going to celebrate together, silly hats and all," she said, placing her hands on his chest as she met his gaze. "I want to experience all these holidays with you, and tomorrow...well, it's about new beginnings, right? About the future."

He smiled and raised a hand, tucking loose strands of her dark hair behind her ear. "The way you described it earlier, it's just another excuse to party."

She smoothed the fabric of his shirt. "Yeah, for most people it is."

Fyran slipped an arm around her, drawing her against him. "But we're not most people."

Avery smiled up at him. She was absolutely radiant when she wore that expression, making him want nothing more than to bask in her glow.

Karak'duun, he could barely believe how much had changed for him since he'd met her.

"No, we're not. And we don't have to have a party to celebrate." Avery's eyes dipped to his mouth. "There's kissing involved. And...snacks. Lots of snacks."

"Oh? I do enjoy snacks." Fyran's gaze dropped to her lips, and that familiar hunger flared in his belly. It didn't matter how often he made love to Avery, he still wanted more of her, still craved her. He lowered his head and buried his face against her neck, growling and nipping at the spot where it met her shoulder, making her giggle. "But I prefer eating you, female."

He slid his hands down to her ass and clutched it, holding her to him as he ravaged her neck. His tail whipped forward and wrapped around her waist.

She writhed against him, her laughter filling his ears as she tried to escape. "Fyran! This isn't fair!"

"I've never fought fair," he said, slipping the tuft of his tail under the hem of her shirt to tease at her belly.

Her squirming intensified. "Fine," she said between giggles, "then neither will I." She turned her head and stuck her tongue in his ear.

Fyran recoiled reflexively, a shiver working up his spine. He released his hold on her to raise a hand to his ear, wiping away the moisture. She'd done a lot of things to him with her tongue in the time they'd spent together, had surprised him more than once, and had even licked his ear on a few occasions, but all that had been pleasurable.

This was totally different. She'd never just...jabbed her tongue in there.

"So, I've finally found your weakness," Avery said, panting. Her mischievous grin brought out the red in her irises.

Fyran snickered, shaking his head. "All I have to do is stand up straight and you'll never be able to reach again."

When he did so, she wrapped an arm around his neck and looked up at him, her eyes so big and beautiful behind those glasses, so deceptively innocent. "You're right." She slipped her finger between her lips, sucking it slowly, teasingly, making him think of that luscious mouth being around his cock, of her tongue gliding over the nodules along his shaft, of her hair falling over his thighs.

His cock stirred in response, stiffening and throbbing.

Avery withdrew her finger just as slowly, letting it tug down her lower lip as it emerged. Without breaking eye contact, she raised that glistening finger closer to his face, and heat flared in his chest. *Svesh*, it didn't take her much to get him going.

"At least not with my tongue," she said just before sticking her finger in his ear and wiggling it around.

"Gah!" Fyran snapped his head away and retreated from her, covering his ear with his hand—a gesture that barely muffled her laughter. "You humans are far crueler than I imagined."

"You weren't playing fair, so I had to play dirty."

"If you wanted to play dirty, *vaerina*, you just had to ask," he said, stalking toward her.

Still smiling, Avery backed away from him, eyes bright with playfulness and lust.

Her phone chimed on the kitchen counter. Her gaze lingered on Fyran as she took a couple more backward steps before she turned and walked to the counter, putting an exaggerated sway in her hips.

Fyran growled and halted. Tempted as he was to take the bait, he didn't want this little game to end yet.

She picked up her phone and turned to lean back against the counter. Her brow furrowed, and her smile faltered.

"What's wrong?" Fyran asked.

"I don't know. I just got a text from Eliza saying she was so sorry."

Fyran frowned. From all that Avery had told him, her relationship with her sister was good, but there were underlying complications. As adults, the two were still trying to figure out how to be close to one another, were still trying to cope with the way they'd been treated, the way they'd been so often pitted against one another by their mother. They were still trying to figure out how best to support each other in living their own, independent lives. But they were on friendly terms. They were trying.

A moment later, a high-pitched, chirping ringtone sounded from her phone. Avery tapped on the screen to accept the Face-Time call. "Mom, is everything okay?"

Fuck. Fyran strode toward Avery, and the passion and lust that had filled him gave way to deep, smoldering anger. Nothing good ever came of Allison Watson contacting Avery.

"Of course everything is okay! Why would you ask that?" Allison said. In the background, a car horn blared.

Fyran positioned himself against the counter, looking at Avery's phone from the side. Allison was outside somewhere, surrounded by dozens of other humans—many of whom were carrying luggage—and a long line of idling vehicles.

Avery's frown deepened. "I don't know. I just got a text from Eliza and then you called." She narrowed her eyes and looked closer at the screen. "Where are you?"

Allison huffed, turned her head, and glared. "Oh, so it took all this time for us to find out, but she told you right away?"

"It wasn't my place!" another woman said from off screen.

"Told me what, Mom?" Avery asked.

Allison looked back at Avery and smiled. "We just landed in Denver!"

Avery stiffened. "What?"

"We're all here. Me, your father"—Allison turned the camera toward a broad shouldered man with brown hair and a short beard who had a cellphone to his ear and didn't even spare a glance at her—"and your sister."

The camera shifted again to another woman. She was tall and slender with flaring hips and her blonde hair pulled back into a ponytail. She looked like a replica of Allison, only younger, but

Fyran saw a faint resemblance to Avery in the woman's facial structure. Her expression appeared contrite, and she only glanced into the camera long enough to mouth *sorry*.

"Why are you in Denver?" Avery asked carefully.

Allison brought herself back into the frame. "To see you, of course! Why else would we leave sunny California to visit such a drab, cold place? Now, I made reservations at a place called Bistro Montagne for tomorrow evening, and you'll be attending along with your...boyfriend. Derek"—Allison looked at Avery's father—"would you *please* hail a cab?"

She rolled her eyes and returned her attention to her phone. "Anyway, Avery, due to it being last minute on New Year's Eve, these reservations were extremely difficult to obtain, and I canceled real plans for you, so the dinner invite will *not* be refused. You will come. Afterwards"—she flippantly waved a hand in the air—"you can show us the apartment you've been staying in. No more hiding like a frightened little girl."

Fyran gritted his teeth, barely holding back a snarl. His hands curled into fists, his claws pressed into his palms, and his tail lashed from side to side, striking the backs of his legs and the cabinets behind him. He understood the courage it had taken Avery to move to Denver. He understood the courage it took to actively seek a new life, to throw everything away to take a chance at the unknown.

She was the only reason he'd found the courage to do so himself.

Without even looking at Fyran, Avery caught his hand and gently pried his fingers open, lacing them with hers. She was comforting *him*.

"I'm living with Hunter now," Avery said.

Allison frowned. "Living with him? As in, you moved in?"

Avery nodded. "We're...basically engaged."

Her mother gaped. "You...you just met him!"

"Really?" Eliza asked in the background.

"What the fuck?" Derek snapped.

Avery shrugged and tightened her grip on his hand. "We love each other. We didn't see any reason to wait."

Fyran's chest swelled with pride, though it only made his anger harder to restrain. Avery was holding her own. She didn't need his help—not yet. Because even though her parents didn't deserve to have her, even though they treated her as an object for them to manage and control, some part of her cared for them. She was too good for them.

He squeezed her hand back, shifting his tail to brush it across her calves.

"Well, your father and I will decide that for ourselves tomorrow night. I'll have your sister text you the restaurant's address, since she seems so fond of passing information on to you."

Allison's image froze for an instant before the screen went black, declaring the call ended, and reverted to the home screen. The background on her phone was the image he'd set it to—him and Avery together in the Denver Botanic Gardens.

Avery lowered the phone and turned toward him, her eyes filled with uncertainty and resignation. "This is going to be a disaster. They probably already have their minds made up to hate you."

Fyran cupped her chin, leaned toward her, and kissed her forehead. "We don't have to go, *vaerina*. We have plans already, remember? The snacks?"

Avery's eyes met his. "No, we do have to go. Because if we don't, my mother will do something crazy, and when she's crazy, it's just enough motivation for my father to get involved so he doesn't have to deal with her any longer than necessary. He could find some kind of obscure law or legal statute that'll force me to come back home or reassert their guardianship of me, or-or try to dig up something on you and get you in trouble."

Fyran stroked his thumb over her cheekbone and put his other arm around her. "Breathe, Avery. No one will take you from me. Not aliens or assholes at restaurants, not the police or the army, not anything in the fucking universe. Not even your parents."

She released a shaky breath and nodded, smoothing her hands over his chest.

He wrapped his tail around her waist and drew her closer to him. "You're *mine, vaerina.*"

FYRAN HOOKED the loose strands of Avery's hair with his claw and swept them out of her face. She didn't stir, even though his knuckle brushed across her cheek, but that wasn't surprising—she'd been well loved.

Avery had thrown herself into their mating with particular passion and abandon tonight, pushing for more and more until even Fyran had been left exhausted. Together, they'd shut out the whole rest of the world for a while, had reveled in each other's bodies, had thrilled in their closeness. Now, she lay in his arms against his side with her head resting on her chest and her face angled toward his. She had one leg draped over his thighs and her arm over his abdomen.

Her features were smooth and relaxed, displaying a serenity that few people seemed to possess during their waking hours. Fyran drew scant comfort from that, though he knew his mate's slumber provided her only a temporary reprieve.

He hugged her closer, stroking her upper arm with his palm and her thigh with his tail. She stirred, snuggling against him, and released a sigh that made her breath fan across his chest before she settled down again.

Fyran hated that the tiny, endearing smile on her lips would inevitably fade after she awoke. Maybe not right away—neither of them seemed able to hold back a smile when they woke together— but sometime tomorrow, their situation would crash down upon her, and the corners of her mouth would fall.

A faloran expression drifted to mind, one he must have heard from his parents in another lifetime—*Valar col san, col tiel.* For all that is and was. He'd never really understood what it meant, not even when he'd heard other falorans utter it well after Fyran had reached adulthood. The saying had always seemed incomplete. It had always implied more words that had eluded him through most of his life. But the meaning had finally become apparent.

Despite everything that was happening and had happened, despite the enormity of the past and present, it was the future that weighed upon a person the most. Because the future was uncertain. It was pain that had not yet been felt, suffering that hadn't been experienced...but it could also be joy that hadn't yet been imagined.

He frowned and lowered his hand from her face, resting it over her forearm and pressing his thumb to the inside of her wrist. Avery's pulse, slow and steady, thumped under his touch.

Here in the dark and quiet of the night, he couldn't stop his mind from trekking back to the event that had nearly ruined their day. Allison's calls always affected Avery. At best, they left her annoyed, and in those cases, she often muttered to herself in a voice that mocked her mother's demeanor. At worst, they'd left her deflated and quiet.

At least that had been the worst before today's call. Allison Watson had triggered a panic in Avery like Fyran had never seen, not even when the ilventyrs attempted to abduct her, or during the car chase just before Christmas. Though Fyran had managed to calm her—and, eventually, to get her mind off her mother—there'd been a far-off look in her eyes for most of the day suggesting that tomorrow's dinner had been eating away at the corners of her mind.

And yet Fyran found himself eager to meet Allison and Derek Watson. All the times he'd seen Avery's demeanor change when speaking with her mother—or just talking about her parents—had left Fyran with a reservoir of frustration and rage that begged for an outlet.

Avery tried to stand up to them. She *had* stood up to them, and moving to Denver had been her strongest, boldest move in that regard. But Allison and Derek didn't respect her. They didn't listen to her.

Fortunately, Fyran knew a few ways to make people pay attention...

Ah, fuck.

This wasn't the sort of situation he could stab his way out of, and he'd never dream of doing so, even if Avery hadn't indicated that she cared for her parents' health and safety. But Fyran certainly wasn't inclined to be nice to them. They'd not extended that courtesy to his mate.

Closing his eyes, he turned his head toward hers, buried his nose in her hair, and inhaled her scent. Heat tingled across his skin, and his groin throbbed. There was something different about her fragrance that went beyond the effects of their mating bond. It was stronger, more potent, impossibly sweeter. It had driven him beyond the limits of his exhaustion as they'd mated tonight, and it was still tempting him. But as much as he wanted to wake her up and make love to her again, he couldn't. He wouldn't.

She needed rest for tomorrow...and he had preparations to make.

Fyran opened his eyes, looked up at the ceiling, and released a long, slow breath. One limb at a time, he extracted himself from Avery. She stirred a couple times as he moved, prompting him to still, but she didn't open her eyes, didn't wake.

When their bodies were finally separated, his gaze roved over her.

So small. So delicate. So beautiful. But also strong, smart, funny, playful, kind. Courageous. Passionate. Driven. Creative.

Karak'duun, I don't know what I did to deserve her, but I'd do it again and again for eternity if that's what it takes to keep her forever.

He took hold of the blanket and drew it up over her naked body, tucking it gently around her to seal in the warmth.

"Back soon, *vaerina*," he whispered.

As he shifted to sit on the edge of the bed, dread pooled in his gut, solid, cold, and heavy. He'd agreed to go to dinner with her parents tomorrow, but he and Avery both knew exactly what risk they'd be taking by doing so.

Khelvar's team hadn't managed to flush out the ilventyrs since Fyran and Avery's last encounter with them.

Gregor and Varketh were still lurking in Denver. Fyran knew it, felt it down to his bones. Going into Denver was the most dangerous thing he and Avery could do right now. It was walking into the lion's living room, or whatever the human saying was. Out of the frying pan and into the fire—not that the frying pan was a great place to be to begin with.

He'd spent time being hunted. He'd known for so long what it felt like to have potential enemies around every corner, to wonder if every sound was a sign of the attack to come, to never feel safe. He wouldn't let that be his mate's life. He wouldn't let Avery experience that any longer.

Fyran dragged his hands over his face, rubbing the weariness from his eyes and sweeping his hair back. Avery had said New Year's was a holiday about new beginnings. He liked that—he loved her hopefulness and optimism.

But tomorrow was New Year's Eve. The last day of the year. If New Year's Day was a new beginning, what did that make the night before but a time of endings?

He and Avery had enjoyed a startling amount of peace in their time here. They'd been free to love one another, to laugh, to be happy...but there was a world beyond these walls. As much as he enjoyed the feeling that he and his mate were the only two people in the universe, that was not the case.

The run-in with the ilventyrs after Avery's birthday, the calls from Avery's mother...those events had been reminders that the world outside couldn't be ignored. That problems wouldn't just disappear if they were disregarded. That there were forces seeking to tear Avery and Fyran apart for no other reason than because they could.

Those events had been a reminder that they would have to fight for the lives they wanted—even if that fight wasn't usually of the sort Fyran had been involved in for most of his life.

He glanced back at Avery to confirm she was still asleep. Her draw on him was magnetic, urging him to move closer to her, to slide back under the covers and take her in his arms again.

But it wasn't the time. If tomorrow was going to be an end to this ordeal with the ilventyrs, he couldn't accomplish it on his own. Whether it had been pride or stubbornness that had always driven him to work alone, Avery was too precious for him to let either prevent him from doing what was right.

Fyran stood and crept over to the hidden floor compartment. Crouching, he opened the hatch, reached inside, and took out the comm disc.

Tomorrow, he'd be bringing his mate directly to his enemies' territory—but Fyran would be the hunter. He would be the lion, the wolf. He would do what was necessary to ensure Avery could have that look of contentment and peacefulness on her face *every* fucking night.

He pressed the activation button the comm disc as he stood and strode for the door.

Though he didn't know much about Earth animals, he knew one thing for certain—wolves always hunted in packs.

THIRTY-THREE

Avery tightened her hold on Fyran's arm as they walked toward Bistro Montagne's entrance. The air was brisk, there'd been a sprinkling of snow earlier, and between the lampposts and the Christmas lights that were still up on the trees, everything was cast in that magical glow she'd enjoyed so much during her night-time walks home from the diner.

Of course, that glow didn't put her at ease tonight.

Her black heels clicked on the sidewalk, and the shin-high skirt of her dark burgundy dress flowed around her legs—the dress was neither overly casual nor too fancy; she hoped it was enough to satisfy her mother. She'd gathered her hair into an intricately braided side bun with wisps dangling to frame her face. Her black eyeliner and mascara would draw attention to her eyes, and she'd painted her lips dark red to match her dress, but she'd forgone the heavy concealer. She refused to cover her freckles.

So which is it, Avery? Trying for your mother's approval or her displeasure?

It was a frustrating predicament. Why was it so hard to break those old habits? Why was it so hard to just...be free, to be herself?

As for Fyran, he wore a pair of black jeans, boots, and a white button-down shirt beneath his black leather jacket. He'd left his hair wild and loose, and the top few buttons of his shirt were undone, granting a tantalizing view of his chest. Avery loved it.

Allison would hate it.

More than once during the drive over, Avery had been tempted to tell Fyran to pull over, to turn around and go home. She'd wanted to say screw it and stand her parents up. She wanted to keep Fyran to herself. But she couldn't bring herself to do it. Avery needed to face her mother.

Of course, it didn't help that just being within the Denver city limits made her skin crawl with an *I'm-being-watched* sensation. Avery hadn't forgotten what else—or rather, who else—wanted to get their hands on her and Fyran.

She shivered and shifted closer to Fyran as they reached the restaurant doors.

Fyran stopped and turned to face her, grazing the tips of his claws across her cheek. "You're beautiful, *vaerina*. And you're strong. You've nothing to fear."

"Sometimes I hate that I care so much."

He smiled down at her and stroked just beneath her bottom lip with the pad of his thumb. "I love that you do."

Avery smiled softly, and her heartbeat quickened.

"The lipstick brings out the red in your eyes," he said. "Will your mother notice?"

"She has before, but she thought it was because I was reading too much. I can always say I'm wearing colored contacts if someone asks."

Fyran delicately tapped the arm of her glasses. "Do humans wear both at the same time?"

With him so close and his hand upon her, Avery's urge to leave resurged. She swallowed it down. "There are nonprescription contacts. Some people wear them all the time to have different eye colors, or for when they cosplay."

He growled, and the low, deep sound went straight to her clit. "I love that you haven't tried to hide them, female. That my mate wears my mark upon her openly."

"And proudly." Her smile wavered as she reached up to brush

her fingertip along his cheekbone and into his hair, where she traced his ear. Though the shell appeared round like a human's, Avery felt what was unseen—its long, pointed tip. "It makes me sad that you have to hide who you are."

"I don't have to for the only person who matters."

The only person who matters.

She was that person to Fyran. He loved her. Every single bit of her.

Warmth flooded her, and tears stung her eyes.

Oh no, no, no, no. No crying! Not now.

She looked up, blinking rapidly, and willed her eyes to dry as she laughed. "You're not supposed to make me cry. I have makeup on."

"And you'd still look beautiful, even with it running down your face. Anyone who thinks otherwise can fuck off." He reached aside and tugged open the restaurant door. "Now let's get this over with. I'm already tired of sharing you."

Avery chuckled as she stepped inside.

A woman in a sleek black dress held the inner door open, smiling at Avery and Fyran. "Welcome to Bistro Montagne."

"Thank you." Avery slipped her arm around Fyran's as they proceeded toward the hostess, who stood behind a tall podium.

The hostess was wearing a black dress of her own, the neckline plunging lower than the other woman's, and her jewelry glittered in the light shining down on her. There was a large arched window cut in the brick wall behind her through which were displayed dozens of wine bottles.

If nothing else, Allison would certainly be at home here.

"Good evening," the hostess said, tapping the display screen on her podium, "and welcome to Bistro Montagne. Do you have a reservation with us tonight?"

"Um...yeah. Watson. Allison Watson," Avery said.

The hostess looked up and smiled. "Ah, yes. The rest of your party was just seated a couple minutes ago." The woman turned her head. "And Angela is on her way back right now. If you would wait just a moment, she'll show you to your table. Would you like us to take your coats?"

"Thank you, and yes please."

After Avery and Fyran had checked their coats, they stepped aside, making space for another couple who'd come in shortly after them. When Angela arrived, she checked in with the hostess, and then Avery and Fyran were following her into the dining area.

The walls were mostly brick, broken up by dark wood accents and borders. Two big chandeliers hung from the angled ceiling, providing a welcoming glow that was enhanced by the lanterns standing at the centers of the tables. The long white tablecloths were simple but elegant, complemented by small flower arrangements with peach and purple roses. The place had that familiar din of conversation, those familiar clinks of silverware, flatware, and glasses, but it was all muted compared to what Avery was used to at the diner.

It was a beautiful restaurant, but places like this made Avery uncomfortable, made her feel like she didn't belong. Such restaurants would always remind her of her childhood. Of being told to sit up straight, to keep her hands in her lap, to smile—but not like *that*. To stop fidgeting, to stop slurping her soup, to stop embarrassing her mother. Places like this would always remind her of a long period of her life that had been unhappy.

She'd prefer a seat at Jerry's over this any day.

When her family came into sight, Avery's stomach clenched. Allison, Derek, and Eliza were seated around a circular table, and of course they were positioned so the two open chairs were apart from each other. Avery had no doubt that was by her mother's design; Avery would have to sit either directly across from Allison or beside her.

Allison lifted her gaze to meet Avery's, and her red lips spread into a wide smile. "Avery!"

That smile was genuine. Whatever issues Avery had with her mother, she knew Allison's smile was real in that moment.

Derek, who was seated next to his wife, flicked his gaze toward

Fyran before settling it on Avery. His expression warmed infinitesimally—which said a lot for him. "You look well, Avery."

"Thanks," Avery said. "Mom, Dad, Eliza, this is Hunter, my ma—uh, my fiancé."

She wasn't sure what felt stranger—calling him Hunter, or calling him her fiancé. Only the latter of the two felt correct.

Eliza's smile was wide and radiant. She wore a black dress with long, sheer sleeves, and her blonde hair was loose around her shoulders. "I heard during your call yesterday. It's nice to meet you, Hunter."

"Even better to meet you, Eliza," Fyran replied, drawing Avery's attention back to him. "Avery's told me so much about you." His eyes shifted to Allison. "About all of you. It's wonderful to meet the people behind the stories."

Allison's smile faltered—because of Fyran's words, or his black, piercing eyes?—but she recovered quickly. "Well, I hope my daughter wasn't too cruel to us in those stories."

"She wasn't. Avery's never cruel. Honest, but never cruel."

"Come have a seat," Eliza said, waving them closer. "I'd love to hear how you two met."

Avery glanced up and met Fyran's gaze. As nervous as she was about this dinner, knowing that he was here with her, loving and supporting her, gave her the courage to smile and extract herself from his side. "I'll sit next to my mother."

He nodded. It was such a simple response, but it was so confident, so reassuring, so solid, that it bolstered her anew. As she walked around to the open seat next to Allison, Fyran pulled out the empty chair between Eliza and Derek.

Derek Watson was a large man, just over six feet tall, and he'd always found the time to get to the gym even if he'd rarely found the same time for his family, but sitting next to Fyran, he appeared small.

Once Avery was seated, she leaned toward her sister and whispered, "Traitor."

Eliza eased closer. "I'm sorry! She came for a surprise visit and saw your address on your birthday card that was sitting on my table." She winced. "Which...I'm totally getting in the mail when I get home."

"What are you two whispering about?" Allison asked.

"Oh, just sisterly stuff." Eliza straightened in her chair and waved a hand in the air. "You know...men, sex, and all that."

"Eliza," Derek intoned.

"What? Mom asked." She picked up her glass, which was already filled with wine, and took a sip.

"Yes, well, we don't need to know the details of *that*, Eliza dear," Allison said.

Pressing her lips together to keep from grinning at her sister, Avery looked at Fyran. Humor sparkled in his dark eyes.

Allison caught Avery's face between her hands and pressed a kiss to Avery's cheek. "It's lovely to finally see you again, Avery. It's been far too long. A daughter really should visit her mother occasionally." Switching her hold to Avery's chin, Allison turned her daughter's face from side to side, studying it. The corners of her mouth fell into a disapproving frown.

Avery dropped her hands onto her lap and clasped them together.

Here we go.

"I can see you never did anything about those eyebrows," Allison said.

"There's nothing wrong with my eyebrows, Mom."

"She's right, Mom," Eliza said. "Natural eyebrows are in."

Allison huffed. "But they're not...elegant. And your eyes are so *red*. Are you on drugs, Avery?"

Avery pulled her chin out of her mother's grasp and drew away. "Really? Of course I'm not on drugs."

"Well, I haven't seen you in two years, what am I to think?"

"We've FaceTimed plenty for you to see me."

"You know that's not the same, Avery. And those cameras aren't very flattering most of the time, anyway. Your freckles look darker in person than they did on the phone."

Avery sighed. "They're exactly the same as they've always been."

Allison rolled her eyes. "Avery, they're darker and you should really cover—"

"They're perfect," Fyran said, his voice deep, calm, and somehow commanding.

Allison turned her face toward Fyran, and her frown intensified.

Avery smiled at him. Her heart warmed, and she wish she was next to him so she could touch him, so she could lace her fingers with his.

"So, Hunter," Derek said, steepling his fingers on the table, "what is it you do?"

Fyran sat back, folding his arms across his chest, which made the fabric of his shirt pull taut around his arms and shoulders. "Private security. Though I'm more or less retired these days."

"Retired? But you're so young," Allison said.

"I went into the field early, and the money was good. Didn't see any reason to continue after so many years."

The waiter arrived, pouring a glass of wine for Avery. Avery didn't miss the slight curl of her mate's lip when the waiter brought the wine bottle around to him.

Fyran covered the glass with his hand and shook his head. "Just the water is fine."

The waiter nodded and smiled. "Are you all ready to order?"

"We still need a moment," Eliza said.

"Of course. I'll return shortly." The waiter retreated.

Avery looked down at the menu in front of her.

"And here I was assuming you were in a rock band that was on the verge of getting their big break if you could only book a few more bar gigs," Derek said dryly. "I suppose security guard is marginally more respectable, at least. What are we talking, shopping malls? Warehouses? I couldn't imagine that paying much."

Fyran chuckled and raked a hand through his hair to tug it back. "When Avery told me you were a lawyer, Derek, I guess I made the mistake of assuming you'd be less prone to jumping to conclusions before having all the information. Mistakes on both our parts, huh?"

Avery's eyes widened as she looked up at Fyran, giving him a pleading gaze.

Derek's eyebrows fell low, and he narrowed his eyes. "Excuse me?"

Fyran locked his gaze with Avery's. She knew he wanted to say more, to put her father in his place, but he simply said, "I worked military contracts, Derek. Spent a lot of time overseas."

The tension bled from Avery, and she reached for her wine glass, taking a long, deep drink.

Eliza cleared her throat. "So tell us, Avery. How did you two meet?"

"Yes, I would love to hear how you met your...*fiancé*," Allison said.

"We met at the diner I work at." Avery smiled at Fyran as she set her glass down. "He looked like he was having a bad day, so I gave him a piece of cherry pie."

"Really? That's it?" Eliza asked, folding her arms on the edge of the table. "You have to tell us more."

"I mean, there isn't much more to say..."

"I was working a contract that was frustrating as hell, and I was reaching the end of my patience," Fyran said, sitting up straight again. "I wasn't in the mood to deal with anyone. But when she set that pie in front of me and I looked up... I forgot everything I was angry about. She wasn't just beautiful, she radiated something from within...joy and kindness like I'd never experienced. I needed to see her again, so I went back for lunch the next day."

Avery pressed her palms to her thighs and grasped the material of her skirt. "That was my turn to have a bad day, and he...he made it better."

The smile he gave her was tender, the sort of smile he only wore for her. "Even though I told myself to keep away, that I had work to do, I kept going back. The food was good, but Avery...she was what I really wanted. I fought with myself about it. Dragged my feet. Until, finally, I decided to go down to that diner and ask her to go out with me. But she wasn't working that day."

His smile took on a mischievous slant. "As I was heading back to my car, I looked down the street, and what did I see? Avery, walking into a little café. So I went inside, and she bought me a hot chocolate. That was our first date."

"Oh my gosh, it was fate," Eliza said, grinning, her eyes bright.

Except Avery knew the truth. Fyran had been following her, stalking her, that whole time. She'd long since overcome her initial shock and anger about that, and now...now she could only look back at what he'd done and be aroused by it. To know he'd wanted her that much, that he'd watched her, safeguarded her, craved her, *needed* her...

There were still times when she thought she was alone only to feel his heated gaze upon her skin. Avery always knew when Fyran was there, even when she couldn't see him. She couldn't explain it, but it was a like a sixth sense, an instinct.

But Avery did agree with Eliza. Meeting Fyran had been fate. She knew deep in her heart that they were meant for one another.

The waiter returned, refilled their glasses, and took their orders. Fyran hadn't even looked at the menu; he simply ordered what Avery was having—baked salmon with a pecan coating and a side of asparagus.

"Hunter, you said you were working a contract when you met Avery," Derek said, swirling his wine in his glass as he sat back in his chair. "Didn't you say you were retired?"

"No, I said I'm more or less retired. I take on work from time to time as it suits me."

"Ah. Home life is dull, isn't it?"

Fyran cast a knowing glance at Avery, and that devilish gleam danced in his eyes. "Not lately."

Derek grunted and took a drink. Avery flushed, taking a drink herself as her family's eyes turned her way.

Once again, Eliza slipped in to steer the conversation in a less awkward direction, asking Avery about work, about the city, about anything the sisters knew was relatively safe. Allison joined in after a bit, and even Derek added a few words in here and there.

Fyran, for the most part, simply observed, keeping a friendly face on throughout. It amazed Avery how easily he'd slipped into the setting, how he'd adjusted the way he talked, how he managed to look so natural despite everything that was happening—and the threat looming over their heads.

Maybe this dinner wouldn't be so bad. Maybe it was possible for her family to have civil conversation, to just enjoy each other's company.

Their food arrived shortly after, and it all looked delicious. Avery unfolded her napkin and arranged it in her lap. The sweet smell of salmon filled her nose, and the flakey meat practically melted on her tongue. It was so strange to be enjoying herself around her parents. Being on her second glass of wine probably helped; she felt warm, but it was relaxing her.

"How is your book coming along, Avery?" Eliza asked as she ate.

"I'm...actually almost done with it." Avery smiled wide. "It's so weird to actually say that. For so long I was writing it in small bursts, whenever I could find the time and inspiration between work shifts or on my days off, but taking some time away from work has allowed me to put more time into writing."

"That's amazing!"

"Honestly, I don't understand these choices you've made," Allison remarked, setting her wine glass—her third—down.

"What do you mean?" Avery asked.

"This silly venture of yours. First you run away from home, and now you're wasting your youth working at a cheap little diner and all your free time on...on...that? A book? Do you *really* think you're going to make anything on that?"

"I'm not wasting my youth or my time."

"Avery, I raised you and your sister since you were babies to be in the spotlight. To go out into this world and take everything you wanted. It's a man's world out there, and your looks are all you can rely on to get anywhere in life. That's all they care about."

Eliza sunk into her chair, taking a sip of her wine. "I guess now wouldn't be the best time to say that I'm only twenty credits away from completing my Bachelor's of Science degree...and I'm going to quit modeling this summer to finish it off and start looking into Masters programs."

Allison's brows creased. "What?"

Eliza grimaced. "Sorry not sorry?"

"I can't believe this! After everything I've done for the two of you? Everything I've given you?" Allison looked at Derek. "Don't you have anything to say?"

Derek shrugged. "What are you majoring in?"

"Astrophysics," Eliza replied.

Allison glared at her husband before shifting her attention back to Eliza. "And what is that going to get you, Eliza? Are you going to spend your life stuffed away in a basement lab under a state university barely breaking the poverty line?"

"No, Mom, it'll—"

Allison waved her hands sharply, silencing Eliza. "No. You and I will talk about this later. I can't believe you would just throw away everything we've worked for all these years. *You*, my perfect, beautiful daughter."

Ouch.

Avery had always known Allison favored Eliza, but to hear her say such things was always a punch to the gut. She swallowed thickly.

"You have years of modeling ahead of you," Allison continued. "You worked just as hard as I did for it. But Avery..." She turned her face back toward Avery. "I am not going to keep quiet about this any longer. You've fought me every step of the way. I've tried everything—*everything*—but you always rebelled against me. I tried to buy you the perfect clothes, tried to get you to do chemical peels so you could have the perfect skin, taught you how to do your makeup, how to style your hair, how to act, and this is the thanks I get? You run off for two years, refusing to tell me where you are, refusing to visit, and throw your life away to what? Work as a *waitress*?"

"There is nothing wrong with being a waitress," Avery said, her chest feeling tight. "And the life you wanted for me wasn't what *I* wanted. It never was."

"Because you never tried. You're an ungrateful child." Allison scowled and snatched up her glass, draining it. "I should have known. You were never like me, never like your sister. And what you're doing now is like a slap in the face."

She glared at Fyran and lifted her chin. "And what is she to you? I don't believe for one instant that she's your...your...*fiancée*. A month? What do you know of her? What does she know of you? You're using her as some plaything, a whore. I mean, I love my daughter, but she isn't a beauty, not like Eliza, and men like you only go after girls like her for one reason. An easy piece of ass."

"I can't believe you said that," Eliza breathed, eyes wide.

"What?" Allison waved her hand toward Fyran. "Look at him! Men like him never went after Avery in the past. They were all vying for your attention."

Avery dropped her eyes to the table and dug her nails into her thighs. Her breath quickened, and her eyes burned from the tears building within them.

Ungrateful.

Whore.

Easy piece of ass.

It had always hurt to know that her mother thought so little of her, but to hear Allison say all that out loud was just...too much. It went beyond anything Avery had anticipated when she'd tried to imagine all the ways this dinner could've gone wrong.

"Are you finished, Allison?" Fyran asked in a low, dangerous voice.

"Don't you dare speak to me that—"

"No. You're done talking now. Time to listen for what I would guess is the first time in your fucking life."

"You need to show some damned respect," Derek said.

"Neither of you have earned my respect," Fyran growled, "and you haven't shown any to Avery."

Allison said, "I don't know who you think you are, but—"

Avery shot to her feet and slammed her hands down on the table, making the dishes rattle. "Enough!"

Allison jumped, and a hush fell over the restaurant.

Fyran had his hands clamped on the edge of the table, knuckles white, and she could see the spots on the tablecloth where his invisible claws were pressing into it. His whole body was tense, the fabric of his shirt was pulled tight around his muscles, and his features were set in a dark scowl.

"I am tired of hearing your insults," Avery said. "So tired of hearing how miserably I've failed to meet your every expectation."

Allision opened her mouth, closed it, and glanced around. "Avery, I never meant—"

"Of course you never mean to, but you do. You never think about what you say or how you'll make someone feel—how you make *me* feel. It's always about you or what other people might think of you." Tears spilled down her cheeks, but Avery didn't bother to wipe them away. Her body was trembling, and her throat burned more with every word she forced out.

"You judge the things I like, the way I live, my *looks*," Avery continued. "God, you can't even perceive someone like Hunter loving me because I'm not pretty enough? Do you honestly not hear yourself?" Avery's bottom lip quivered. "Why can't you just love me for who I am? Why can I never just be good enough?

"But *I've* had enough. Today, right now. I've had enough of this. Enough of this abuse, enough of you and this fake...this fake... whatever it is, because it sure as hell isn't a family."

Avery stepped away from the table, but stopped when Eliza caught her wrist.

"Avery..."

"I'm sorry, Eliza," Avery said quietly. "I'm not mad at you, but I just... I can't right now. I'll call you later, okay?"

Wearing a pained frown, Eliza searched Avery's eyes. She nodded and released her hold.

Ignoring the stares, Avery hurried across the restaurant, wanting nothing more than to leave. She never should have come. Why couldn't she have been strong enough to just say no? Why hadn't she listened to Fyran? Why hadn't she just ignored her mother and stayed home to enjoy New Year's Eve as she'd planned with her mate? Why had she thought tonight would have been any other night she'd spent with her parents? Why had she been so naïve?

Because despite everything, I still love my parents, and I hoped tonight would be different. That we finally could've started moving forward...

God, she'd been so blind, so stupid. But no more. She was done.

Avery swiped her hand across her cheeks. She should've been relieved to get all that off her chest, should've felt victorious for speaking her mind for once, for putting an end to it, but all she felt was the weight of her sadness and pain.

THIRTY-FOUR

Fury boiled inside Fyran like magma building toward an eruption as he watched Avery walk away. It was fire in his veins, acid on his tongue, a crimson stain over his vision. It made his tail coil tight, and his claws lengthen, and he had to clench his jaw to hold in a roar.

He didn't care who it was—he couldn't stand *anyone* talking to his mate that way. But even in his rage, he wouldn't harm her parents. He'd come for Avery, not them.

"She's right," Eliza said softly. "You've always treated Avery horribly, and your marriage is a complete farce."

"Eliza!" Allison gasped, her face still slack with shock.

Derek's face had turned red, though Fyran couldn't tell whether it was from embarrassment or anger.

Fyran shoved his chair away from the table and stood. His every instinct told him to go after his mate *now*, to catch up with her immediately, to forget Allison and Derek Watson, to leave them to their wine and their expensive meal.

He stuffed his hand into his pocket and pulled out his wallet. His entire body thrummed with pent-up aggression, with the urge to strike. He could feel Avery moving steadily farther away as he separated several bills from the cash in the wallet's sleeve, and his skin itched in his need to go to her. Pinching off four or five one-hundred-dollar bills, he pulled them free.

Allison and Derek both looked up at him, their expressions mixtures of bewilderment, hurt, and anger. Fyran met Derek's gaze first, holding it for a few seconds before shifting his attention to Allison.

Karak'duun, the words he longed to say, the curses he yearned to hurl at these people.

The *blood* he wanted to shed.

"Avery is the most beautiful person I've ever known. She's like the stars in the night sky, sparkling, constant, mesmerizing. She's like the sun, fierce and fucking passionate, warm and welcoming. And she's like the moon, quiet, calming, always smiling even when she hurts inside. She's all that despite you. Your best fucking efforts couldn't destroy her, because she's more than either of you could ever be. And she is *mine*." He tossed the money onto the table. "Enjoy your fucking meal."

As he turned, he looked at Eliza and offered her a tight nod. "Nice to meet you, Eliza."

He felt eyes upon him as he stalked toward the front of the restaurant, and he didn't care. Fuck Derek and Allison Watson, fuck these people, fuck this whole situation. None of them mattered. Or at least he wished they didn't matter.

Because the hurt his mate had suffered, that was real. Avery's love for her parents, love they truly did not deserve, was real. Fyran couldn't ignore any of that. And as proud as he was of her for speaking up for herself, for standing up to her mother, he couldn't shake his anger, and he couldn't pretend that anger was useful.

How would he ever be able to keep his cool when someone brought tears to his mate's eyes?

His claws had nearly broken the skin on his palms, his jaw ached, and his tension hadn't eased in the slightest when he reached the front of the restaurant. Avery had already donned her coat, and stood alone near the exit, lips still quivering, with Fyran's leather jacket hugged to her chest. Her eyes rose and met his gaze. They were red-rimmed, and her makeup was smudged and ran black down her cheeks.

She was still the most beautiful fucking thing he'd ever seen.

Fyran strode toward her, his urgency increasing with every step, and drew her into his arms the instant she was within reach. She embraced him, whimpering as she buried her face against his chest.

His mate cried silently, her tears soaking through his shirt, and he held her, shielding her from prying eyes and smoothing his hand up and down her back as soothingly as he could manage.

"You're all right, *vaerina*," he rasped. "It's done."

She sniffled. "I know."

He pressed his lips to the top of her head and breathed in her scent. "I love you, Avery."

She hugged him tighter and tipped her face up. His shirt clung to his skin where her tears had dampened it, and black splotches stained the white material fabric.

"I love you, too, Fyran. Thank you. For being here for me."

Fyran caught her chin and gently stroked her jaw. His heart ached at how bright her eyes shone, their mix of blue-gray and crimson glittering through her tears. "Always, *vaerina*."

He leaned down and kissed her slowly, tenderly, caressing her lips with his as though it could soothe away all her pain. He wished he could have prevented the hurt she'd suffered tonight, that he could've taken away the hurt she'd suffered through her whole life and annihilated it, ensuring not even its memory would remain to haunt her.

But that wasn't the way people worked, whether human, faloran, or otherwise. That wasn't the way the universe worked.

Reluctantly, he broke the kiss, fingers flexing on her jaw. His tongue slipped out to run across his lips; they tasted faintly salty, a whisper of flavor from her tears. He wiped away the remaining moisture and dark streaks of makeup from her cheeks. "Are you ready, Avery?"

Her nostrils flared with a sharp exhalation, and her brows knitted as she pressed her lips together. "You sure we can't just...

ask them to reschedule? I think I've hit my emotional breaking point tonight."

Fyran chuckled, as much out of despair as humor. "I don't think I have their number, or I already would've canceled."

A tentative smile curled onto her lips, warring briefly with the uncertainty in her eyes. She whispered, "And here I thought you were supposed to be this meticulous assassin who paid attention to every detail, no matter how small."

"Might've exaggerated a little to impress the female I wanted as my mate."

Smile widening, Avery dropped her gaze and stepped back. Fyran released his hold on her.

She held up his jacket. "Guess it's best to get this over with."

Fyran accepted the jacket, swinging it around his back to pull it on. "We'll be all right, *vaerina*. You've got me, and we'll have backup this time."

Avery nodded. "That's if they even take the bait, right?"

"Yeah." His fucking heart ached, and he didn't know how to make it stop. He'd asked himself a hundred thousand times if this was really the right course of action, if this was really worth the risk, and though his answer hadn't changed it remained unconvincing.

His instincts just couldn't accept the contradiction—that using his mate as bait for the ilventyrs was the best way to eliminate his enemies. He was supposed to guard her from harm, not put her in its path.

Once his jacket was on, Avery took his arm. One of the restaurant's employees held the inner door open for them. Fyran led Avery through it, and they paused together at the exit door while Avery steeled herself. Fyran moved only when she did.

The night sky was dark, the air was cold and crisp, and the golden decorative lights seemed a mockery of what had happened —and what may yet happen. Fyran kept his gaze in constant motion, scanning his surroundings as he and Avery started toward the car, which was parked along the curb a few blocks away.

As much as he wanted to end this ordeal with the ilventyrs, he couldn't help but echo Avery's sentiments—not tonight. Part of him just wanted to bring her home, watch a movie, put on his ridiculous tiny plastic hat, eat snacks as they counted down to midnight, and make love to his sweet mate. That would've been the best way to make up for the disastrous dinner with her parents.

Halfway between the restaurant and the car, Fyran knew they'd get no such reprieve. A vehicle turned onto the street not long after Fyran and Avery had rounded the corner, and the sound of its tires on the pavement prompted Fyran to glance back. The sedan was black, its windows tinted dark, and it was rolling down the street slowly enough to match Fyran and Avery's pace.

He wasn't sure whether he should've felt relieved, enraged, disappointed, or anxious, but each of those emotions roiled to the surface regardless.

"Is it them?" Avery asked without looking up.

"Think so," he replied, quickening his stride slightly. When she held him tighter, he placed a hand over hers, squeezing.

The black car remained behind them as they crossed into the next intersection, maintaining its speed. Between the security cameras on the downtown buildings and the groups of humans walking along the street—undoubtedly on their way to New Year's celebrations—Fyran didn't think the ilventyrs would make a direct move.

He hoped they wouldn't.

But as Fyran and Avery reached their car, another black vehicle pulled up behind the first—a familiar black SUV.

It was likely Fyran's imagination, but he was certain he felt a hateful gaze upon him, hot and seething.

Fyran unlocked the doors, and he and Avery climbed into the Hellcat. They buckled their seatbelts quickly as Fyran started the engine. He reached into his back pocket to remove his phone. "Turn off your phone."

Avery picked her purse up from the floor and set it on her lap. With hands only slightly shaking, she dug her phone out of it. "What if we need to call for help?"

"There's no one we can call with these that can be any help tonight, and we don't want any cell towers pinging our locations considering what's going to happen."

As Fyran powered off his phone, the black car pulled up beside the Hellcat, stopping fully. Parked car in front, parked car behind, enemy vehicle to the left. They were blocked in.

"*Svesh.*" Fyran glanced to the right, where pedestrians were walking along the wide sidewalk.

The doors of the black sedan opened, and several familiar faces emerged—not just Gregor's crew, but Gregor himself. Fortunately, Varketh wasn't amongst them.

"Guess it's one of those nights, isn't it, *vaerina?*" Fyran twisted the wheel all the way to the right, shifted into drive, and slammed his fist on the horn before hitting the accelerator.

The Hellcat jumped the curb. The front driver's side fender scraped against a tree, making Fyran growl, and the vehicle rocked wildly. Pedestrians scattered, their screams and shouts of protest and fear muffled by the closed windows.

"Oh, my God," Avery gasped.

Fyran gritted his teeth, tightened his grip on the steering wheel, and straightened the car to head down the sidewalk. He'd always taken care to learn what he could about his targets and their behaviors, but it always came down to guessing in the end—because nothing was certain.

Nothing except his love for Avery.

How wrong had he been in assuming the ilventyrs wouldn't try anything in the middle of downtown Denver? How far were they willing to go?

Keeping the horn blaring, Fyran drove off the sidewalk at the corner crosswalk, taking a hard right turn onto the intersecting street. There'd undoubtedly be surveillance footage to track down and delete to ensure this didn't come back on him, but Khelvar's team would handle that backend work.

Avery twisted to look out the back window. "Do they not even care about witnesses?"

Fyran glanced into the rearview mirror to see the black car

turn the corner and resume pursuit, followed closely by the SUV. Both vehicles gained speed, closing the distance between themselves and the Hellcat.

"Apparently not." Fyran's muscles tensed as the black vehicles drew closer. These streets were about the last place where he'd wanted to get involved in an aggressive chase.

"We need to be careful," Avery said, turning her face toward Fyran. "Most cities have extra police units on patrol on New Year's Eve to look out for drunk drivers."

What difference did one more complication make?

He pushed his car faster, weaving through traffic to keep as much of a buffer between the Hellcat and the ilventyrs' vehicles as he could. The ilventyrs followed, but they backed off when a police cruiser pulled up to the stoplight at the next intersection.

The traffic signal turned red. Fyran brought his car to a halt at the white line, watching in the rearview mirror as Gregor's sedan stopped behind him. The ilventyrs inside were shadowy figures thanks to the headlights of the SUV behind them shining through the cab of their vehicle.

The cross traffic set into motion, and the police car rolled across the intersection, the blue badge painted on its white body gleaming briefly in the Hellcat's headlights.

At the corner of his eye, Fyran saw Avery trembling. He extended his right hand to her, and she took it in a strong grip.

Fyran's insides twisted, and his blood filled with fire. Once they made it through tonight, he was going to shower her with so much love and affection, was going to pamper her so thoroughly, that she'd forget all this forever.

The light turned green. Fyran returned his right hand to the wheel, and the Hellcat darted across the intersection with a growl.

The chase continued through Denver, carried out not through speed but maneuvering. More than once, the SUV broke out from behind Gregor's car and the two black vehicles lurched forward in an attempt to box Fyran in. He narrowly avoided their trap each time.

When they reached the freeway, some of the tension eased

from Fyran. It would be easier to keep ahead of the ilventyrs on the relatively open and straight road, though the danger of getting caught behind slower vehicles remained real.

Avery's tension, on the other hand, persisted. Her eyes bounced repeatedly between the side mirror, Fyran's face, the speedometer, and the road ahead. Her skin looked paler than normal thanks to the dark smudges around her eyes and the ethereal glow of the dashboard.

"Soon, Avery," Fyran said. "Not much longer."

"I know," she replied softly. "This...this is going to work, right?"

Yes. Such a simple word, such an easy answer. But it seemed too simple. Too...absolute. Seemed too much like a comforting lie.

"We'll make it work. No matter what."

Avery nodded, facing forward. "If your people are even a little like you...I know we'll be okay."

"There's no one like me, female." Grinning, Fyran guided the Hellcat into the next lane, blasting past a pickup truck. The ilventyrs' vehicles followed suit.

Keep following, fuckers. I'm as eager to end this as you...

When the sign for the highway junction came into view on the side of the road, Fyran shifted on his seat to pull the comm disc out of his jeans pocket. He activated the device without looking at it. The instant it had verified his identity, he sent the mental command to pair the device with his neural transceiver and did something he'd not done in years—activated the device's tracking beacon.

He dropped the disc into his jacket pocket and tore across the freeway to take the exit ramp.

"The others know we're on the way now, right?" Avery asked. The headlights from the pursuing vehicles fell across her face as they rounded the curve of the exit ramp, granting Fyran a clear view of her freckles.

How the fuck could anyone think those little marks needed to be covered up?

"They do. They'll be tracking our location. And when we

reach the rendezvous...they'll take care of everything. You just keep your head down, okay?"

"Okay." She grasped her purse, which was still in her lap, twisting the strap in her white-knuckled hands.

Not long after getting onto the highway, the road went dark. They were flanked by low, snow covered hills on either side, the white broken only by tufts of brown grass and weather worn wooden fenceposts jutting up from it.

Fyran picked up speed, gaining a lead on their pursuers, but he ignored his instinct to push his car to its full capabilities. He needed to keep the ilventyrs on his tail, but he needed to do so without making them suspicious. Thankfully, there were a few other cars on the road, providing just enough of an obstacle to slow Fyran occasionally. Each time he had to decelerate because of another car, the ilventyrs caught up a bit.

The Hellcat blazed across miles of dark Colorado highway, and the ilventyrs pursued.

This was going to work. There'd be an end to the threat... and the ilventyrs would face some sort of justice for all their wrongs.

At last, the turn came into sight ahead—the main road that would lead directly to their destination. The final main road before all this was over.

Fyran slowed his vehicle just enough to drift around the turn onto the narrower two-lane highway. Avery half-screamed, half-giggled, the sound full of nerves more than humor. Maybe under different circumstances the two of them might've enjoyed the thrill of driving like this—but the extra threat posed to their lives by the ilventyrs was too much.

He led their pursuers through the hills and up a winding road, pushing into the mountains. The scrubby grass that stuck through the snow in some places was joined now by pine trees, and the slopes grew steeper and more imposing.

And there were no other vehicles in sight.

Ten minutes, and they'd be there. Just ten more minutes...

Gregor's sedan put on a sudden burst of speed. The Hellcat

jolted forward as its rear bumper was hit by the other car. Avery threw her hands out, bracing herself on the dash.

"Fuck." Fyran pressed harder on the accelerator.

"Are they trying to kill us?" Avery's voice rose in pitch with her building fear.

"Don't know," Fyran replied, baring his teeth in a grimace as he guided the car around a sharp bend, barely keeping the tires on the road. "Probably trying to scare us into stopping."

The faloran ambush wasn't going to work if Fyran and Avery were run off the road miles before reaching the location.

As the road straightened out again, Fyran accelerated, hoping to put some extra distance between them and the ilventyrs. It was too dangerous to let them get so close; it didn't matter if they suspected a trap at this point.

The gap between the Hellcat and the sedan widened gradually. Fyran's heart thumped wildly. All he wanted to do was hold his mate and assure her that everything would be okay, that he would keep her safe, but the distance between their seats felt impossibly large.

A second pair of headlights emerged from behind the black car, their glare making Fyran squint when the rearview mirror reflected it into his face. The SUV's dark shape loomed behind those headlights; it had pulled into the left lane to speed past the sedan.

A big, shadowy figure leaned out of the SUV's passenger window, features obscured in silhouette but for two—his bald head and the fur lining around his coat's collar, which was flapping in the wind.

Varketh.

Something flashed in Varketh's hand. Fyran barely registered the telltale plasma bolt before it zipped through the back window of his car. It passed him closely enough that he felt the sting of its heat on his ear and cheek before it exited through the windshield.

"*Svesh,*" he growled, jerking his body aside.

Avery screamed, ducking in the opposite direction.

The melted glass from the entry and exit holes sizzled. The

Hellcat weaved across the road, and Fyran fought to maintain control as another plasma bolt zipped past the driver's side window. The bolt struck the pavement far ahead, leaving behind a small point of glowing orange on the otherwise black road.

"Get down, Avery," he commanded.

She clamped her hands over her head and bent forward, curling over her purse. She cried out as another plasma bolt struck the back of the car with a high-pitched *ping*. Metal hissed, having been melted instantly by the bolt.

"Fuck. Fuck, fuck, fuck." Fyran glanced in the rearview mirror again to see the SUV directly behind them. Varketh's single eye glinted with reflected light.

The ilventyr seemed to be firing at Fyran, which was better than him aiming for Avery, but the risk to her was just as great. If Fyran were killed or injured enough to lose control, she'd come to great harm—whether from the ensuing crash or at the hands of the ilventyrs afterward.

He swerved into the left lane as two more shots went off, each casting a faint glow in the cab as it flitted by just outside the windows.

On this highway, they were blocked on both sides by those steep hills, all dark, snowy, and still. He could outrun the ilventyrs, but how many more shots would Varketh get off before Fyran and Avery were clear of the danger? When each shot could mean the end of his mate, Fyran couldn't risk it. He couldn't give his enemies any more opportunities.

His gaze fixated on something up ahead—a turn-off, a path cutting between the thick pine trees where the snow was worn down into twin ruts. An unmarked access road.

"Hold on, *vaerina*," Fyran said. He threw the car into the turn, letting the rear wheels slide into another drift, the entirety of his mind focused on precisely controlling the vehicle. The slightest overcompensation could result in overshooting the turn-off and spinning out, whereas just a touch too little compensation could mean a deadly rollover.

His muscles tensed and his stomach lurched as the high-speed turn amplified the effects of gravity. The tires screeched, scraping over the pavement. They found traction just as the front of the car was angled directly toward the access road.

He slammed down on the gas pedal, and the car surged forward onto the snowy road.

In the rearview mirror, he saw the SUV skid past the road opening. Another plasma bolt flashed through the air, going wide of the Hellcat and hitting one of the trees lining the access road with a tiny burst of flame. Gregor's car managed to stop within sight, its wailing tires echoing off the surrounding hills.

The Hellcat rocked and bounced as it tore down the uneven surface, jostling its passengers. Fyran guided it around a curve in the road, losing sight of the highway and the ilventyrs' vehicles. That didn't put him at ease, but at least there were trees enough around here to provide some cover.

"I'm going to be sick," Avery groaned. "I'm going to be sick all over myself, and then I'm going to die."

"You're not dying tonight, *vaerina*," he said, raising his voice over the noise of crunching ice and snow. "And you are *not* going to vomit in this car when I just cleaned it the other day."

"Oh, that wine was a mistake..."

Fyran's attention shifted forward as they reached the end of the road. It opened into a large lot filled with dormant construction equipment and stacks of materials, most of which looked to be concrete. A big, partially constructed building stood at the center, a concrete and steel skeleton fenced off by flimsy orange netting and warning signs.

Construction materials were piled under tarps on the open floors, and the building was surrounded by scaffolding and temporary platforms.

He slammed down the brake pedal. The car slid to a halt, its back end whipping around so Avery's door was facing the building.

"Out." Fyran shifted into park and threw off his seatbelt.

Avery lifted her head. Her eyes were rounded behind her glasses and her skin was pale. "Out?"

Fyran twisted toward Avery, slapping the release on her seat-belt and reaching over her to open the passenger door. Thankfully, she set into motion, hurrying out of the car just as the ilventyrs' vehicles rounded the bend and their high beams fell on her. The whisper-crunch of tires over snow became loud and clear.

Scrambling across the seat, Fyran tumbled out through the passenger door. He regained his feet quickly and threw his arms around Avery. She clung to him as he lifted her off the ground and engaged his cloaking field. He was already running when Gregor's sedan and the SUV pulled up to the Hellcat, hiking Avery's legs up to wrap them around his waist.

Car doors opened, and boots crunched on the snow. Fyran darted through an open doorframe, entering the shadows of the unfinished building.

"Did they just disappear?" someone asked from outside, speaking the harsh Ilventyrian tongue.

"They're here," Gregor replied in the same language. "Hiding like rats in the building. Those tracks are fresh."

Heavy footfalls stomped toward the building. "I'll fucking flush him out," Varketh snarled.

Avery buried her face against Fyran's neck. Her body trembled against him, and her hold grew tighter and more desperate.

The fire inside Fyran roared, building in heat and intensity, flooding his muscles with restless, bristling, violent energy. No one was allowed to make his mate feel this way. No one.

He turned onto a wide set of stairs and began his ascent. Wind howled through the building's bones, flapping loose tarps and spraying flecks of ice and snow.

"You'll stay right here," Gregor snapped. "You've fucked this up enough already. Are you trying to kill the damned human, you idiot?"

Though Varketh's response was low, it somehow carried over the rumbling of idling engines and the wailing wind. "He took my fucking eye."

"And he took a fuck of a lot more from me, Varketh! We need

the female alive if we want to recover from this, just like I fucking told you a hundred times. It'll be more than your eye if we don't deliver!"

Fyran bounded up the steps three at a time, rounding the flights until he'd reached the uppermost level—the fourth floor. The voices of the ilventyrs sounded more distant from so high up, but his hearing was sharp enough to make out the words.

"You stand right the fuck here," Gregor continued, "and make sure they don't take any of these vehicles. Understand?"

Fyran crept toward the front of the building, taking cover behind a pile of wooden planks as he peered down at the ground. Avery's breath, warm but shaky, fanned over his neck, and she clung to him tighter still.

Gregor and Varketh were the closest to Fyran's car, staring at one another. Five others were positioned nearby, watching intently. Each carried a firearm; it was difficult to tell for sure from this distance and with the harsh light of the headlights, but Fyran doubted those weapons had originated on Earth.

He backed away from the opening and hurried to the farthest corner of the floor, where several large power tools stood beneath plastic coverings.

Outside, Gregor ordered his associates to move in.

Fyran carried Avery to the stored power tools and set her down on the floor amidst them, where the shadows were thickest. He released the cloaking field and looked into her eyes, which were big and full of fear.

Karak'duun. Fyran, you damned fool, just use the cloaking field to keep you both hidden.

No. Need to end this. Now.

He activated the comm disc's emergency beacon through his neural transceiver. The disc pulsed briefly in his jacket pocket.

Ten minutes before help arrives.

"What are we doing?" Avery asked, bracing her hands on his chest. She was so, so beautiful, but he couldn't stand to see that fear on her face.

"You're hiding here," he replied as he drew his *Exthurizen*-issued plasma pistol from the hidden holster under his pants.

"What about you? You're not—" Her brows drew together in an agonized expression. "No. No, Fyran."

Boots thumped and scraped one of the lower floors, the small sounds amplified as they reverberated off bare concrete.

"One last time, *vaerina*. The final chapter of my old life, so we can start anew."

He stepped back from her, gently guiding her hands down. She stared at him, her pupils blown wide, and shivered. Fyran turned the plasma pistol so the grip was toward her. Grasping one of her hands, he moved it to the weapon and closed her fingers around the grip.

Avery shook her head. "I can't."

"You will do what you must, my brave, strong female. Hide. Stay low, stay still, stay silent." Fyran released both her hand and the barrel of the weapon and rolled his shoulders back to shrug off his jacket. The biting wind pierced his shirt immediately. "If another faloran finds you, tell him you are mated to *Althicar* Fyran Voltanix, and ask for Khelvar."

He whipped the coat around so it was behind her and settled it over her shoulders. When she opened her mouth to speak, he quieted her with a finger over her lips.

The footsteps downstairs grew louder; the ilventyrs were starting to work their way up. They'd sweep the entire building long before the other *althicars* could arrive, and they'd sniff out Fyran and Avery if it came down to it, cloaking field or not. Fyran refused to let them get that close to his mate.

"Low, still, silent. I *will* be back, Avery. I promise you this." He slid his finger to her chin, tilted her face up, and kissed her.

Something metallic clanged on the concrete below, making Avery jump, but Fyran held the kiss through her startlement. He breathed her in, and it took everything within him to tear his mouth from her lips; his every instinct demanded he stay right here and defend his mate.

When he withdrew from her, it was far too soon, and her lingering taste on his lips was even more fleeting than that kiss. He kept his eyes on her until she crouched in the shelter of the covered equipment. A guilty, devastated pang pierced his chest as he turned away from her.

This time, he wasn't abandoning her. Never again. This wasn't the same.

The cloaking field crackled across his skin as it reactivated. Fyran tugged up his sleeves, drew his knife from his boot, and strode toward the stairs.

Seven enemies. Isolated location. At least eight minutes before the other *althicars* arrived. And his mate's life was in danger.

There was only one way this could end—with a pile of dead ilventyrs.

THIRTY-FIVE

Fyran crept downstairs, the claws of his free hand extending as though eager for blood. He stopped on the steps just above the second floor, sinking into a crouch. His lines of sight were broken by beams, pillars, and partially constructed walls, but he could make out shadows moving in the deeper darkness. Even his sharp faloran eyes couldn't fully penetrate this gloom, but his enemies wouldn't have such trouble.

Ilventyrs were made to hunt in the dark.

Footsteps sounded below Fyran—on the flight of stairs coming up from the first floor. It was the whisper of someone treading slowly, carefully. Fyran shifted his position to look down the stairwell.

A lone ilventyr was ascending, his eyes reflecting the scant light that managed to spill into the building from outside. His nostrils flared as he sniffed the air. He slowed his pace further, brow falling low, and raised the butt of his plasma rifle to his shoulder.

Fyran sank into a crouch near the edge of the steps. The air here reeked of the ilventyrs—but he had no doubt they'd scented him and Avery just as easily as he had them. As soon as the ilventyr's head was above the level of the steps upon which Fyran was perched, Fyran lunged forward.

He caught the side of the ilventyr's head with his free hand and thrust his knife into the ilventyr's throat.

The ilventyr stiffened, eyes rounding. His lips peeled back as he released a choked grunt. Fyran twisted the blade. Dark blood bubbled through the ilventyr's teeth and trickled down his chin. The plasma rifle slipped out of his hands and hit the stairs, its heavy clattering echoing through the building.

Fyran tore his weapon free and hurried down the remaining steps as the other ilventyrs rushed toward the disturbance. The mortally wounded ilventyr fell forward, catching himself on one arm and clamping his other hand to his throat. His dark blood flowed between his fingers and splattered the floor beneath him.

Keeping low, Fyran moved around the concrete wall to the outside of the stairwell, entering a long corridor.

"*Grag tark,*" one of the ilventyrs growled as he reached the stairs. "That bastard hit Irgan!"

By the sound of the footsteps in the stairwell, more ilventyrs had arrived at the scene.

"What the fuck is he?" another ilventyr asked.

"A faloran," Gregor said. "I knew that stench was a fucking faloran."

"Smells like ilventyrian blood to me," Fyran said. He darted farther away from the stairwell.

The ilventyrs growled and cursed, their footfalls heavy as they followed his voice. Fyran slowed his pace and circled back around toward the stairs.

"Where are you hiding with your fucking tail tucked between your legs, *jattosh?*" Gregor called. "I am going to tack that fucking tail to my wall when I'm done."

Fyran entered the stairwell again. Irgan was face down and motionless at the top of the steps, abandoned by his comrades.

Six more.

Retracing his own steps, Fyran walked past the stairs and

rounded the wall. Two ilventyrs were moving along the wide corridor, their weapons at the ready—and their backs toward him.

"You can't hide for long." Gregor's voice boomed from farther away, masking the sounds of Fyran's rapid advance. "But I will take a long, long time killing you."

Count yourself lucky that I won't do the same for you.

Fyran switched his knife into his left hand as he drew up behind one of the ilventyrs. He stabbed down into the back of the ilventyr's skull, puncturing bone with a dull crack, even as he reached around to his victim's front with his right arm. His hand clamped over the ilventyr's, which was wrapped around the grip of the plasma rifle, and Fyran pressed his claws into flesh.

Spitting a curse, the other ilventyr spun toward his companion. Fyran swung the dying ilventyr around, forcing down his victim's trigger finger.

Plasma bolts blasted from the barrel with a series of high whines. The first three went wide; the next four hit the adjacent ilventyr in the chest before he could bring his weapon to bear.

The shouts of the remaining ilventyrs echoed along the corridor, and their footsteps drew rapidly closer. The stench of scorched flesh filled the air, and the soft hiss of smoldering plasma burns was just audible over the wind. The smoking ilventyr stumbled backward and fell onto his ass, his back propped up against the wall behind him. Fyran braced a knee against the sagging ilventyr's back, meaning to pull his knife free, but fresh plasma bolts blazed across the hall.

Fyran shoved the dead ilventyr onto his fallen companion and dropped low, hurrying away from the bodies. More plasma fire arced through the air behind him. Fyran reached back to draw his human-made pistol, the last of his weapons.

Something metallic clinked on the floor behind him, bouncing several times before rolling.

"Ah, *svesh.*" Fyran dove through the nearest opening into one of the partially constructed side chambers.

A blinding light filled Fyran's vision. There was a sound—there had to be a sound—but Fyran didn't register it. He couldn't.

A wave of energy blasted through him, making his every muscle lock up simultaneously and his hair stand on end. An electric jolt coursed over his skin, and there was a sharp, searing pain in his head. His vision went white—whiter than the light of the explosion—and flickered to black.

He was on his hands and knees when his vision recovered a moment later, staring down at his fingers. As his eyes refocused, he couldn't miss the black claws at the end of his fingers—fingers that were quite visible to his naked eye.

When he attempted to reactivate the cloaking field, nothing happened.

His neural transceiver, which had been a part of his mind for half his damned life, was unresponsive.

Amongst *althicars*, the sort of charge that had gone off behind him was usually called a neural neutralizer thanks to this very effect. On intergalactic black markets, they were usually known as blackout bombs or nulls. Humans called them EMPs.

Fuck.

Gregor growled from somewhere on the other side of the corridor. "Now we see how you do without your fucking tricks."

Exthurizen neural transceivers had fail-safes built into them to prevent damage to both the devices and their users in such cases; Fyran's would reboot eventually, but he couldn't rely on it anymore.

Just four more.

Soon, vaerina. *Soon.*

Fyran tightened his grip on the pistol, willed the natural glow of his eyes to diminish, and crawled forward, working his way behind a large coil of metal-sleeved electrical wiring. He clicked off the pistol's safety and listened.

The wind remained the predominant sound, but there were so many others to sift through—the whisper of rustling pine needles outside, flapping tarps, spatters of loose snow and ice, the low rumbling of engines. The latter sound was a good sign; it meant the blackout bomb had been a relatively weak one.

And then he heard what he'd sought—the slide of a boot over the floor.

Fyran emerged from behind his cover, swinging his weapon toward the sound. His eyes fixated upon a dark figure in the corridor that was just within view through one of the open sections of wall. The ilventyr was approaching Fyran's position. Fyran fired three rounds in rapid succession. The gunshots boomed, reverberating off the surrounding concrete to become deafening. He barely heard the high *tings* of the metal casings hitting the floor.

He dropped behind his cover again and rolled aside.

The ilventyrs returned fire, their plasma bolts tearing through the electrical wiring as though it were made of melting butter.

Their weapons were clearly high quality if their power cells had endured the blackout bomb. It was a shame that neural transceivers couldn't be shielded in the same way, but it apparently would have interfered with the devices' ability to interface with their users' brains.

One of the ilventyrs cursed in his native tongue. The scent of fresh blood wafted to Fyran on the wind, though it was barely noticeable over the acrid odors of hot plasma, molten metal, and gunpowder. He hurried into an adjoining chamber and rounded the corner, pressing himself against a large concrete support column that butted up to the main corridor.

He peered into the hallway.

Gregor and another ilventyr were advancing toward the room Fyran had just left, weapons raised. Their companion was still on his feet, but he was propped against the wall, one hand clutching his lowered rifle and the other pressed to his chest. Even in the gloom, it was apparent that the ilventyrs' disguises had also failed; their hairless, grayish skin was unmistakable.

"You know the things that will happen to your female?" Gregor asked in thickly accented English before firing a couple more shots into the room in front of him. "You know what *I* will do to her before I pass her on?"

Grasping the pistol in both hands, Fyran leaned out of his

cover just far enough to take aim. He squeezed the trigger again and again, filling the corridor with the pistol's thunderous registers.

Gregor and the other ilventyr started and dove forward to take cover in the chamber. Their wounded companion jerked as though he'd taken another hit. He staggered backward, but managed to swing his rifle high enough to fire a burst of plasma at Fyran.

Fyran shifted behind the column again. Plasma bolts blasted through the concrete beside his head, spraying his cheek with bits of superheated stone. The shots ceased abruptly, followed by the telltale sound of a rifle clattering onto a hard surface.

Fyran swung into the hall again and fired twice more. The shots struck the wounded ilventyr in the face, making his head snap backward. He collapsed in a heap.

Three.

Something whispered across the floor just around the column from Fyran.

The barrel of a plasma rifle appeared around the corner, but Fyran was already in motion. He caught the barrel before the weapon was trained on him and forced it aside. The ilventyr holding it stepped forward, baring his pointed teeth in a snarl as he wrestled against Fyran's hold. His two-handed grip on the weapon provided him an advantage, and he threw his weight behind the weapon.

Fyran ducked under the barrel, moving to the ilventyr's opposite side and adding force to the swinging weapon. The rifle struck the column hard enough to send a jolt up Fyran's arm.

The ilventyr smelled of blood. Fyran registered the bullet wounds on his enemy's shoulder and abdomen even as he angled the pistol toward his foe's head. The muzzle flash illuminated the ilventyr's face three times in rapid succession. A little less remained of his features with each shot.

Two.

Gregor's cry was wordless, a furious, desperate sound that destroyed any advantage he might've claimed. Fyran shoved the dead ilventyr toward Gregor's voice and darted aside just before a spray of plasma bolts cut through the body and filled the airspace Fyran had occupied an instant before with superheated death.

Gregor came into view, standing about twenty feet away. His inhuman eyes blazed with the reflected light of the plasma bolts.

Fyran fired the last round in his pistol. Gregor grunted, and his plasma pistol ceased firing for an instant. He turned the weapon toward Fyran.

Fucking soon, Avery.

Charging forward, Fyran threw his weapon. It struck Gregor on the chin with a dull *thwack* just as the ilventyr fired his weapon again. The force of the blow snapped Gregor's head aside, and his body twisted along with it, sending his shot into the floor far to Fyran's right.

Fyran leapt at his foe. He slammed into Gregor shoulder first, knocking the ilventyr off his feet. They landed hard. After a brief, frantic struggle, Fyran tore the plasma pistol out of Gregor's hands. The weapon flew aside and hit the floor somewhere across the room. Fyran positioned himself over Gregor and rained blows upon his foe. His claws shredded flesh, his fists pummeled it, and soon his hands were wet and sticky with blood.

Fyran growled, striking harder, faster, the crimson light from his eyes making Gregor's blood glisten. The ivlentyr's attempts to shield himself weakened.

A sound echoed from one of the floors above, barely audible over the wind but piercing straight through Fyran's rage. Laughter. Deep, gravelly, malicious laughter.

Fyran's heart skipped a beat, and he turned his face toward the sound, body going still.

Avery. Avery was up there, and the only unaccounted for ilventyr was...

Karak-*fucking*-duun, *no.*

Something hard and heavy slammed into the side of Fyran's head. The impact rattled his skull and blasted pain through his brain. He reeled aside, tumbling away from Gregor. His ear was ringing, his vision unfocused, and a rapidly throbbing ache permeated his whole head, and yet somehow the worst part was that the tip of his ear had been crushed between his skull and the object that had hit him, and it fucking *stung*.

He shook his head, willing away the confusion and dizziness. Gregor, battered and bloodied, dropped the cinderblock from his hand, rolled over, and half-crawled, half-stumbled away. Somehow, the ilventyr gained his feet, trailing blood as he loped for the open side of the building.

Fyran rose to give chase reflexively, but he hadn't even closed half the distance before Gregor reached the opening and leapt out into the snowy night.

"Fuck," Fyran snarled.

He needed to be sure Gregor was dead, needed to know this was done. But none of that mattered if he lost his mate.

With another sharp shake of his head, Fyran turned and raced for the stairs.

Coming, vaerina. *Hold on.*

THIRTY-SIX

Though Fyran's jacket had blanketed Avery in his warmth and the comforting familiarity of his scent, it couldn't ward off the biting cold. Her legs were freezing, and her toes were going numb in her high heels. She couldn't imagine how cold it would be out in the open with nothing to break the wind.

But Avery's shivering was the result of a lot more than the weather. The fear that had spread through her was icier than this mountain air, penetrated deeper than that cruel wind, and it was tying her insides into knots, tighter and tighter with each passing second.

She adjusted her grip on the faloran gun Fyran had given her, keeping it under his jacket. It felt impossibly heavy in her hand, weighed down not by gravity but the weight of what she'd have to use it for if the situation worsened. With her other hand, she tugged Fyran's jacket closed more snugly over her chest. That gesture soothed her more than any weapon ever could.

She'd closed her eyes what felt like an eternity ago. Every sound had made her start, every blast from a plasma gun had made her heart stutter, every moment had been dragged out into a thousand years of uncertainty and maddening worry. Was Fyran all right? Was he winning? She had to believe he'd be okay, that he would come back to her, but her mind wouldn't stop following the what-ifs.

What if he was hurt? What if he...if he didn't... What if this was their last night together, and they'd spent it by having a falling out with her parents and getting chased by hostile aliens? What if—

No. No more of that.

The voice that had spoken in Avery's head was hers, but it was stronger, bolder, and more confident than usual. It had been empowered by Fyran. By his trust, by his quiet, solid, unconditional support, by his faith in her. And she had just as much faith in him.

Fyran will come back to me.

She jumped when gunshots—the really loud kind made by human guns—went off somewhere below, and her eyes snapped open. Those gunshots sounded like someone banging against a big door with rapid, powerful blows.

In her imagination, she was huddled in the Mines of Moria from *The Fellowship of the Ring* as orcs and a cave troll hammered on the stone doors; she was trapped in a dark, dead place with enemies all around. But she didn't have Gandalf, Aragorn, or Legolas to save her—and her real hero, her alien assassin, was out there amidst the monsters.

"I can smell you, human," someone rumbled from nearby.

She knew that voice. She'd heard it the night of the attempted kidnapping, very close to her ear, and again on the day Fyran had taken her shopping on Sixteenth Street. The day they'd been chased by a black SUV.

Well, the first day they'd been chased by a black SUV, anyway. That was becoming a habit she could do without.

Varketh.

Avery's eyes darted from side to side, searching, but it was so dark that everything just looked like shadows amongst thicker shadows. Her hand trembled, making the zipper of Fyran's jacket rattle faintly. The sound was overpowered by blaster fire from below—which was far more menacing and unsettling than any sci-fi movie's sound effects department had ever made them.

"Maybe I'll take out one of your eyes," Varketh said, his boots thudding on the floor from somewhere much to close by. "You're the reason one of mine was taken. Would only be fair."

Her imagination shifted again, this time drawing from real memory—Varketh behind her, his large, rough hand clamped over her mouth, and all her attempts to fight back proving futile... The fear that had seized her that night surged back, compounding with the terror of the present.

Stay low, stay still, stay silent.

Avery curled her lips in and bit down on them. She struggled to keep her breathing even, to keep her heart from bursting out of her chest. All the while, her eyes continued moving, but the only movement she could make out was the fluttering of the plastic coverings around her.

More thundering gunshots sounded downstairs. Avery turned and sucked in a sharp breath as the skin on her back flared with sudden heat, making her swear something was behind her.

But nothing was there except darkness and a dormant table saw, its covering too reminiscent of a funeral shroud for Avery's comfort. One of those blasters fired again. God, she hoped these bad guys had stormtrooper aim.

Something crunched softly in the nearby darkness, like a boot coming down on some loose dirt or gravel atop the concrete.

Avery snapped her head toward the sound. How could her palms be clammy when she was so cold?

Varketh laughed. A shiver crept up Avery's spine, and her breath caught in her throat. She'd heard a lot of evil laughs in movies and TV shows, some of which had even been unsettling, but this was the first time she'd heard a laugh that was bone-chillingly, stomach-churningly terrifying.

"Found you," Varketh whispered hoarsely from much closer than before.

Avery spun toward his voice, barely holding in a cry. Her wide eyes searched the shadows beyond the nearest piece of equipment as she fell onto her ass, pushing herself backward with her heels.

If she survived this, she'd have to have a laugh about wearing a nice dress and heels for the first time in years only to find herself in a situation like this. Maybe she would after—or between—some sobbing cries.

A figure seemed to coalesce from the darkness itself—bald head, thick neck, wide shoulders.

With a stuttering, scraping groan, the piece of equipment in front of her jerked aside. Avery clutched the jacket around her even tighter. She was pretty sure she screamed, but it was hard to tell for sure with all the noise.

The dark figure crouched, still looming large before her, and set something on the ground. There was a click.

Avery slitted her eyes against the sudden, intense light, quickly realizing that it was cast by a portable electric lantern, the kind people often used for camping.

And it granted her full view of Varketh. He had a rifle laid across his thighs, the barrel thankfully pointed away from her. His torso was bare, and his powerful muscles were bulging, making his corpse-gray skin look too tight. Intricate black tattoos in strange patterns ran across his chest, arms, and shoulders, up his neck and to his face.

Her eyes widened, and her mouth went dry.

That face...it was almost human, but the differences were unnerving. It was hairless, just like the rest of his body, with pointed ears that looked far more bestial than Fyran's elflike ears. His eyes were sunken, one of them gleaming devilishly in the lantern light, the other a pit of blackness crossed by jagged scars. But worst of all was his smile. His thin lips stretched wide, far too wide, revealing a mouthful of pointed teeth that could make a shark look friendly.

"Good," he growled. "You understand. You humans are prey. Now stand the fuck up, *gethuk*."

She could almost feel his hands on her again, so powerful and indiscriminate, so brutal and uncaring, but he hadn't reached for her yet...

Avery remembered two things in that moment. Firstly, that her struggles the night of the attempted kidnapping hadn't been in vain. She'd bought precious seconds for Fyran to arrive.

Secondly, she was armed with something a bit more significant than pepper spray this time.

She drew in a deep, steadying breath and forced herself to shift onto her knees, ignoring the hard, freezing concrete floor from which her nylons offered no protection. Somehow, Varketh's disconcerting grin only grew.

Avery released her hold on the coat, letting the sides fall open as she angled the blaster toward Varketh. His good eye rounded, and his grin shifted into a grimace.

She pulled the trigger.

She'd expected some kind of kickback, expected jolting recoil up her arm, and had braced herself for it. No such thing came. Just a flash of light, that disquieting plasma-bolt whine, a pained grunt, and a hiss. Her eyes shut reflexively.

She opened them what couldn't have been even a second later to see Varketh stand upright, growling. He staggered back a step. A tiny wisp of smoke curled out of a hole low on his abdomen, immediately swept away by the wind.

He raised his rifle. "You fucking—"

Avery angled her gun higher and pulled the trigger again, firing another shot that grazed Varketh's shoulder and left a divot of blackened, smoldering flesh in its wake. He recoiled, stumbling backward another step, but his aim was only slightly thrown off— and now he was correcting it.

Avery's life didn't flash before her eyes. She didn't reflect upon her every sin or draw comfort from her good deeds, didn't feel regret, didn't feel the crushing, paralyzing despair of impending doom. All she saw in her mind's eye was Fyran, and she felt...strong.

She felt *loved*.

Avery fired one more shot at her assailant, but it darted past his cheek, succeeding only in reddening his skin. He opened his jaw wide, far wider than any human could, giving her a glimpse of all those sharp teeth and his long, pointed tongue as he released a bestial roar.

"Fuck you," Avery said.

A dark blur moved behind Varketh. Avery saw a flash of crimson before there was a heavy *whoosh*, and something slammed into the side of Varketh's head with a dulled *thwap* and a wet crack.

The gray alien's head snapped aside, and he fell, twisting away from Avery. His weapon clattered onto the floor.

The blurred figure took shape as it positioned itself between Avery and Varketh. She knew those glowing crimson eyes, knew the faint light cast by the flowing tattoos beneath that white dress shirt. She knew that wild hair.

Fyran met her gaze. His expression was hard set, with his face spattered with blood and his eyebrows angled sharply down toward the bridge of his nose, but something softened in his eyes for an instant.

He turned his back to her, blocking all but Varketh's legs from her view. She caught sight of the weapon in his hand—a long piece of rebar with a noticeable bend in it—before he set it to work on the fallen alien.

The plasma gun fell from her hand. Avery squeezed her eyes shut, turned her face away from the carnage, and tried to focus on something, on anything, other than the sound of that metal bar coming down on Varketh again and again, on the sound of flesh and bone yielding to the force.

When the rebar clanged on the concrete floor, Avery released a shaky breath. Tentatively, she opened her eyes and looked up at her mate, who was again facing her. His eyes were alight with more emotion than words could ever express—with lingering fear and simmering fury, with hunger and relief, with love.

He dropped onto his knees before her and reached toward her with both hands. Avery reached for him, too, her chest swelling with the overwhelming need to touch him, to hold him, to be held by him. Fresh tears welled in her eyes, their sting enhanced by the chill wind.

"Ah, fuck," Fyran rasped, pulling away from her abruptly before they could make contact.

Avery swayed, catching herself on one arm. It felt like...like he'd just pulled the world out from beneath her. Brow furrowing, she watched as he hurriedly tore off his shirt—literally ripping the fabric and breaking off a couple buttons—and used it to wipe off his hands and face. The garment was immediately stained dark with blood.

Avery laughed. She didn't know why; maybe it was because she'd almost died, or because they hadn't died, or maybe because after all this he was still thinking about her so thoroughly that he refused to touch her with soiled hands. Maybe...it was just because of *everything*.

Fyran looked at her quizzically, and she only laughed harder. All the tension inside her flowed out with that laughter. The pressure in her chest was suddenly released, warmth danced on her cheeks, and her tears flowed freely.

She threw herself at her mate, and he caught her in his arms, crushing her against his broad chest, cocooning her in his heat, his scent, in the rhythmic beating of his heart. She didn't care about the blood. All she cared about was that he was *alive*.

Avery wasn't sure how long they clung to each other; time didn't matter, and neither the cold nor the howling wind could penetrate the tiny bubble she shared with him in those moments.

"Are you hurt?" he asked, voice rough.

"No. I'm okay."

"*Karak'duun, vaerina*," he rumbled, "let's never do this again."

She laughed more, shed a few more tears, and buried her face between his neck and shoulder. "I love you, Fyran."

"Love you, too, my brave, sweet female."

Something crunched through the snow outside, the faint sound carried up to them on the winter wind.

Fyran growled. "Gregor."

He dropped an arm to grab the discarded plasma pistol, stood up—helping her to her feet in the process—and took her hand.

She followed him toward the front of the building, where he held her back for a second as he peered outside. When he allowed her forward, Avery glanced down to see a lone figure staggering through the snow below, face glistening in the glow of the SUV's headlights as though it were covered in a dark, wet substance.

Something pulsed gently in the pocket of Fyran's jacket. Frowning, Avery withdrew her hand from Fyran's and reached into that pocket. Her hand emerged with the small device he'd called a comm disc held between her fingers. There was a small, solid red light glowing on its face.

"You left this with me?" she asked, looking up at Fyran.

"For just in case." That tender gleam was back in his eyes again. He tipped his head toward the outside. "They're here."

Avery followed his gesture with her eyes, gaze immediately fixing upon movement along the access road. A vehicle sped into the open lot a moment later, a black pickup truck with an extended cab and no lights on.

Gregor, halfway between his car and the building, hesitated in his unsteady trek.

"You don't need to watch this, *vaerina*," Fyran said gently.

"I know," Avery replied. "But...I just need to know it's done."

Fyran said no more; he simply put his arm around her shoulders and held her close, giving her the support, the foundation, that she appreciated so much.

The truck slid to a halt. All four doors opened simultaneously, and four big men hopped out. Gregor turned as though to flee. The foremost pair of men fired their weapons. At least a dozen plasma bolts struck Gregor in the back.

Gregor collapsed face-first into the snow, smoke wafting off his body like fog burning away under the morning sun.

One of the newcomers looked up at Fyran and Avery and made a gesture. Avery didn't see Fyran's reply gesture, but she saw the others moving toward Gregor's car and the black SUV, weapons raised.

Fyran turned away from the opening and walked toward the stairs at an unhurried pace, keeping his arm around her to lead her along.

She hugged Fyran around his middle, leaning against him as they walked. Her skirt fluttered around her legs in the wind. She shivered. "Aren't you cold?"

"Freezing. Wish I had a coat."

"Oh, crap! Sorry!" She shifted, meaning to push away and shrug off his jacket, but Fyran held her in place.

He chuckled. "Keep it. I'll survive. I've got you to warm me, *vaerina*."

Avery smiled as she looked up at him, but that smiled faded when he crossed into the lantern light and she saw the scrapes on the side of his face and the blood seeping from the tip of his ear. More blood was matted in his hair.

"Is it all really over?" she asked.

"Yeah, it's over."

"What about all...this? The...evidence?"

Fyran paused at the top of the stairs and glanced over his shoulder. "The others will take care of it. No one else will ever know what happened here tonight."

He tipped his head down and met her gaze. The glow of his crimson eyes intensified as he cupped her chin and stroked his thumb over her jaw. "This is the end of my old life. I clung to it so hard because I never knew anything else, because I never thought I could have anything else. Until I met you. And I never want my old life to come in contact with you again. I never want to feel what I felt tonight, while you were in danger. Now we start anew, *vaerina*. No more running, no more hiding, no more fear. Now we will *live*."

"And love."

"Ah, my Avery, I'll never fucking stop loving you."

Avery slipped her arms around his neck, and Fyran bent down, capturing her mouth in a kiss. As his hands dropped to her hips, Avery leapt up, and he caught her. She hooked her legs around his waist. With a low growl that sent delicious vibrations straight to her core, he wrapped her in a tight embrace and held her close.

His lips caressed and ravaged hers. They were tender and urgent, ravenous and sensual, yielding and demanding, showing how fearful he'd been of losing her, conveying the infinite depth of his love for her, and she returned the kiss just as fiercely.

They didn't need to wait until midnight for the new year to begin. They were starting their life together now, and it would finally be on their own terms.

EPILOGUE

Six Months Later

FYRAN LOWERED himself into the Beetle's driver's seat, one leg sticking out the door, and started the engine. The vehicle rumbled to life without so much as a stutter. He pressed down on the gas pedal, coaxing a fresh growl from the car, and used his neural transceiver to activate the sound dampener he'd installed in the engine compartment.

The growl became a purr, deep and distant but full of promise and potential.

They'd have to get the Beetle out on the road to ensure everything was functioning properly—and so Avery could test its new capabilities.

But that could wait for tomorrow.

He turned off the car and pulled himself out, closing the door behind him. He strode to the front of the vehicle, where he paused for a moment to look over his work. The modified engine gleamed under the garage lights. It looked out of place in Avery's little car, looked like it was far too much for the Beetle to handle, but it fit just right—and he knew the vehicle wouldn't have any trouble with it. Especially not since he'd torn the whole thing apart last month and reinforced the passenger compartment with lightweight but incredibly strong faloran metals he wasn't necessarily supposed to have on hand.

He closed the hood.

There was probably some metaphor or something to be made about it being whatever was on the inside that counted, but Fyran's mind threatened to turn it into sexual innuendo, so he shrugged the thought off.

Karak'duun, he'd been out here too long.

He glanced toward the Hellcat, which was parked in its usual place beside the Beetle. The two vehicles made an odd pair. And yet, to Fyran, they fit together perfectly, complemented one another in just the right ways. That seemed another opportunity for a metaphor—about life, perhaps, or his relationship with his mate.

"Damn it, my female's writer talk is really starting to rub off on me," he muttered.

Smiling to himself, he turned and walked into the adjoining laundry room. He washed his hands in the basin sink, dried them, and plucked his ring off the nearby shelf. The gunmetal gray band looked smooth and unadorned until he slipped it onto his left ring finger.

Flowing faloran script appeared around the band, matching the color of his eyes perfectly. *Mine to claim. Mine to love.*

He only removed the ring when he worked on the cars, unwilling to risk getting it scratched or covered in motor grease and grime. Avery had surprised him with it on the day they'd married, having apparently conspired with Khelvar to have it made.

Fyran left the laundry room, emerging in the kitchen. Even after a couple months, he was still getting used to this house. They'd decided to relocate not long after the year had begun, purchasing a home on a more isolated stretch of land in the foothills, where they'd have more privacy than even their former residence on the outskirts of Westminster. They were farther away from Denver now, but that was all right. Neither of them minded taking a longer drive when they didn't have to worry about being chased by homicidal aliens.

His eye caught on something scrawled on the calendar hanging on the kitchen wall. He stopped to look. In the box marked the thirtieth of June, Avery had written a note in her small, scrawling handwriting.

Lunch with Allison/Mom???

Avery had already discussed the tentative meeting with him, and he would support her no matter how she decided in the end. The dinner with the Watsons on New Year's Eve had been both liberating and exhausting for Avery, but she'd moved on admirably. Avery standing up for herself had triggered change for her parents, also, and the news had been passed on via Eliza a few weeks after the dinner that Derek and Allison Watson were separating.

In the months since, Allison had tried several times to reach out to Avery, and Avery had ignored most of those attempts. But Fyran's mate wasn't unfeeling, and some part of her still cared about her mother. They'd begun speaking to one another again last month. Fyran had been...skeptical, but Allison's demeanor had been different on that first call. She'd apologized to Avery—the first genuine apology Avery had received from her mother in her entire life.

Allison was apparently going to therapy now, trying to work through her issues, and had asked for another chance to be in her daughter's life. To start over again. Avery maintained her own suspicions, but she hadn't been able to hide the glimmer of hope in her eyes that things had finally changed, that she'd finally be able to build a meaningful relationship with her mother.

Fyran wanted that for her, too...but he'd be ready, regardless, to help his mate through it if things went poorly again. He would never fault her for her kindness and compassion—but he would stand by to ensure no one ever took advantage of it, even if that meant protecting her from her own mother.

As he continued on through the dining room and into the

living room, he slowed his pace, running his gaze across the framed photos they'd hung on the wall. Every time he walked by, his attention was drawn to the picture they'd taken on their wedding day. In it, the two of them were standing together, Avery in a brilliant white dress and Fyran in a black suit, his hair down as usual. Her cheeks were rosy, her eyes sparkling.

It didn't matter that the picture had been taken in front of the courthouse, where they'd made their mating bond official in the eyes of the human government. It didn't matter that they hadn't had an elaborate ceremony with dozens of friends and family in attendance, like so many humans seemed to do. Avery hadn't wanted any of that.

Instead, they'd invited a few of her friends from the diner— Noah, Brandy, and the elderly couple, Harley and Mary. Jerry had walked Avery down the aisle to stand before the justice who'd performed the brief ceremony.

Avery had jokingly called herself the winter queen that day as she'd climbed onto one of the mounds of plowed snow at the side of the street; he had agreed to call her *his* queen forever after.

The smile she wore in the photo was so bright, so stunning. He'd only once seen it brighter—on the day she'd discovered she was pregnant.

Had it really already been six months since she'd found out? Had it really been five months since they'd been married?

Had he *only* known her for seven months?

It felt like she'd been his mate, his wife, his love, for all his life.

Fyran climbed the stairs and walked to their bedroom. Her scent washed over him, sweeter and fuller than when they'd first met. It had become more enticing, more alluring, and its effects on him were stronger than ever. He halted in the open doorway, settling his gaze on his mate.

Avery was lying on the bed, her back propped up on a thick, armed pillow, with a black tablet in her hand. Her other hand was resting atop her rounded belly, where their child was growing. Beau was curled up against her side, a ball of fur identifiable as a cat only because one of his legs was sticking up in the air, its little toes splayed.

Drawing in a soft breath, Avery flicked her finger across the screen. Her eyes widened, remaining fixated on whatever she was reading.

Though he yearned to join her, to lie beside her and hold her, Fyran kept himself in place. He'd always enjoyed watching her; that would never change. And over the time he'd known her, he'd seen Avery blossom into someone more beautiful than he could've imagined—and she'd already been the most beautiful thing in his universe. She was still his Avery, but she was so much more. She was so much more *herself*.

She curled her toes and shifted her legs, making her fluffy pajama pants ride up and reveal the smooth skin of her ankles and the glint of her silver anklet.

Soon, vaerina...

She'd finished writing her first book months ago, and she'd done all the research to market and self-publish it. Seeing her excitement as people bought, read, and raved about the story had filled Fyran with delight and no small amount of pride. His mate had accomplished her dream, had overcome every obstacle that had been set in her way.

But she had received a few negative reviews, too. To say that she'd taken them better than Fyran would've been an understatement. Avery had taken them in stride, even though she'd winced as she'd read a few of them, and ultimately said those reviews would lend her some credibility. She'd called it *earning her stripes*.

And when she'd caught Fyran digging to uncover the identities and locations of the harshest reviewers, well...she'd proven that she was just as capable of administering *punishment* as he was.

Beau released a huff and rolled in place, nuzzling his face against Avery. She moved her hand over to scratch his chin without ceasing her reading. The feline purred; Avery smiled.

After a moment, she flicked the screen again and returned her hand to her belly, smoothing her palm over it slowly.

Fyran leaned his shoulder against the doorframe and drew in another lungful of air, relishing her fragrance. They now knew that the changes to her scent, which he'd first noticed half a year ago, were a result of her pregnancy—and something about it drove him not merely to heightened levels of lust, but a sharpened state of protectiveness. Even leaving her to go down to the garage for a few hours was almost too much, even that distance was nearly too great.

Her scent had been the first sign that she was with child, though he hadn't understood that when he'd first noticed. Even now, part of him couldn't comprehend that there was a life growing inside his mate—a life they'd created together. It seemed unreal that, in a few short months, he was going to be a father. All the checkups and tests from the faloran medical team over the last several weeks, the surprise visit from Khelvar, her growing stomach...none of it had been quite enough to make reality sink in for Fyran.

Fuck, he was so nervous. What did he know about children, about parenting? What did he know about setting a good example and nurturing a young life?

He lifted his eyes to find Avery looking at him, her smile wider than it had been a moment before. Looking into her eyes, he knew everything would be all right. He knew that, together, he and his mate could overcome any challenge.

"Are you waiting for an invitation?" Avery asked.

Fyran grinned as heat rippled through his chest and flowed through his veins. The effect this female had upon him hadn't diminished even slightly in the time since he'd met her.

"Ah, *vaerina*, I don't need an invitation. I'm no werewolf."

She chuckled, setting her tablet aside on the bed. "Definitely not. You're not hairy enough. But it's vampires that need an invitation. You were close."

"Don't know how anyone can keep all these made-up creatures straight," he replied, shaking his head.

"Same as you keeping all those real aliens straight, I guess." Avery patted the bed beside her.

Karak'duun, she was absolutely radiant, even in her pajamas with her hair up in a messy bun.

"Now are you coming, or are you going to make the pregnant lady get up and drag you over?" she asked.

"Can't say I'm not tempted…" Fyran pushed away from the doorframe and stalked toward her. Though Avery's eyes sparkled with humor, something else smoldered in them now—a hint of hunger and fire.

He crawled up onto the bed and stretched out beside his mate, nestling his cheek against her stomach. He put one arm around her back and placed his hand atop her belly.

Avery beamed down at him, combing her fingers through his hair. "You didn't blow up my car or anything, right?"

"Some things are best left unknown, female," he replied, brushing his fingers over her stomach. There was a tiny movement beneath his hand, the faintest hint of pressure.

"Baby says hello," Avery said softly.

"Hello, baby," Fyran whispered, stilling his hand. *Karak'duun*, he felt so full, so awed, so…fortunate. But that word wasn't enough. It couldn't begin to encompass the infinite number of chance occurrences that had culminated in him finding Avery, in him claiming her, in their surviving everything that had been thrown their way.

They remained like that in silence for a while, Avery caressing Fyran's hair, him stroking her belly and marveling at the minuscule movements beneath his hand.

"You didn't have to hole up in the garage all afternoon, you know," Avery said.

"I know. But I wanted to let you relax, *vaerina*. You've earned it."

"Pfft. All I've been doing is reading and making teasers for the next book while the editor finishes up. That's hardly strenuous work."

"But it's work nonetheless. Perhaps we should go out tomorrow and enjoy the sunshine."

"Tomorrow's Sunday."

Fyran arched a brow and counted off the days in his head. It felt nice to lose track of time every now and then—especially when the reason for it was his mate. "So it is. Maybe we can go to Lookout Park after Jerry's and take a walk?"

Their new year—their new lives—had begun with a new tradition. Though Avery hadn't returned to work at the diner, she and Fyran had gone to Jerry's every Sunday for lunch even though it was almost an hour away. She said it was because the place was special.

He couldn't argue that; it was where they'd met. Her old co-workers were always happy to see her, and Fyran and Avery had shared their table more than once with Harley and Mary, who adored Avery like she was their own granddaughter.

"Eww, no." Avery scrunched her nose. "Make it before. No way am I going to walk around on that hill with my stomach full of burger, fries, and milkshake."

"We're taking your car, so I don't care if you puke in it."

Avery laughed. "I only did that once in your car! And since you'll never let me live that down, I will remind you that it's partly your fault. You contributed to my morning sickness."

"Hmm." He lifted the hem of her shirt, exposing the pale flesh of her belly, and settled his hand back in place with fingers splayed. "Worth it, I'd say. Even if the smell never comes out."

"You can't still smell it!"

"Faloran nose, *vaerina*. Much more sensitive than yours."

"Don't you have some special faloran cleaning solution to get out lingering odors and stains?"

"I was an assassin, Avery, not a chemist."

She chuckled. "You weren't a mechanic, either, but that hasn't stopped you." Her brows creased and she turned her face, giving him a sidelong glance. "Wait...*should* we take my car tomorrow?"

He growled, flexing his fingers on her belly. "I wouldn't put my mate and child in danger."

Avery placed her hand upon his, her smile softening. "I know. I'm going to have the safest little bug around."

"*Nothing* will harm what's mine." He pressed a kiss to her

belly, growled again, and tickled his female's sides, making her erupt in giggles and laughter.

"*Fyran*! No! Oh my God, stop!" She squirmed in an attempt to escape his assault, sliding down from her sitting position and wiggling farther down the bed.

Beau, having been disturbed by the commotion, leapt off the bed with a disgruntled huff.

Fyran seized the opportunity. He crawled onto her, straddling her thighs and bracing himself over her on his arms.

Avery lay beneath him, panting, with her cheeks flushed and wild strands of hair having worked free of her bun. She placed her left hand over the center of her chest, making her ring sparkle in the light. He glanced at it for a moment. The white gold band had a sapphire as its centerpiece, flanked on either side by tiny rubies. The employee at the jewelry store where Fyran had had it made told him that diamonds were usually what human women wanted and had tried to convince him to go with that, but he'd refused.

This ring was perfect for his mate.

She raised her other hand, placing it on his shoulder. "I never get tired of this view."

"Dodo."

Avery giggled again. "You mean *ditto*."

Apparently, this was what he got when he tried to rely on his neural transceiver less often.

Fyran glared at her, lowering his face and putting extra grit in his voice as he said, "Female, if you correct me one more time..."

Her grin took on a wicked slant, and a heated, mischievous gleam entered her eyes. "That's *Queen* to you."

He arched a brow.

"Okay, so being called *female* gets me wet. You caught me," she said with mock exasperation.

Fyran's nostrils flared as he breathed her in. Desire laced her scent, making him groan. "Ah, my Avery, you are all I ever needed. If only I'd known sooner, I would've raced across the universe on my own to find you."

She smiled up at him, her eyes shining behind her glasses. She caressed his cheek and tucked his hair behind his ear, her fingers lingering to caress its pointed tip. "You found me and have me now. I'll always be yours."

Fyran dropped his mouth and slanted it over hers. He groaned as she opened to him, allowing his tongue to enter and coax hers into a sensual dance. Angling his mouth, he kissed her harder, deeper, craving more and more of her sweetness. Craving *her*. She was madness, she was a drug, and he'd never get enough.

She moaned and delved her fingers into his hair, capturing his head and arching against him. The delicious fragrance filling the air strengthened. He was lost in her, surrounded by her, and she was just as lost in him. He'd happily wander forever by her side, drinking in her essence.

Their hands roamed each other's bodies, yanking and clawing at their clothing until every scrap had been removed and there was nothing separating them. And when he entered her, thrusting deep into her tight heat, he felt her at his core, felt her in his heart, felt his love combine with hers to become something so much greater and more beautiful than the most fantastic dreams could've produced.

"You're my obsession, Avery," Fyran growled as he broke their kiss and met her gaze. He pumped his hips, surrendering to the lust crashing over him as he listened to her soft moans of pleasure. "My purpose, my desire, my need"—he drew back and drove into her again—"my hope, my everything."

He caught her jaw in his hand, pricking her skin with the tips of his claws, and snarled, "And you're all fucking mine, female."

AUTHOR'S NOTE

Thank you so much for reading *Stalked by the Alien Assassin*! We sincerely hope you enjoyed it! I adore Avery so much, and Fyran... Rawr! I have such a weakness for heroes like him.

If you have a moment, consider writing a review! If you'd like to help us even more, spread the love in your favorite book groups on social media!

Thank you all again!

<u>**Tiffany Roberts - Unleashed**</u>

<u>VENYS NEEDS MEN COLLABORATION</u>

<u>**Tiffany Roberts - To Tame a Dragon**</u>

<u>**Tiffany Roberts – To Love a Dragon**</u>

ABOUT THE AUTHOR

Tiffany Roberts is the pseudonym for Tiffany and Robert Freund, a husband and wife writing duo. Tiffany was born and bred in Idaho, and Robert was a native of New York City before moving across the country to be with her. The two have always shared a passion for reading and writing, and it was their dream to combine their mighty powers to create the sorts of books they want to read. They write character driven sci-fi and fantasy romance, creating happily-ever-afters for the alien and unknown.

Sign up for our Newsletter!
Check out our social media sites and more!